A BROOD
OF DUCKLINGS

BY FRANK SWINNERTON

PART ONE

CHAPTER I

FERDINAND AND HIS FAMILY

I

ABOUT five o'clock one February afternoon a few years ago, an elderly man—obviously a gentleman—was walking at a leisurely pace through the large London square which is known as Lincoln's Inn Fields. He had come from one among the narrow streets of the neighbourhood, had paused awhile before the window of a shop claimed as the original of Charles Dickens's "Old Curiosity Shop," and now, with a faint smile upon his thin face, was preparing to skirt the central garden. Dusk was already upon the City, and was made the darker by heavy rainclouds which covered the sky. A strong, bitter wind carried a few flying splashes of rain to the square flags of the pavement. It blew headlong dark smoke from a tall chimney in Holborn and dispersed it high above the buildings visible to our friend. In passing him, it twitched the flap of his overcoat just below the bottom button, and, by its assault upon the modestly striped trousers thus revealed, it disclosed the thinness of the legs within them.

Turning up the collar of his coat and fixing his hard felt hat more securely upon his head, Ferdinand Meadows showed by the unconscious shrugging of his shoulders that this bleak and mischievous blast troubled him. He even shrank slightly as the wind, resolved apparently to tease and pursue the solitary stranger as long as he remained vulnerable, battered him again and again. But as this struggle continued the clocks in the Strand began audibly to chime the hour; there was an increase in the visible life of Lincoln's Inn Fields; and the wind, perhaps distracted by the change, fluttered into docility. Lights popped up in some of the windows of the tall buildings; the street lamps peered yellowly; men and women came, at first singly or in twos, and at last in a moderate stream, from the narrow alley known as Great Turnstile for which Ferdinand had all the time been heading. He met the stream at the neck of the Turnstile, and as soon as he had been submerged by it he was thankfully sheltered from the wind. Nevertheless, he had not been driven to hasten his steps, but had preserved throughout the air of tranquillity which was characteristic of his port.

Tall, thin, grave, rather gray, scrupulously dressed, Ferdinand Meadows had the aspect of a lawyer, and some of those who met him only in the street were apt to imagine that he might even be a judge. In reality he was unconnected with the law, of which he had the greatest distrust. It was by accident that his daily walks so often led him into the region of the Courts and the Chambers, and if he had supposed that false impressions of his character rose in flashes to the minds of those who saw him he would have been full of nervous deprecation. With his hand raised to his lips, and possibly with his fingers lightly pressed against them, he would have pleaded: "Please, *please,* don't think any such thing about me. Indeed, I am no *attorney!*" He would have pronounced that last word in the gentlest of tones, but his gentleness would have emphasized his disquiet. The law, for him, was no "ass," but a terribly menacing conspiracy against all whose object it was to live unjargonized at peace with his fellows.

By this time Ferdinand had emerged into Holborn, where the shattering noise of the traffic bewildered him, as it always did, and caused him to be a little undecided in his movements. He glanced this way and that, made an attempt to cross the street, saw danger, abandoned his attempt, walked a little way westward, tried again to detect a possible path, and once more relinquished his design. It was during this second period of hesitation that, with the instinctive effort of the nervously discomfited person to hide his discomfiture, he turned away from the curb and gazed into the window of the shop that he unexpectedly found before him. And as he did this, Ferdinand gave a start of pleasure. He did not remember ever to have noticed until to-day the existence of a florist's shop at this point in his journey, and the sight of flowers upon so drab, so gusty an evening, when disagreeable noise and ugliness oppressed him, was magical in its solace.

He looked upward, and read the name BALTHAZAR in blue lettering upon a cream ground. It had been newly painted. The wooden frame of the window, also cream-coloured, had been likewise newly painted. Flowers and a little fine fruit could be seen within, demurely displayed, as if to charm and tempt the eye or the palate, rather than the purse, of any beholder. Ferdinand smiled as he relished the colours thus gathered together, the brown of beech leaves, the gold of young mimosa, and the blue of the African iris, so lately blooming amid sunshine in the South of France, and now brightening the dreariness of lingering winter in London. He smiled, but with a faint air of sadness, as if he regretted that these beauties should have been transported from their natural surroundings. Then his eye brightened once again, for he had just caught sight, behind these brighter hues, of something even more lovely than they. It was a rush basket brimming with Parma violets. The enchanting delicacy of that pallid blue intoxicated him. Without hesitation Ferdinand walked straight into the shop.

Within, the subtle effect of the flower scent was so strong that he was quite dominated by it. He fell into a reverie, as one fainting, and the flowers seemed to billow about him, secretly lustrous and divine. From some hidden bower be-hind the flowers and the palms had advanced—he knew not how—a slight and charming woman—not a girl, but a woman, very small, very fair, with blue eyes, a curiously delicate and doll-like complexion, a manner quiet, almost stealthily, watchfully quiet, an expression like that of a Virgin limned by Perugino. Ferdinard stammered a little before such beauty and heard his own voice asking painfully for some of the violets; but he did not cease to regard the woman before him. She was dressed very plainly in black, and when her blue eyes were inquiringly raised it seemed to Ferdinand that the droop of her little mouth was entirely pathetic. Her hair was wavy, and worn long; her white throat was plump; her slender shoulders had a quality which ensnared the eye. He felt an immediate interest in her, an interest that quickened unexpectedly into pity, conscious regret that somebody so delicate should be forced to battle with life, shame that a civilization created by men should still permit such anomalies as the struggle of helpless women with what he called the harder facts of human nature. She was lately bereaved—as her dress showed. Perhaps this shop represented her brave effort to avert disaster. Ferdinand with difficulty checked his apprehensions.

"Good-afternoon," he said hesitatingly. "I wonder whether —you have some Parma violets in the——"

Helplessly he abandoned his intention of asking in a firm voice for the flowers he preferred. His thin fingers rose to his lips. He was silent. The blue eyes which had been lifted to meet his own dropped quickly. The face was still. Seen thus, it was plumper than Ferdinand had realized. The tip of her nose was sharper. But the lashes were very long and silky, and the air of sadness was accentuated.

"How many would you like?" She had a charming voice, low and clear. Her words were pronounced—so fastidious was he in such matters—with an accent which delighted him. The tone was exquisite. Ferdinand had desire to engage the owner of such a voice in conversation, but for the present he was too shy to yield to that desire. Instead, therefore, of talking, he became deliberately businesslike, as a shy man does, and frowned a little, discussed with uncertainty the size of the bunch he would buy, paid for it, and was about to leave the shop when a recollection seemed to strike him. He returned.

"I—I think I should like to take another bunch," said he, awaiting hesitantly the surprise which he felt his demand would create and yet obstinately determined to brave criticism of his own vacillation.

There was the merest flicker of her eyelids, the merest pressure of her lips—not a smile, but a thought.

"The same size?" questioned the lady, with the most tactful avoidance of surprise.

Ferdinand considered. It was so difficult to decide such a problem in an instant—in such company—with such responsibilities as he had. And yet not at all difficult, as his tongue, which in some matters was wiser and more alert than Ferdinand himself, soon demonstrated.

"The same size, please," he answered breathlessly, inclining his head with firmness, as if there had been no doubt at all.

A few moments later he left the shop carrying two bunches of violets (they were in size almost bouquets) which in every particular were exactly alike. It chanced that at the instant of his departure the street before Mrs. Balthazar's shop was clear of traffic, and Ferdinand accordingly ran across the open space and resumed his more leisurely walk upon the farther pavement. He was so absorbed in his purchase and in his thoughts of the charming lady at the florist's shop that he forgot the wind and the threatening rain and did not think to cast a glance back in the direction from which he had come. If he had looked—it is often done—over his shoulder, he might have observed that the lady herself was standing close to the shop window, and that she had with interest—almost with thoughtful demureness—watched his rather nervous flight across the roadway and his subsequent progress, marked as it was by a most suggestive air of abstraction.

II

He had still some way to go, for Ferdinand and his family lived in an old house in Woburn Square; and with the falling of the wind it was clear that rain would shortly follow. Still, however, he continued to stroll, the violets lightly held to his side, for Ferdinand never hurried. Indeed, now that the wind no longer buffeted as it had done, he had relapsed into that state of reflectiveness which made his life so pleasant. The clanging tramcars in the Theobalds Road did not arouse him. He passed unheeding the litter in the gutters of Devonshire Street. Only the shapeliness of these old houses, now so defaced, so dulled by the wear of a century that they were like shadows from an older time, created an atmosphere of tranquillity which was in harmony with his mood. It was in the past that Ferdinand lived, in the past and in a faint, dreamy present to which his thoughts gave something of the sweetness of memory. He did not realize it; but he was more free from anxiety than almost all the human beings against whom he unconsciously brushed in his progress.

At length he reached Woburn Square and admitted himself to a very sedate house upon the eastern side. It was a well-kept house, the bricks tawny with age, with an ample stone portico, a little balcony before the first-floor windows, discreet curtains of net, and a delicately green front door bearing a knocker and letter box of polished brass. The heavy door closed gently behind him, with small sound. Within, amid rich darkness, there were thick, silent carpetings, dull walls upon which hung fine engravings, a wide staircase leading to the upper floors. Elegance, ease, and silence marked the house. No sharp noises disturbed the air. Everything was still and full of the peace which indicates a well-ordered establishment. Unconsciously grateful for the encompassing calm, which he was too much of an epicure to take for granted, despite his familiarity with it, Ferdinand hung his coat and hat—slightly spotted with rain—upon a Victorian stand of superb quality which shone sombrely in the gloom, repossessed himself of the Parma violets, and made his way up to a room upon the first floor of this tranquil house.

Here, standing in the semidarkness by one of the long windows overlooking the square, was a very slim dark girl in the early twenties. Her hair was almost black, her hands very white and without rings, her dress short, simple, and lustrous. She had drawn aside the heavy velvet curtain and was looking anxiously downward, as if she strove to command, not only the farther pavement, which was open to view, but also that one which led directly to the front door below. She had not, it was clear, heard the faint sound of Ferdinand's entrance, since she did not immediately turn to greet him; and Ferdinand himself drew such delight from the unconscious picture thus presented to him that before speaking he stood for an instant contemplating that delicate figure. The half-raised arm which supported the curtain gave clearness to the charming line of her body; the attitude of expectancy revealed his daughter's slimness and the unthinking grace which distinguished her. Ferdinand smiled.

"Why, Rhoda," he said in his gentlest tone.

Instantly she stood erect, the tenseness of her pose relaxed, and faced him in radiant welcome. Her lips were parted, and her eyes, which he could not clearly see, widely open.

"Father! I was looking for you. It's raining hard." No voice was as sweet as Rhoda's! It had all the music of emotion, the gentleness of love and beauty. Eagerly she came forward. "Are you wet? I was beginning to be quite afraid."

Ferdinand laughed away her fear.

"Is it raining, then? I hadn't noticed," he said, with a kind of agreeable derision. "No, I'm perfectly dry." As he spoke, he switched on the softly screened electric light, and the room was in a glow. "You're quite pale, my darling," he exclaimed. "Are you well? So much afraid? Surely you——"

She made no response to his comment upon her pallor. Her eyes were fixed upon the flowers he carried. Ferdinand could now clearly see how those beautiful eyes shone in the oval, delicate face, making it quite startlingly full of ardent expression, and how prettily her parted lips disclosed the small, regular teeth. Her very dark hair was fine and curly, although, after the current fashion, it was worn short; and the slenderness of her neck was that of a flower. She was dressed in a plain afternoon frock of amber colour which enhanced the loveliness of her complexion, and when she moved towards him, smiling, with her arms slightly raised to receive the violets, the length and the delicacy of her hands, it could again be seen, were remarkable.

"What enchanting violets!" Rhoda cried, with the vivid stress that natural emotion gives even to words lightly spoken.

"I saw them in a most unexpected shop," Ferdinand answered, in the same tone, fastidious yet eager. "A jolly shop!" He smiled as he spoke. They both smiled, in common delight and understanding. "They were so pretty that I couldn't resist them."

"For me?" Her brows were raised. She was delicious.

"Some of them. Half of them." He separated from its companion the bunch which he had brought for Rhoda. The other bunch he laid upon a table beside the door.

"Lovely!" She took the flowers from his hand, and held them to her face. "Incredibly lovely!" There was something really passionate in her gratitude, her vivaciousness. It was as though she had been athirst for flowers; and the consciousness of this made Ferdinand's heart soft with tenderness towards her. He felt swiftly that he was never sufficiently thankful to God for having spared him this beautiful daughter to love, to idolize, and to protect from all evil.

"Do you like them?" he asked, with fresh satisfaction in his own gift. "I'm sure you do."

"*Like* them? They're exquisite!" She was archly indignant. "I love them. How kind of you, Daddy!" She caught him playfully by the sleeve and with gravity kissed him.

"This new flower shop—I must show it to you. It was quite by accident——" Ferdinand's voice faded. His ear had caught a sound somewhere outside the room, and it was a habit of his, when anything distracted his attention, to forget what he was saying and leave his speech—like a perfume—suspended, evanescent, and finally forgotten by himself. He listened. And as he listened his eye strayed round the room in which they were standing. He did not know that his own figure was as full of grace and distinction as Rhoda's. He had no sense of the picture that they made together. But he loved this room, which was as sober as any in the house, and as charming.

It was, in the first place, a very large room, and the walls were of a light brown, the colour of canvas. Upon two of them were original paintings which Ferdinand believed to be genuine Vermeers, delicately hued, each marked by characteristic cunning of light and shade and perspective, each domestic in theme and revealing a vista of cobblestones, doorways, and subtle greenery. Of these the larger and more beautiful represented an old woman spinning. He head was covered with a linen cap, her placid face was lighted in the most exquisite fashion from a window to the left of the picture. The smaller, less beautiful, showed a young woman standing at the door of a small room—perhaps a kitchen—her face averted. She was listening. Ferdinand never tired of contemplating the pearly quality of these two paintings, and their ravishing blues and yellows. They were his delight. To some extent the room had been furnished in such a way as to emphasize the beauty of the two pictures, for the armchairs, the curtains, and a large ottoman or settee which lay between door and fireplace were all covered in richer shades of green and gold. A grand piano stood between the fire-place and the second window, and above it was what Ferdinand knew to be only a copy of a study by Verrocchio. It hung there because of a fancied resemblance between the features portrayed and those of his dead but still very tenderly loved and remembered wife. The floor was covered with large and splendid rugs. A bright fire was burning in the grate, and above it was a finely carved mantelpiece which Ferdinand had been fortunate enough to find in the house when first—ten years earlier—he had made it his home. Higher still was an old oak-framed mirror, so tilted that the greater part of the room, and in particular the larger of the two paintings, could be seen reflected in its depths.

And as his eye flitted over these secretly approved furnishings and rested with pride upon the Dutch painting which he considered to be the finer of his two reputed Vermeers, Ferdinand saw that his quick ear had not been at fault. The door swiftly opened, and a second girl, his daughter Catherine, came from outer dimness into the delicate radiance of the room.

"Oh, you're home," she exclaimed. The tone, at once less soft and less ardent than Rhoda's, was equally welcoming. To both these girls, indeed, the return of their father—even though it should be only from an afternoon walk upon a blusterous February day—was an agreeable event, for both loved him very dearly; but Catherine, who was fair, and brisker in all her movements than Rhoda, was less demonstrative than her younger sister. Having, as it were, cheerfully announced the fact of his return, she at once looked away from Ferdinand to the darkening windows, and before she moved towards the fire it was her first thought to draw the blinds and shut out the dreariness of the rainy evening. Ferdinand's eyes did not follow her—as those of a younger man must inevitably have done, so extraordinarily light and graceful was she—as she went to the windows. He seemed once again to have fallen into a dream. And yet if Rhoda was beautiful so also was Catherine. Her expression was calm, but there was no lack of quickness and vivacity in it. Indeed, with all her good-nature, she did not want personality, and could never have been ignored in whatever company she might find herself. She was no taller than Rhoda, and was equally slim; but her cheeks were plumper, and her smile was quieter, less radiant than Rhoda's. She looked as if she had more humour, as if secret laughter sweetened all her responses to the human comedy; and more repose, as if she knew a tranquillity to which her sister might never attain. She was twenty-four and was the senior by perhaps a couple of years.

"Look what Daddy's brought!" cried the irrespressible Rhoda, with a quiet unconscious childishness of delight and impulse. She was alight with pleasure. A flame seemed to burn within her. It shone from her radiant eyes.

"How lovely they are!" agreed Catherine, as pleased as she. And added: "You must put them in water before they droop." She lowered her face, close to the proffered flowers.

In his dream Ferdinand was conscious that something had jarred upon him—some uneasy intimation, some memory— he knew not what. Perhaps it had been a lightness, a kindness, an unsuspected detachment in Catherine's tone, or an unwelcome practicality in the suggestion which she had made? He could not tell. Everything that was utilitarian was anathema to Ferdinand. He would prodigally have heaped flowers upon Rhoda; perhaps, then, the thought of their careful preservation hinted at some niggardliness of spirit? He stirred slightly, glanced at the two girls who, with their heads together, were bending over the violets; and he was filled anew with awareness of his love for both. For *both*. Then recollection came to him.

"Oh, Catherine," he said, starting forward, stabbed by conscience. "I beg your pardon. Here are some for you, too."

He raised hastily from the table upon which they lay the

violets bought from the florist upon a second impulse, and in some confusion placed them in Catherine's hands. As he did so he met the wise smiling hazel eyes, saw the straight little nose and almost roguish lips, and once again realized, not for the first or second or third time in his life, but nevertheless with a pang of surprise, as if he had again forgotten the truth, that Catherine, his elder daughter, was no less beautiful and no less attractive to the eye and the spirit than her younger sister.

III

Having, therefore, received her warm thanks for the gift, Ferdinand—he knew not how it was, unless for the reason that he was never wholly at ease with Catherine—turned away from his daughters, and took a seat by the glowing, cheerful fire. He stretched his thin hands out, indeed, towards the warmth. Was there sometimes a criticism of himself in that refreshing glance of Catherine's? He could not guess. He knew only that the simplicity, the unreserve of Rhoda gave him no comparable discomfort. Yet he appreciated the fact that he owed much to Catherine. It was she who protected him. Protected? It was too strong a word. Nay, it was a wrong word to use regarding the relation of a daughter to her father. He himself, he was sure, being of the male sex, was born to protect, to guide, and to guard these two delicate natures from every ill. What a burden, what a responsibility that was! It sometimes frightened him. Two lovely girls, entirely lacking experience, and without female connections, wholly dependent upon himself for their understanding of life, for every shade of worldly wisdom, were they not sufficiently a charge to alarm the most experienced of men? And if anything were to happen—to them—to himself—— Uncontrollably Ferdinand sighed. In an instant Rhoda was at his elbow.

"Daddy!" she urgently exclaimed. "You sighed!"

"Did I, my dear?" Ferdinand shrugged his shoulders. "I was thinking. Or, rather, I *wasn't* thinking. I've nothing to sigh about."

"You *should* have nothing," Rhoda meditated. "Should he, Catherine?"

"Perhaps he's bored, Rhoda." It was a teasing response. "Or the wind may have tired him."

At the word "bored" Ferdinand had shivered with distaste.

"The wind, yes, the wind. For the other—*please!*" He shot a little reproachful glance at Catherine. She knew—she must know—how much he disliked the word "bored." It was a word that had no place in the vocabulary of this household. "I am never bored."

The sisters exchanged a smile which Ferdinand did not see.

"I'm *often* bored," cried Rhoda.

"Oh, Rhoda!" Catherine was laughing at an absurdity. Her sister turned indignantly.

"It's true. I *am*. You don't know. You don't know me." The glowing eyes challenged defiantly.

"But you're so interested in everything."

"For a moment. And then——" Rhoda gave a little nervous grimace.

"This is terrible," murmured Ferdinand, greatly disconcerted. He appealed to Catherine, who shook her head at both of them.

"Don't take any notice of her, Father," she said reassuringly. "Rhoda, you're frightening him with your nonsense."

"Darling!" Rhoda was filled with vehement self-reproach. "Am I frightening you?" She came nearer to Ferdinand. "Of course I don't mean what *you* mean. When I say 'bored' I only mean——"

"Happy," interjected Catherine, with mischievous intention. "Mournfully happy!"

"No. That the interest has passed."

Ferdinand was bewildered. He could not imagine Rhoda bored. For a moment his thoughts were confused. Then, with an effort to control the fluttering of his apprehensiveness, and as if to distract all their thoughts from so painful a theme, he said in a more animated, less fastidious tone:

"Let me see, is anybody coming to dinner to-night?"

Even here he was unfortunate, for his confusion led him into error. The consequences were again discomfiting.

"Father!" Rhoda's cry was full of rallying, frowning protest. Your memory must be failing. Surely you know perfectly well who's coming!"

"Do I?" Ferdinand made a feeble effort to recapture his recollection. With a shaken head he confessed his failure. "I've forgotten. Or perhaps *you* forgot to say anything to me about it. You've taken to a habit of inviting——"

"That's quite impossible." Rhoda was imperious. She surveyed him with displeasure. Ferdinand was the more alarmed.

"Tell me, then," he coaxed, his head inclined, so that it was quite close to her shoulder.

Rhoda was now kneeling upon a hassock which she had drawn to his side, and Ferdinand—once his fears were allayed—loved to be scolded thus affectionately when Rhoda was so near.

"First," said Rhoda, "there's Jerry." She indicated his place in the order by pressing one slight forefinger against the other.

"Jerry," echoed Ferdinard obediently, bending his head over that childish hand, pink-rimmed against the glowing light of the fire. As he did this he smiled in content. "Jerry's always a welcome guest."

"And Mr. Piercy." There was no spoken response to that name, but the head was again slowly nodded, and another finger was pressed. A slight pause came in the list before Rhoda continued, rather less distinctly: "And Joe Gascoyne and his sister."

"Whether Father quite *likes* Joe," began Catherine disconcertingly, "I can never be quite sure."

"Of course he likes him!" Rhoda flamed with indignation. Her eyes flashed back at Catherine, quite fiery in their reproof. But Catherine was unwithered. She said:

"I'm never perfectly sure. But he likes Gwen, I think."

"Well, we *all* do." Rhoda's eye flashed again, but less brilliantly. She was laughing, and the firelight caught her happily excited face. "Don't we, Daddy?"

Ferdinand cleared his throat. That nervous left hand of his was raised and pressed against his lips.

"My dears," he began very hesitatingly, "I *do* like Gwen and Joe. They seem to me to be—both of them—bright, cheerful, lively companions. Very. Of course, I may be wrong—perhaps I am—but I only feel, with regard to Joe——"

"Daddy! Be careful!" Rhoda's seriously reproachful face terrified him. Ferdinand's hand fluttered painfully in the air. His eyes were cast upward in concern; then, entreatingly, they sought the brilliant eyes at his side.

"No, no. Don't misunderstand me. I feel——" He was so conscious—although he could not see it—of Catherine's smile that for an instant he could not proceed. That smile wounded him, whereas Rhoda's gravity sent shock after shock of alarm to his heart. "I consider him admirable. Admirable. I do him every justice," concluded Ferdinand in desperation. "I like him. I admire him. He's honest. Full of ability. Full of confidence. He's—he's amusing."

"But he annoys you, Father." It was Catherine who spoke —Catherine, who had come to his other side, so that Ferdinand was between two searching, incalculable fires. "He annoys us all."

"Yes. Yes," said Ferdinand more hopefully. "I think I can admit so much. The best of men have had this—this slightly irritating effect. And yet 'annoys'——" He shook his head. To be annoyed was to be impatient, and impatience was unphilosophic. Catherine, disregarding the protest, continued, still calmly:

"Even Rhoda, who defends him. But we're very fond of him."

"*Very* fond," added Rhoda, with unexpected quietness. She was for a moment deeply thoughtful, until she burst out impulsively: "Oh, Daddy, I wish you liked him!" Her eyes seemed, in that bright firelight, to gleam, and to Ferdinand's affrighted fancy the gleam hinted a possibility of inexplicable tears which he would never be able to charm away. He capitulated, with immense mental reservations.

"I do. I *do*," he urged. Then he was inspired. "I think perhaps it's only that he's—what shall I say?—could it be called irreverent?"

"Irreverent!" exclaimed Rhoda wonderingly. Such a thought apparently had never occurred to her.

"Well, *that's* true," Catherine put in, before anything further could be said. "I suppose it's fashionable nowadays to be irreverent."

"Fashionable!" Ferdinand pronounced the word with deepest loathing. "Oh, dear, I hardly know——"

"Edmund Piercy's coming, too, Father," supplemented Catherine, as if she had resolved to take in hand the announcing of other names. Rhoda whispered hastily: "I'd told him that," and Catherine, without comment, proceeded: "And Mona Talbot."

"Ah, Mona," peaceably remarked Ferdinand. "Now, there can't be any two opinions about Mona. She is really a most sensible girl. Not, I think, particularly—— But a most sensible, a most *sensible* girl."

There was no reply from either of the sisters. They did not look at each other. They did not so much as hint an objection to this bland approval or the significantly abandoned parenthesis.

"Mona is bringing her cousin, a young man whom you've never met, Father," continued Catherine. "A *Mr.* Talbot.

We've met him at Mona's house, and she begged that he might come one evening."

"Excellent," said Ferdinand, who by this time was frightened into approval of every name that was to be spoken. "I hope he resembles the charming Mona."

"You'll be able to see for yourself," exclaimed Catherine calmly.

"You like him?" asked Ferdinand, in his gentlest tone.

"Oh, *awfully*," cried Rhoda, with bitter ironic emphasis. The colour rose suddenly to her cheeks. Her fists were unconsciously clenched. *"Tremendously!"*

Ferdinand—although, having missed the irony in her tone, he was very much afraid lest the vigour of Rhoda's response should indicate romantic infatuation for the young man—showed himself to be not entirely without wit.

"How ominous that sounds!" he murmured, rather drily.

"In fact, Father," Catherine said, as if she pierced to his fear, "Rhoda can't stand him. But I think he's interesting. He's got a very good head."

"And very bad manners!" flashed Rhoda.

"Very good manners," proceeded Catherine. "Though he made Rhoda rather angry."

"Extremely angry!" Rhoda declared, trembling anew at recollection of the original cause of her anger, and rising—as if she could no longer bear to keep still—from the hassock upon which she had been kneeling. "It makes me feel warm just to think of him. A rude man! I wish he weren't coming. However, I shan't show that I don't like him. It will be good discipline for me. I shall be quite polite. As nearly frigid as I can manage to be. It's the only way. Frigid. Frigid." She said these last words to herself, quietly, as if impressing them upon her mind, willing frigidity. Then she impulsively stooped, resting her hand upon Ferdinand's shoulder in the most fleeting of caresses. "You won't like him, either, Daddy. I'm sure of it. He'll tread on all your most bigoted and irrational opinions. You see if he doesn't!"

"Mine!" stammered Ferdinand, for a moment doubtful if he had accurately heard what she said.

"Anybody's. And you won't like him any better than you like Joe, who is *really* very nice indeed, for all you and Catherine may say about his being fashionable and irreverent. He's not a bit fashionable or irreverent, but the kindest——"

"My darling!" Ferdinand would have defended himself; but before he could begin to do so Rhoda had thrown her arms about his neck with a little smothered ejaculation of love, had kissed him, and had run out of the room.

Ferdinand did not see her face and was too slow to catch her by the hand and search her eyes so that he could ascertain the truth of her mood. As he looked after her, deeply concerned, he saw Catherine, apparently quite undisturbed by the scene, gathering together all the Parma violets, as if with the intention of reviving them in water. Instead, therefore, of speaking, Ferdinand rubbed his chin. His fingers stole up to his mouth and pressed against the long, sensitive lips. This entire conversation had been completely unexpected—nay, it had been frightened in many of its vagaries; and he had an anxious feeling that it was most necessary for him to turn it well over in memory, that the meaning of some of its more perplexing issues should be fully disclosed.

CHAPTER II

VISITORS

I

THE father of Ferdinand Meadows, a clergyman, had lived in one of the western counties of England, where he had possessed (by the will of his late wife) a good deal of not very valuable land and a considerable income from investments in government securities. At his death Ferdinand, the only child, inherited perhaps fifty thousand pounds, and, having sold his father's land (the house was small and inconvenient), he settled in London. There, ignoring the political strife which surrounded him, and making very few acquaintances, he tried to give effect to his ambition, which was to become an artist. In vain. He had skill as a draughtsman, but he never could satisfy himself in the matter of subject. His conceptions were intellectual rather than imaginative, and he was thus condemned to æsthetic sterility. Nevertheless, experience caused him to become something of a connoisseur; he bought pictures, cultivated a taste for letters, and lived the comfortable, solitary, self-engrossed life of a bachelor; until, at the age of forty, he fell in love with, and married, the beautiful daughter of an elderly artist, whose talent had always been greater than his assiduity.

Ecstatic happiness followed for Ferdinand and his wife. The father (something of a reprobate), after luxuriating for a brief period in his son-in-law's fortune, was one morning found dead in bed; and with his disappearance from the scene the only obstacle to Ferdinand's entire contentment was removed. Within four years of the marriage both Catherine and Rhoda were born. Thereafter Ferdinand's wife lost strength year by year, until, when the children were just old enough to go to school, she slipped gradually out of life, leaving her husband at the beginning of middle age with two enchanting little girls upon his hands and without near relations of any description.

Ferdinand's dread regarding his daughters had been that they might grow up delicate. His dread was groundless. Both were healthy, and while neither was robust he had never had occasion to feel any further anxiety as to their physical state. He had sent Catherine, who had seemed the stronger, to a school upon the south coast of England, where she had been taught to hide her feelings, to keep her hockey stick low, to respect conventions, to speak French and Italian, to read George Meredith and Henry James, and to think for herself. Rhoda, meanwhile, owing to supposed greater delicacy, had been kept at home for a space, with a governess, and subsequently had been sent for a very short time to another school upon the south coast of England, where she had been taught to read poetry, whisper during lessons, work spasmodically, and in accordance with mood, paint, embroider, and make delicious chocolate fudge. Illness had led to her return home, and she had never again been sent to school. But she had shown no aptitude for domestic management, so that while Catherine, at the end of her school days, had been put in charge of the household, Rhoda had continued, unoccupied, as the apple of her father's eye. Of late she had attended art classes, but wilfully and occasionally; while Catherine, having her mind full of home affairs, was unsuspected by her father of any extra-domestic ambitions. Much else went to the composition of the family life, as the following chapters will reveal, but in the main the relations of father and daughters remained ostensibly as they had been for some years, unchanged.

II

Two hours after the scene which has been described, Ferdinand was back in the drawing room, standing before the fire and gravely regarding the larger of his two much-treasured paintings. He was dressed in his customary garb for the evening—striped trousers, evening shoes, a black waistcoat, a silk shirt, and a black velvet jacket with silk lapels; and in order to read a couple of newspapers which he held in his hand he had donned a pair of horn-rimmed spectacles. He thus became a slightly fantastic but perfectly dignified figure, slim without emaciation, ivory-faced, reflective, faintly æsthetic in appearance. Refinement was his characteristic, and the long thin hand which held the newspapers was that of an acutely sensitive person. The serious tender, short-sighted, half-humorous eyes behind the horn-rimmed spectacles admitted one to many secrets of his nature. Few human beings would have gone out of their way to affront Ferdinand; no little urchin would ever have hesitated to ask him the time.

He had glanced through the headlines in the papers, had smiled over one cartoon, and frowned over another which seemed to him to be in poor taste, and was about to refold both papers and set them down when the door of the drawing room opened and a maid admitted two persons. The more noticeable of these was a tall young man with a long thin nose, a quick black eye, and a very droll expression; the other, shorter, plumper, less droll, but with possibly greater brightness of manner, was evidently his sister.

"Ah, Gascoyne," cried Ferdinand, in his most courteous manner. He laid aside the horn-rimmed spectacles before taking two steps forward. "And you, my dear, how are you? We're the first, you see."

"We're early because we had a taxi," explained Gwen rather proudly.

"Gwen insisted on a taxi," added her brother.

"I have a prejudice against taxis," said Ferdinand, with the air of one who begins: "I am old-fashioned enough to ———" He did not expect—or wish—to be believed, since he disliked prejudice in other people. Nevertheless, what he said was true. He had a prejudice against taxis.

"It can't be greater than mine," Joe assured him. "But for some reason Gwen loves them. She now says: 'Shall we have a taxi?' just as she used to say, when she was a baby, 'Shall we buy a sugar stick?'"

"Well, I can't afford a car," retorted Gwen. "And you can say what you like, walking in the rain is horrid; omnibuses are frowsty and make me feel sick; and I'd sooner die than travel underground. One burial in a lifetime is quite enough."

"I can think of no other alternative," ventured Ferdinand archly, "except flying."

"And that I shouldn't like because I believe it's very wobbly. But the truth is, Joe is mean about taxis. Like most other men—not you, Mr. Meadows—Joe's a mixture of generosity and meanness," pursued Gwen, sitting down abruptly as she spoke and crossing her legs. "He'll give you almost anything you want—except the comforts of life. And those are really just the things that matter."

"Gwen's motto is 'when in doubt, talk volubly about yourself. And keep on talking until you're interrupted,'" Joe said. "Take no notice of her, Mr. Meadows. Besides, she has no sense whatever of comfort. I doubt if many women have."

But he did not speak seriously. He was lost, Ferdinand noticed, in contemplation of a small bowl which stood upon the piano, filled with the Parma violets which Ferdinand had bought that evening. He seemed to be magnetized by these violets, as if they had some message for him, some secret unknown to his observer. Ferdinand saw Joe's head sink. Never previously had he noticed an expression of humility upon that droll face. He was deeply interested in the phenomenon.

III

A moment later Catherine was in the room, immediately
followed by both Rhoda and a very good-looking fair boy;
and at the coming of these three the atmosphere of the room
grew noticeably more kindly. To Ferdinand, the sight of the
newcomers was a relief, for the boy—Jerry Anderson—was
an especial favourite of his, to whom he could talk without
feeling that what he said might be very strictly measured.

Jerry smiled in the doorway, as he always did, and blinked
his eyes nervously before approaching Ferdinand. He was
perpetually deferential, full of constrained grace which often took the form of excessive politeness akin to that of the
shopkeeper; but he was popular wherever he went. A young
man of some means, he acted as secretary to a famous
author, and hoped to be one day a famous author upon his
own account. But as to that prospect Ferdinand was less optimistic than the young man himself, although he did not declare his opinion.

"An escape, I see," Ferdinand said, taking Jerry's hand
cordially in both his own. "I presume the great man doesn't
actively function this evening."

"Oh, I'm not a *companion,* you know," explained Jerry,
in a weak, languid, high-pitched voice, and with a particularly delicate pronunciation. He looked very frail, almost
effeminate, with his big blue eyes and his mild expression of
naïveté. "We've finished our work for the day. That is, if
you consider that our work is work." He smiled with sweet
sadness and said, not "work," but "weuk."

"What a curious assumption it is that writers and artists
do not work," Ferdinand remarked. "You remember the little
ragged girl who watched a landscape painter for some time,
and said, 'My father *works* when he paints.' A barbaric survival. And very widespread, of course."

"*Quite* absurd," agreed Jerry, with exaggeration of the
adverb. "*Perfectly* absurd!"

"We're all absurd, I'm afraid," consolingly said Ferdinand. "If that is any comfort. I confess that it isn't always a cheering thought to myself."

"But our absurdity," Jerry complained, "is simple. Theirs is compound."

"On the other hand, the spiritual rewards of the artist——"

"I never know what a spiritual reward is," objected Jerry. "I believe it to be like the reward a policeman doesn't get for taking home a lost dog."

"The policeman's reward," Ferdinand laughed, "is not so much spiritual as mythical. And, speaking of the law, I see Edmund." He touched Jerry upon the elbow with one hand as he extended the other to his new guest. "Well, Edmund, we're speaking of the law; and as the embodiment of the law here you are. 'The law is the true embodiment of everything that's excellent'—how does the song go?"

"I don't know how it goes," Edmund said in his sonorous voice, which in time to come would waken many a juryman to a sense of his duty; "but the excellence of the law is much mitigated by the shortcomings of the lawyers." He smiled triumphantly, as if he had created a mot.

"And *is* the law excellent, Edmund?" pleaded Jerry, blinking his eyes and drawling.

"I'll tell you when I'm Lord Chancellor, Jerry," answered Edmund. "At present the law and I are comparative strangers. We hardly know each other. I wish it were not so, because my tastes (unlike yours, my dear Jerry, as I perceive from the tie you are wearing, which is a most admirable effort, if I may say so), because my tastes"—he recovered himself adroitly after the lengthy parenthesis—"are expensive."

Edmund's rolling tone was belied by his statuesque appearance. He was a tall, thin young man with high cheek bones, cold gray eyes, and a habit of drawing the whole of the lower part of his face upward rather pompously when he made a

jocular remark. There was something of the actor about him,
but the shape of his head suggested considerable intellectual
power. And although his eyes were cold they were not the
eyes of a selfish or unfeeling man. If Ferdinand did not love
Edmund, or admire him, at least he felt that Edmund had a
separate existence. He might have dreamed Jerry, but he
could never have dreamed Edmund. He had the quality
of slate.

"I passed the Law Courts to-day," Ferdinand ventured,
slightly shrugging, and jerking his head—it was a way he
had—gently to one side as if he were listening to the spheres.
"And in fact—forgive me, my dear Edmund: I know this
will be painful to you—I *hurried* past the Bankruptcy Court,
of which I have a peculiar horror. All of them, indeed, make
me exceedingly uncomfortable—as an innocent man—as an
innocent man. I imagine to myself the falling of that giant
arm, my own helplessness, the terrible array of skilled intelli-
gences. I can never remember where I was upon a particular
day or at any particular time. I can never 'answer the question, "yes" or "no." ' And I should be sure to be convicted.
So, as I say, I'm invariably frightened. Whereas you, I suppose——" He turned, smiling, to Edmund.

"They're his Mecca," suggested Jerry. "Or, rather, his
oyster."

"They're my office." Edmund was bland.

"The ladder by which you ascend to higher things?"

"Exactly."

Ferdinand was oppressed by the knowledge that Edmund
was at all times a little ponderous, and in listening to Edmund he was always aware of some strain upon his nervous
endurance. He occasionally caught a faciful glimpse of Edmund in middle life which made him fastidiously shiver.
The cold eye, grown colder, a little glassy, the chin longer,
some fat under the eyes and under the chin, the cheeks length-
ened so that they hung. . . . And the voice . . . It would not
have mattered if Ferdinand had not been haunted by a

dream. Again and again he had dreamed that Edmund was married to Rhoda.

Thought of that dream crossed his mind at this instant. In a panic, he looked across the room to where Rhoda sat by the side of Gwen Gascoyne, describing the size of something by holding her hands wide asunder. This glimpse of Rhoda was reassuring; but what a stab had gone to Ferdinand's heart!

IV

It was with some difficulty that he readjusted himself to the conversation of the two young men at his side. They were speaking more seriously than they had been doing earlier.

"When you're Lord Chancellor, I wonder where the rest of us will be," Jerry was sighing pensively. A seraphic smile showed that he was thinking of his own future. Well, was Ferdinand wrong? Was it to be a great one?

"My dear Jerry, this is a daydream," Ferdinand said very kindly.

"When I'm Lord Chancellor, Punch Teed will have shot himself," said Edmund deliberately.

"What!" The exclamation was drawn from Ferdinand by a sense of amazed horror. "What makes you say that?"

"Because I think it's true," Edmund said coolly. "I *know* he'll do it."

"But, Edmund!" Ferdinand was appalled. "What a terrible thing to think—to say." He was greatly agitated. The face of Punch Teed rose before his eyes, young, ruddy. "I really——"

"Don't repeat what I say. Above all, don't tell Punch. But I've always felt he'd do that."

"You've no reason?" Ferdinand stammered.

"Only my conviction. By the way, I see Punch isn't here to-night. Isn't he coming? No: I remember he said he wouldn't be coming. He's got a first night at the Globe.

Naturally I wouldn't say that about his end if I supposed for one moment it would come round to him. I should feel beastly. You won't, of course——"

"Goolawd, no!" ejaculated Jerry. "Make my hair stand on end." He turned away for an instant, his face distorted.

"I'm very much shocked at what you say," Ferdinand murmured, and shook his head in distaste. "I don't like it. There's a hint of necromancy, Edmund. The Black Art. In the Middle Ages you'd have been burnt. Dear, dear!"

Edmund's cold eye seemed to probe him.

"Well, it's a beastly thing to have said. I oughtn't to have said it. I can't think why I did."

"Perhaps you ought not," Ferdinand agreed. "Although, as you have done so, I must confess I should be very interested to know why you *think* it. Is it something Punch has *said* to you?"

"I don't think so. It's in his face."

"To you. Not to us."

"His voice?" demanded Jerry excitedly. It was on account of his odd, Punch-like voice that the man of whom they spoke went everywhere by his nickname.

"No, face. And to me, because——" Edmund stopped thoughtfully. His tone was sunk, lest any hint of what he said should reach the happy talkers who were farther across the room than themselves. "If I were to say that when I was a boy I saw the same expression in another man—— It's not wholly that. It's colouring, temperament, habits, tricks——"

"Oh, but *come,* Edmund!" Ferdinand was slightly impatient. "We live in a world where such things don't go by rule."

"After all, statistics show that so many people, every year, *do* commit suicide. The variation is extraordinarily small."

"Oh, you're a bally statistician, Edmund," began Jerry, with great discomfort. "These police rules of thumb are disgusting. They're an affront to human nature. And, anyway, let's get off Punch, for God's sake! The worst dramatic critic in England. Damn it, I shall see his corpse in every line." Jerry wavered as if he were tempted to run away. Curiosity, however, mastered him, and he returned, his eyes shining with a new interest. "But as you know so much," he said, "let's try another test. What about *me*, Edmund? D'you suggest that I shall do the same as Punch?"

Edmund shrugged, smiled, and shook his head.

"Oh, my dear boy, I don't pretend to be second-sighted. I expect you'll be a literary god and your portrait in all the papers."

"Rather good, what?" smiled Jerry. "A literary god, eh?" He jerked his head. "Well, then, what about old Joe there?"

"Old Joe will get anything he wants in life. No shooting for him. A nice long sleep when he's eighty or more." Edmund looked quickly down at his feet. "He'll outlive us all," he said.

In spite of his incredulity Ferdinand shuddered at this apportionment of futures.

"A *very* grisly seer," he murmured. He had been comparing the length of Jerry's fair eyelashes—which were so often dropped, as if in shyness, as he spoke—and the great size of his smiling blue eyes with the sculpture-like outline of Edmund's mouth and chin when Mona Talbot entered the room.

"Hullo, who's this?" Ferdinand heard Edmund say with some abruptness—as a dog may growl at a stranger.

It was not, however, to Mona that he referred, for Mona's tall figure and her plain face, surmounted by a great deal of old-fashioned hair which resembled the stuffing of an antique sofa, were perfectly well known to them all. It was another figure, that of a man, who was at first partially hidden by Mona's angular lines, which stirred them all to curiosity.

Ferdinand, who had the clue to the puzzle, saw one who was not very tall but who was unusually broad for his height. It was not for this reason an ungainly figure, but there was

strength in it rather than grace. The head was large and fine,
as Catherine had said, and it was surmounted by vigorous,
closely cropped curly hair of a particular rich chestnut colour. There was a suggestion of power in that firm brow, of
great intelligence in the clear eyes. But upon the mouth
there was a bitterness, a determination, emphasized by a
strong line at either side of it, which struck Ferdinand with
something like dismay. Such a mouth, in such company,
seemed to him to be out of place. It was as if a ragged and a
starving man had appeared suddenly amid revellers.

The introduction—for which Ferdinand moved forward
—took a moment only. To neither of them was it agreeable,
if he could judge by the stranger's manner, for at his courteous words of welcome Jabez Talbot merely bowed, gave
one inclusive glance at Ferdinand, which took in his clothes
and air as well as his features, and for the rest ignored him.
Brusque, gauche—the words sprang to Ferdinand's mind.
Then there was a stir in the room. Awaking from his little
dream, Ferdinand saw a white-capped maid—she was called
Annie—at the door, knew that dinner was served, heard and
felt about him the pleasant jostling of mind and tongue and
convivial interest. Speechless, he joined the others as they
moved towards the dining room.

As he approached he overheard the newcomer, in a harsh
voice with a Northern accent, and with an odd movement
of his arms and hands, say contemptuously to Catherine:

"Of course, I'm not used to this sort of thing. I *work* for
my living."

That was all; but Ferdinand drew his breath quickly in
surprise. This sort of thing! It was a condemnation. His own
home, with its beauty and carefully maintained comfort!
What *sort* of fellow, then, was Mona's cousin? "I *work* for
my living!" It was contemptuous enough. Ferdinand, with
narrowed eyes, watched the stranger descend the stairs.
Then, when all were gone, he followed, a little acid twist
upon his smiling lips.

CHAPTER III

A THEFT, A FRIEND, AND A LETTER

I

UNLIKE the room which they had just left, the dining room in the Meadows's house was gaily coloured. It had been designed by Rhoda. A concealed lighting made the painted ceiling look very brilliant, while the walls and the pictures were very brightly coloured. Candles standing, lighted, upon the polished table had small, cheerful shades of decorated parchment, the plates and dishes bore an extremely fanciful design in colour, and the little mats and doilies matched them in a vivid display. Ferdinand, seated at the head of the table, between Mona and Gwen, smiled to himself at the noise and cheerfulness which were all about him. He saw the two maids making their rounds among the diners, heard the voices and laughter, and thought unexpectedly to himself: "How much I like the company of young people!" The reflection so cheered him that he was stimulated to conversation.

"Your cousin," he said agreeably to Mona, "he has a very striking face. I should say a man of strong intellect. Is he a professional man?"

Mona's mouth, which had been slightly open, closed suddenly. She smiled at Ferdinand in a friendly way.

"He's everything," she said. "You'd be surprised."

"I am indeed surprised," remarked Ferdinand, smiling. "Your description is so inclusive."

"So is Jabez," promptly answered Mona. "You know, don't you, that he's a Labour man?"

32

"Labour?" Ferdinand's thumbs pricked. He was filled with alarm. It was as though she had said that Jabez was a commissar. "Ah! No, I didn't know that. Did you mean——?"

"A Labour organizer. He'll be an M.P. at the next election. They think the world of him."

"They," breathed Ferdinand. Yes, he could now understand the expression upon the stranger's face. Mortification had begotten pride, a craving for power. Retributive power. It was all there. "Is he—is your cousin what would be called *extreme?*"

"I don't know. What *is* extreme?" she asked, in the most innocent way.

"It's what we're all very much afraid of," retorted Ferdinand. "Those of us, at least, who have any desire to conserve civilization."

"Oh, you mean property?"

"Not only property."

"I feel sure he's not an extremist," declared Mona loyally. "He always takes his hat off when they play 'God Save the King.'"

"Oh," said Ferdinand, much relieved. "Then he's a democrat, like myself."

"He's wonderful!" exclaimed Mona. Her dull face glowed with enthusiasm. Below her ruche of hair there were two extremely intelligent brown eyes; the rest of her face, with its coarse skin, was disappointing. Her colour was bad, her mouth and teeth were misshapen, and she carried herself awkwardly. But Ferdinand liked her because she was not only kind and sympathetic but sincere and without affectation.

"I don't remember that in the past you and I have ever spoken of him," Ferdinand ventured. "Though we've talked of many things."

"Perhaps not," she agreed. "He's not often in London. He goes about speaking."

"Ah, yes." Ferdinand's thought was: "Then we fortunately shan't see much of him"; and he brightened slightly.

"And it's only since he came to stay with us about a month ago that I've got to know him really well."

"Quite," assented Ferdinand. "Quite."

"In that time I've come to realize why it is that he's so popular. I mean, being a relation, one's naturally a bit suspicious. But now that I know him I *do* see it. He's really got a power of understanding what you say to him. That's more rare than one imagines, because people's minds distort so. It needs real sympathy. And when he talks to a man or a woman he's *really* interested in them, not shamming, as the good workers generally are, and wondering how they can get something for their horrid collecting cards. He quite separates that man or that woman from all the others. You know what I mean. It isn't just an art, but something—— It's very charming."

"It's a very rare gift," said Ferdinand thoughtfully, "if he's successful. Is he never guilty of a mistake?"

A light came into Mona's eye. The ugly lips spread apart, disclosing her irregular teeth in a jagged smile.

"Oh, yes. He wouldn't be human if he didn't make mistakes. He made one with Rhoda the other day."

"Indeed?" said Ferdinand quickly. This was what he had wanted!

"You hadn't heard about it? It was really nothing, but it was rather funny and provoking, because it was so unnecessary. She was talking politics in the way she has——"

"I didn't know she——"

"Didn't you? Mona raised her brows in surprise, but not in disbelief. She nodded confirmingly. "Yes, she constantly does. She seems to be sort of sentimental Conservative—I don't know *what* she is." Ferdinand's brow contracted. He strove to look guileless, listening carefully as Mona continued: "She began talking with horror of utilitarianism. She

was talking—you know how she does—very impulsively and
hotly against that man Ben Lever——"

"Oh, that fellow," Ferdinand shiveringly said. "Yes, yes."
He allowed Mona to glimpse his own extreme distaste for
Ben Lever, a Communist who had recently been sent to
prison for some harangue.

"And so Jabez told her this man was a friend of his."

"And is he?" Ferdinand was anxious.

"Apparently. In that way that every sparrow is and every
tramp. And Jabez asked her if she knew all the facts. He
wasn't debating with her. He never debates with people. But
I think Rhoda thought he was. So she was very outspoken,
and Jabez said finally—quite nicely—that she didn't know
what she was talking about. Well, she didn't, you know, Mr.
Meadows; and one doesn't like to be told one's a goose when
there's a reason for it."

"A reason," murmured Ferdinand, under his breath. "A
goose."

"Unfortunately, though Jabez was as nice as he could be,
he was too blunt for a short acquaintance. You know what
I mean, don't you?"

"Quite, quite," Ferdinand said, still thinking: "A goose!"

"So I asked Catherine if he could come to-night to—well,
to make it up."

Ferdinand smiled appreciatively and nodded in approval
of Mona's reconciliatory scheme; but in spite of this he was
not sure that he enjoyed having it said so humorously that
his daughter was a goose. After all, Rhoda was the product
of his own teaching. . . .

"He never debates with people." "He's wonderful."
Clearly Mona was a partizan of this fellow. Was she a convert to his ideas? Had he that terrifying power over the
human mind? Was *nobody* safe from him? Ah, danger,
danger! They were so young, so inflammable. . . . Ferdinand was very silent for the rest of the meal. He had much
to occupy his mind.

II

He would have liked to steer this dangerous young man into the study, seat him, and in that good-humour which indicates absolute self-confidence begin to rally him upon some of the points which had been suggested by Mona's discourse. In vain. Coffee was served upstairs, and to coffee they all must troop. Meanwhile, he found himself alone. Catherine, Mona, and Jabez, before the larger of the two Dutch paintings, engaged in contemplation of its loveliness.

"Ph!" It was a breath of impatience, almost a "pish"! He turned away and set his empty cup and saucer upon the tall mantelpiece. In doing this he glanced upward and found that in the old oak-framed mirror which hung above his head, slightly tilted, he could just embrace that interested group at the other end of the room. Catherine, who was shorter than the rather angular Mona, was as tall as Jabez. Their heads were upon a level. His breadth, however, made her appear slight, a pink Malmaison carnation among commoner flowers. And the perception caused him to look, still in the mirror, a little anxiously for Rhoda.

She was safe! Gwen and Jerry were near—Jerry lazily listening, his pale lids very languidly half closed, his head thrown back, golden in the reflected light; while Gwen delivered a breathless, vivacious, endless speech. How her hard little tongue rattled, and her brisk eyes, full of humour, gave the impression that she entirely lacked repose! Ferdinand smiled, with some malice.

The brother? Yes, Ferdinand was reminded of Joe. Where was he? What was he doing? He glanced again into the confiding mirror, quite casually—not with the slightest wish to spy or pry—and by this curious chance he became the observer of an inexplicable incident. In the mirror he saw Joe at some distance from him, upon his left, standing alone, near the grand piano, upon which rested the book of prints at which he and Catherine had been looking earlier in the

evening. It was a quite natural situation, and Ferdinand
would have thought nothing of it. But as he caught sight of
Joe standing there he saw Joe take a swift survey of the
room behind him. First he looked at Catherine and her companions, and then at Rhoda and the others. Seeing that all
were occupied, and apparently forgetful of Ferdinand's
existence, Joe put his fingers into the bowl which contained
that great bunch of Parma violets. Hastily he abstracted
three or four blooms, touched them with his handkerchief,
as if slightly to dry the wet stalks, drew out a pocketbook,
and popped the stolen flowers between its covers.

It was done in an instant, not stealthily, but with a nervous
promptitude which suggested that the theft—if it could be
called theft—was due to sudden impulse. At the sight, Ferdinand wheeled round, quite astonished, so that he frankly
faced the room, his eyes wide open, even his lips parted in
amazement; and Joe, in replacing his pocketbook, simultaneously glanced up, straight before him, straight at Ferdinand.
The eyes of the two met, Ferdinand's kind, smiling, and very
much mystified; Joe's smiling also, but with a brightness, a
gleam, that was unaccountable. Seeing that his action must
have been observed, Joe smiled more deeply, put a finger to
his lips, and picked up the book of prints which lay near the
violets. His air was one of nonchalance, but there had been
haste, there had been an arch and puzzling air of guilt.

Guilt? thought Ferdinand. Nonsense! No guilt. That was
impossible. Besides, the theft was trifling. If he had asked
for the flowers he might have had them. There could be no
guilt. But there was certainly mischievousness, some ruffling
of emotion, of haste. What did it mean? A game? Love of
the flowers? A sentiment? Unthinkable. Ferdinand shrugged.
A moment later, Joe moved towards him.

III

"One thing I can never understand," said Joe, "is the
modern passion for remaining upright. I like to sit down.

There isn't a soul in this room who is sitting down or who *wants* to sit down."

"By all means, let us sit down," hastily responded Ferdinand. "I beg your pardon."

"Oh, it wasn't a reproach," Joe assured him, as they sat. "It was an observation."

"Quite," said Ferdinand. "But a true, a pointed observation. And so you think it is a modern custom not to sit down? And yet our ancestors had most uncomfortable benches and wooden chairs."

"I don't believe they stood as much as we do. They had *time* to sit down. Now, we've no time to do anything. We're always going on to the next thing. I suppose Jerry will go on to a night club from here, and Edmund will sit over a dummy brief. As for Talbot, I expect he's got a midnight meeting in the vaults of the House of Commons."

"The vaults——" stammered Ferdinand. He leapt at the opportunity of further enlightenment regarding his guest.

"He and his fellow conspirators, making red crosses of rage on a manifesto, swearing death to every plutocrat."

"He's a red?" questioned Ferdinand. "But Mona says he is no such thing. You alarm me."

"I don't think you're so easily alarmed," soothingly replied Joe.

"Still, he's a newcomer to the house. I feel a little responsible. Honestly, Gascoyne, do you know anything about him?"

"Only that he's one of the people who live in order to lecture to the world. He's always saying 'Woe, woe!'"

" 'Woe, woe!' " echoed Ferdinand. He made a slight, very delicate grimace.

"He wants to grind our bones to make the people's bread. Does that terrify you? Most of these chaps are very peaceble in private life. He won't grind any of *your* bones."

"Or my daughters'?" asked Ferdinand. "It's on their account——"

"They can look after themselves."

"Catherine, perhaps. Not Rhoda. Or, at least, I *think* not Rhoda."

"It's a question," Joe seemed for a moment to grow serious. His long face assumed, at any rate, a graver cast. "You probably know them better than I do."

"As their father, perhaps I *ought* to do so," Ferdinand said, with an air of lightness which indicated a rather poohpoohing irony.

"It doesn't follow. The looker-on sees most of the game."

"Isn't that just what I am?" interposed Ferdinand. "A particularly privileged looker-on?"

"In the sense that you're not a submerged participant—yes. But you're a good deal involved, aren't you? I mean, they're a little of your own hatching. You're not absolutely indifferent."

"Far from it," Ferdinand said warmly. "But I admit—Gascoyne——" He was carried involuntarily into this almost abject candour with a young man whom he had hitherto feared—the one young man known to him in the company to whom he did not feel superior. Never before had he said as much to another person. Never previously, perhaps, had he been in a state to conceive the thought which he now expressed. "You speak of a brood. That word has associations. Have you an analogy in your mind? Are you by any chance thinking of me as an old hen clucking on the edge of a pond? Tell me, was that your meaning?"

A quick smile crossed Joe's face, and instantly vanished.

"I shouldn't have any right to say a thing like that," he answered. "My use of the word was accidental. But supposing your chicks *did* show a taste for the water? What would you do? I haven't the least wish to offend you. I'm tremendously afraid of doing so."

"You're afraid of wounding—of speaking your mind?" Ferdinand exclaimed. "My dear boy, forgive me, but fear of that kind is the last thing one would associate with you. I also mean no offence, as I hope you know. But are you *really* afraid?"

Joe nodded. His eyes gleamed, as they had done when he took the violets.

"I'm afraid of everything," he said. "I see you all at the verge of a crisis——"

"A crisis!" Ferdinand caught him up, with a sense of thrilling excitement in his breast. He might have seen his own hands trembling as they were raised to the region of his heart. "You say a crisis? That is really most inexplicable! At this time? Now? But you're not afraid *for* the girls. You've said that they could look after themselves."

"Yes; but will you allow them to do so?" asked Joe. He was still unusually animated. "Actually, I think Rhoda is one of those people who inspire the protective impulse, who are always sure of protection—except from her worst enemy. I may be wrong. Most likely I am. Still, it's a view. But Catherine——"

"She has great sense, great self-command. She doesn't *need* protection in the same degree. Don't you admit that? She doesn't, I mean, need protection from herself."

"I don't think that's true," Joe said quietly. "It *is* the point of disagreement between us. Or at least, it's one of the points. What I'm really wondering is this: you haven't known any of us"—he indicated the groups—"for a great while—except Jerry. And you don't know Jerry at all. Until a few months ago, your girls knew nobody but a few school children. They're none the worse for that——"

"I'm glad you say so," Ferdinand murmured. Joe did not heed him.

"Now they're making friends hand-over-fist. You think you can absorb as fast as they. You can't. They'll leave you behind. Already they're doing it. And then, what? Rhoda can float in any society. She's self-centred, emotional——"

"Exactly. Isn't the emotional temperament the dangerous

one?" Ferdinand had not interrupted earlier, but he could not pass what seemed to him to be a glaring error in rudimentary psychology.

Joe shook his head.

"Self-contained people have a tendence to explode," he said. "If your emotions are always flowing it's different. Because some people bottle their emotion it doesn't follow that they're frigid. That's one of the vulgar errors of this vulgar age. Emotion has to be seen to be believed. So it's simulated by all the people who can feel nothing at all. That's my view of Catherine, at least. And, as I said just now, I'm quite likely to be wrong."

"I feel sure you are," said Ferdinand warmly. "Sure of it. I can't help feeling sure of it. I admit a great deal of what you say. It's very shrewd. But——" He was emphatic. Then he was less emphatic, and more appealing. "There must be so many things known to me that you can't possibly know. Something the other way, too, perhaps; but I think you'd admit a balance. You see——"

He paused in thought; and before he could resume they were interrupted by a breaking up of the groups and by the advent of Rhoda, who came towards her father and claimed him as her own property, linking her arm in his, and as if possessively remaining at his side while the general talk proceeded. A large, all-embracing group was formed, with Ferdinand in the centre of it. There was accordingly no opportunity for more private talk between Ferdinand and Joe, and the exceptional warmth of cordiality between them died down.

It was not until later that Ferdinand, thus distracted, realized how entirely he had been prevented from gratifying his strong secret desire to ask why Joe had stolen the violets.

IV

He listened in almost complete silence while all these voluble young creatures expounded their notions of life. Joe was adventurous, Rhoda incoherent, Jerry in agreement with everybody. Edmund, who knew nothing about the law, spoke at length upon the theory of music, while Gwen, who knew nothing about any subject in the world, was defiant in her strictures upon various national heroes of the past and present. When the newcomer, Jabez, made any comment at all, it was brief and was uttered in a low tone; and in general, although he listened attentively and was often appealed to by Mona, who desired that her cousin should shine as a bright light, he said nothing whatever. In this silence he was emulated by Catherine, who was no talker in general company.

Ferdinand, now that he could scrutinize Jabez's face at leisure and without rudeness, availed himself of all his privileges. If he could not talk to the stranger, at least he could observe him, and he did this with an emotion that was, if not jealous, certainly rather hostile. It was a good face, he was forced to admit, and the eyes had that almost bluish purity of white which heightens an effect of intelligence. Nor were the eyes themselves those of a fanatic. Far from it. They were very clear, a dark gray, and the pupils were no larger than normal. Also, they were full of expression. They travelled from one face to the other in sympathy and understanding. A little serious, Jabez might be (because those who are very humorous are rarely guilty of ardour in their political convictions), but he was not odd. He evidently had much self-control, as well as much frankness, and his rare smile was without bitterness or malice.

"But in *spite* of that, I don't like him," thought Ferdinand defiantly. The man ruffled him. He felt much as a cat does who is disregarded by a dog of unknown temper.

The party came at last to an end, and as the servants were all, according to custom, in bed, Ferdinand personally superintended the departure of the visitors. The girls accompanied him; and all three stood upon the front doorstep looking out into the darkness. No blustering wind, no flying rain marred

the mild dignity of the evening. All was very black except
for the street lamps in the square. There seemed to be no
moon, or, if the moon was there, it was hidden by clouds
invisible to the watchers below. Sedately the members of the
party went off together in comparative silence, while Ferdinand and his daughters withdrew into the warm house.
Ferdinand was the last to enter, and he had his back to the
girls for an instant as he closed and bolted the front door.
He therefore saw only the conclusion of a scene which gave
him a faint shock.

As he prepared to walk from the door he became aware
that Catherine was by the small table which stood beside
the big old Victorian coat-and-umbrella stand. Rhoda was
behind her and nearer to himself. Catherine had stopped
and was bending her head to look at an envelope lying upon
the table, a letter which had reached the house by the last
post of the evening. The bright light from above caught her
fairness as she straightened herself and looked strangely at
Rhoda, who in turn stepped forward to read the writing
upon the envelope. Then, to Ferdinand's surprise, as Catherine, without speech, proceeded upon her way, Rhoda snatched
the letter from its place upon the table, crushed it quickly in
her hand, as if secretively, and ran up the stairs in Catherine's wake. The silence, the singular fixity of Catherine's
glance, the swiftness and suddenness of Rhoda's action,
her concealment of the letter, were all charged with significance.

CHAPTER IV

NIGHT AND MORNING

I

ALTHOUGH Ferdinand, tired out, slept as soon as his head rested comfortably upon the soft pillow, his daughters did not so easily take leave of the day. They called good-night to him as they went, and a moment later, with a brief word, they separated. Each disappeared into her own little bedroom; and thereafter the house was silent.

When Catherine had closed the door she stood still, just inside it, her hand outstretched behind her, as if she thought to reopen the door and step out, across the landing, to that other room which was so unlike her own. The minutes passed; she seemed to listen, to hesitate; then the hand fell slowly to her side; she advanced farther into the room, the door fast as before. Evidently that first impulse was not to be obeyed. A second impulse, stronger than the first, had conquered.

This room of Catherine's, which was not above sixteen feet square, was furnished in a way to contradict Joe Gascoyne's estimate of Catherine's character. It was very plain. The small bedstead, the chairs, and the two tables were simple in design, as he would have expected; but the furnishing and arrangement of the room had nothing in it to support Joe's theory of suppressed emotion. The room, in fact, was thoroughly homely—cheerful and free from pretentiousness, but hinting at very simple tastes and an enjoyment of life. There were some books upon a small set of shelves, all of them in the original cloth bindings, bright and clean, all of them the obvious reading of a girl of the day; there was a long cheval glass with a green frame; the bed and a cane-seated chair were likewise painted green, the bed with a design of small pink roses upon its foot; while an exceedingly comfortable tub-shaped armchair with a bright cretonne loose cover had its feet firmly planted upon the warm hearth-rug. The walls of the room were papered—again with a gay little rose pattern—and a flowered eiderdown lay upon the bed. The carpet was a plain dark green, soft to the foot, inconspicuous to the eye.

Amid this cosiness (for a small fire burned in the grate) Catherine presently took off the powder-blue frock which she had worn for the evening, wrapped her slender body in a rose-coloured dressing gown, and sat in the tub-shaped armchair by the fire. Her fresh young cheeks were as clear as ever; her brow was unpuckered. As she breathed, her breast rose and fell slowly, and her lips met demurely over the small, regular teeth which showed only when she smiled or spoke. Catherine was entirely calm, entirely unruffled. If she had painful or alarming thoughts she gave no sign of any such thing, but sat quietly and without any appearance of trouble or apprehensiveness. But she was not smiling. She was noticeably grave, as if, quietly and gently, she were considering something which had happened and deciding what course she would presently pursue in connection with it.

Seeing Catherine thus, Joe must have reconsidered his judgment of her character. He could not have failed to admire her beauty and to speculate upon her wisdom. But he would have learned nothing from her outward aspect as to the feelings which were in action below that appearance of tranquillity and thoughtfulness. He could not have supposed that Catherine had been deeply agitated within the previous few minutes, and he would thus have been compelled to decide that she was ordinarily calm as the result of natural and constantly exerted self-control.

Presently Catherine began to undress, bathing her face

in the warm water which had stood for half an hour, carefully covered by a bath towel, in a brass hot-water can. Within ten minutes she was lying in bed, in the darkness, listening acutely for any sound which might come from within the house, until at last, lulled by her own soft, regular breathing, she fell asleep and dreamed—it was the first hint in support of Joe's theory—of Rhoda in the clutches of a terrible monster with unseen face and long, horrid clawlike hands.

II

In the other room, the one across the landing, which in size and shape so closely resembled Catherine's, a very different scene had been enacted. Rhoda had controlled herself with vehement effort until she had parted from Catherine, until she was alone, with her door swiftly, silently made fast, the key turned. Then, trembling, she had opened her hand —the hand in which she had so lately crumpled the letter snatched from the hall table. It lay, an almost unrecognizable ball, in her slender palm, marked by the convulsive pressure of her fingers; and as she stared at it the ball slightly untwisted itself, now that the pressure was relaxed, moved as if it had stubborn life, and fell silently to the floor. Not unheeded, for Rhoda continued to stare at the letter as it lay there, but a crumpled travesty of what it had been a few moments earlier.

Still staring, Rhoda backed away from the letter, until she reached her little white bed. Her hand crept round behind her; the fingers touched and wandered about the foot rail of the bed; thus guided, she sat down, watching the letter, the dark, enormous eyes glowing in her white face, her lips bitten by the little teeth which showed milklike against the darker colouring of her cheeks. She breathed very quickly. A flush came and went in her face, spreading painfully to her neck, leaving her paler than before. She did not cry. She was too excited to cry while the moment of discovery

persisted. A letter; a glance; an error—and her present fear.
Instead of crying Rhoda looked tremblingly at the door, as
if she expected to see the stealthy turning of its handle, as if
she thought Catherine might still, by some force unknown
to her, be able to enter. Catherine had seen the letter, had
recognized the handwriting, had said nothing—in surprise.
Catherine, whom Rhoda loved. She shuddered.

Minutes passed. The small gilt clock upon the mantelpiece,
under her Medici print of Botticelli's Venus rising from the
Sea, ticked them busily. The smouldering cinders rustled as
if they might be coughing behind their hands, huskily. The
whole room, white in its hangings and its paint, was silent,
breathless. She felt that it was listening, watching, while she,
breathing rapidly, and ever more rapidly, was struggling
against an impulse to break into heavy sobbing, the sobbing
of a child in distress, bitter, inconsolable.

Once Rhoda started to her feet. The expression in her
eyes was one of terror. She clearly had thought to run into
Catherine's room, where Catherine, not yet sleeping, awaited
her. But as she stood she caught sight of the twisted letter
lying upon the floor, and with a gesture of desperation she
sank again to the bed, lower, lower, until her face was hidden
in its soft covering. Very quietly she began to cry, her shoulders moving, the tears wetting the backs of her hands.

III

So she lay for perhaps an hour, half slumbering when the
tears had spent themselves. But at the end of that time,
languidly, reluctantly, she drew herself up and sat once more
upon the bed, her hands raised mechanically to her tossed
hair. The clock was ticking away as if it were trying to hurry
the world into the next day; the fire had sunk to a grayness
in which red could hardly be seen. Rhoda stared before her.
The drawn face, the pathetically puckered mouth, were those
of a little girl who was afraid and full of sorrow. It was

more than half-past one. Everybody but herself in this large, quiet old house was fast asleep. Only Rhoda, not daring to look at the letter, was wide awake. If she had been pale, as her father had noticed when she turned from the window to greet him, she was paler now. Her hands were white, but her cheeks were whiter than they.

At last, miserably, she stood erect, incredibly childish, and stooped and picked from its place upon the floor that dangerous, that terrible letter which she had not opened. Then, very gently, she smoothed out the bitter folds into which she had crushed it and laid the letter—still unopened—upon her dressing table. The writing upon it was bold, rapid, and clear; the letter within must be equally so. But Rhoda had not the courage to open the envelope. Having smoothed its creases, having stared at the direction to herself, with a faint little half smile upon her lips, she too (as Catherine had done) removed her evening frock, which was much crushed, and took from her wardrobe a dressing gown. But she did not seat herself by the fire, but returned to the dressing table, once more looked long upon the envelope, and then at the reflection of her own face in the mirror. For a few moments she did not speak, but at length her lips were uncontrollably parted.

"Poor Rhoda," she said softly, shaking her head. "Poor Rhoda!"

The mirrored head shook mournfully in time with her own; the mirrored lips echoed her whispered word of pity. As if she had been consoled by this sympathy, Rhoda looked again in the mirror, long and tenderly, until the colour began to return to her cheeks and a more natural light to her eyes, until her lips lost something of their melancholy droop. The letter, lightly brushed by her elbow or by the hanging lace in the sleeve of her dressing gown, fell silently to the ground, where it lay for several minutes, unheeded, until Rhoda straightened her body, looked down, and restored the letter to its old place in front of the mirror. Still, however, she did not seek to learn what message was hidden within its envelope, but seemed content to pretend that she already knew what her lover had written.

IV

In the morning, at breakfast time, a low-toned gong summoned the family downstairs. At that hour Ferdinand had already been for some time in his book-lined study, standing idly in front of the burning fire, and drawing a particularly soothing kind of delight from the contemplation of between four and five thousand books. Catherine had been in the lower part of the house, engaged in some of her morning duties. Only Rhoda had risen late, tired by the excitement of the previous night. But when they all assembled for the meal it was Rhoda who bore the most tranquil expression. She entered the room hastily, after the others, dressed in a plain blue cotton frock, as fresh as love-in-a-mist, and went directly to her father, whom she lovingly kissed.

"Good-morning, Daddy," said she. "It's a lovely morning, I see."

"Good-morning, my dear," Ferdinand replied. "I hadn't noticed it was lovely. Possibly because something has given me a headache. It makes me incapable of taking much interest in the weather. But I *do* feel, now, that the sun's shining."

"That's because *I've* come!" announced Rhoda gaily.

"I was intending to convey that impression," responded Ferdinand. "And you look particularly charming, I think. Charming." He kissed her again, still holding the hand which she had given him. "And as it's a fine morning what do you say to coming for a walk with me? We might go and see the squirrels in Regent's Park."

"Oh, Daddy!" Rhoda flushed deeply. "I'm so *awfully* sorry. I can't."

"Never mind," Ferdinand gently answered. "Another day."

"You see, I'm going out," stammered Rhoda.

"Quite," said Ferdinand, not looking up, but patting her hand.

"I'd really *love* to come with you——"

That made him raise his eyes and smile reassuringly.

"I'm sure you would. And I should love you to come. I'll go and see the squirrels by myself."

"In Regent's park?" faltered Rhoda. "Oh, but you wouldn't see them. They wouldn't——"

Ferdinand could not understand that deep flush, the tears which had started to her eyes. But he could tell that she was distressed at having given him pain.

"We'll go to-morrow, instead," he said cheerfully, "won't we? I shouldn't like to see them without you. You're quite right."

Was there relief in Rhoda's eyes? He could not tell. Involuntarily he looked across at Catherine, who sat behind the coffee pot at the end of the table. She was reading a letter which had come that morning, and she did not appear to be listening to their conversation. But as Rhoda went to her place Catherine did look up, and in meeting Rhoda's glance it seemed as though she very faintly, and in disapprobation, shook her head. Rhoda's glowing eyes held no secrets from her sister, who, although she had not read the letter which Rhoda had received upon the previous evening, knew perfectly well the very simple secret of its contents.

CHAPTER V

WORKERS AND DRONES

I

So PASSED a few days, while the wind raged and the mornings and evenings grew markedly lighter. Ferdinand, playing as he did, from time to time, with the notion of some work which should give him an object of concentration, conceived the notion of writing a book; but as he could not decide upon the theme for such a book he was once more discouraged from beginning work upon it. He wondered why men should spend their lives in writing books when already there are so many books which can never be read; and he comforted himself with the assurance that writers, upon the whole, are an inferior class of persons. They are not thinkers, but improvisers. They catch the current vogue and give it expression. Well, things were different long ago, in the days of giants.

The days of giants were gone, Ferdinand believed. That was partly because nobody expected nowadays to meet a giant. Or desired it, perhaps? A giant would be a great inconvenience in modern life, where so much is standardized. He would be what is termed an "O. S." Where there is a high degree of civilization, monsters are not much in demand. Certainly there was no room in the house in Woburn Square for a monster. The more Ferdinand considered that question, the more thankful he became that he and his daughters lived obscurely, conscious of their smallness, happy and contented.

And yet it seemed as if, unawares, they had admitted to

their company—or had had forced upon them—a kind of lesser monster. Unpleasant as a monster could be, a lesser monster might be sufficiently disagreeable; and in Jabez Talbot they had found somebody who introduced disharmony to their table and their fireside. Not content with that first appearance, upon the occasion of which he had affronted Ferdinand by describing the house as "this sort of thing," he visited them a second time. And at the second meeting he was even more outspokenly disagreeable than he had formerly been.

Dinner was over: they were in the drawing room. Subdued light played upon them all, and Ferdinand, who was accustomed to the respect of all who visited the house, was surprised to find himself the subject, first of extremely fierce glances, and then of sharp speech, from Jabez. He was amazed by first the glances and then the speech. In his amazement he did not at once hear correctly, but in a dream looked at his assailant, wondering how those bitter lines could ever have been engraved in the broad cheeks. It was a stern face, he thought, a face which might very well subdue an audience. Leaning back, he could imagine Jabez Talbot facing an audience. The hall, he thought, would be well filled; and all faces upturned. He could realize something of that aspect, because he had upon several occasions sat behind the orchestra, facing the general public, at Queen's Hall, upon a Sunday afternoon. And by his habit of pictorially envisaging any scene he could imagine both Jabez and his listeners, passing his eye, as it were, from one to the other of them. Some person, perhaps—for Ferdinand merely one of the white faces, ghastly under the lights of the hall —had shouted an interruption. Kindling, Jabez was about to answer it. His face was drawn, as pale as all the other faces; the lines in his cheeks were deepened; his bitter mouth —the lips were not thin, but they were hard, as if brazen— was tightly closed before opening the retort. Then——

"I've been wondering," said the Northern voice, "if you ever saw a slum, Mr. Meadows."

Ferdinand struggled out of his dream, opened his eyes widely.

"I beg your pardon. You mean——"

"I mean a slum. A place where people are crowded higgledy-piggledy together—four or five or six in a room, living and dying there."

"I never did," Ferdinand said confusedly, after a moment's thought. He was still so far from having expected this remark that he could not persuade himself that it had been made. The silent room, with the exquisite pictures, and with that little group—of Rhoda, Catherine, Mona, and Edmund Piercy—by the piano, seemed to be so far distant from questions about slums. And yet Ferdinand was by no means inhumane. "I belong to the countryside, though my middle life has all been spent in London."

Jabez nodded. His face was grim.

"I should like to take you through a slum, Mr. Meadows," he said. "You'd get a shock."

"Yes," Ferdinand answered. No more.

"It seems odd to me, Mr. Meadows, coming as I do from among the workers, to get into this atmosphere."

Ferdinand courteously inclined his head.

"It must be very odd," he agreed; but he still did not quite follow the train of Jabez's thought. "Poor creatures; their lives are full of ugliness and suffering."

"You may well say that," responded Jabez. "You can't wonder at what they think and feel."

"Indeed, no," said Ferdinand thoughtfully.

"D'ye ever feel uncomfortable, Mr. Meadows?" pursued the harsh voice. "In all this?" Jabez waved his hand—it was the free gesture, Ferdinand recognized, of one who was well versed in the art.

"I?" asked Ferdinand. "Oh, you mean—as a humanitarian, or as"—he smiled—"one of the so-called idle rich?

As one of the idle rich I don't feel uncomfortable. I'm not ostentatious; I live simply; I merely am fortunate in being able to gratify my taste. But as a humanitarian, I do feel extremely uncomfortable. At the same time, I must ashamedly admit to a great personal repugnance to—what I suppose you would call the proletariat."

"I call them the workers," said Jabez bluntly.

"The *manual* workers," Ferdinand answered, a little drily. "That, of course, is a very old fallacy. There was somebody here the other day—I forget who it was——" He left the sentence suspended.

"As opposed to the idlers," persisted Jabez, looking fierce.

Ferdinand could see that vigorous frame, impressively muscular, under the plain dark tweed suit. He knew that as a man Jabez could crush his bones with a single hug of those iron-strong arms. He smiled, rather timidly, at the knowledge and at his own immunity. But under his smile there was a sense of aversion. He was fastidious, and he resented not only the topic but the aggressive physical toughness of his interlocutor.

"I pity the idlers more than I pity the workers," he answered quietly. "They must be the less happy. I can imagine nothing more disagreeable than idleness."

"Yet you've brought your daughters up to it, Mr. Meadows," came the rough reply.

Ferdinand looked in silence at Jabez—not at him, but past him. He did not speak. It was not fitting that he should speak. He was quivering secretly, it might be with resentment or with distaste; but he had lived enough in the world to know that one should never appear to notice impertinence. And having, by his silence, indicated indisposition to discuss his daughters with a stranger, he was relieved when his daughters, with the two other members of the party, came closer and interrupted the *tête-à-tête*. To Rhoda, especially, his swift glance of welcome was eager.

II

To Rhoda, especially, his glance was eager. To Rhoda, because she, too, he knew, had found this fellow offensive. To Rhoda, because he loved her. To Rhoda, because he knew that she was being what she hoped was frigid. To Rhoda, because, with the memory of their former encounter (it seemed to Ferdinand) still in his mind, Jabez gave her none of his attention. During the meal, when they had been side by side at the table, so much had been clear, for his shoulder had been turned to her almost all the time. Catherine, it appeared, was so greatly to his liking that he had conversed with her throughout dinner. Rhoda, with equal distaste, had behaved more correctly. Only to Ferdinand, who knew all, did her coldness—which was uncharacteristic—cause understanding and amusement.

Rhoda was the first to come to the fire, but the others were at her heels. She was in a beautifully embroidered dress of rich tawny red, which made her clear skin seem as white as milk. Beside her, Catherine, who was in gray, had no comparable richness, but appeared demure. It was impossible, as a result of this demureness, for Ferdinand ever to discover whether Catherine was bored; but he thought her very slightly constrained this evening, as if something had gone amiss. Mona, as usual, was untidy, enthusiastic, candid, silly, and sagacious. Edmund was merely agreeable.

"Daddy," said Rhoda, "Mr. Piercy wants to pretend that the Riviera is an intolerable part of the world. He's very much down upon it. I think we ought to go there one winter."

"What!" cried Jabez, in harsh disgust. He turned away his head.

Rhoda, ignoring that involuntary exclamation, proceeded:

"Can we go next winter? I should love to go where all the swells go."

"And the snobs," Mona added.

"I suppose we might go," hesitatingly agreed Ferdinand. "Yes, I should think——"

"There must be lots to paint," Rhoda said.

"Miles and miles of mimosa!" put in Catherine. "I love mimosa."

"Oh, yes!" exclaimed Rhoda. "So do I! Just imagine mimosa *growing!* Delicious!"

"Think of the society, the rich Jews, the profiteers, the snobs, the gamblers," said Jabez bitterly. "Fancy being mixed up with the scum of the idlers!"

Rhoda turned upon him.

"I think you're very puritanical, Mr. Talbot!" she cried warmly. "Supposing these people *do* go there, what does it matter to us, to you? They've got the money. They're spending it for the good of the workers. I suppose there are horrible people among the poor, too. I'm sure there are. *Horrid* people!"

"Aye, there are horrible poor people," agreed Jabez dourly.

"Besides, why should we starve ourselves of beauty and sunshine?"

"I won't argue with you," answered Jabez.

"You're as bad as Thomas Carlyle, who seems to have been——"

"Oh, Rhoda darling!" groaned Ferdinand. "Not a disquisition, I hope!"

The argument collapsed. They all laughed bubblingly, with the exception of Jabez, who looked down at the floor and ignored their further talk.

III

Jabez was the first to show—shortly after this—a restless desire for departure; and as soon as Mona had grasped and acted upon his rather anxious hints the disintegration of the party began. By eleven o'clock—quite early for the Meadowses—the visitors had left the house. There remained of the day nothing but that untidy fragment in which nothing can be done. And yet Ferdinand did not dismiss his daughters to bed. With the going of their guests he was ready for conversation, and it was only when he saw that both of his girls were unwilling to listen to his conversation that he ceased to make attempts at something which fell short of sprightliness.

"After all," he thought, "I'm growing quite middle-aged. But then, although I have the middle-aged person's respect 'for the young, who are so peremptory, I feel that my conversation *ought* to be worth listening to. Clearly it is not. But whether that is due to my prosiness or to their insensibility I shall not decide at this moment."

It was enough occupation for him to observe Rhoda as she sat pensively near the fire. The long lashes made a shadow upon her delicate cheek; the warm, impulsive lips were parted. One hand rested upon the other, and both were supported by her knee. She was half smiling as she sat there, spellbound by some memory as to the nature of which Ferdinand remained ignorant. So pleasant a picture caused him also to smile, in sympathy, and he turned thereafter (with some slight curiosity) to see whether Catherine had noticed what he had seen. Catherine, however, was not looking at Rhoda. With a rather serious expression, she was gazing across the room, straight before her.

"Probably thinking that we need new curtains," was Ferdinand's cruel surmise as he saw this direct and apparently objectless gaze. But he was wrong, it seemed, for presently Catherine in her turn smiled faintly, and thus disposed of the theory that she was thinking of curtains.

At last the silence grew too long for them all, and simultaneously they changed position. A glance among the three of them led to a general uprising from the chairs.

"I can't refrain from saying," observed Ferdinand, as they stood, "that I feel I shall never like Mona's cousin. He is brusque, gauche——"

"He's terrible!" agreed Rhoda, with her accustomed ardour.

Only Catherine did not respond to the condemnation of Mona's cousin. Without either frowning or smiling, she listened calmly to the general flow of opinion. At last she said:

"You're both very tired. It's high time for bed. Good-night, Father."

The comedy, for one day, was ended.

CHAPTER VI

MRS. BALTHAZAR

I

THE following evening Mrs. Balthazar was about to lock
the front door of her shop, after lowering the blind which
concealed the whole of her floral stock from the public eye,
when a shadow, thrown by the figure of a young man, came
sharply across the doorway. Mrs. Balthazar jumped at the
suddenness of this unexpected shadow and frowned; but
when she saw the face of the intruder her frown disappeared.
Her blue eyes twinkled into a smile of welcome; her doll-like
face became instantly animated. From that cold air of fra-
gility and suffering which had caused Ferdinand to feel so
apprehensive regarding Mrs. Balthazar's ability to struggle
with the world emerged a surprising liveliness of pleasure.

"Oh, it's *you!*" cried Mrs. Balthazar, in a rallying tone.
"Can't come in! Shop's shut! Call again, please. When I'm
out! What's that?" She pretended that she was not going to
admit her visitor.

"Damn you, Minnie; open the door! I'm in a hurry!"
asserted the young man, forcing the door open with a push
which he—with equal gaiety—pretended was far more vigorous than in fact it was. "Here's a fine way to greet a customer!" He was within the shop now, a large tweed-clad
figure, considerably above middle height, rather burly, crisp
haired, and rubicund; and the door was shut behind him.
He leaned against it for an instant, surveying the scene with
great contentment. Then, among the softly scented flowers
and the cold hanging leaves of the plants which stood dis-

played for sale, he caught the laughing Mrs. Balthazar in his arms and kissed her, while she, struggling as if to resist him, pressed the closer, and was evidently amused and delighted by his robust embrace.

"Now, now! That's enough!" she cried, averting her face and resisting him in earnest. "You'll have people looking in through all the slits. Come inside and behave prop'ly. Sh! sh! There's Auntie inside."

The visitor exclaimed at that piece of news, and put up his hand to ward off an imaginary blow.

"Auntie, by Jove! Help! Can I—I mean, can I face her?"

"What nonsense! You've done it before, haven't you? Auntie won't bite, you silly boy!" She gave him a little touch, teasing, encouraging, such as a mother might give a shy child who is hesitatingly about to meet a stranger. "Come along, I'm going to switch off this light!"

The light was switched off; but it was a moment before the two of them reached the room behind the shop. When they did so it was to see a rather cramped, comfortless, odd-shaped little space, separated from the shop only by painted matchboarding, poorly furnished with a rug, a curtain (both of them of red and blue in curious combination), a plain table, and a couple of deal chairs. Some empty boxes or cases, in which plants had been carried, stood against one of the unadorned walls; and in the middle of this so-called "room" sat an old woman with a comical resemblance to Mrs. Balthazar, who was reading a woman's paper by the light of a single and particularly feeble electric light bulb.

"Aun-tie!" shouted Mrs. Balthazar. "Hey!"

"What, dear!" whispered the old woman, dazzled by the change from a white printed page to the comparative darkness which enshrouded the two others. She peered towards them.

"Here's a visitor!" shouted Mrs. Balthazar gaily. "You know who this is, don't you?"

Again she spoke as if to a child. That refinement of

speech which Ferdinand had noticed was now less observable. Mrs. Balthazar was more at ease than she had been in the presence of a customer; and her articulation was thicker, less precise. There was even, at times, a slight twang of commoner speech. Her gestures were more unconstrained. Her whole demeanour was less demure, although she still wore the plain black dress in which Ferdinand had seen her. But whereas, in talking to Ferdinand, she had looked downward with something of the inscrutable expression of a cat, she now lifted her head freely and with vivacity towards the tall stranger's face, following all its play of humour and mood with absorbed tenderness. Seen thus, Mrs. Balthazar was no longer doll-like, no longer masked and hidden. As for the old woman whom Mrs. Balthazar addressed as Auntie, she was also dressed in black, but over her black she wore a knitted shawl of crimson wool, while crimson mittens protected her wrists from the cold. Her face was round and plump, as was Mrs. Balthazar's, but it no longer held any attractiveness and was red and swollen. Her eyes, which received the aid of spectacles, had lost their blueness, had begun to protrude and to look rather like highly polished gooseberries.

"Ay?" whispered the old woman. She lowered her head and looked over her glasses in the direction of the visitor thus announced.

"Don't you know him? Here's Mr. Teed come to see us. Mr. Teed. *You* know!"

"How d'ye do, Mr. Teed," said the old woman. She thrust forward a gnarled hand that was as rough as a file. "Ain't seen you for a long time. Sem months or more, ain't it? How you keeping?"

Punch Teed groaned in anticipation of the effort which this conversation was going to cost him.

"Splendid!" he bawled. "And *you're* looking fine, too!"

"I'm not," grumbled the old woman. "I may *look* it, but I ain't what I *should* be."

"We none of us are!" shouted Punch. "Born to sin and sorrow."

"It's not *that* I mind," said she. "So much as my stomach. And this light, Minnie. Awful, it is. I've got spots crawling about in front of my eyes, reading. I shall be blinded, soon enough, as if being deaf and dumb wasn't enough. My life's a misery to me. Ain't you ready to go home?"

"Presently, Auntie!" called Mrs. Balthazar. "Shan't be long now." In a lower tone, she added: "Take no notice of her, Georgie. She can't hear, poor old soul. She'll go back to her book—all about earls and countesses and what not. She still likes that sort best. We'll send her along home presently. Sit down." She stopped, looked at him brightly, and then, almost as if she were breathless, and much more softly, she asked: "You going to take me somewhere to dinner?"

He started, towering above her with his hands in his trousers pockets and his face in the darkness. There was the smallest pause. Then:

"Sorry, old girl," he said smoothly. "I can't, to-night. I'm most fearfully busy. Absolutely fearfully busy. I just looked in to see how you were. Saw the light on——"

Punch Teed did not look away as he spoke, as liars are supposed to do, but it was as if something fixed and deliberate had come into his glance. Or possibly the very easy, almost glib way in which the words of excuse had come from his lips caused Mrs. Balthazar to suspect him of untruth. Whatever the cause of her reply, it was clear that she did not believe that he was too busy to take her to dinner.

"Oh, well," she said quickly, "I only asked," and then turned away, not pettishly, but as though she had been greatly wounded. Punch stood there, watching. He was a very good-looking young man, with a reddish, clean-shaven face and a clear eye. His shoulders were broad, and he looked well fed, athletic, and as if he were successful in most things to which he set his hand. The glance which he now cast upon Mrs. Balthazar was shrewd, ironic, and confident.

"Cross?" he asked coolly.

"No," answered Mrs. Balthazar, less coolly. The shadow which had passed over her face had left it pinched. Her nose was pinched at the tip, her mouth was pinched at the corners, the curve of her cheek was less round. All this Punch must have seen, for it was obvious. But he did not look uneasy, although the smile had left his eyes and rested only upon his very clean-cut lips.

"I wish Auntie *was* blind, as well as deaf. Have you got any nice plants in the shop?" He looked suggestively into the semi-darkness behind them, through which the big brown holland window blind could be seen, quite light against the distant brilliance of one of the Holborn arc lamps. Now and again, for it was past eight o'clock in the evening, and few people are in Holborn at that hour, a sharply moving shadow was to be seen leaping across the blind, as a pedestrian hurried by, to east or west. Then again the pale light shone silently through the blind, as if the world were asleep. Punch backed towards the door, one eye upon Auntie. But Mrs. Balthazar shook her head.

"No, you're too busy," she said. "I mustn't ask favours." The word was very slightly emphasized. Her tone was dry. "Besides, Auntie and I are going home." She turned from him once again, bent down to the old woman's ear, and called, "Come on, Auntie! Time to go!"

"Yes," grunted the old woman, as if to herself. "Ah!" She did not immediately move.

"Don't be an idiot, Minnie," said Punch, in a low tone. "You're not in such a hurry as all that. Nor am I. It's one thing to stay for a few minutes. Quite another to go out to dinner."

"Yes," said Mrs. Balthazar, motionless.

"You don't believe me?"

"Well, what you say is true," she answered. The tone was without life and colour.

"But—?" he prompted.

"Well, I haven't seen you lately; and you're here. I thought perhaps you'd come to take me out somewhere. I haven't had much fun——" She was looking at him again, but at a point below his eyes; and her cheeks were white and her voice had a tired roughness in it. "I don't know what the good of it all is."

Punch swore under his breath. He was now perfectly serious. A heaviness had come into his face.

"Well, I ought to *work*," he cried, as if despairing. "Isn't that what you've always told me? Gosh, if you knew what I've got to do!"

"I'm not stopping you," said Mrs. Balthazar.

Auntie was struggling slowly to her feet, breathing rather hard. The spectacles had slipped some way down her lengthening nose, towards the point, and her mouth was gaping wide open in a yawn which she did not try to disguise, and which showed the yellow inside of her under lip and the toothless bottom gum at the front of her mouth.

"These *earls!*" she was ejaculating thoughtfully. "Well, I'm a working woman, meself, thank God for it!"

"And *I'm* a working man," grumbled Punch, in echo, and showing his teeth. "God damn it!" Mrs. Balthazar said nothing. "No, you're not stopping me, are you!" he continued, in bitter rumination, looking at her. "Not a bit of it. You're *helping* me!" He gave a sniff of pretended laughter. With a complete change of manner to extreme gentleness, he went on: "But you're upset, and you know I can't stand that."

"Oh, well, we all have to stand *something*," answered Mrs. Balthazar. She did not move as he approached her. Her arm and waist were rigid to his touch.

"I'll come," Punch whispered. "Don't be cross!"

There was an immediate but only partial slackening of the rigidity.

"I'm *not* cross!" The tone was intense. "And I don't want you to come—not like that!"

"Well, I'm coming." He shrugged, stood aside while Auntie heavily tramped over to her thick overcoat, which hung against the wall; and, as soon as she was ready, he helped Mrs. Balthazar into her own silky coat of gray squirrel. Even in that wretched light it lifted the beauty of her soft hair into higher radiance and enhanced the brightness of her eyes and the creamy fullness of her neck; and although she would not then suffer him to take her hand, no opposition arose, as they went through the darkened shop, with Auntie leading the way, to his bestowal of a sudden, vehement kiss upon the rather cold cheek nearest to his own.

Then they were all in Holborn, and Punch turned up the collar of his overcoat so that his face was almost entirely hidden.

II

An hour later the two of them were sitting together in Monaddi's, one of the large, brilliantly lighted restaurants in the West End of London which cater rather for the suburban and the visiting provincial than for the cosmopolitan epicure. Great masses of ferns and flowers, brilliant many-coloured lights, an orchestra, and a dancing floor gave diners many of the sensations of luxury and splendour, but not quite all of them. Owing to the lateness of the hour the restaurant was half empty, and Minnie Balthazar and Punch Teed, at a discreetly retired table behind some enormous palms, were served with interest by several waiters. They could see groups of others in the great mirrors which, by their reflections and counter reflections, multiplied the flowers and the lights and the empty white-covered tables many times over, until the restaurant seemed to shine as one incessant firework display.

Mrs. Balthazar had changed the black dress which she wore during business hours for a heavily beaded frock of cyclamen pink. She was slightly rouged, but not too evidently. And her eyes sparkled, her lips were parted, as she watched the cocktails being mixed and shaken by a spruce young man in a white jacket and listened to the playing of the orchestra, beating time secretly beneath the table with one hidden foot. All his discontent at Punch's first unwillingness to give her this treat appeared to have gone, and she was full, evidently, of the happiness of the moment. Punch, too, had cast off whatever gloom he may have felt and smiled jovially upon the world. In this dazzling light it was possible to see that the colour of his cheeks spread to the roots of his curly and shining fair hair. His eyes and teeth flashed; a ring upon his little finger gleamed; he looked good-natured, a trifle sensual, as if he lived well and was much in the open air. It was impossible to pass him without a second glance of interest.

Once, indeed, as Punch sat beaming, the rather frizzy-haired girl who pushed a trolley bearing chocolates and cigarettes permitted herself just such a second glance, and he responded with a bright, arch sparkle that was as nearly as possible a wink. The girl remained sedate and wandered on, so that Punch, still beaming, turned again to Mrs. Balthazar, who had watched the incident with all the composure proper to the feminine equivalent of a man of the world. Minnie had received very similar greetings from other men; she knew something of both human nature and what may be called social finesse; and she had few illusions. Nor did she, as prudes do, appear to exaggerate the viciousness of such pleasantries and convert them into matter for moral disapproval.

"Nice girl, that," she remarked.

"Is she?" Punch yawned. He was not really interested in the girl who pushed the chocolate wagon. Having seen that Minnie was handed her cocktail by the waiter, he took his own. "May as well mix us another, waiter." He set his glass back upon the tray at once, empty.

"Well, I thought so. I thought *you* did, too. You smiled at her, and she seemed to like it all right. However, I expect you were dreaming. Or perhaps it's me. My, but this is good! Ay, I feel better! You've no idea what a time I've had, Georgie. Those old furnaces where I am—the radiators are icy, most of the time. I've had to have an oil stove. Fancy *me* with chilblains! Well, I've written to the landlord about it."

"Tell him off," lazily said Punch.

"I thought—as it's all Auntie's money, really——Well, I thought she'd better not be frozen to death, you know. Might be awkward. However, trade's been better than I thought for, and I've got orders for quite a lot of—well, good sort of houses. And I've got some new regular customers calling, too. One funny old bean came in—do you remember pointing out an old man one night in the theatre, and saying you knew him, and keep my head down?"

"My dear child, I know five thousand old men!" he cried. "Each one a bigger bore than the last. All prize winners. What about this one?"

"I don't remember what his name was. Only that you said you knew him, and he'd be shocked if he saw you with another man's wife."

Punch shook his head. His face was overcast with slight heaviness, but he still smiled.

"They'd all be that," he said.

"Oh, well, it's different, now, isn't it?" She sought his eye. "Georgie!"

"Absolutely different," he assured her smoothly. "Of course it is."

"You wouldn't be——"

"No, no, no!" cried Punch. He put his head back and laughed. Minnie could see all his fine white teeth and the mischievous shining of his eyes.

"I'm so glad," she said quietly. "Well, this man—I can't think where it was we saw him, but I knew him at once.

He's a thin old stick. Looks like a judge. You *do* remember him, don't you?"

"Not I!" swore Punch.

"I thought you looked a bit queer when I said he looked like a judge."

"I was thinking of the black cap!" teased Punch.

Minnie shuddered.

.."Don't, Georgie!" she cried. "Give me the creeps! This old chap came in the other day and bought some violets. To-day I saw him looking in the window again. But he didn't come in. I don't think he'd got the courage."

"What, to buy a few flowers?" Punch was not listening. "Yes, it wants a lot of nerve to do a thing like that. Here, what are we going to drink?" He took the elaborate wine card from the waiter and looked it over with the confident ease of the man who is used to dining out. "Red or white? Can't afford fizz to-night. I'm broke."

"Really broke?" asked Minnie, when the waiter, smiling incredulously, had gone. Her face had grown grave. "Why didn't you *say*, Georgie? I mean, I'd never have let you bring me——"

"That's all right, old girl. I was joking about being broke. Absolutely! Cheer up!" He fixed her with his gay eye until Minnie's smile returned. "It's only that I haven't got much *on* me. And my Dad's getting a bit stingy. He thinks I ought to be—— However——"

"Yes, it *is* 'however,' isn't it!" echoed Minnie. "I wish I could help you."

"Good Lord, no!"

"You wait." She nodded at him. "When Auntie——"

"Ah, yes, Auntie! Good old Auntie!" He put his head back and laughed again, like a boy. Minnie raised both head and hand as if she appealed to the heavens.

"Auntie's as provoking as an old hat!" she declared. "She's terrible, Georgie! Really *terrible*! Poor old soul, she can't help it, you know; but being deaf's made her so grumpy and grizzly that she's hard to stand, sometimes! And these old tales she reads—all about the aristocracy—little old-fashioned penny books full of earls and countesses with black moustaches and snapping eyes. They *make* her cross. I think she b'lieves they're true, you know. She tells me the country's in an awful state. Regular Gloomy Dean, she is. But she's not a bad old sport, really."

"This fish is tough," remarked Punch. He yawned again, and when he saw that she had observed the yawn he smiled. "Up late last—this morning," he said. "Oh, I tell you, I'm *working!*"

"What on?" She was full of eager interest.

Punch did not reply. His attention had been diverted. He was looking over his shoulder at a man who had just strolled past at a little distance. Like Punch, this man was dressed in a tweed lounge suit, but, unlike Punch, he seemed to be alone. Minnie, having followed her companion's gaze, also watched the figure as it slowly disappeared. The man was tall and thin, and his legs were very straight. His head was long, and the hair at the back of it seemed to have a sort of curly whorl at its centre. Both head and figure were those of a youngish man—of a man, she thought, not above thirty years of age. But she could not see the man's face, even in one of the many mirrors, and did not remember him as an acquaintance.

"Who's that?" Minnie asked.

"Nobody." Punch seemed momentarily uneasy. "Nobody I know."

"You looked as if you knew him."

"Well, he's rather like a chap I know," admitted Punch. "But I don't think it's the man."

"Did he see you, d'you think?" Minnie's eyes were a little dark, but what her thoughts were concerning the stranger, or, in face of his declaration of a few moments earlier, concerning Punch's uneasiness, could not be guessed from her still animated expression.

"I dunno." Punch spoke carelessly. It was clear that he was thinking about the man who had passed.

"What's his name?" pleaded Minnie.

"What? That chap? I don't know. I don't believe it's the man I thought it was."

"But the man you *thought*——"

"I've got him on my brain a bit. I think my pater knows something of him. Nothing serious. Cheer up, old girl!"

"Georgie! What's his *name?* I want to know." She spoke earnestly, obstinately.

"His name's Gascoyne," said Punch a little sulkily. "He's a friend of some friends of mine."

"Oh, friends of yours," said Minnie in a low voice. The corners of her mouth quivered. Then, quickly: "Golly, this fish *is* tough! I didn't know fish could *be* so tough. It's preserved. I shan't eat it."

She looked again into the glittering distance as if to be sure that the man who had passed them—this man who resembled, but who was not, the friend of Georgie's friends—was indeed completely out of sight.

III

The flat which Minnie shared with her aunt was in one of the streets which run north of Shaftesbury Avenue and lay up several flights of stairs, at the top of the building. The floors below were occupied for the most part by business concerns, and it was without fear of observation that Minne and Punch Teed went back to the flat when their meal was finished. Minnie led the way, peeped into the sitting room, beckoned Punch to follow her, and stepped noiselessly to the door of another room. She returned, humming, and Punch had a glimpse of her own lighted bedroom, in the doorway of which she stood for an instant silhouetted.

"Auntie's in bed and snoring," Minnie said, smiling back over her shoulder with delight. "She's dropped her book and gone off to sleep in the middle, with the light on. What a waste! I've turned it off. Shan't be a minute."

She disappeared; and Punch, standing in the sitting room, stooped and roused the dying fire into life. It was not a large room, and the furniture in it was old and shabby. He had known it for years—before the death of Sam Balthazar, before Auntie had come here to live with Minnie—and for Punch as well as for Minnie these chairs and that great maroon-covered settee with the green, golden-fringed cushions, the dark, dreary pictures upon the walls, and the odd, brightly coloured Russian toys upon the mantelpiece, held many memories. High above his head the grimed ceiling of the room received little tongues of light, reflected from the leaping flames in the grate below. All was dark, dim, full of hints and murmurs, like the recesses of a crypt. From the street below he heard the sharp noise of passing footsteps. From a little distance came the vibrant sound of omnibuses and automobiles passing the end of the street. Punch Teed's heart sank a little. He was listening to all these indications of man's activity upon the earth.

And while he stood thus, intent upon the sounds from without, he felt Minnie's arms about him and her body pressed against his own with a clinging, gentleness such as she had always given him from the time of their first trembling excitements of discovery.

"Come and sit down," she was whispering. And, as he obeyed, she sank to his knee, and held his head close to her breast. Punch's arms closed about her. He listened no longer. Minnie had changed her many-beaded dress for one that gave her greater ease, and now that they were alone she no longer troubled to disguise the ardour of her love, but kissed him, sometimes lightly, sometimes with passion, murmuring her old eager expressions of endearment, as a mother will fearlessly, unconcealedly caress and delight in her baby. "My boy," she softly said, her face against his. "My blessed boy. You haven't loved me like this for ages. Love me, Georgie;

love me, my honey, my great boy. . . ." She was crooning; she was shivering; and yet all the time, while Minnie was wooing him, and smiling, holding his head so lightly and tenderly against her bosom and bringing her lips to his, she must have been remembering the day when Punch had told her to keep her head down because that old man in the stalls knew him, and she must have been thinking of the stranger who had passed them that evening in the restaurant, and recognizing quite well some part of the meaning of Punch's uneasiness at the encounter, for—hidden from her lover—the smiling lips drooped and the loving eyes held steely bitterness.

"Georgie." It was so barely uttered, so much breathed sweetly and gently into his ear, that at first Punch did not seem to know that she had whispered his name. "Georgie . . . You do love me, don't you? . . . You love me a little . . . a little. . . ." He nodded comically, exaggeratedly, as if he were indeed the boy that she often pretended. "And one day, Georgie . . . one day . . ." She was still whispering low in his ear.

"One day," said Punch obediently.

"Hold me tighter. Say it; whisper it in my ear, Georgie." She bent her head so that her ear was close to his lips, so that his breath tickled her cheek and made her smile. And at last, in a whisper as soft as her own, she heard him say:

"Love you . . . darling." And then, nothing.

"And one day," she prompted, her eyes hidden, tragic.

"And one day," whispered Punch, holding her very close and kissing her until both were breathless and their hearts beating fast and thickly. "Yes; one day, please God!" There was no sound in the flat but the soft thudding of their hearts. Below, a taxicab skirred suddenly into life and went grinding down the street until the noise of its engine was lost in the general murmur of noise. Then silence.

CHAPTER VII

A WALK AND A TALK

I

CATHERINE, closing the heavy door of the house behind her with the gentle click of a well-oiled latch, stepped out into the square and turned south. The trees were all naked, their branches still black and barren, laced across the forbidding sky. She looked up, fearing that rain would fall, for although the afternoon was yet young there was a darkness overhead. A wind was sweeping the pavements bare. But Catherine was warmly clad. A little gray velvet hat was set upon her head; a short gray coat of Persian lamb with a raised collar protected her body from the cold, and her short trim skirt was of smooth tweed. Beneath the skirt her slim straight legs took their short strides with a firmness which was in keeping with her character. She did not sway as she walked, as do those who dance continuously, but stepped out as though she found pleasure in the exercise. And upon her cheeks there was a natural flush of good health which did credit to the London atmosphere.

It was a Saturday afternoon, and Catherine was making an excursion alone. To-day, however, she was not destined to go without company, for within three minutes of leaving the house she came face to face with Joe Gascoyne.

He hailed her triumphantly, his eyes twinkling, his long face gravely polite.

"I was just going to call on you," said Joe.

"Oh." She was sedate. "Shall we turn back? Father and Rhoda are both at home."

"But you were going out," he ventured, looking down from his great height.

"But I can go back," she assured him. "It's quite a short distance."

"On the contrary. Why shouldn't I come for your walk, too?"

"Because I thought you would rather do what *you* had planned, and not what *I* had planned."

Joe fell into step beside her, perhaps not displeased with her comeliness, for her coat and hat were both charming, and the little face which the hat was too small to conceal was delicious. They crossed the road in order to obtain what shelter was possible from the sweeping wind, and walked quite rapidly between the rows of rather dull, plain, stucco-fronted houses, since, although Catherine's steps were necessarily shorter than those which the length of Joe's legs made habitual, their briskness was greater.

"The unfortunate Gwen belongs to a club that takes rambles," Joe said as they walked. "She's gone to the top of the Monument, or some other high and windy place; and she'll probably be blown away. I really promised her that I'd ask you to come and see us this evening; but whether there's any chance of Gwen's survival——"

"I don't think we can," answered Catherine. "Father has a friend coming to dinner. I'm sorry."

"Oh!" exclaimed Joe, apparently carried out of all his customary calm by the announcement. "*Has* he a friend? Isn't that extraordinary! I beg pardon—I don't mean it's extraordinary that he should have a friend. It's not at all extraordinary. By *no* means extraordinary. But we've never chanced——"

Catherine listened gravely to his rather confused explanation. Then she said:

"Well, it *is* extraordinary."

"What's extraordinary?" demanded Joe, with an air of

indignant protest. "Only my folly in thinking of him as friendless. It was extremely impertinent."

"He hasn't any friends," interrupted Catherine. "That's what is extraordinary."

"You amaze me!" cried Joe. He did really look amazed. His comical black eyebrows, which were frequently in motion, and added much to the droll expressiveness of his face, were raised. His eyes were serious. His mouth—the lips were thin, and as capable of infinite contortion as those of a comic actor—was quite straight.

"I don't amaze you at all, Joe," said Catherine frankly. "You're not amazed. You don't know *how* to be amazed."

"How unjust!" he murmured.

"I'm not unjust. I'm truthful. You're quite right. This is a man Father knows. They've got a common interest—some particular book, or some particular edition of a book—I forget what. But Father has no friends. He can't make them. He's too reserved, too—something. Even Rhoda and I haven't any friends——"

"Catherine!" He was wounded. His protest was sharp.

She checked herself, looked up into his reproachful face. One glance, a smile, and then, almost impulsively, she nodded.

"You see? I'm ungrateful. It's no wonder we haven't any friends!"

"You don't do yourself justice. You couldn't be talking as you've been doing unless you felt I was a friend. Has it struck you?"

II

It was Catherine who spoke first.

"I hope you don't think I'm really ungrateful, Joe," she ventured. "I shouldn't like you to think that. It would hurt me. And it wouldn't be true."

"I don't know if you're ungrateful or not." Joe had the appearance of thinking aloud. "It doesn't matter."

"It does." He saw her quick, fierce stiffening; but it did not check him.

"No. One gives friendship because one can't help it."

"Love. Not friendship," said Catherine.

"Don't be absurd! That's just the sort of thing Gwen would say!"

Catherine laughed unexpectedly.

"But listen, Joe!" she said. "And be serious, because I'm serious just at this minute. You talk about friendship. Rather sentimentally, I think——"

"Well!" He was aghast. "What effrontery! You insult me!"

"I *do!* Not insult you, but think that you talk sentimentally at times. But supposing friendship *is* what you say, what does it do? What do we really know of each other?"

Joe shrugged his shoulders. They were walking less rapidly. By some instinct they had escaped being run over by a highly polished taxicab which rushed from a side street just as they were about to cross; and Joe's hand, at Catherine's elbow, guided her down this side street, westward, before a row of elderly houses with trim doorsteps and dark railings and gloomy basements.

"How intimate are *any* human beings?" he grumbled. "What d'you want to be told? You mustn't expect English people to behave like the characters in a novel by Dostoevsky. They haven't got either the self-knowledge or the fluency. Besides, it's not the details that matter, but the confidence."

"That's quite true," Catherine agreed. "But just lately I've been thinking a good deal. It's very salutary."

"It's very *dangerous*," he interposed half teasingly, half alarmed. "And you—you *personally*—don't want these gushing emotional relationships. Everything laid bare. Gush, gush, gush! 'I'm so this, and you're so the other.' That sort of thing's horrible."

Catherine did not take his reference to herself. She brushed it aside, and continued:

"It *is* horrible, and it's not at all what I mean, of course. You know that perfectly well; only you're very unscrupulous. What I've been thinking is this: Take us, the Meadowses. It seems to me that we've been leading a very narrow sort of life—until just lately. And it's suddenly broadening. Not broadening, but widening. Some people would say deepening, but I don't think so. We're meeting more people and getting to know them—or at least, getting to know things *about* them, such as that *you're* never really surprised at anything, for instance." She was roguish in that instant, which brought an answering smile to Joe's face. "But it seems to me that we're still on very polite terms with all the people we meet. And they're the same with each other. They talk about all sorts of things—facts and ideas"—by this time she was breathless—"but never about the things that they must think when they're alone. Never about the things that keep them awake at night. Never about the things that *frighten* them. They're all wearing a sort of fancy dress and pretending. They're all giving each other a lot of whacks with toy balloons and a lot of gossip; but always affectedly, self-consciously. Never the reality."

"When they're in groups, yes," said Joe. "It's better when they're separated."

"Even then, they're posing and pretending," objected Catherine. "Or we never see them natural."

"You can judge by yourselves," suggested Joe. "You're natural enough."

"That's not very heartening," said Catherine. "For although I suppose we're what would be called a happy and affectionate family, it seems to me that we're strangers to each other. Rhoda and I, for instance, were sent to different schools—Rhoda was mostly at home with Father. All our experience has been different. We're sisters, and I think sometimes that I understand her—but it's not likely. We're not really together. And we're both growing up, you know." She smiled rather sadly. Then she said: "But we'd better not talk about such things. You didn't come with me this afternoon to be bored."

"I'm not bored. I'm very much interested. I'm glad you should feel that you can speak to me. Can I say, without being what you call sentimental, that I'm proud? I'll risk it. I *am* proud. And I'm perfectly glad, because it gives me an opportunity of saying something that I wanted to say." He hesitated, looked serious, and after a pause proceeded: "I feel very fortunate in having met you. I wanted to meet you and to talk to you alone; and that was why I was determined to ask you to come and see us to-night."

"You *said* it was Gwen who asked us!" Catherine reproachfully cried. Her eyes shone with laughter. She looked adorably radiant in her cunning little velvet hat and the gray coat. Those who passed could not restrain smiles of sympathy with such gaiety. For although she had been in earnest Catherine had not been carried away by her own eloquence into solemnity.

"Gwen, prompted by me," returned Joe, untroubled. "I'd counted on walking home with you alone."

"But Rhoda——"

"Rhoda wasn't included in the invitation. I should have made that clear if you had thought you would come. It's not as though you and Rhoda were Siamese twins. And it's about Rhoda that I want to speak to you."

"Ah!" She sighed, walking with fresh sobriety at his elbow. Her head was lowered so that Joe could not see the change which had come over her face. It was as though she already knew what he was about to say, and as though, while she acquiesced in the necessity of his confidence, she was none the less reluctant to receive it.

III

Without knowing whither their steps led, the two of them had crossed Tottenham Court Road and were in the dirty streets south of Fitzroy Square. It was not at any time a neighbourhood for cheerful thoughts or cheerful conversation, but under this February pall of gray cloud it was stale and horrible, as if the dreary lives of dwellers in these mean streets cast their own stifling blanket over all human intercourse. Men and women—Italians, French, and Jews, as well as native Londoners—some of them clean, some of them foully dirty, stood in dreary groups before the windows of shops which were grimy, untidy, and full of cheap, shoddy clothing, greasy food, ugly kitchen ware, and the corpses of last summer's flies. Untidy children played screamingly in the gutters and across the pavements, while girls and boys, very little older, stood leaning against railings or lamp-posts in the first stages of precocious love-making. Presently Catherine and Joe would emerge into Great Portland Street, and would thereafter find themselves in a district of great houses, expensive limousines, and medical consultants; but for the moment they were penetrating what might be called Greater Soho. They were moved to hasten their steps, so frowningly did the shabby houses lower, and Joe's communication was delayed as for a few moments they fell into anxious silence.

Joe hesitated to the last.

"Catherine," he then said abruptly, "I don't want you to suppose that I've got any of the habits of a private detective. I loathe them as much as you can do. So you won't think that, will you?"

"No, Joe." Catherine's head was still down. Her tone, although not fervent, was entirely reassuring.

Again silence, while Joe appeared to falter over innumerable conversational openings. At length, abruptly, he said:

"Your father dropped into a sort of confidential talk with me the other night."

"Father did?" She was surprised. Her spirits mounted suddenly. She could not restrain a delighted smile. "Oh, Joe! It was awfully clever of you!"

"I daren't tell you how it happened," Joe replied. Nevertheless, he, too, smiled. "But it happened. You probably know the sort of thing——"

"Was it about Rhoda?" Catherine interrupted, more gravely.

"About you both."

"How extraordinary!"

"Principally Rhoda."

"Yes," said Catherine. "They're great friends." And looked away from Joe.

"But about you too." She did not press him to disclose the nature of the confidence regarding herself; but Joe continued: "I tried to alarm him a little about you."

Catherine's curiosity was perfectly plain. She was not indignant, but she did not approve.

"You shouldn't have done that, Joe," she thought. "Poor Father! Besides there's nothing that he *ought* to be alarmed at."

"That's what he said. I told him that I thought Rhoda could always look after herself, but that you—couldn't."

"But that's absurd, Joe!" Catherine cried warmly. "It's the opposite of the truth."

"Wait a minute."

"You've got a crotchet. A bee in your bonnet! And I don't think you ought to have said such a thing to Father. It will worry him dreadfully."

"No. It won't do that," Joe said thoughtfully. "He's too sure of the opposite. And yet I don't know that I was wrong —about you, I mean."

"You *were*," said Catherine. "I'm the safest person in the world. I never lose my head or my nerve. I'm practical, unimaginative. My blood pressure's normal."

"What I told him was that you might flare up like a rocket," persisted Joe.

She became superficially impatient—almost superficially despairing.

"This just illustrates what I was saying a moment ago. Well, several moments ago. We don't know each other."

"Or ourselves," said Joe. "Anyway, that was what I said. And I reassured him about Rhoda. I said that people would always see that she didn't have a nasty tumble. She'll always have protectors. People will always be anxious about her. I am, myself. That's what I'm coming to. You *do* see what I mean, don't you, Catherine? About yourself—you give the impression of needing no support. One day you'll want some support. It *may* be so, at any rate."

"I can look after myself, Joe," Catherine assured him. "But Rhoda——"

"Well, that's just it. Was I wrong about Rhoda?"

"Are you *asking* me? Or just meditating?"

"Both. The fact is, I'm not so sure about Rhoda."

"Since when?"

"Since the day following the talk I spoke of."

Catherine reflected. Then she nodded her head, Joe observing her all the while.

"You know what I mean?" he asked.

"Joe, Rhoda's very young——"

"If anything went wrong, they might blame *you*. They'd think you ought to have spoken to her, looked after her. You're older than she is."

"I know. I *have* spoken to her; but she's so emotional that I can't——"

"Of course, it's awful cheek of me; but I'm so fond of her—of you both——"

Catherine's head was down again. Joe could not see her face at all. But he knew that she was not unmoved. Not smiling, this time; not amused. There was a rigidity in her shoulders, in her hands, which proved as much.

"I wish you would tell me," she said at last, "exactly what it is that you have seen or learned."

"It's little enough. A flash. Catherine, it's probably nothing; but he's a wrong 'un. He's a chap who never could go straight and never will be able to. I mean, there's nothing in it for her. Except a lot of—either suffering or excitement. I saw her, with Punch Teed, in a taxi——"

"Joe!" Catherine was protesting sharply. "There's nothing in that. Surely she may ride——"

"She can do anything she likes," he answered. "I'm not thinking of that aspect of it. Only of *her*. She's riding for misery if she's in love with him."

"But what reason have you got for thinking she's in love with him?" Catherine was quite pale. She was defensive.

"I saw her face as he kissed her," Joe said. "Just as the taxi slowed up alongside. It alarmed me."

He too was rather pale. The dry little smile which as a rule played upon his lips was gone.

IV

A long silence followed his assertion. They walked along heedlessly, both looking disturbed, both entirely preoccupied with what had been said and with what both of them had envisaged as the sequel. Catherine was the first to speak.

"You're *sure?*" she questioned. Her voice was a little thick, as though throat and tongue were dry.

"Quite sure," said Joe.

"I knew nothing of that. All I knew was that she didn't seem well, and I asked her about it. She was restless. And then, when you had all gone the other night, there was a letter from him that made her very confused. I knew she must be going to meet him. But there isn't anything in that. I simply thought that she was hiding something from shyness. Joe, are you sure that Punch is horrid? I mean really *sure*. He seems quite—I don't like him very much myself—but I've always thought——"

"I shouldn't have dreamt of saying anything if I hadn't been sure. I hate that sort of scandal-mongering as much as you can do. But the circumstances here are exceptional.

I don't know Punch well, but I've known his father for a good many years, because his father's at the head of my department. So I've heard a good deal about the son. He's very experienced, and Rhoda's an innocent. So I thought something ought to be done. I might have spoken to your father——"

"Oh, *hopeless!*" cried Catherine. "No!" She shook her head very decidedly. "No; that would do no good."

"Then there are the three others. Yourself, Rhoda, and Punch. I'll talk to Punch, if you think that best."

"What good would *that* do?"

"I don't know. It might stop him. No, I don't think it would."

"Not if she's in love with him."

"Well, then, Rhoda?"

"Rhoda would never forgive you if you interfered," Catherine said quickly.

"I know. That's just what I can't stand," Joe answered, as quickly as she.

It was an admission. The words seemed to echo in the air. At least he was not indifferent to Rhoda.

"Joe——" Catherine checked herself. He saw how white she was. Even her lips were suddenly white, as though she were enduring terrible strain. But the lips were closely pressed together, and Catherine's eyes, although they were darkened by pain, were wide open. Nothing would rob her of her courage. "I must think," she said, at last. "What you've said alarms me very much."

"I hope you'll forgive me for hurting you," he implored.

"Forgive you . . ." she repeated, with a strange smile.

"I thought that together——"

"Together? Oh, no; it's I who must—— I think we'd better go home again, now. I'm—I feel I want to be there and see that Rhoda's safe."

"Do you think there's anything at all that I——"

"Only to *kill* him!" cried Catherine, trembling. Then she

relaxed. "That was awfully silly of me," she added. "I couldn't help it. If anything happened to her—— Let's go home!"

She shook her head, fiercely defensive of Rhoda, and began to walk rapidly back in the direction from which they had come. Joe kept pace with her, equally ill at ease. They spoke no more for a long time, and were walking in silence when the first spots of rain began to fall. Within a moment the deluge was upon them.

CHAPTER VIII

FERDINAND IN A SHOWER

I

CATHERINE had not known that precisely at the moment at which she closed the front door behind her, Ferdinand was descending the stairs from above. Ferdinand had been sitting alone in his study when he had noticed the hour chiming by his silvery-toned little clock. With his horn-rimmed spectacles on his nose he had been examining a copy of Sir Thomas Browne's *Religio Medici;* but at the chiming of the clock he set this aside, rose, and prepared to go out of doors. The house was quite tranquil, and he would not have been aware that Catherine was in front of him if the door, in opening and shutting, had not sent a faint reflected light about hall and staircase. A moment later he, too, was walking slowly away from the house, while Rhoda watched from the window above.

Ferdinand was still recalling some words upon which his eye had alighted as he turned the pages of *Religio Medici:* they were those in which the Doctor asserts that "there are wonders in true affection; it is a body of enigmas, mysteries, and riddles, wherein two so become one, as they become two"; and they made him think of Rhoda.

The wind caressed his face and made his clear gray eyes kinder and more grave. He did not regard the houses he passed or the human beings who came for a few instants into his neighbourhood. He was thinking of Rhoda, his love for her, his trust in her, and of her love, so ardently given in return. For the whole of her life, through delicate childhood until the present hour, she had been under Ferdinand's tutelage. Until quite recently they had been little separated. Her thoughts had been given to him with freedom, and he had watched their fitful growth from childishness and the seeming wisdom of early youth to the greater restlessness and the more evident immaturity of what seemed to be the other day. Of late there had been a change. He still loved and trusted her; but he had been disquieted by other signs. Only within the past few weeks had he felt the need of winning her demonstrative love by effort. Was she no longer his little girl? Had he lost her? "There are wonders in true affection," said Sir Thomas Browne. "It is a body of enigmas, mysteries, and riddles." Yes; that was true. But did the affection of a child for her father gradually wane? Had this affection in fact waned? His own had seemed but to increase.

Meditatively Ferdinand followed his customary path in the shadow of these tall Victorian houses, which held in their looming shapes, he felt, the hint of many sorrows, many lost affections. He sighed as he strolled, and looked neither to the right nor the left. For if Rhoda's love should be withdrawn from him Ferdinand knew that he would be indeed poor and indeed lonely. He was not happy. The warning of his intuitions, and even the explicit warnings of Joe Gascoyne, filled his ears and his mind. He had never been so bereft of confidence.

"Strange," he thought. "Does growth mean parting? Shall I lose her? *Have* I lost her?"

There was no answer to these questionings. The gloomy sky depressed his spirits still further. The deserted silence of the mid-London streets at this hour upon a Saturday afternoon served to emphasize his present solitude and to hint deeply at that other, more unwelcome, loneliness which the withdrawal of Rhoda's first fresh engrossing love and reliance upon him would bring. Ferdinand's steps became slower. His sadness increased. Even the sharp noise and bustle of Theobald's Road, where crowded shops and loaded purchasers presented a scene of activity to the eye, did not serve to rouse him from the depression into which he had fallen.

II

He had crossed Holborn and was almost abreast of the florist's shop which he had so lately noticed for the first time when the earliest dreary drops of rain scattered upon the pavement. The drops, no more than harbingers of the storm, alarmed Ferdinand, and he looked apprehensively skywards. His fears were justified. Within an instant the pavements were running, and, acting instinctively, Ferdinand stepped aside off the roadway to take shelter in the square porch of Mrs. Balthazar's shop. Beside him, as he stood, the blinds of brown holland were lowered. The shop was closed, sealed tight for the week-end. As far as Ferdinand's eyes could reach along the rows of other, and familiar, shops, they saw nothing but shutters, blinds, and locked doors. The booksellers' windows into which he made it a practice to peep as he passed were hidden. Hissing, the rain bounded viciously up again from the solid flags, and ran in the gutters, curdling there and streaming onward. Ferdinand pressed farther back into his shelter, catching a glimpse within the florist's shop, through the chinks left between the blind and the framework of door and window, of a faint greenness where moss and fern escaped from the shadow.

It led him to think of the violets which he had bought here only a few days earlier. Especially it made him think of the little lady who kept the shop, who was so slight, so frail as to suggest that she could never with success fight her desperate battle against poverty. Poor lady! thought Ferdinand. Compared with such as she, how fortunate must Rhoda be considered! She was sheltered, protected by his love, his anxious wisdom. . . .

It was as this reflection crossed his mind that he heard a soft sound behind him, turned, and beheld Mrs. Balthazar, who had opened the door of her shop and was checked in the porch, evidently, by the unexpected sight of the rain. She seemed aghast, and stood with one hand upon the door, looking doubtfully at the street before her. As Ferdinand glanced round in surprise their recognition was mutual. And as the lady smiled, Ferdinand's hand was courteously raised to his hat in salutation.

"Good-afternoon," Ferdinand said in his precise, gentle voice. "I hope I'm not trespassing. The storm burst just as I was near here, and I was thankful to find a shelter in your porch."

"You're welcome," said Mrs. Balthazar reassuringly. Her smile was shy. *"Isn't* it a shame!"

"I don't think it can last long," began Ferdinand. "At least, in its present fury. I *hope* it can't."

"You're getting splashed," said she. "Come farther back."

The bouncing rain was, indeed, splashing the legs of Ferdinand's trousers, as he saw when his attention had been called to the fact by her quicker eye.

"Oh, thank you!" He backed a little deeper, while Mrs. Balthazar made way for him. They stood together against the partially open door of her shop, looking out at the bitter rain and the deserted pavements. Ferdinand could not think of anything more to say, but the lady was less speechless.

"I was going home," she announced. "But that's no good for an idea in *this,* is it?" She was very cordial, as if they had often conversed.

"Perhaps, when it slackens, I could get you a taxi. Or one may come along——"

Mrs. Balthazar shot a quick glance at Ferdinand, in which sweetness and derision were mixed inextricably with pathos.

"Oh," said she. "Taxis! I can't afford them. They're as bad as the other kind of taxes, it seems to me. Do *you* like them, Mr. ——?" The prefix seemed to slip from her lips. Then, as if to justify the slip, she proceeded, "I remember your buying some Parma violets the other day. Lovely flow-

ers aren't they! I hope they were liked. I think most
ladies——"

Was there an arch hint?

"They were for my daughters—my daughters," stammered
Ferdinand.

"Daughters——" He was amazed at the expression which
crossed her face. It was as though the word had given her
a severe shock. Suspicion rushed to her eyes and was instantly gone, replaced by a smile of complete naturalness.
"Pardon me," said Mrs. Balthazar. "But I——" She checked
herself. The smile deepened. "It didn't enter my head that
you—— Silly of me! Are your daughters very pretty,
Mr. ——?"

"My name is Meadows," answered Ferdinand. Then, smiling in return, he answered her question. "I believe they
would be thought pretty," he said rather shyly.

"And—and I suppose if the *younger* men was—were
asked," continued Mrs. Balthazar, her breath coming quickly,
"they'd be sure of it, wouldn't they, Mr. Meadows?"

"It hadn't occurred to me," returned Ferdinand, with a
quickening heart. "But—but—it's very possible, of course."
He forgot the rain, the cold, Mrs. Balthazar's gentleness, in
sudden fear. Was *that* the meaning of Rhoda's change of
feeling to himself? Could it be that she was as conscious of
the passionate link between beauty and admiration as this
woman immediately showed herself? He trembled. He was in
haste to be gone. But the rain forbade. It came slanting
down, gray and merciless, making the air dank and the town
dreary.

"You'll wonder, perhaps, why I asked you," she went on.
"But the fact is——"

"I suppose it's a very natural thought," Ferdinand said,
making his own apology for her.

"Look here, why should we be standing out here in the
rain, Mr. Meadows? Chilly, isn't it! Why not come right
into the shop? I can turn on a light. It's warm in there."

"Indeed, no; thank you," protested Ferdinand. "Thank you; no. This is—I shall——"

"Come along." She spoke very gently and retreated, opening the door quite wide and revealing the shadowed greenery. The warm air from within reached Ferdinand, tempting him. But he had been alarmed in his thought of Rhoda and was filled with dread. He had seen a strange expression upon the face of his new acquaintance. He was vaguely ruffled, restless. It was with difficulty that he so far overcame his repugnance as to move within the door.

But the movement was enough for Mrs. Balthazar. She drew forward a light chair and bade him sit down. The lighting of the shop, if not brilliant, gave to the ferns and palms an almost electric quality of greenness. Soothed by all that he felt about him, and by the very curious and attractive scent which so many flowers gathered together poured into his nostrils, Ferdinand sat rather stiffly in the chair, while Mrs. Balthazar seated herself at a couple of yards' distance. She had thrown open her fur coat, thereby baring her throat and neck; and she looked instantly younger and more pathetic than she had done with her coat closed. It was the light, perhaps, which made her cheeks appear sharper and the cheek bones higher; for the light was very dazzling and made odd shadows everywhere. But as Ferdinand glanced hesitatingly from the cheeks to the soft lines of Mrs. Balthazar's neck he thought she seemed to be regarding him with peculiar intentness and at once averted his own eyes.

"Yes," she continued, as if casually, although her eyes were glittering. "I was interested in what you said about your daughters, Mr. Meadows. I've no children of my own; though I'd give anything to have a girl—you know, just somebody to talk to, and love——"

"Your husband?" Ferdinand ventured.

"He died six months ago. Very painful." She nodded sympathetically. "And so I have to *work* for my living now."

"You're very plucky," said Ferdinand.

"Well, I always *did* work, as a matter of fact, even when my husband was alive. There's nothing like work, is there? Keeps you from grizzling, I always think."

"If the work is congenial," agreed Ferdinand. "I suppose you're very fond of flowers."

"I love them!" she exclaimed with fervour. Though, poor things, they die——"

"We can none of us escape from that tragedy," observed Ferdinand, smiling.

"No," sighed Mrs. Balthazar. Her lids dropped softly over her eyes for a moment. "Oh, yes"—she seemed to recollect something—"I was going to say—the reason why I asked you that—about your daughters——"

"Yes, yes." Ferdinand could not keep still under the conflict of that lightness of tone with those intent eyes.

"I think I know a friend of yours, Mr. Meadows. He's often spoken to me about"—there was a perceptible delay— "about two beautiful girls he knows. Often. I think they must be your daughters. It's a Mr. Teed. . . . Mr. George Teed. I think his friends call him by some horrid nickname. Something to do with his voice, is it?"

She sat back in her chair. The artificial light, which has such odd freaks, threw into relief a part of her throat which had been bare since she had thrown open her squirrel-skin coat. A nerve in this part of the throat was throbbing very rapidly; but Ferdinand, absorbed in his own discomfort, did not see it. He was thinking of the horrible prophecy made by Edmund Piercy, and for a moment he could not respond to her question. When at last he did so he was led by politeness to impart to his tone a cordiality, almost an enthusiasm, which he was far from feeling.

"Ah, yes," said Ferdinand. "Punch Teed. A delightful fellow. Yes, indeed; he's a great favourite of ours. So you know him? Extremely interesting. Extremely."

Then he peeped out through the open door of the shop to see whether the rain was slackening, for he was now very anxious to escape from the discomfort of his present situation.

III

"I wonder if you'd care to have a cup of tea, Mr. Meadows?" asked Mrs. Balthazar soothingly. "I hope you don't think it's great cheek of me to suggest such a thing; but I've got tea here——"

"I really think I ought not to," Ferdinand said, with a desperate glance. "My daughters——"

"They're expecting you. Oh, yes." She nodded wisely.

"The rain seems to be slackening."

"Well, it seems to *me* to be falling faster than ever," retorted Mrs. Balthazar frankly. "But you're a bit nearer the door than I am, so perhaps you can see better."

"No, you're quite right. It *is* faster."

Gloomily Ferdinand stared out through the open door. A wind was blowing the rain very disagreeably, and the ferocity of its downpour was unabated.

"Dear, dear!" Ferdinand clucked his tongue. "I'm afraid I shall have to——"

"Give it another five minutes," urged Mrs. Balthazar. "But perhaps I've been talking too much——"

"Good heavens! No!" Ferdinand turned to her imploringly. "You make me appear very ungrateful, Mrs. Balthazar. After the extremely kind shelter. . . . After all your kindness. . . . Forgive me! And tell me, do you think that you'll be able to make this shop a great success? I hope so. It seems to me to be a very precarious——"

"Well, but what else was I to do, Mr. Meadows?" She spread her hands. "My husband left me no money. As a matter of fact, he never had any money to leave. And I've got no friends." Her voice dropped.

"No friends," echoed Ferdinand soberly enough. He nodded slowly and sympathetically.

"When you come to think of it, Mr. Meadows, the number of people who've got friends—and those to look after them—well, it's not very big, is it? And we can't all be lucky! If we were, it would be monotonous."

"Perhaps it would," agreed Ferdinand, impressed by her philosophic acceptance of misfortune.

"I can't help thinking your daughters are lucky girls, you know," she continued. "With you to look after them, and lots of friends and young men always round them. Are they fair or dark, Mr. Meadows?"

Before Ferdinand could reply she rose quickly and went to the door. Her ear and eye, quicker than his, had detected the arrival of a stranger who was proposing to enter the shop.

"We're closed," Ferdinand heard her say. "No, I'm sorry. Yes, I know the door's open. Pardon? Oh, no, it's *quite* all right. I'm only sorry. . . . What was it you wanted? Perhaps I could——"

The murmur of a man's voice from without reached him. He could not hear what was said, but peering out he caught sight of a stoutly built young fellow with a brown mackintosh buttoned to his chin and a heavy cap pulled over his eyes. This man stood out in the rain, and his mackintosh and cap were quite blackened with it. He continued so to stand, even when Mrs. Balthazar left him to reënter the shop.

"Customer!" she whispered to Ferdinand, smiling. "Poor young chap! Wants some flowers for his girl, I expect. Pardon me just a minute, will you?" She spoke as though she and Ferdinand were old friends.

Ferdinand, alone, saw no sign of the storm's abatement and watched the drops shivering and scattering from the stranger's mackintosh. As his eyes travelled up from the stout, wet boots to the drenched figure of the waiting man, he thought, amiably enough, of the kindness shown by Mrs. Balthazar in serving a customer after hours, and then recollected that the sale would take some of her dying stock and put money in her pocket. He resolved that he also would buy some flowers, and upbraided himself for not having thought earlier of the possibility.

"Come inside, will you?" called Mrs. Balthazar, wrapping tissue paper around some yellow flowers that Ferdinand did not identify before they were hidden from him.

"I won't, thanks. I should only bring the wet in with me."

"Oh, that wouldn't matter—I'm afraid the mimosa will get soaked. Pity, isn't it?"

The purchase was made and the stranger departed. And, as he went, there was an obvious improvement in the light; the rain was silvered; its fall flickered, grew thinner. . . . Ferdinand rose to his feet, and Mrs. Balthazar continued to stand, showing by her action that she also had observed the slackening.

"That young man," stammered Ferdinand. "He put into my head——"

She laid a hand upon his arm, instantly divining his thought.

"Don't you bother about that," she said, with good-nature. "You buy flowers when you want them. And when you're passing, if you've got a few minutes . . . You see, I don't see many people—not to talk to, I mean—and, well, it's *nice* to talk to somebody like you. I feel you're—you know, sympathetic."

"I hope I am," said Ferdinand wistfully.

"I'm sure you are. And it's a real treat. Only what I'm afraid of is that I've been too cheeky, asking questions, and all that——"

"Oh, no! Please, no!" begged Ferdinand. "I really——"

"No?" She looked smilingly at him. "Sure?"

"You've been most kind. I wonder if you—— I really must go. I think we ought both to take advantage of this stoppage."

"Well, good-afternoon, Mr. Meadows. It's been so nice. Oh, by the way——"

Just as Ferdinand had stepped to the door he was detained

by her sudden call. He returned, very cheerful over the cessation of the storm, prepared to answer a question, knowing that her friendly manner was not assumed for the sake of business.

"I asked you something just as that fellow came in." Mrs. Balthazar was demure. "A question. Do you remember? About your daughters. If they were dark or fair."

"Yes, yes," smiled Ferdinand. "I remember. The young man came just at that moment. Now, let me see: the answer to the question is that one is fair and the other is dark. The fair one is the elder."

"Fair and dark." Mrs. Balthazar nodded. "And the dark one's the youngest. I'll remember. Thanks so much. You'll pardon my curiosity, won't you?" She followed him rather breathlessly to the door. "Thanks so much. Good-afternoon!"

IV

The streets were very wet, and the water was gushing through the bars of the gutter drains. Over the shops in Theobald's Road the canvas blinds which had been drawn out to protect exposed goods were sodden and a melancholy trickle splashed down from their corners. Outside a butcher's shop sawdust had been strewn, and those who clustered about the trays of meat carried away with them, for a few steps, traces of the butcher's sawdust. These traces did not go far, however, for the number of people who passed quickly churned the wet pavements into mud, and with chill in the afternoon air and bad light caused by the premature darkness of a wet February afternoon Theobald's Road was an unpleasant experience for Ferdinand. He would have hastened from it if he had not been thinking amusedly of Mrs. Balthazar. Amusedly and pityingly. Perhaps a little quakingly. Ferdinand could not deny that there were disadvantages as well as advantages in that friendly manner. Disadvantages, also, in the response to that manner.

He picked his way along the muddy streets, glad when he realized that each step brought him nearer home. Walking more rapidly than was his wont, he overtook a man who was going in the same direction as himself and did not notice that this man, who was a good deal shorter than Ferdinand, and who wore a soaked brown mackintosh and still more sodden cap, carried in his hand, wrapped in paper, a bunch of mimosa. The mimosa shed here and there its tiny golden balls of flower, and the young man from time to time looked a little ruefully at his burden. As Ferdinand passed, this young man, who was Jabez Talbot, stopped sharply in the middle of his stride, and remained stationary until Ferdinand was out of sight in the gathering murk of the afternoon. Then, impulsively handing the bunch of mimosa to a little ragged girl who had gaped enviously and admiringly at it, he turned his back upon Ferdinand and disappeared in the direction from which both had come.

Ferdinand, still unconscious of all that had so swiftly happened, arrived within a few moments at the door of his own house, admitted himself, and proceeded up the stairs. His shoes being wet, he went first to his bedroom, where everything was as it had been during his wife's lifetime. Dry shod once more, he returned to the drawing room, thereby interrupting a conversation between two young people who appeared to have been standing close together by the fireplace. They were his daughter Rhoda and Punch Teed.

Nothing would have struck Ferdinand regarding their proximity if Rhoda had not moved confusedly towards him, her face suddenly scarlet and her eyes brilliant. It seemed as if the innocent glance of Ferdinand had produced in Rhoda an altogether unusual self-consciousness; and he was concerned first of all to put her at her ease.

"Hasn't it been an afternoon!" he exclaimed, clasping her fondly by the arm as he passed onward towards the florid form of Punch. "Ah, Teed! You escaped the wet, I see."

It was an innocent remark; but there followed it, upon the

part of Rhoda, a silence so expressive that even Ferdinand was surprised.

"I was lucky, sir," answered Punch. "My luck's in, to-day." He laughed cheerily and sank back into a chair. But Rhoda, looking from Punch to her father over and over again, had lost that sudden flaming colour; and by the time Catherine and Joe, who had been sheltering from the rain, reached home upon Ferdinand's heels she was very pale indeed.

CHAPTER IX

MONA TAKES A HAND

I

In a tall and shabby house in one of those hilly roads which lie between Swain's Lane, Highgate, and the Junction Road, Upper Holloway, lived the Talbots. John Talbot, a retired furniture manufacturer with a passion for cultivating his own little oblong of back garden; his wife, Jane Talbot, who had no passion for anything in the wide world, but only an amiable interest in all that concerned her husband, her daughter, her home, and her own comfort; and their angular, plain, sensible, silly daughter Mona, likewise devoid of passion, but not therefore devoid of eager interest in everything but herself. Mona had been at the same school as Catherine Meadows, and had won prizes. She now thought a great deal, was very kind and untidy, and consumed immense quantities of printed matter in the shape of books, pamphlets, and even leaflets such as those issued by every type of propagandist. But Mona never remembered anything she read, and while she was sensible with the wisdom of the innocent and unselfish, she was particularly ill informed. For all that, however, she was happy. She was a good and loving friend, and in fact there were few better women to be found in the immediate neighbourhood of her home.

While Mona, owing to her selfless devotion to many interests, went into all sorts of houses, her heavy but equally kind and ignorant parents received in return visits from almost every kind of human being. They endured this late change in their social habits (which had always been narrow and best-parlour-ish) with creditable equanimity, and adjusted themselves very agreeably to the needs of the hour. Both had given up going to church on Sundays, because the hills troubled them and because they were both home-lovers; and they now listened together upon Sunday evenings, unless there were visitors in the house, to the non-denominational service which they could hear by wireless from the London station of the British Broadcasting Corporation. Wireless, indeed, filled much of their lives. They listened solemnly to the news bulletins, nodding their heads, looking askance at each other, repeating aloud the numbers of those killed in accidents and ejaculating: "Fancy . . . a little boy! Oh, his *mother* . . . seventeen . . . Burnt!" Mr. Talbot, in particular, enjoyed the twenty-minute lectures to be heard at intervals throughout the day, and if he never learned very much from them, owing to the unintelligible speech of those Irishmen, would-be-aristocratic Englishwomen, and Oxford and Cambridge intellectuals who provided the lectures, at least they helped to fill Mr. Talbot's waking hours, which otherwise (especially in winter) might have been wearisomely undiversified.

Mr. Talbot, upon the Saturday afternoon in February which has been already described, was listening to the running commentary which was being broadcast upon a football match. He was a thin man, who looked like a University Professor, and had a high, hairless head and sunken temples which threw into high relief the prominent bones of his forehead. With the head phones formidably binding his face he seemed to be imprisoned in a kind of skull-stocks. A drooping ash-coloured moustache hid his mouth, and his chin was feeble; but his nose was large and bulbous, and his eyes were the eyes of a shrewd and cautious man. They did his character no injustice, for John Talbot had made his small but snug income by manufacturing and selling good tables and chairs at reasonable cash prices, a fact which

showed commercial wisdom so greatly in advance of Twentieth Century practice as to be remarkable.

His wife sat calmly near him with an open novel in her
two hands, which rested in her lap, and her eyes artfully
shut behind her big spectacles. She spent much of her time
thus, and was never known to betray herself by snoring.
There are some to whom her way of life will seem ideal.
She, too, was thin; she, too, looked honest—as she was; her
nose was thin, her skin and her blue eyes were pale, her teeth
protruded slightly; and both she and her husband were much
at home in a roomful of solid, ugly furniture. They were not
old people—neither of them was yet sixty—but they had
grown indolent with modest prosperity, and sat down a great
deal in the comfortable chairs made years before in Mr. Talbot's factory.

Upon this day Mr. Talbot, vice-bound by the head phones,
now and then jumped in the air as the noise of a big crowd
roused to much excitement caused great vibration in his ears,
and communicated to his being a similar, but second-hand,
excitement. There were two commentators, also, whose
words came brokenly upon the atmosphere, and who played
upon Mr. Talbot's feelings. These two were as fire and
water, opposed to each other in temper and speech. Where
one of them was all enthusiasm, so that he became ejacula-
tory and inarticulate, the other, who said less, was precise
and biting, as if he had neither heart nor bowels of compassion. Where one seemed to bark, the other seemed to
sneer. Mr. Talbot hated the sneering voice, and schemed
retorts to its owner which were very ironical and effective.
But he never really made them. His attention was always too
urgently recalled to the exciting matter in hand. Besides, the
enthusiast was always imperturbable by the cynic, and Mr.
Talbot was gratified at the way in which the enthusiast
ignored all interruptions.

Now the game was in progress after a stoppage. Mr.
Talbot, his mind as it were upon tiptoe, was absorbed in its

wayward fortunes. His eyes glared with animus. His head was sunk between his shoulders. His lips were pursed. And the enthusiast described the play to the accompaniment of a low roar from the multitude.

"Brown has the ball now. He has taken it very cleverly from Haggard. He's lost it. Haggard now has it. He's passed it to Dobbs, who puts it out to Lemon. Lemon has trapped it cleverly. He is tackled by Smith. He recovers and keeps the ball. Oh, well done, sir! That was awfully good!" The commentator grew excited.

"A little lucky, I think," said the cold voice of the cynic.

"Shut up!" exclaimed Mr. Talbot.

"By Jove, that was awfully good!" insisted the enthusiast. "Lemon has tricked Jocks. He's tricked Todd. He's going through! Will he do it?"

"Square five," observed the cynic.

"He's passed Burge, controlling the ball cleverly. By Jove! This is exciting! There's only one man between him and the goal. The crowd is tremendously excited. Can you hear them? All the players are running down the field. Dacker is coming out to defend his goal. Shoot, shoot, man!"

"Square seven," interposed the disgusted voice of the mathematician.

"Shoot! O-oh!" came the voice of the crowd.

"Shoot!" cried Mr. Talbot, kicking his right foot convulsively. "O-oh!" He groaned, looking ashamedly, vicariously ireful at his wife as she opened her eyes and raised her book with an automatic gesture. "Robbed!" he said mournfully. "Just at the last minute, as he was going to shoot!" He brought his fist down upon the table in indignation.

"Good gracious!" sighed Mrs. Talbot, her whirling mind among the millionaires. "Who?"

"Lemon," said Mr. Talbot. "Can you hear them shouting?"

Mrs. Talbot picked up her head phones, from which proceeded a raucous bray.

"Who's winning, dear?" she asked.

"Nobody!" snapped Mr. Talbot, intent once more upon the game which he was overhearing. "I don't believe in this chap Lemon. Spectacular! Pretty tricky play; but he finishes badly. Give me good solid work, and none of this modern gimcrack. The curse of modern life, it is. Cleverness! Smartness!"

He settled down, rather ruffled, to the game; and his daughter Mona, hearing that raised voice and looking into the room, caught only the last sentences, agreed with them, smiled lovingly at the thought of this old couple settling between them the character of the world at any point in its progress, and went into the room facing this one, upon the opposite side of the square, tiled entrance hall of the double-fronted house. Here, where there was only a gas fire beneath the dark marble mantelpiece and immense gold-framed mirror, and where a canary drooped in a gilt cage near heavy green bob-fringed curtains of plush, she seated herself at the long mahogany dining table, in the middle of which a well-cultivated aspidistra spread its green leaves. Taking up a pamphlet issued by the True Temperance Association, Mona set herself to imbibe information with the avidity of a drunkard.

II

Upon the mantelpiece ticked a large marble clock; and just as Mona began to suspect that True Temperance was something different from what she had supposed and that it had no connection with those frightening advertisements which she sometimes read commending secret and tasteless cures for alcoholism, the clock struck the half hour. In twenty minutes Anna, the Talbot's housemaid, would be bringing tea, and Mona had this pamphlet to finish, and another one defining the differences between Communism,

Collectivism, Socialism, and the Coöperative Movement to read before she could conscientiously accept tea. She was going to read this pamphlet upon the 'isms in order that she could ask intelligent questions of Jabez; because she felt that the questions which she ordinarily asked him were really too silly for words.

"I think I must be the silliest person in the world," thought Mona, putting down the pamphlet which she was reading. "Oh, dear! Isn't it getting dark!" She forsook her pamphlet with a rather guilty conscience.

"Tweet," said the canary, hopping along his perch and looking through the bars of his cage.

Well, the question was whether one didn't do more good by following one's inclination and talking to Dickie than by trying to understand what Bishop Somebody had said about houses that were tied and houses that were untied. Jabez said she wasn't to bother her head about theory, that what she was intended for was salvation by works. He considered she was better in action than in thought. "Actions, not Words!" thought Mona, kindling to the phrase. Then she jumped up and went to Dickie's cage and saw that he had really most cleverly drawn her attention to the emptiness of his water cup.

"And he hasn't got a lump of sugar or any green stuff!" exclaimed Mona. "It's too bad of Anna, because I asked her if I should do it! She doesn't like anybody to look after Dickie but herself; and yet she doesn't—— However, I expect she's been too busy. I wonder if she'll mind my filling his cup."

Feeling quite bold, she opened the small shutter which protected the water cup and took the cup out. It was at this moment that she realized for the first time how fiercely it had been raining. The window pane was streaming, and the earth in the window box and in the garden beyond was pounded to a muddy paste. The rain was over now, and there was a patch of blue almost directly above the house; but

Jabez, who had been in town for luncheon, had not returned home. Pausing in the window, Mona became clairvoyant. She thought: "I know he was lunching with Edmund Piercy, because I arranged it. Edmund lives in Chancery Lane. They may have gone together, after lunch, to the Meadowses'." Now, why Mona should think thus she did not know; but the mere fact that she had thought it crystallized the supposition into a certainty.

Quickly her imagination ran on. She saw the two of them arriving at that sedate house in Woburn Square. She saw them going up the stairs to the drawing room, saw them being greeted by Ferdinand. And she picked Jabez out—with cousinly loyalty—as the centre of the group. She liked Jabez. She admired and trusted him. And she wanted him to make friends in that house. She thought it would be good for him to know her two best friends. She wanted him to fall in love with Catherine, but she would not mind if he fell in love with Rhoda. One or the other would make him a beautiful and attractive wife; and either would do something which Mona desired. She wanted Jabez to be made less serious. Her instinct—or her secret wisdom—told her that he must be made less serious. And this change, she believed, could be effected best by marriage. To marriage as the grand solvent Mona, as a woman, pinned her faith.

She was still standing in the window, looking out at the gloomy dusk and holding in her hand Dickie's little water cup, thinking of all these strange and (to Mona) romantic things, when her crystallized certainty was shattered and her dream made insignificant by the appearance of Jabez, alone, at the gate. His cloth cap and his mackintosh were black, as if both had been soaked by the heavy rain. His face she could not see, although it flashed into her mind at once that his head was carried low, as if in dejection. Mona's brows moved together for a fleeting instant, and immediately she was again perfectly placid. She watched her cousin enter the gate, heard his key in the front door, heard him pass the

room where she was and go quickly upstairs, while she stood
all the time near the canary's cage. Knowledge of the failure
of her intuition concerning his possible movements did not
impress her adversely. She merely went to the door, carefully carrying the water cup in her hand, filled it from a tap
in the ground-floor lavatory, replaced the cup in Dickie's
cage, and remained standing by the window until Jabez once
more came downstairs and discovered her.

III

His entry satisfied Mona that her impression, drawn from
the carriage of his head at the gate, had been accurate. There
was a look of pride upon Jabez's face which she had seen
only twice before—and on each occasion this look had followed a rebuff. His lips met closely; the lines in his cheeks
were intensified; the air of ruggedness and indifference was
heightened. Now Mona thought that an air of indifference
was always assumed. She had found it so with others, and
she had now been observing her cousin closely for several
months. Nevertheless, her first remark to him at this time
did not convey any hint of what she was thinking. It was for
that reason even more disconcerting than a more deeply
planned speech would have been. Said Mona:

"I wonder if you ought to wear glasses, Jabez."

Jabez, perhaps prepared for something else, started. Mona
saw his face very clearly, in spite of the darkness which was
everywhere gathering. Before he could answer her with his
tongue she had read even more in that sensitive face than
words could have told her.

"That's just come into my head," she continued conversa-
tionally. "You know how things do, don't you? Just seeing
you." To herself she was thinking: "Poor dear, he's unhappy!"

"I expect you're right," Jabez said, and looked away. She
saw the line of his large obstinate nose. His hair was thick

and strong, brushed straight back from the forehead. It was a fine face, and not the face of a weakling. Yet Mona had perhaps not been wrong in thinking that the expression which it wore was that of a sensitiveness, a discouragement, known only to those who accept a certain kind of defeat.

"Afraid you had a wet walk," Mona said. "It's been pouring here. I've been reading a drink pamphlet. But I'm so silly that I can't understand it. And besides, you know, I hardly ever *do* drink anything, so I suppose that kind of thing wouldn't in any case mean much to me."

"Perhaps not." Her cousin turned indifferently to the canary's cage; and with his mouth grimly set endured the candid gaze of Dickie's cocked eye. "Besides which, I don't see why you should bother yourself with a lot of stuff that doesn't interest you."

"Yes, but how's one to know *anything,* Jabez?" demanded Mona. "I mean *all* learning's terribly difficult. Unless you happen to have a brain, which I haven't."

"You've got enough brain to understand your own affairs," retorted Jabez, looking at her squarely. "And a bit over. And that's different from me, who have no such thing."

"You could understand anything," Mona protested.

Jabez shrugged.

"I'm disposed to think just at present that I understand nothing whatever," he said.

"Wasn't your lunch with Edmund a success?"

"Perfect," Jabez reassured her. "We didn't touch on anything I wasn't sure of. Oh, it's not *that* that troubles me. I'm in doubt, Mona. I'm wondering if I've got any useful function in life at all."

"You're in love," thought Mona. Her face expressed nothing but the mildest and most gentle interest in what he was saying.

"All my ideas seem to be shifting. My notions of what's to be done."

"You're growing," she said quickly. "That's nothing to

worry about. You *want* to grow. You're the kind of man who does. You don't want to stick in the same place all the time."

"But I want to be consistent."

"Well, I don't see why. What I think is that the notions men have of consistency and honour and dignity are generally very silly. Women don't have them. They're too sensible."

Jabez gave a short laugh.

"If you mean," said he, "that women are all inconsistent, undignified, and dishonourable, I don't agree with you. They're better than that."

"That wasn't what I meant," answered Mona calmly.

"Nor did I mean by consistency anything as silly as you pretend. What I meant was 'logical.' I want to go onward but not to skip. And I don't want to find myself unable to account to myself for my opinions. That's the position I'm in now. I've always believed that if the world were run on logical lines everybody would be happy. Now, that seems to me to be the most absurd assumption I ever heard of. I've always believed that the control of industry by the workers was the logical path to happiness for all. Now I'm inclined to think it may be the ruin of industry. How can I go on trying to persuade everybody that one set of opinions is true when in fact my own opinions are changing so that I don't any longer believe what I'm saying?"

"You can't," Mona remarked. "But what has made you change?"

"I don't know. Something in the atmosphere, perhaps." He tried to speak lightly. "In the last few weeks I've been meeting people whose opinions are different from my own. And I've been thinking about what they say. I can't help listening to them. There's Gascoyne, for example. He's an intelligent chap, although I don't care much for him."

"Not like Joe!" Mona's exclamation was positively crowded with amazement. "Why, Joe's a dear!"

"I expected you to say that. I admit there's something about him that one likes at first. I don't *dis*like him. But I don't understand him. He's not sincere in argument. You can't hold him to a thing. And yet he's got brains; he's got ideas. I don't deny that. I can't. He's said one or two things that have set me thinking. They aren't anything much——" Jabez spoke grudgingly—"but as he says them they certainly have a kind of effect. For example, he said there was no room for him in my world, whereas there was room for me in his. It's a nuisance, but that's quite true. There's no room for people like Gascoyne in a really efficient world; and yet I can't get away from the fact that even in Utopia there ought to be a few jokers." He spoke almost bitterly, as if with contempt; but there lurked in his eye something that was neither bitterness nor contempt.

"Poor Jabez!" said Mona, with pity, with sympathy, and with a smile and a shake of the head. "I'm sorry you're troubled. And yet, you know, the explanation's quite simple. You're just a little—just a *very* little jealous of Joe."

The charge produced a sort of earthquake in that quiet room.

"Who, I?" Jabez frowned at her. "Nothing of the kind." He was emphatic. And Mona was unmoved, because she had expected the denial.

"I'm afraid you're a fraud, my dear," she told him. "And I'm sorry for that, because, although I'm fond of Joe, I think you're probably better than he is. A more important man——"

"For God's sake!" cried Jabez. "What a word!"

"To the world, I mean. Because you're the kind that wants to alter, and Joe's just an old conservative. But you're jealous of him because you don't know him."

"Nonsense!"

"Not wickedly jealous. I don't mean that. But you're impressed by him. More impressed than you ought to be. You think he's cleverer than you are, and more attractive."

"Attractive! Good heavens! What's that got to do with it?" Jabez spoke almost loudly in his unwonted excitement. "What on earth have you got into your head now?"

"Don't you know?" said Mona innocently. "I should have thought you did. I meant that people aren't as a rule jealous of other men's opinions. Nor their qualities. Only of something else altogether. And it's generally attractiveness."

Jabez stared at her.

"I should like to know what you mean," he said in a bewildered way. "But I can't make head or tail of it. As far as Gascoyne's concerned——"

"You think some people would like him better than they'd like you."

"Why not?"

It was Mona's turn to shrug, and she shrugged.

"Well, I'm just saying what I feel," she said. "I don't think you're very fond of yourself. And supposing you were to fall in love, you'd have a very bad time, because you'd feel that everybody else had a better chance than yourself."

"Oh," murmured Jabez, unprotesting. "So you think that."

Mona saw that he had crimsoned; but as they were at this moment called to tea she could not ascertain anything more of her cousin's state of mind. Feeling rather naughty, she led the way into the other room, where Mr. Talbot, still bound by his head phones, looked solemnly into space, listening to the referee's whistle and the wrangle of the commentators, and where his wife, by a series of fidgetings, was working her chair nearer to the tea table (with much squeaking of the castors) in order that she might pour out tea for all. Jabez sat down near to his aunt. The one glance which he gave in Mona's direction was charged with uneasiness.

IV

"Bah!" said Mr. Talbot presently, squeezing out of his head phones and laying them upon the table at his side. "It's ridiculous. To my mind, it's ridiculous. Here are sixty thousand people, a good many of them standing in the rain, watching twenty-two men—twenty-five, to be precise, if one includes the referee and the linesmen—running and slipping about in the mud for an hour and a half. And at the end of that time neither side has scored a goal. I've wasted my afternoon listening to a lot of rubbish——"

"And you'll do it again next Saturday, Pa," Mona assured him.

Mr. Talbot was entirely unaffected by her rebuke.

"Simply because I'm an old fool," he answered. "And because the world's full of men like me, who busy themselves with rubbish because there's nothing else for them to do. When's the Millennium coming, Jabez?"

"Not in time for you, I'm afraid, Uncle," said Jabez. "We're doing all we can to hurry it up."

"Pooh! Morris dancing," said Mr. Talbot cryptically. "Maypoles. Inspectors. It won't work. And even if it did, what is there for me in it all? I can't dance round the maypole."

"You could inspect the furniture, Father," suggested Mona.

"Benches, I suppose, Jabez. No upholstery, eh? No time for soft goods in the ideal world. This William Morris pattern stuff, now—d'you like it?"

Jabez shook his head.

"I imagine there would always be fashions," he said.

"Just what we want to get rid of!" exclaimed Mr. Talbot. "Fashions bring gimcrack. Surely, that's obvious? You get the latest; but it mustn't last. No, no. Solid benches and tables——"

"You *must* have beauty, Pa!" remonstrated Mona.

"You talk like your friend Mr. Meadows," said her father. "He's all for beauty, I understand. What he and his kidney will never understand is that the most beautiful thing in the world is a straight line."

"Well, there's something in that," observed Jabez thoughtfully.

"Something in it! Did you hear that, Mother?"

Mrs. Talbot nodded. She never spoke unless it was to ask a question.

"Something in it!" repeated Mr. Talbot, with a melancholy air. He gave a single wheeze of ironic laughter.

The two younger members of the party were not attending. Mona had said, half under her breath, and bending towards her cousin so that they should not be overheard:

"I thought I'd go down after supper and see Catherine. Would you like to come?"

Jabez endeavoured to look unconscious.

"I almost went there this afternoon," he answered.

Mona's heart gave a triumphant throb. Her intuition had been vindicated.

"Almost?" she inquired archly. "Why not quite? Frightened to go alone?"

Jabez's lips were pressed together for an instant. Then he responded quite frankly:

"No, not frightened. But I saw Mr. Meadows, whom I can't stand, and somehow I—well, I felt I didn't want to go when I'd seen him."

"Don't you think you're rather intolerant, Jabez?" smiled Mona. "And I've told him you're such a—such a thoroughly respectable man, as of course you are."

"He stands for all I detest. Money, ease, culture, and uselessness. He's never done a hand's turn, never suffered for a single minute. He doesn't know what it is to work or starve, or watch others starving."

"Who's this?" asked Mr. Talbot.

"Never mind, Pa," Mona answered briefly. To Jabez she added: "You're quite wrong."

"He doesn't like me, either. I'm poisonous to him." Jabez spoke in a lower tone. His face was quite flushed. There was an uneasy, strained look in his eyes, as there might have been if he had been holding his breath almost to suffocation point.

"You're terrible, Jabez!" murmured Mona. "And if he's done nothing else at all, Mr. Meadows has brought up the two nicest girls I know. Catherine and Rhoda——"

"Oh, Catherine and Rhoda!" said Mr. Talbot, who had been listening, trying to catch the subject of their talk. "Now, Rhoda's a little hasty; but she——"

"Will you come?" asked Mona, her brows arched. "You needn't talk to Mr. Meadows till you know him better. You can talk to Catherine."

She intentionally hesitated for the smallest fraction of time before pronouncing Catherine's name—not maliciously, for Mona was never malicious, but with a slightly mischievous enjoyment of her own capacity for teasing. Jabez looked very serious. For a moment she was afflicted by the fear that she might have hurt him by such clumsy, hoydenish rallying. Mona at times regarded her own methods as flat footed and ill bred; and she was always apt to be seized, as she was at this moment, by remorse and timidity.

"*Do* come," she urged. "I want you to get to know my friends properly."

No hint there! No suggestion of anything but kindly feelings.

"After supper?" asked Jabez. He was as sober as a judge. His face had assumed a sternness which permitted only serious speeches to be made. Then he nodded. "Very well," he concluded, after causing Mona's heart to flutter to her throat. But while his face was set Mona was convinced that his heart, released from constraint, must be dancing. Her own gladness was intense. Mr. Talbot, finding himself ignored, replaced the head phones and began to frown; his wife's head gave a little jerk downwards.

CHAPTER X

ÉCLAIRECISSEMENT

I

EVERYBODY had gone, and Ferdinand was alone in his study. He had switched off the lights excepting only one small lamp which stood upon the table by the arm of his chair. A book was in his hand, but he was not reading. Instead, he stared directly at the dying fire in the grate, which he made no attempt to revive. In the darkness above his head the outline of a large portrait of an unknown man, the work of an Eighteenth Century painter, lurked unseen; about him were the many tall shelves of books, his constant friends.

As Ferdinand sat thus in silence, the books seemed to him to crowd closer, the shelves to expand and heighten, himself to shrink, until he became quite tiny, and the book in his hand a Lilliputian volume. It was the hour for ghosts. The silver chime of his clock had sounded midnight. There was silence. Ferdinand's eyes closed.

And then, out of his dream he started wide awake, for the faintest, smallest sound had struck his ear. Ferdinand sat upright in his chair, looking straight before him, sensitive to the slightest change in the atmosphere. A draught of cooler air—no greater than that which would come by way of a gently opened door—struck his cheek. Still he did not look round, but continued in his chair near the fire, while the draught vanished. There was a rustle which Ferdinand's ear hardly caught, a light creaking which anybody may hear in a still house at night, a whisper.

"Daddy."

Rhoda's voice. Was he dreaming?

"My darling." She had glided across the room, was at his side, kneeling. Ferdinand saw her white face, the slender hand upon the arm of his chair. Was she real? His own arm, thrown out, embraced her shoulders, hardly covered by the thin silk dressing gown that she wore. His ear heard her hurried breathing, as if she had been crying, or were about to cry.

"Why, Rhoda," he whispered in return, holding her gently, feeling that she trembled. "Are you ill? Not ill?" His disengaged hand had taken hers, and he felt it covered by Rhoda's other hand, so that they seemed to be doubly met together in love and intimacy. "What is it, child? You're trembling."

"I'm afraid," she said softly. She seemed to be struggling with tears. Presently her head sank lower until it rested upon their clasped hands. The shoulders within Ferdinand's embrace quivered. It was as though she shuddered.

"You're cold," Ferdinand protested. "Wait; I'll stir the fire."

"No." She clung fiercely to his hand, lest he should move.

"Frightened? You've been dreaming?" He held her more closely, but still in a very gentle way, to reassure her against fear.

"Yes, I've been dreaming," Rhoda said in a low tone. Then, shivering, the words coming unsteadily, as if her iips trembled. "Daddy, I must tell you something."

"Anything, my darling," Ferdinand whispered in reply. "Are you unhappy?"

"Yes." It was hardly spoken. Then, much louder: "Dreadfully unhappy. Daddy, I've been deceiving you." Again that shivering. Ferdinand said nothing. His cheek rested gently upon the soft hair of the head which was so near his face. "I'm horrible!"

She was a child, with a child's exaggerations; Ferdinand was sure of it. He did not fear.

"Not as bad as that," he teased, smiling faintly in the darkness.

"Don't laugh," Rhoda whispered. "That's worse than——"

"If it's something you can tell me," Ferdinand said, "it can't be so very bad."

A pause. He heard her breathing. Then, lower if possible than before:

"It's very bad. I've deceived you. I'm unhappy."

"Unhappy because you've deceived me? Unhappy because of something you've done?"

"I'm ashamed." Her shoulders trembled anew. She pressed within the shelter of his arm.

"Then?" asked Ferdinand, after a moment. No answer. "Aren't you going to tell me?" Still silence. He continued. "You see, darling, I love you. Nothing you could tell me would alter that."

"Wouldn't it?" Her voice was faint. The warm cheek had been raised so that it was against his own. There was another hesitation, prelude to a great effort. It was prolonged. Then gaspingly, with the desperation of one who seeks extremity of self-commitment: "It's Punch."

"Punch?" Ferdinand did not grasp her meaning. He had a vague sense that somebody had said something of Punch which caused him to feel dislike and discomfort at any mention of that name. But he did not link Rhoda with Punch. As the instants flew, however, he guessed something more. His heart quickened. The arm about her shoulders grew a very little more tense. "My darling?" Still he questioned.

Rhoda drew away from him. She knelt upright, pressing his hand, but withholding her head. No longer whispering, but in a dry voice, quite audible in the silent room, she said:

"Daddy, I've been letting Punch make love to me."

It was out, and Ferdinand was a little dazed.

"Punch?" he stammered. "You've . . . Do you mean . . I suppose you mean he wants to marry you? Is that it?" A heavy sigh rose to his lips. He gripped her hand tightly. He was alarmed, startled. . . . What could he say? What could he say? What could he say that would temporize, that would not hurt her? The notion of such a marriage— such imprudence . . . "My dear, you're so young."

"No, Daddy," came that hoarse little voice, which was so much a part of her shamed rigidity. "No, there's no question . . . No, we don't want to marry each other. It's just that I've been letting him make love to me."

"But, Rhoda!" exclaimed Ferdinand suddenly, vehemently, with aversion. He started violently, realizing too late that the movement of repulsion, which had been instinctive, would be misconstrued. He had lost her. Her hands, too, were gone from him. She was altogether apart, miserable, ashamed, alienated.

"You see?" she said.

"My darling!" He sought again to reach her. In vain. She was quite withdrawn, driven by misery and sensitiveness into despairing reserve. But presently, as if she forced herself to speak, she went on:

"That's why I'm ashamed. If he'd wanted to marry me, or if I'd wanted——" Ferdinand heard her heavy sigh, the sobbing intake of her breath.

"What *did* you want?" he asked. A horror seemed to have taken possession of him. This his daughter, his Rhoda? This his darling, whom he had lovingly imagined to be yet a child, unspoilable?

"I wanted to be made love to," he heard her say.

"But by a lover," he urged.

She was shuddering.

"Well, I've told you," she said drearily. And added immediately afterwards: "I knew that if I didn't tell you Catherine would."

"Catherine." Ferdinand was appalled. "What does *she* know about it?"

"She knows I've been meeting him. She guessed."

"You've been meeting him," repeated Ferdinand, quite at a loss. "But my dearest——"

She was upon her feet, standing near him in the pale light, a faint slender figure, like a ghost against the background of all those old books with their warm, rich bindings.

"Do you hate me?" she said quickly. "You're horrified."

"No, no, no!" cried Ferdinand, springing to his feet. "Never that!"

"You do." Rhoda shook her head miserably.

"I'm alarmed," Ferdinand said. "I'm bewildered. I don't see——"

"You don't understand?" she asked. "It seems to you horrible? It *is* horrible, I suppose." Her tone was exaggeratedly meditative, as though she were pretending to be detached, to enter into his feelings. There was the strangest air of condescension.

"I've thought of you as falling in love one day with some fine young fellow."

"Yes," she whispered, her head lowered. "You see, Daddy, I can't talk to you about that."

"But you're not in *love* with him, my dear!" exclaimed Ferdinand, coming close, insisting upon taking her hand, which was without life.

"Oh," she drawled, as if indifferently. "Yes. A little, perhaps. A little. Half. Enough to——"

"Enough!" That was just Ferdinand's difficulty. That was what filled him with dastaste. Was it *thus* that young people felt nowadays? No ecstasy? All experiment? But Rhoda—it was impossible. "Enough! Good God! What does Catherine say?" It was a cry of conscious inadequacy. Then he guessed, and was repelled by, something that resembled a bitter, distorted smile upon that white face—a sneer at his naïveté.

"Catherine? Nothing. She doesn't know more than she's guessed."

"She's said something?"

"She's warned me. She's done her duty. She's been the elder sister," Rhoda said painfully, with distaste. "I didn't listen. I just smiled at her for her trouble."

"You mean you have secrets from Catherine?" Ferdinand was overwhelmed.

"Of course. From everybody," said Rhoda quietly. "From myself, even."

"But from Catherine!" He could not restrain his amazement. "Don't you love Catherine?"

"I suppose I do." It was dubious. Her hardness was appalling. Much lower came the words: "I'm sure I do." Did she sob? Under his breath Ferdinand exclaimed something of his horror. There was a sudden mounting of excitement between them—a breaking of pride—a collapse into truth of confession. The threatening hardness, so precariously sustained in face of disapproval, gave way before a flood of emotion. Rhoda's next cry was forced from her by anguish. "I love you best, Daddy!" It was broken, despairing, the last word she could bear.

She was in his arms, sobbing in agony, pressing him to her with little convulsive jerks which told their tale of endurance strained to extremity.

"My darling, my darling!" protested Ferdinand, distracted. "What can I *do?*"

"Love me still!" she groaned, her body convulsed with dreadful sobs.

"I do!" He felt her head shaken. Frantically, he went on talking, trying to soothe, to calm her. "I do! Nothing could change that. Nothing on earth. But I'm quite overset with this, you know. It's so unexpected. It's so unlike anything I'd looked forward to. You see, you're growing up so suddenly, and I hadn't noticed it. You've surprised me. You've given me so much to think over. I'm not used—— I'm really——"

"Poor Daddy!" she caressed him, her face held tightly to

his cheek. "I've frightened you. I've disgusted you. Poor Daddy!"

"You've frightened me," Ferdinand confirmed. "And bewildered me. For I don't see—— My darling, have you thought how this is to end?"

He felt her start.

"No," she said, in a low tone.

"You've met him. He's kissed you. Nothing more than that?"

There was the slightest pause. It seemed to Ferdinand that his heart stopped beating.

"Nothing that I could tell you. Oh, no, no. Nothing, nothing!"

She was now sobbing desperately, as if she were broken-hearted. Ferdinand, dumb and full of terror, glimpsing unknown sequels of horror and despair, held her close, as he had done when she was a baby.

"Hush," he whispered. "Hush, my darling. You'll be ill. You'll be ill."

II

Gradually her fit of bitter sobbing spent itself, and only the shudder which shook her body from time to time showed that she was still within its power. Ferdinand continued to murmur in her ear and gently to pat her shoulder; but this he did automatically, for he was all the time struggling to conquer his own despair. Was this the end of all his happiness? Had he lost her forever? What could he do? What could he say?

"Weak . . . weak . . . weak . . ." he was thinking to himself. "I'm weak. Another man would know what to do. She's been meeting . . . But not in love, not in love. That's what I can't understand. It horrifies me. I'm not fit to meet such a thing. And the man—Punch, of all men. I can see why. He's handsome, ready . . . but coarse. Coarse! That Rhoda——" His mind was full of darting thoughts,

apprehensions, disgusts, half-formulated resolves, self-re-
proaches.

"Come and sit down, my dearest," Ferdinand said very
gently, drawing her towards the chair in which he had been
sitting at the moment of her entry. "Come and kneel by me
as you were doing."

Rhoda gave a weary cry of unwilling submissiveness and
suffered herself to be led. She sank at his side, shivering,
while Ferdinand stirred the fire and once again enfolded
her within his embrace. The little clock ticked audibly. Rhoda
held back her head, so that her face was outside the radius
of the pale light; and, at recognition of this, Ferdinand
pulled down the shade and at last extinguished the light itself. The room was illumined thereafter solely by the flicker
of one dancing flame behind the bars of the grate. Shadows
trembled upon the ceiling above them and darted hither and
thither, mysteriously, and at last ceased altogether as the
flame died out and the cinders rasped together in hollow
collapse, while Ferdinand and Rhoda continued silent as
before, crouched in the darkness.

But the silence grew painful to them both; and as Rhoda
recovered composure, with the sense that the worst was told,
she began to speak in a low voice, as if she were glad of this
relief from secrecy and constraint.

"It began a long time ago," she said. "Not very long, but
it seems a long time. And you and Catherine knew nothing
about it and never seemed to think of it at all. And Punch
was very kind to me and told me about himself, and how he
wasn't very good, and I said—I said I was glad of that, because I wasn't . . . I wasn't quite—quite altogether good,
myself." Her head was jerked a little downwards, and Ferdinand heard that she was crying softly. He felt that he must
exert all his strength to prevent himself from pushing her
agitatedly away, from rising and walking about the room in
horrified frenzy. This had been going on; and he had been
unaware of the danger, unobservant and concerned only with

his own thoughts and his own interests. All the time that he had supposed himself protective he had been allowing this danger. But the deceit, the duplicity. It was nothing; the love of a child for mystery. The search for sensation. The opportunity. The man. Punch Teed had been given free access to her.

"But you *are* good, my darling!" protested Ferdinand, in agony. "You *are* good."

Rhoda shook her head sadly in the darkness.

"Not as you and Catherine are," she whispered.

Catherine. Was Catherine? Ferdinand was tortured by a maddening suspicion. What if Catherine——

"Nonsense," he cried. He could not keep still. "You're both good. It's this *beast* who's responsible." He trembled as he sought refuge from his agitation in abuse of Rhoda's partner. His voice was out of control.

"Who, Punch? Poor Punch!" she sighed. "He's only a little boy. He can't help himself. He's always been looking for somebody like me. Just fancy; all his life."

"My dearest!" groaned Ferdinand, beside himself.

"It's been exciting, you know," she told him, in that little hoarse voice of confession. She might have been a child who had just been found after running away. "Awfully exciting. But I've been unhappy, too. Unhappy; and yet I couldn't give it up. Oh, I'm wicked. I'm wicked!" The sobs shook her a little. She was silent. Then: "Not really wicked, either. And the thought that I was deceiving you was horrid. I don't know how long I should have gone on. . . . Do you know, as soon as you'd gone out this afternoon—you and Catherine —I knew you'd be out a long time. . . . Only the rain came down. As soon as you'd gone I telephoned to Punch and said I was all alone and miserable——"

"Miserable, my darling!"

"He said: 'Oh, we'll soon put that right. I'll get a taxi.'"

"Rhoda!" groaned Ferdinand.

"That was why I had telephoned to him. I wanted him

to come. And he did; and—and he said I wasn't to be miserable any more, and I said I wasn't. And then it seemed as though you came in at once, and Punch walked away from me, and I looked at you; and you looked so innocent that I couldn't bear it any more. I just felt hot all over. And I went on feeling worse and worse all the evening; and I couldn't hear what anybody said because I was feeling so bad. And when we went to bed Catherine came and called to me from outside the door——"

"Catherine," said Ferdinand, half to himself.

"And I took no notice, because I guessed what she was going to say."

"But Catherine came in after I did," protested Ferdinand. "At tea time."

"But she looked very white. She was more suspicious than you. And when she came and called me I took no notice at all, and she was afraid to call too loudly because she thought she'd wake everybody up; and at last she went back to her own room, and I waited till I thought she must be in bed, and then I came down here to you."

"You're getting cold. Your hand's quite cold," Ferdinand said, chafing it. The fire had sunk to gray and black, only one dull patch of red remaining in the midst of the embers. A chill began to hang upon the air, numbing them both.

"You see, I didn't mind deceiving Catherine," continued Rhoda, in a voice that seemed to have no expression but to be only a tired drone. "I didn't like it; but I didn't really mind it, because—— But you looked so innocent——"

"Now that you've told me——" began Ferdinand.

"You despise me," she went on, quivering afresh. "I knew you would. *Knew* it!" Her cry was resigned, contemptuous, despairing. She could not understand his horror, his shock, but was engrossed in herself. What could he say? How put the blame without alienating her? But *blame*—it was a word, not the primary duty. Love must come first. There must be no diminution of warmth, of intimacy. And yet, how difficult, in such distress as he was feeling, to be at the same time a diplomat.

"Come, Rhoda," said Ferdinand. "There's no question of despising you." Despising, indeed! When he was in deadly fear for her safety.

"You see? You see? Your voice tells me——" she cried aloud, almost hysterically.

"Sh! sh!" Ferdinand tried to calm her. "My dearest!"

"I know. I *know*. You're thinking I'm—— You're think-ing Catherine would never——"

She had gone so far, gaspingly, when a sound checked the words upon her lips. Both heard the door open, both looked round, both simultaneously saw Catherine in the doorway, silhouetted against the light upon the landing without. That slim black figure with the dim golden glow behind her sent a shock to the two who were in the study. Catherine, like Rhoda, was in her dressing gown and slippers, and her ankles were bare. She bent forward to peer into the room, as if, coming from the lighted staircase, she were blinded by the darkness before her and so could not see the two figures which were huddled together between herself and the dead fire.

"Are you there, Rhoda?" called Catherine softly. "Rhoda, darling!"

III

Rhoda jumped to her feet, facing Catherine. Her teeth were chattering.

"Don't turn on the light," she called in reply. "Daddy's here. I've been telling him——"

There was defiance; but defiance of a different quality. Catherine's coming had made a great difference to the situa-tion. Rhoda was instantly more composed.

"Yes, I'm here, Catherine," Ferdinand said.

"I'm so glad. It was only that I was alarmed about Rhoda. I didn't mean to interrupt you." She was retiring, closing the door, as if this scene were one of the most ordinary and as if it had no concern for her.

"Catherine!" cried Ferdinand. "Don't go."

"Let her go," whispered Rhoda imploringly. Then: "No, I don't want her to." In a louder tone, she said: "You'd better stay, Catherine. Don't you want to hear what I've been telling Father?" There was jealousy in her voice, some feeling which Ferdinand could not catch. All he knew was that he depended upon Catherine's wisdom. He would have clung to her had she been nearer, begging her to aid him in this moment of distress.

"No, I don't mind what you've been telling Father," came that cool voice. "So long as you're both safe. But this room's rather cold, and I think you both ought to go to bed before you catch chills."

"Chills!" exclaimed Rhoda. "I'm burning."

"Good-night," called Catherine from the doorway. She was gone.

The two who were left in the darkness looked blindly at each other. Constraint had fallen upon them. They both felt suddenly very cold and tired, as if all emotion had been drained out of them.

"You're quite right," whispered Rhoda. "I'm a beast, and he's a beast. Both beasts. Both horrible! *Horrible!*" It was as though a sudden realization had come upon her. She raised her hands vehemently in emphasis.

"Rhoda!" Fear surged again into Ferdinand's heart lest despair should drive her thus to link herself with Punch, lest it should carry her into flight with that unscrupulous lover and ultimate irretrievable ruin. It was of this that he was most in dread. He had always dreaded her flight. She was of the kind that yielded to disaster and sought to escape from its consequences. If she ran away, if in desperation she——

"Don't be afraid," Rhoda said, as if she could read behind his cry the thoughts which it crystallized. "I'm quite sensible again. There's nothing to be afraid of. Poor Daddy, how frightened you are! And all over me, isn't it! Poor Daddy. Daddy, you'll go on loving me just the same, won't you? If you didn't, I couldn't bear it."

She took his hand, kissed it with her soft lips, and ran to the door. An instant later she had followed Catherine. Ferdinand, alone, fell back in his chair and put his long hands to his face. His head was throbbing. His vitality was exhausted. For the first time for many years, he felt old and overwhelmingly weary.

PART TWO

CHAPTER I

FERDINAND BUYS SOME FLOWERS

I

IT WAS a month later. February had gone and April was almost upon the town. The black old trees in the London squares, which are often among the earliest in southern England to respond to the year's changes, were already showing signs of reawakening life. For days Ferdinand had been conscious of the fact that the tracery of their branches had subtly developed, so that a fine web seemed to be mysteriously warming the winter hues into colour. Now he was sure that leaf buds were swelling. Here and there, upon a warm day, he imagined that he could detect the first tender green of spring. A faint ecstasy charged the atmosphere and made the hearts of all sensitive persons rise in ardour. Ferdinand himself breathed more deeply and was aware of new and wonderful restlessness within him, as if he, too, had been frozen and were awakening from slumber to new energy. The days were lengthening, and those murky evenings were going which he had so loved in the first days of winter, and which he had since found so unbearable.

From the window of his study, as he stood there with his hands in his pockets, he could see the square patch of garden, behind the house. Above the garden, and below the gray, cloud-laden sky, were the dark bricks and darker tiles of other houses and the sombre gloom of the small, barren gardens belonging to them. By craning his neck Ferdinand could watch the manœuvres of a large tabby cat scheming the capture of certain sparrows which chirped vigorously about the garden. He grew afraid lest the sparrows should fall under those eager claws, and threw up the window, clapping his hands, and scaring birds and cat alike, so that all disappeared. This done, he remained for a time at the open window, inhaling the air of the spring morning and thinking about recent happenings and the hidden future. He could neither read nor think, this morning. Therefore it was necessary that he should go out of doors and walk about in the drab streets, enjoying the sunshine, and listening to all those lovely echoes which are so subdued in winter and which begin to expand under the buoyant air of spring.

He left the house. His steps upon the pavement were light, firm, and regular. He held his head high, smiling gravely upon the town. A gusty breeze fanned his cheeks and carried little whirls of dust along the streets. It rattled the windows and drove the clouds so rapidly that their shadows seemed to whisk blithely before Ferdinand as he walked. With every step he grew more happy and less inclined to dwell upon those thoughts which had lately disturbed the tranquillity of his waking hours. He was young again, young and shy and confident, as if he had never felt old. And for this reason he was the less inclined to dwell upon his thoughts and the more ready, for once, to observe the scene about him.

The first thing he noticed was that the women and children had begun to wear clothing of brighter colours. Their cheeks were clearer under this cheerful breeze, and although flying particles of dust filled their eyes they were noticeably more gay. The shop windows were newly decked; the red omnibuses glittered; outside one of the houses he passed, two house painters, swinging, as it seemed to him, precariously in their cradles, were whistling blithely as they whisked their brushes to and fro. There were all sorts of interesting sights, from the road menders to the window cleaners; and high above the houses, the sound of its engine almost unheard in the busy noise of the streets, an aëroplane roared northwards.

Close to Ferdinand, as he lowered his eyes again, a stout, florid-faced, fur-coated woman with ringed hands and a feather-laden hat sat upon a chair beside a little stall, upon which were displayed violets and daffodils.

"Lovely violets," sang the woman. "Lovely violets."

Ferdinand started. His heart was touched by memory. Once he had bought some violets, but not here. He thought of the flower sellers at the foot of the steps leading to the Trinità dei Monti in Rome, and those who made a bower of the Port of Cannes. He thought of Mrs. Balthazar. And as he did this Ferdinand diverged from the walk he had planned and resolved to act upon the impulse which had overtaken him. He would turn eastwards and would go to see the little lady in whose fortunes he had lately begun to take so much interest.

Turning abruptly and with enthusiasm, he directed leisurely steps towards that shop which he had first entered a month earlier. He was smiling with anticipation.

II

However, Ferdinand was not to reach the shop of Mrs. Balthazar without an interruption; for as he crossed to the shade-darkened side of New Oxford Street he saw before him a face that was both familiar and unwelcome. It would have been difficult for him to say why he so much disliked Jabez Talbot, and yet there was no doubt as to the constraint which affected both Jabez and himself whenever they chanced to meet. In the present instance Jabez was walking slowly in the opposite direction, and the meeting was unavoidable. Ferdinand, quick to estimate mood in others, observed that Jabez looked tired and dispirited. The lines in his cheeks were deep; his mouth was set; his eyes were lustreless. Also, there was an air of shabbiness about him, as though his clothes were old and as though Jabez did not care whether they were old or new. The contrast between clothes carelessly worn and clothes fastidiously chosen was not less striking than the discrepancy in the carriage of the two men. Ferdinand was tall and thin; his hard felt hat cut his brow rigidly a little above the eyebrows and sharpened his features into an almost emaciated severity. The erectness with which he held his body, the neat cut of his light overcoat, the strict crease of his trousers, all combined together to emphasize his scrupulousness. Jabez, much shorter, much broader, much more clumsily and sturdily built, was without an overcoat. He wore a soft felt hat of an undistinguished gray; his suit, a dark gray with a speckle of lighter shade, was not so much ill cut as ill worn. The boots which Jabez wore, moreover, were stout, mended, and square toed; whereas Ferdinand's boots were Lobb-made and caused his slender feet to look exceptionally trim and delicate. There was calm in Ferdinand's face, and much almost tortured expression in the face of Jabez; a reserved pleasantness in Ferdinand's greeting, and reserved unpleasantness in the greeting of Jabez.

"How disagreeable he is!" thought Ferdinand. "As if he had the taste of quinine in his mouth." Aloud, he said, with much affability: "Ah, Talbot! Enjoying the fine morning, I see!"

"It's fine enough," admitted Jabez grudgingly. Then he smiled and his face became beautiful. "It's fine according to your mood, Mr. Meadows. Anybody can see that you're pleased with the world."

"Am I?" There was a chill in Ferdinand's voice as he answered. Was the man forever criticizing him? Did his bitterness persist even in the commonplaces of greeting? "I wonder if I'm pleased with the world. With the world of man, no. But 'there's the sun, moon, and stars, brother, all sweet things.' Are you insensible to those?"

It was Jabez's turn to pause under criticism. He glanced quickly at Ferdinand, but he did not smile as he replied.

"No," he said quite seriously. "No, I'm not insensible to those. But they don't feed men and women; and that is my chief concern nowadays. It's been a hard winter, Mr. Meadows, with much suffering among those who have no fire and no warm clothes; and I'm taking a dreary number of sad stories along to my committee meeting. I'm now on my way; and I've been thinking of what I have to tell. That's why I'm enjoying the fine morning a little less than you can do."

"Quite," said Ferdinand. "I understand." His heart was softened. He was filled with pity for all who suffered. "I'm afraid you think me little concerned with the misfortunes of others."

"I think of you as very comfortable, Mr. Meadows," answered Jabez unsmilingly. "But I think that if you saw as much and knew as much as I do about what goes on— elsewhere—you'd feel it as much as I do—more than I do, very likely, because I'm a bit hardened. But I mustn't keep you."

Ferdinand, touched by the frankness of what Jabez had said, held out his hand for the parting.

"I want to know more," he said warmly. "Will you believe that?" Jabez did not look at him, but away. Ferdinand saw the roughness of that dark skin and the dullness of the flush that rose under it. He was stirred by something that he could not explain to add: "Come and talk to me about it. I'm not insensible—only ignorant. Come to dinner to-night. Will you? Do!"

Later, when they had separated, and when Jabez was out of sight among the varied crowd, Ferdinand was amazed at his own conduct.

"Now, *why* did I do that?" he asked himself, in some consternation. "Why *on earth* did I do it? I've let myself in for something! I must be mad!"

Shaking his head and hesitating whether to resume his

walk or to return home, he continued, almost without will, to walk in the direction of Mrs. Balthazar's shop.

III

Within its window, which was slightly steamy with the condensation of moisture, he saw the flowers lying in their boxes, or arranged in ugly dull-coloured vases such as florists use. They were bright and fresh, yellow and white and blue. Spanish iris from abroad; daffodils from English gardens; early anemones; great white Arum lilies; and multi-coloured cinerarias decked the shop and made it gay. The scent, also, as Ferdinand entered, was heavy. It started a thousand memories, because mankind, having developed a brain from its original sense of smell, is still, despite every vagary of civilization, more quickly and powerfully affected by scent than by any other channel.

Before him sat an old woman who bent low over a novel-ette. Black-rimmed spectacles were set halfway down her nose, towards the tip, and Ferdinand could see her lips mov-ing as she read. The skin of her face was brown, and the face was not so much wrinkled as worn and bloated. Her hands, rather dirty, were like the branches of an old apple tree. There was an expression upon her brow that spoke of con-stant dejection. When her attention was caught by some movement of Ferdinand's, and she looked up over her spec-tacles, her heavy lips drew apart, and he saw a gap in her yellow teeth. The hair upon her head was gray and coarse; her shabby old dress peeped from above and below an equally shabby pinafore of dark blue. As she stared at Ferdinand her upper lip twitched a little, as if in distaste.

"Yes?" she demanded, in a loud, hoarse voice. "What?" Ferdinand's customary tone did not reach her hearing. "Oh, I can't hear," said the old woman impatiently. "'Arf a min-ute. Shop!" she bellowed.

And with that she rose painfully from the chair upon

which she had been sitting and staggered off, showing a creased skirt within the folds of her creased pinafore. Ferdinand, nonplussed, moved nervously about the shop, looking first at these flowers and then at those, inhaling their odours, marvelling at the brilliant golden stamens of the Arum lilies, the waxen beauty of the anemones, the adorable loveliness of the yellow daffodils. He turned again at the sound of a slight rustle and beheld Mrs. Balthazar as she came alone from the inner room.

She was very white. There were darknesses under her swollen eyes. Her lips were pale, and with her teeth she bit the lower lip as though she sought thereby to restrain herself from crying afresh. Without realizing what he was doing, Ferdinand gave a little exclamation of pity, stepped forward, and took her hand. It was a perfectly natural gesture, and Mrs. Balthazar was apparently unaware that Ferdinand had thus, for the first time, shown his interest in her. She suffered her hand to remain enclosed in his; he heard her breath quickly and shudderingly drawn. For an instant they stood thus, while Ferdinand noticed how wearily her head and shoulders drooped; and then Mrs. Balthazar withdrew her hand and did her best to stand upright and to smile.

"Why, you're quite a stranger," she said lingeringly. "I'd begun to think I was losing all my old customers."

"Yes," murmured Ferdinand. It was a very low-toned "yes," so pitched as to suggest inquiry. He went on: "I've been busy—or rather, I've been occupied, because unfortunately I'm never busy. And my walks have taken me in other directions."

"Aren't you a deserter!" reproved Mrs. Balthazar, with pathetic archness. "You know I said you wasn't to wait until you wanted some flowers. After that rainy day I don't feel you're just a customer, you know."

"But I really *want* some flowers to-day," Ferdinand protested. He smiled slowly and reassuringly, and as his teeth were very white and very perfect, and as his lips were so trim, his smile was always an encouragement. "I should like some advice from you as to the choice of them."

Mrs. Balthazar seemed to have difficulty in speaking. When she succeeded, the faint lightening had left her face, which had become inscrutable.

"Are they for your daughters?" she asked. "You know I'm always interested in them. You must excuse me asking. I know it's not at all——"

"Please!" Ferdinand stopped her with his very fastidious hand. "Yes; the flowers are for my daughters."

"Are they quite well?" Still she had that difficulty in speaking. Her voice was smothered.

"Quite well, thank you. What are those charming blue flowers with the yellow——"

"Those? They're cinerarias. They're very nice for vases. I've got them in pots, too." Into Mrs. Balthazar's tone had come a different quality. It was sharper, more eager, almost businesslike. "I don't know if you'd like them. See, they stand——" She pulled aside from one of her shelves something that resembled a miniature gateway, and revealed behind this screen an ordinary flower pot in which the cinerarias were growing. "Or I've got them cut. They're very nice, and quite fresh. Fresh this morning. Well, they *all* are. And I've got some nice fresh violets still. You like those, don't you?"

Ferdinand knew at once what he was going to buy. He knew what Catherine would prefer. Catherine—how strange that he should think first of Catherine! How *very* strange! Into that peculiar world of rumination in which Ferdinand lived, a new bewilderment was thrown. He was conscious that Mrs. Balthazar was looking at him expectantly, that her hand was stretched back towards the cinerarias.

"I'll take daffodils," he stammered. "And some violets." Daffodils, he thought, for Catherine; violets for Rhoda. Rhoda would bury her face in the violets and lose for a time her new expression of rather haggard strain; while Catherine, confronted with the golden daffodils, would reward him sufficiently with a single word, a single glance. "Yes, yes. Daffodils and violets. What could be better?"

"Don't you like the others, then?" asked Mrs. Balthazar. She was hurt! She was looking anxiously at him. She had wanted him to buy the other flowers. Not these beautiful flowers, grown in the open air, but those others, from the hothouse. Why was that? Ferdinand was puzzled, troubled.

"They're beautiful!" he cried enthusiastically. "Beautiful! But my daughters——"

"Oh, yes." She was alive again. "Of course, I understand. They've got their preferences, same as all of us; and you really can't go against them. I often think if somebody gives you an expensive—not that anybody—you know what I mean. But it's what you *fancy*, and not the——"

"My daughters both love these spring flowers."

"Lovely, they are," agreed Mrs. Balthazar, busying herself with tissue paper and beginning to lift the tender blooms from their baskets. "You like these Emperors, do you?"

Ferdinand's mind had been distracted from her appearance, but now, as he followed her movements with his eye, he saw that Mrs. Balthazar's hands were trembling. Once, indeed, her face puckered violently, and she was forced to lay the flowers and tissue paper aside in order that she might recover her composure. With a soft heart, Ferdinand averted his head. Was it sorrow or fear that troubled her? Was it some perplexity which he could in any way relieve? Could he? Should he? No, no. All his breeding dissuaded him from the admission that he had seen anything unusual. And yet his heart——

"Mrs. Balthazar," said Ferdinand impulsively. "Forgive me; but I can't help seeing that you are unwell—unhappy. Will you let me say how sorry I am? If it were anything—anything that I could help to put away from you——"

Her head was so turned that her eyes were hidden. A hand was raised, and the fingers of it were pressed hard against her lips. Her body was shaken by a single convulsive sob.

"Thanks." It was painfully forced from her. "I'm sorry. Thanks. No, I'm all right. I'm silly, that's all." She began to dry her eyes.

"I'm sure you're not silly," said Ferdinand slowly. "Unhappy, I think."

Again that terrible difficulty in controlling herself sufficiently to allow of speech.

"Yes." It was a voice full of tears. She nodded.

"Nothing I can do to help?" asked Ferdinand very gently. "Forgive me."

"No. . . . Nothing." For a moment or two Mrs. Balthazar, with her head kept low, struggled to regain her ease. Then she began once more to fumble with the tissue paper and the flowers; and after a time she seemed, although subdued, to carry herself with something of her usual air. The flowers were laid together, and were then wrapped so that their brilliant nodding heads were sheltered. When they were ready, the violets had to be gathered from their basket and similarly treated; and when both daffodils and violets were in Mrs. Balthazar's hands, passing from her to himself, Ferdinand saw that she would not meet his glance, but kept her eyes down, protected by those long and beautiful lashes.

"You're sure there's nothing?" he ventured, laying the flowers down upon the same chair upon which the old woman had been sitting when he entered the shop.

"Yes, sure."

"I should be so glad to be of assistance," Ferdinand said. "I feel—I feel that for a woman like yourself, so alone——"

"Yes, alone," she echoed, with a quick breath. "That's the worst of it." Then, after a pause: "You're very good," she said. "You're lovely. I'm ever so grateful. Thank you. You're really lovely."

Ferdinand had taken the hands which had been there for

him to take; and was lightly holding them in order to emphasize what he was saying.

"You must tell me——" he began. And then he looked up, and immediately released Mrs. Balthazar's hands, for the hideous old woman had returned to the shop and was standing in the doorway of the inner room regarding the two figures before her. She did not say anything, but looked over her black-rimmed glasses in a kind of disapproval. "Let me know," said Ferdinand. "If there is anything at all——"

He picked up his flowers, bowed, smiled, and left the shop. There was the uncomfortable sense that he had left overhurriedly, without learning the nature of Mrs. Balthazar's trouble; but he had been disconcerted by the appearance of the ugly old woman and had not been entirely a master of his own movements. And, at any rate, he remembered, Mrs. Balthazar had acknowledged his final salute with a glance of gratitude which, if it was not smiling, was full of meaning.

CHAPTER II

HE DISCOVERS A DAUGHTER

I

PAUSING as he strolled for tea that afternoon from his study into the picture-dominated drawing room, Ferdinand looked up the shallow stairs which led to the upper floors of his house. Catherine was descending, a lightly clad, self-possessed figure, her fair hair deepened in colour by the semi-darkness of the staircase. He waited until she was by his side, and thereafter followed her into the room, closing the door and taking his accustomed place near the fire.

The picture before his eyes was charming, and it was one for which Ferdinand had especial relish. The bright little fire in the grate; the fine old fireplace, surmounted by that oak-framed mirror in which he had watched Joe Gascoyne's theft of the violets; the pale light of the early April afternoon which made every pearly tone in the two big paintings more luminous than ever; and, before the fire, drawn close between two armchairs in soft green velvet, a little table with tea things spread very temptingly upon it. And Catherine to do the honours, sitting quite erect, indescribably graceful, as if she had stepped from one of the Vermeers, and as if she were a part of the general picture. Ferdinand smiled in contentment. He was well pleased. It occurred to him that tea with Rhoda would have been very different from this. She would have moved more, spoken with more animation, glanced up and sideways with a brightness which sprang from every eager impulse.

"We're alone for tea to-day, Father," Catherine announced. "I forget if you knew we were going to be."

"Alone, eh?" Ferdinand moved his chair a little nearer to the fire. "Where is Rhoda, then? She goes out more now than she used to."

"She's having tea with the Talbots. She'll be home in a little while."

There was a long silence, while Ferdinand meditatively stirred his spoon round and round in the cup, looking in the meanwhile at the bright little fire, and seeing in it all the castles and quaint faces which he had loved since childhood. His mind was elsewhere, for he was recollecting what had happened during the morning, when he had encountered Jabez Talbot and had visited Mrs. Balthazar. At last, disconcertingly, he plumped out the question which had been troubling him for so long, and for which this solitary tea with Catherine gave him the first opening.

"Catherine, as we're alone—— Let me ask you, do you think Rhoda is happy?"

Catherine smiled.

"I think she's always rather happy, Father," she said. "Even when she's unhappy. But whether she's thinking of Punch or not I can't tell you, because I don't know."

"And yet you see her. As I do, it's quite true." Ferdinand shook his head. "It was disagreeable. Extremely disagreeable. I don't like such things. However——"

Catherine appeared to be quite content to allow that to be the last word. She sighed and turned to something else.

"Jerry gave me the manuscript of his novel to read last night," she said. "I've been reading it this afternoon when I ought to have been sewing. It's a great rigmarole, but it's very amusing."

"Jerry," murmured Ferdinand, idly scratching at his under lip. "Does it give you the impression of any fundamental brain stuff?" he asked.

"*Jerry* doesn't, Father," demurely responded Catherine. "Does he give *you* that impression?"

"No." Ferdinand spoke wonderingly. "No, I must admit——"

"I think he's just the usual clever, silly boy. And his novel is a good deal the sort of thing you'd expect Jerry to write. There are lots of little obscure jokes in it. *I* like them, because I like Jerry; but I've got a suspicion that anybody who doesn't know Jerry would think them just silly."

"Quite," murmured Ferdinand. "Quite."

"He's got a horrid caricature of Jabez Talbot in it. Quite unjust, and beastly——"

"Oh, dear!" began Ferdinand, wrinkling his nose in distaste. "That man's name—— I wanted to ask you, Catherine—— What were you going to say?"

Catherine, slightly subdued, thought back to her own speech, which she had forgotten in continued remembrance of the lampoon.

"Oh, only that I think you're as unjust to Jabez as Jerry is, Father."

He seems so conceited; so mulishly to go on his own path."

"You know that Mona says he's shy."

"Oh, shy!" laughed Ferdinand. He was inexpressibly tickled by that word. "It's a strange word to use of *any* young man of the period."

"Father, they're *all* shy, with you, for various reasons. Don't you realize that? Jabez is different from the others. *They're* generally shy from conceitedness. They feel you don't think highly enough of them. You see, you haven't followed their private reputations. They feel you've never heard of them. And they can't explain to you how awfully good they are, because that would be bad form. Nothing is *more* galling."

"But *you*," said Ferdinand. "I see you getting on with them quite easily."

"Oh, but I'm always tremendously impressed."

It was Ferdinand, upon this occasion, who was impressed. He blinked at her gay readiness.

"Catherine, are you *artful?*" he cried presently, in some consternation. "It's an extraordinary—a horrible—thing to say, I admit; but I'm sometimes quite unable to make up my mind——"

Catherine laughed outright at this. It was a merry laugh, Ferdinand thought. It made her face wonderfully attractive.

"Doesn't it seem terrible that you—above everybody else—should suspect me!" she remonstrated. "I think it's really unforgivable of you, Father. Of *course* I'm not artful. The idea! I'm ashamed of you!"

"But you're not in the least ashamed of *yourself*," mused Ferdinand, not altogether without shrewdness. "I think on the whole I trust you." He smiled suddenly, quite whimsically. "I must confess that you and Rhoda have both given me some shocks lately. I sometimes feel, after all, a little out of my depth with you clever young things——"

"Father!" protested Catherine. "It's the most dreadful thing to call a person clever!"

"And yet you *are* clever."

"If you mean *by design,* no. But if you mean—otherwise, I don't know." She was momentarily thoughtful. "One can't tell. And if you mean that I'm cleverer than others, I'm not."

"I think you're cleverer than anybody I know," Ferdinand said mildly, almost in surprise, as though his declaration were entirely unpremeditated. The more he thought of his own verdict, indeed, the truer it seemed to be. He repeated, more surprised than ever: "Yes, I think you are."

Catherine did not falter. She did not seem even to be impressed.

"Then you have your own definition of cleverness, Father," she said, with serene disrespect. "For you wouldn't get anybody else to agree with you. No, I'm not clever. I can't talk or write. But I can listen. That's what made you think I may be artful. But you don't think I'm artful when I listen to *you*."

"Quite true. I think sometimes that you're very patient," declared Ferdinand rather pathetically. He looked steadily at her. In face of such speech Rhoda would impulsively have jumped up, run to his side, and cajoled him into the rediscovery of happiness. Catherine did no such thing. She smiled, not unkindly or in ridicule, but as though he had said something which did not require an answer. Her smile did not ease Ferdinand's mind, because when the words had been said he felt that possibly they might be true.

II

He continued to feel this, and his heart sank a little. The admiration—not only the love—of his two girls had been so much a matter of course in past years that he had come to rely upon it. If that admiration ceased, or if it was impaired, he would have no command over them. Love without respect, he well knew, becomes a thing of labour, and when love becomes disrespectful it grows destructive. No human being can stand against such ridicule. And yet, how could he recover his old ascendancy?

"There's something I wish you could tell me, Catherine," he said presently. They were quite alone, and the idle meal of tea, which is no meal, but an excuse for gossip, gave him an opportunity which might not recur. But having demanded her attention, Ferdinand lost himself in a dream and did not continue. Catherine waited. At last Ferdinand, groping his way through the clouds, became aware of her expectancy. "I beg your pardon," he exclaimed. "Yes, I wish you could tell me something." It was beautifully quiet and warm here, and Catherine was lovely as a picture. "You see, it has always been my hope that nothing would ever come between you and Rhoda and myself. Nothing tangible has come—with the exception of Punch, who is tangible enough. But even Punch is no longer tangible, because we don't see him. And yet the effect of him may be lasting. I can't discover exactly what influence he still has over Rhoda's mind. Have *you* any idea?"

"I don't think he ever had any influence, Father," declared Catherine. "I think he simply offered."

"You don't think Rhoda was serious?"

"Yes, I think she was serious; but not over Punch. If she'd been in love with Punch——"

Ferdinand's hand stole to his lips. Catherine had touched the very cause of his deepest distress. To passion he felt he could forgive much, because he supposed passion, in the last resort, to be invincible. But where there was no passion——

"If she'd been in love with Punch," he said, "it would all have been very different. Unfortunately, that's one of the things that takes me out of my depth. I feel that I'm not only very much more simple than you youngsters, but that I'm very much——" He broke off. Could he say it? With that fresh young face before him and the clear, unbewildered gaze that indicated a clear, unbewildered mind, he was confronted with something which he could not reconcile with his theory. "Very much less *tough*," he blurted out. "That's it. That's what troubles me. The young people I see—so egotistical, so complicated, not at all subtle, and so disagreeably *tough*."

"You mean insensitive, Father?" asked Catherine.

"Superficially sensitive," he agreed. "The neurotic always are. Of course, I think of them as sophisticated, and I mean, by that, raw underneath the polish; wary and self-conscious above, and undeveloped below. But also something more than raw—a toughness of moral fibre. Insensitive, if you like." He shrugged at the word. From criticism of others he fell to criticism of himself. "I wonder if I'm not what would be called 'an old woman,' " he added. "I'm afraid of that, too."

"I'll tell you where I think you're wrong," Catherine said, with the utmost candour. "And that is in thinking yourself typical. Typical, I mean, of your generation. I don't think you are. Just think of the appetite of some old women—both sexes—for horrors. Aren't people of your age as coarse as the younger ones?"

"Coarse?" Ferdinand speculated. "Would you say coarse?"

"I think it may be a question of convention and nothing more. A certain way of talking and thinking and behaving."

"But you and Rhoda, my dear!"

"We catch the tone, perhaps. I don't think we're coarse."

"No, no! The word's none of mine. It was your own. And yet Rhoda——" He could not express his intuitions.

"You were very much offended by the thought that she should be having an affair——"

"You see, you use the phrase 'an affair' as if the practice were normal. Not even 'a love affair,'" cried Ferdinand. "There's all the difference in the world. Can't you see that? Your mother and I didn't have 'affairs.' We fell in love with each other. There wasn't the selfishness, the crudeness—if you like, the coarseness——"

Catherine mused. Then she said:

"It's the thought that Rhoda was cold-blooded. That *is* it, isn't it? Well, she wasn't, Father."

"She spoke of it—" began Ferdinand—"she spoke of it in a way that made *my* blood run cold. As if she defended herself, and yet as if she despised me or was ready to despise me if I disapproved. That was one of the worst features——"

"Think of her vanity. You ought always to remember it. You *must!*"

"Is she vain, then?"

"Aren't we all?"

"Well, really, Catherine!" Ferdinand fidgeted, and his brows were drawn together into an expression of distaste. "There's something cynical——"

Catherine smiled, shaking her head at his agitation.

"Then that's *my* fault," she said composedly. "I think Rhoda is young, very secretive——"

the ruddy firelight, her face like that of a statue, clear-cut, unfaltering, mysteriously cold. He was secretly amazed at her composure. Such a woman would hide everything. She would be indomitable to the last. There was no question, for him, of her superiority to Rhoda. "I'm so tired that I'd just closed my eyes. Poor Father——"

"I'm here," Ferdinand ventured.

"Haven't you been talking?" asked Rhoda. She switched on the light; and was herself the most conspicuous object in the room. Ferdinand's eyes absorbed the effect of her white face and those half-angry, searching black eyes in contrast with the vivid orange of the scarf about her neck. "About me, I mean."

"Not for a few minutes," Catherine said, rising also, and as if consciously opposing her own slimness and her own will to her sister's. Catherine might be cold, but there was pride in every gesture. She had poise and quality. All this Ferdinand understood, with admiration. He realized also the rebuff to Rhoda. There was something gratifying to him in that rebuff; it repaid some of the contempt which Rhoda had shown for his judgment. A strange flame of cruelty leapt up in Ferdinand's heart as he watched the two of them. He saw Catherine frankly meet Rhoda's suspicion, saw Rhoda, darkly glancing at himself, nonplussed. A moment later she was gone; but her jealousy had been apparent. She was too quick ever to have a quiet mind and heart; too vehement not to imagine rivalry in every action of Catherine's; she would read and misread forever, poring upon incidents, silences, and expressions until they yielded their torturing satisfaction. All this Ferdinand guessed in that moment of clairvoyance. He had learned much within the last hour, and was to learn more in due time.

CHAPTER III

JABEZ PAYS A CALL

I

Joe Gascoyne and his sister lived in a small flat in Bedford Row. It is not a district favoured as a rule by responsible Civil Servants, who commonly patronize the Kensingtons and other lurking places of the intelligentsia; but Joe, who had been born not far from Bedford Row, loved it. To him, it was "home." But then Joe was in the habit of pretending that he did not belong to the intelligentsia, because the more fashionable and falsetto-voiced section of that class displeased him, and he did not choose to frequent the society of those who have been expensively taught. It pleased him to believe that he belonged to a different kind of being altogether, which was one of those fantasies in which men of quick wits normally indulge. The truth was that Joe had been a day boy at a London public school, had entered the Civil Service at the appropriate age as a Second Division Clerk, and had received the successive promotions due to his years and his efficiency. He was thirty, was perfectly competent as a public servant, and his interests were wide and flexible. He knew a good deal about the history of his own country, was familiar with the literature of three nations, knew the names of most of the principal first-class cricketers and most of the leading boxers, statesmen, and men of letters, occasionally visited the theatre, held a multitude of indefensible opinions (which he defended with much address) upon many subjects, and was both shrewd and kind-hearted. He was thus a typical member of the English middle class of his day, even in his ridicule of the class to which he belonged by birth and employment.

His sister Gwen (they were orphans) was likewise typical. She kept house for both in their small flat, with the aid of an experienced charwoman; and she also preserved her independence by earning her own living as stenographer in a neighbouring office. She wore her hair short, smoked cigarettes, ground her teeth when she read attacks upon "the modern girl," and was much more sophisticated in speech than in thought. She had read the works of Freud, Jung, Havelock Ellis, Shaw, Wells, and Bertrand Russell, and spoke with much certainty about all of them; but she innocently adored her brother, was romantic, and thought a good deal less of her own sagacity than, at this time, do many of her sisters. She was also, in her style, quite pretty, powdered her face, made her own dresses (with skill), and had as much grit and sense as her brother. She was twenty-three. The two lived happily together, had common friends, and rarely quarrelled. When they quarrelled they lost their tempers quickly and recovered them again as soon as the ridiculousness of their quarrel became apparent to both. Neither Joe nor Gwen suffered from "repressions," but in anger plumped out whatever was in their heads and took the world as they found it.

Upon the evening of the day already described, they had arrived home about the same time. They found the fire alight in their one living room, and cleverly banked up with damp ashes by the admirable Mrs. Chubb, while tea things were spread upon one end of their large dining table. The room was as unlike Ferdinand Meadows's drawing room as could be imagined, for it was very barely furnished. Books new and old—but mostly old—lay about on shelves and tables; a brass travelling clock ticked rapidly upon the mantelpiece, flanked by a small bust of Mozart and a few table utensils of pewter; there were small reproductions of pictures by ancient and modern masters upon all the walls. The carpet was faded, the heavy curtains, which could be drawn across the windows at night, over those of white net which hung there during the day, were old, and pale with many cleanings. But the really remarkable thing about this comparatively small room was the number of armchairs which filled it. There were six of them, all odd in size and shape, and in the mass they were indicative of the kind of social life enjoyed by the Gascoynes. At night young men and girls would extend themselves in these armchairs; the room would be full of smoke; Gwen would have coffee for all; and the talk would represent truly the mental chaos of our day.

No visitors were present as Joe and Gwen sat down to their tea. The two were alone, and it could thus be seen how strongly contrasted they were. Gwen's brisk manner and the activity of her movements were those of a terrier. She had the same intelligent cock of the head. Repose was unknown to her. A little round face, a half-open mouth, the noisiness of quick walking in sharp-heeled shoes, an unconquerable impetuosity, made her seem ever in movement. Joe, towering above his sister, with his long, qauint face, his quietness, his expressive black eyebrows and mischievous lips, was silent, full of reserve, full of a kind of fastidiousness. Yet he was in no sense repressive. Although Gwen felt the greatest respect for him, and although she would at all times be sensitive to his judgment, she had no fear. It was Joe's grief that nobody feared him. "I ought to inspire fear," he said, "not derision." If he had really desired to inspire fear the power would not have been wanting, and the fitful wish to which he thus gave expression was another of the fantasies which flitted in and out of Joe's mind from hour to hour, from moment to moment.

Gwen, as they took tea in silence, was reading a letter which filled about twenty hastily scrawled pages. A frown was upon her face, a frown which made her appear to scowl.

Her nose was wrinkled with impatience. She went so far, at length, in turning to the last page of all, as to sniff.

"Idiot!" ejaculated Gwen. "I don't know what the stupid thing wants me to do!"

"They're *all* so stupid," Joe murmured, "it seems to me, when they write to you."

"Priscilla is," frowned Gwen. "This is Priscilla Deenor. She wants to come and see us. At least, I suppose it's that, by the way she avoids saying so. I don't know what she *does* want!"

"Does *she?*"

"I wonder if she's in love with you!" Gwen stared at him, open-eyed. "By Jove! I believe that's it!"

"It sounds probable enough," sighed Joe. "Poor child!"

"Stranger things have happened."

"Your mind is positively packed with strange things, my dear Gwen."

"You don't believe me. But Priscilla's just at the age. It's not *you*, I mean; but *somebody*."

"Green-sickness, in a word. That was why I said 'Poor child!' I say it again." He did so, with melancholy emphasis. "Poor child!"

"You know what I mean, don't you? I dare say if you were to marry her she'd be entranced for the rest of her life. D'you like her?"

"Priscilla? Let me see, which is she? She's not Gertrude. Oh, *that* girl—the skinny one!" Joe shook his head. "I'm afraid it won't do, Gwen. I'm very sorry. You see, the woman I marry——"

"More tea?" Gwen interrupted his rapt look which betokened sentimental thought. "I don't want you to tell me about the woman you marry. Though I *do* want to say this, that if you want to get married, any time, you—I mean, it's *all right*. I mean, as far as *I'm*—I mean——" She faltered. It was evidently a difficult thing to express.

Joe's eyebrows, having been raised, drew together.

"Why should I get married?" he demanded.

"Because it would be good for you. You'd be happy. So would she. But whether——"

"Whether?" gently prompted Joe, his expression impenetrable.

"Well, there you *are!* I mean, I don't *know.*" Gwen was looking at him with a very guarded, dubious air. She was considering.

"What is it you don't know?" inquired Joe, still respectful, still indulgent, still unmoved by Gwen's mysteriousness, her doubts, her avowed ignorances. "D'you think you could tell me?"

"I could *tell* you, all right," said Gwen frankly. "Though whether you'd thank me—— You see, I'm not so sure that she loves you." Gwen's cheeks coloured slightly. Great discomfort entered her eyes.

"She?" asked Joe, smiling with mischief. It was the most baffling expression in the world.

"And I'd just *hate* her if she made you unhappy. I'm not sure that I don't hate her now; but that's probably only jealousy. Joe!" Gwen made her appeal for candour. Impatiently, she went on: "I see so much more than you think I do. You annoy me inexpressibly by poking your head into a bag and pretending I'm blind."

Joe shook his head—perhaps to show that at this moment it was not in a bag.

"You see more than is there. As you would say, you're 'just at the age.' You mustn't be so sentimental, Gwen. You think that love and marriage is the only thing in the world. How false that is! There are ideas! Ideals! Work!"

"All of which boil down to love and marriage, as you call it! There's the Life Force, Joe!"

"True." He appeared handsomely to admit her assertion.

"Besides"—Gwen hoisted her shoulders in a shrug that made her look like a very young girl. Her eyes were dark with knowledges—"I don't want you to tell me anything. I know you're not breaking your heart, or anything of that sort. But you can't hide from me the fact—well, that you *like* somebody."

"I try to love the whole world," answered Joe suavely. "It's difficult; but I make the effort. Nobody can accuse me of not making the effort. I'll try even to love Priscilla, as you seem to want me to do it."

"Pooh! Priscilla! Priscilla's name isn't Meadows!" In her momentary slight exasperation, Gwen had been led to declare herself. Still glowing, she faced him, her face expressive of the baffled triumph which struggled in her mind.

"Meadows. What an extraordinary notion!" declared Joe. He was absolutely unaffected. No telltale flush, no frightened glance, no jump of astonishment and alarm confirmed her guess. His long face, so droll and melancholy remained as calm as before. "I hope you're not making an idiot of yourself by hinting to others——"

"Joe, I wouldn't *dream!*"

"I'm thankful to hear it. Anything more preposterous——"

"I *know* I'm right." It was Gwen who was flushed. "And that's why I'm worried. Because I'm so afraid——"

"Afraid?" At last Joe had looked sharply at her. At last she thought she could detect the first rising of emotion in his mysterious face.

"Well, have you thought of Jabez Talbot?" demanded Gwen. "I'm so afraid that *he* may——"

"Your head," remarked Joe, with complete nonchalance, "must be crammed with as much rubbish as any head in this great city. I *used* to think you were a sensible child; but I see that you've been running to seed since we last had any conversation. I must look into this and get you back into condition."

"I don't care what you say!" cried Gwen defiantly. "You just watch out!"

Then, rather ruffled by the unsatisfactory sequel to her disclosures, she poured herself out another cup of tea, shrugged her shoulders, looked across the room to the window, listened, and fell into a brisk and disconcerting silence. She had spoken, and she was finished. No more was to be said. Only her rebelliously peeping eye revealed the discontent which seethed within Gwen's mind, and this discontent was in no way appeased when Joe, taking from his pocket a small volume, proceeded to make a note in it, as if his thoughts had already taken flight in quite another direction.

II

Matters were still as they had been when a subdued knocking came at the front door of the flat. Gwen jumped up from her place at the table; Joe looked inquiringly at her; both heads were shaken. Their visitor was evidently unexpected. So Gwen, with a housewife's quick glance about the room, answered the door, and found waiting there none other than Jabez himself. The sight of him made her start.

"Isn't that remarkable!" cried Gwen. "We'd just spoken of you!"

Jabez came slowly and hesitatingly into the room with the distempered walls and the heterogeneous mixture of prints and pictures. He had his soft hat in his hand, and his thick strong hair looked as if it had sprung up with the removal of the hat. The roughness of his clothes and the sturdiness of his carriage did not seem to be so much out of place here as they had done while he spoke with Ferdinand. The faint Midland accent was hardly noticeable. He did not offer to shake hands with Joe, and indeed his greeting was rather gruff and lacking in warmth; but he stepped over towards the fire with plenty of alacrity.

"I've come at a bad time," said Jabez. "You said I might."

"No time is bad," Joe assured him. "This is good."

"Tea, Mr. Talbot?" interrupted Gwen. "It may be rather stewed."

"No, thanks. I wanted to see your brother."

"Not me?" Gwen at least had the satisfaction of seeing him look confused, and of hearing him stammer, and she was by no means displeased with his honesty.

"Well, I wanted to ask him something. I'll ask you, too. Only I felt it wouldn't so much interest you, you see." Jabez took the chair they pushed forward, and Joe swivelled round from the table, crossing his legs, and leaning back, much as Sherlock Holmes used to do when clients called breathlessly at his rooms in Baker Street. Indeed, he was tempted to place the tips of his fingers of one hand against the tips of the fingers of the other hand, in the manner of his model, but restrained himself, lest the visitor, who obviously did not like to be laughed at, should be offended. Gwen merely gave an encouraging smile. But Jabez, having seated himself, and having turned from one expectant face to the other, had a difficulty in proceeding. He made one attempt and failed. At last he blurted out:

"It's like this, you see. I'm all wrong."

"Universal," Joe responded blandly. "Nothing whatever to worry about."

Jabez glowered.

"I don't mind that," he said bluntly. "I'm not worrying. It's myself I mind. However, that's not the point. I'm not asking you to sort out my mind for me. You couldn't do it. Nobody could. But what troubles me is this. You know Mr. Meadows. You know him well."

"We're on speaking terms," explained Joe.

"No more than that?"

"We're not intimate."

"Is that so? I thought——" Jabez, missing Joe's habitual raillery, which led him at all times to fastidious understatement, was puzzled. "But you know him. You know him better than I do. What d'you think of him?"

The tone was nearly savage. It was supported by an expression which was both exasperated and agitated. More, evidently, lay behind Jabez's question than curiosity as to

Joe's view, or indeed interest in Ferdinand. Such pallor and such sharpness appeared in Jabez's face as to suggest a thousand possibilities. Gwen bent forward in great enjoyment of this conversation. It fascinated her. She looked as if she thought she understood a great deal more than either of her companions. Such confidence is the special privilege of the young.

Joe, as if he saw nothing of all this, and as if the question addressed to him represented nothing but the most ordinary interest, answered with perfect calm:

"Mr. Meadows is a shy, timid man, a bit of a scholar, a bit of an artist, a great deal of a dilettante. He's honest, sentimental, quite intelligent. If he let himself go, which he never will do, because he's temperamentally cramped, he'd be almost interesting."

"Honest, eh?" was all that Jabez said in reply. He was thoughtful.

"Very honest and very humane. He's the son of a West Country clergyman, and through his mother's family he's always had money. How much, I don't know; but you see how they live. He wanted as a young man to be an artist; but, after a good deal of experiment and expense, he found he hadn't the talent to do what he wanted; so as an alternative he married the daughter of an artist—an old man called White, whose water colours you may have seen—pretty good in their way, but fudged over with a shaky hand. The rest you can see for yourself— *have* seen, in fact." He broke off, smiling; but Jabez gave no sign that he had noticed the significance of Joe's phrase or his smile. Instead, he growled out:

"I'm going there to dinner to-night. He asked me to."

"We're going there to dinner, too," put in Gwen eagerly, her eyes sparkling. She had her own reasons for wishing to be present at this momentous party.

"Oh, that's a comfort!" Jabez spoke with deep relief. He leant back in his chair, and his sigh was audible. "Yes, I say, that's a comfort! You see, there's something in Mr. Meadows that I can't *stick*."

There was a silence after that pronouncement. To the Gascoynes, a silence of amused irony.

"What strikes me," observed Joe, at last, "is that it's wonderful that any of us, as you might say, can stick *any* of us. Here we are, all egomaniacs, bumping into others all the time. We all like ourselves a little. Or if we don't *like* ourselves, at least we thank God we're not like other people."

"Well, I don't like myself much," Jabez said stubbornly, making two words of the pronoun. "And I'll tell you why. I'm at war with all the flummery that I see in the world, and I see a lot of flummery in myself. Only not as much as I see in Mr. Meadows."

"You *ought* to like yourself," rebuked Joe. "Flummery and all. It's characteristic. After all, it's fairly distinguished nowadays to have some genuine personality instead of the sham Gothic of the intelligentsia. Besides, if you don't like yourself, how can you expect others to do so? You have to give them a lead, you know. Self love is the most attractive thing in the world."

"H'm," grunted Jabez. "I expect you can't go against your own nature. Up in the North we think plenty of ourselves, but we've got no time to be indulgent. We leave that to the South. Well, as I was saying, there's something I can't stick about Mr. Meadows; and I want to know—if you can tell me—what his good points are. You say he's honest. Well, perhaps he is; honesty's a very funny thing, and it's got a lot of funny fashions. But can you dig into him and find anything but mush?"

"You can dig into everybody and find exactly what you want," said Joe. "Hence friendships and marriages——"

Jabez laughed at that.

"You're an optimist," he returned, with bitterness. "With most people, if you dig deep enough, you find a stuffy self-satisfaction. That's what I'm out against."

"What do you find in yourself?" asked Joe quickly.

"Ah!" Jabez threw back his head. "Confusion, mostly."

"At bottom?" persisted Joe.

"It's a fair question," Jabez admitted. "I suppose I find self-righteousness. It's the same with most preachers." He was immediately defensive under this attack, ready to say the worst, for fear it should be charged.

"I'll tell you what you *do* find," Joe told him. "You find Mr. Meadows."

"Good God, no!" declared Jabez, thumping the arm of his chair.

Joe's answer was a most sinister nodding of the head. He looked like a magician.

"Good for you, Joe!" cried Gwen, full of pride and elation. "You're *terrible!*"

III

The silence now was impressive. It indicated that Jabez, sickened, was slowly digesting the news conveyed to him by the philosopher of the party, and confirmed by the most nimbly observant of them all.

"If that's true," Jabez said, after a long pause, "which it isn't, I'm more wrong than I thought for. I don't see how it *can* be true. It can't!" He shook his head vigorously from side to side. "I'll tell you. My dad was a navvy. He worked over a pick. There were six of us kids, and I was the youngest. Most of the others are dead. Well, Mother made up her mind that I was to be a black-coat. She made me go to school, even when I didn't want to go, and she made a fuss of me, and my cleverness, and my prizes, and what the teacher said; and as soon as I was fourteen I turned out and went as what they call a junior clerk in a big business in Walsall, where we lived. But I'd caught the infection from her, you see. I thought I was as clever and as brainy as she always said I was. And I read and I listened. I got on. But they didn't like me—at this place where I was—going to Labour meetings, and they didn't like me—in the end—speaking at those meetings. Because that's what I did. So they pushed me out. I'd quite a difficulty in getting another berth. It was a rough time and I'm not likely to forget it." His face darkened at the memory.

"I began speaking more. I used to go here and there, speaking. I didn't know much; but I'd got hold of all the claptrap, and I used it. I was quite sincere. I told the boys unemployment was the result of capitalism, and that the capitalists fostered it so as to get plentiful cheap labour. I told them capitalists were bloated bloodsuckers, and working men were poor fools to put up with slavery. All the usual stuff. I suppose I got popular. In the end I got a paid job as a speaker. I've made progress since then; I've read a lot and I've learnt a lot; and I don't talk in that way nowadays. I'm less popular than I was. But I still feel I've got a lot to learn. I come to London now, and I meet a good many of the men who take charge of the movement. It's been a blow to me. There's so much politics and jealousy among them—as much as there is in every other party. And there's a lot of insincerity, too. I suppose you can't have leadership without sham, because there's such a lot you can't make the rank and file— all in a lump, I mean—understand. They don't know enough. They've got to be thrown raw lumps of propaganda and abuse or it's too subtle for them. That's one of the sickening things. They're not educated to understand their own strength. And you can't teach them by battle cries.

"However, what I was going to say was this: Since I've begun to learn something of the mechanism of the Labour movement I've grown angry. I'm turning away from the official movement. To my mind there aren't any ideas there. Only claptrap and funk. Labour leaders seem to me just as bankrupt as the other leaders—the Tories and the Liberals. They're tired. They want to keep their jobs. They can't promise anything. What is there to promise? We've got all the older Socialists demanded, and a bit more. We've got most of the things that were demanded all through the Nineteenth Century—shorter hours, higher wages, votes, payment of members, unemployment insurance, pensions, and so on; and in spite of it all we haven't got, and we can't promise, happiness. So we're offering to keep the poor by robbing the rich, which means making every man a pauper. And in all this dreary stuff, got up by the educated sentimentalists in the party, I've been thinking more and more of my own class. They may be stupid and uneducated and full of wrong ideas, but they're honest. Honest in a way that such men as Mr. Meadows could never understand. They're up against real life from the moment they're born. I think they're the salt of the earth.

"But since I came to London a few months ago I've met my uncle up at Highgate, and some of his friends and *their* friends; and I've met people like yourselves, and a hundred or two hundred others, all different, and all, in a way, just the same. The whole lot of you going on as if my people up North don't exist. It isn't that you ignore them or despise them; you just don't think of them. They don't exist for you; and you don't exist for them. My uncle's a kind, silly old man, who's made quite a lot of money honestly, treated his men well and his customers well, and has retired. I can respect him. You and most of the others down here get on with your own jobs and don't bother about anything else. I can understand that. I don't blame you. My lads care nothing for you any more than you care for them. You're better taught than they are, but you're made of the same stuff. You all work for your living, and there's that much in common. I'm a blackcoat myself. I know a lot of blackcoats, and I know that a good many of them are just as much afraid of losing their jobs and starving as the people I was brought up among. Just as much.

"Then I see this Mr. Meadows, who's never done any work and wouldn't know how to begin; and he seems to me to be soft all through. I see his daughters, and I can understand that they're the product of the leisured life they lead, kept and sheltered by the father——"

"A *good* product," interposed Gwen, with some sharpness.

Jabez raised his shoulders. His eyes glittered; the deep lines beside his mouth were accentuated.

"I'm not saying otherwise. I'm coming to that," said he. "I was going to say that there must be hundreds of men like Mr. Meadows, all over the world, all parasites, all soft, somehow thinking they're entitled to live in comfort, with pretty pictures all round them, feeling what they call tender compassion for the workers, and hitching their skirts away from them, as if the people I know to be the best of the bunch were all thieves and cut-throats, and dirty into the bargain. Well, it's my impulse to treat Mr. Meadows as a parasite. I'd like to tell him he's got no right to walk about in his best clothes all the time, never doing a hand's turn. He and his tribe seem to me to represent the fat they skim off the top of soup and throw away. But when I go to his house—I've been a lot, lately—and sit down in all that comfort, I'll admit I have a sense of taste and a sort of dignity, and I think to myself that the whole world ought to have a chance of enjoying the same taste and dignity; and then I know that nothing would ever bring that about. Utopias such as More and Morris described won't do in the modern world. They're just romances. They're just escapes. We're in a different kind of community, and we're bound to work *from that* to something better. It's no good thinking of a rustic world when the world gets steadily more urban. It's for an urban civilization we've got to cater. And yet when I think of what public picture galleries are like, and public libraries, and public baths—it sounds crazy, I dare say—but my heart sinks. I can't see my dad happy in that house, even if he had it. He wouldn't know—poor old man—where to spit. I don't know that I should feel comfortable living there myself; and yet it's—to me—a lovely place, the loveliest place I was ever in."

He ceased talking for a moment, and a look of hopelessness made his face haggard. Then, rousing himself, he concluded:

"So I go back to my dislike of Mr. Meadows, not because I think he's a representative capitalist or a parasite, or because he grinds the faces of the poor; but because I think he's a foolish, weak, tender creature, who's no good to anybody—doesn't understand. And now you say that he's—that I'm——"

Jabez broke off abruptly as his honest, heated argument was dwindling into incoherence. He recovered his breath, staring at the other two, who, although he had ceased, were still listening attentively.

"You'll think it funny that I should talk like a youth," he said, in disgust. "I think it's funny, myself. I think it's soft. But there's something about Mr. Meadows——" He shrugged his shoulders, grimacing.

"That you can't stick," added Joe. "And I expect there's something about you——"

"That's true enough," exclaimed Jabez, with energy. "He always looks at me daintily, like a spinster looking at a drunken clod. And yet, in the ordinary way, if I met him in the street, I shouldn't notice him. It's just going to his house, and meeting him——"

"You could always stop going to his house, if he annoys you," said Gwen suddenly.

So suddenly that Jabez started a little.

"Well, he can't *help* going," answered Joe, turning to Gwen. "There's a sort of fascination in it, as far as I can see."

"That was exactly what I meant," said Gwen in a dry tone. "Strangely enough."

Joe brushed aside her innuendo.

"It's perfectly easy to explain. If, as I say, Talbot and Mr. Meadows, at bottom, are the same, they're bound to attract and repel each other."

Gwen smiled satirically.

"Oh, you think *that*," she observed.

"They're both artists *manqués*. When Talbot goes to Woburn Square he says to himself, 'Here, but for the grace of God, dwell I.' Or 'This is the sort of home *I* ought to have. Why haven't I got it?' There isn't an answer; or, at least, Talbot isn't the one to give it."

"You sort me out very nicely among yourselves," Jabez observed, looking malignantly at them from his place in the chair. "I've told you I don't think I could bear to live there. It would stifle me. I'd be frightened of breaking the furniture. I'd be frightened of losing my temper and kicking it all to blazes. The orderliness of it, the luxury—— There may be something in what you say, but not a deal."

"It's half true," said Gwen decidedly, with a sneer at her brother and the suspicion of a tossed head. Her upper lip was slightly curled. "I think you *do* envy Mr. Meadows *some* of his possessions. And what Joe says about that is reasonable. It's not the whole truth. People with their heads in bags can't expect to discover the whole truth. Even if the bags were off, Joe's a reasonable being, and not at all intuitive; so he couldn't possibly understand what's immediately clear to a woman. I'm sorry for both of you."

"Both!" cried Jabez. "Why, what's——" He started upright in his chair. His swarthy face flushed a deep crimson. He looked at Joe with a sudden fury, struggling with himself until his knuckles were white. Grimly, as he relaxed, he muttered: "So there's two of us, eh?" And thereafter sat glowering at Joe, his lips gray and his brow deeply furrowed.

"There may be more," observed Gwen, shrugging. "There may be dozens. Who knows?" There was no immediate answer, and so she concluded: "Well, it's a rum world."

That last remark seemed to sting Joe to retort.

"But it's not an imbecile world, Gwen," he said, unconscious of the hatred in Jabez's glance. "It's fortunately not a world that can be understood at a glance by the juvenile mind."

"Imbecile, it may be," muttered Jabez, turned ever so little by this temperate reproof from preoccupation with the cause of his suppressed excitement. His face was still distorted, but he was calmer.

"Joe doesn't mean what you mean, Mr. Talbot," said Gwen, sparkling. "Joe doesn't care twopence about the world. He's bored by the world. He's got none of the reformer in his blood. All *he* wanted to do was to snub *me*. And he wouldn't want to snub me if he thought I was altogether wrong. He'd pity me. He'd be sorry for me and try to hush it up. He's sorry for *you*, Mr. Talbot."

"Sorry for me, is he?" Jabez, bewildered by the expression, was startled once more into close attention. His watchful eyes seemed to be asking: "Is there more than raillery in all this?" He caught something of the loving recalcitrance of Gwen's manner, and followed to its destination the glowing line of her defiant gaze. But he could have read nothing in that mask-like face of Joe Gascoyne's for he fell back upon what appeared to be either a platitude or a threat. "Well, better that than sorry for himself, I suppose, Miss Gascoyne. Or sorry for *you*, perhaps."

"Very much better," agreed Gwen quietly.

Jabez was not listening to her. His thoughts were evidently elsewhere. His mood had changed. He glanced sideways at Joe from time to time, in distrust. A gleam was in his eye. His face had lost its savage expressiveness and had become once again threateningly morose. For his part, Joe continued to sit, as he had done all along, with his head bent forward and his legs crossed. He gave no sign that he had comprehended any of the meaning of Gwen's rebellious speech.

Gwen, exasperated at the quietness of both her companions, jumped up with a vicious stamp of her heels upon the floor.

"I must go and change my dress," she said, "if we're to

be in good time for dinner. For I suppose we shall walk, as usual."

She was gone. When the door had closed, Joe uncrossed his legs.

"The trouble about women," he remarked in a light tone, "is that they spend their lives in guessing."

"H'm," answered Jabez, inattentive to his companion, because he was deep in thought.

"If they guess right," continued Joe, offering a box of cigarettes, "they're so amazed that they lose all self-control, and talk ecstatically about intuition. They're born gamblers with life, miracle hunters. If they guess wrong, they forget. They're all superstitious, believing in the dark stranger and the lucky dip. Stars, cards, and palms—always dark strangers and journeys, love and fate and nonsense. As if you could read your life in the bottom of your teacup. Poor things! They love the shadow world! Their lives are spent groping in the darkness of the human spirit."

Jabez returned no answer to this. He was sitting as one stunned. Perhaps he did not understand what Joe was talking about; certainly he could not guess at the feeling behind this quietly offered series of reflections upon the feminine mind and its common obsession.

CHAPTER IV

COMBAT

I

THE company gathered beneath that brightly painted ceiling
in the Meadows's dining room was a comparatively small
one. Ferdinand, at the head of the table, had Gwen upon his
right hand and Rhoda upon his left. Catherine, at the foot,
facing Ferdinand, was between Joe Gascoyne and Jabez.
No others were present. It was just such a party as Ferdinand liked; for it was small enough for general conversation,
and large enough for the interchange of intimacies. Candles
were alight upon the table; the large central electric light,
suspended from the ceiling, was extinguished. Everything
made, therefore, for friendliness and pleasure. The extremely simple dinner itself was certainly an assistance to
this end, because it had been chosen and cooked with a taste
which did credit both to Catherine as housekeeper and Catherine's cook as cook. The wine, as usual, was good; the soup,
the delicately golden sole, the tournedos, the marvellous
soufflé, were all as they should be; and Ferdinand, mellowed
and comforted by the sense of well-being which follows an
agreeable meal, was prepared to be genial even with the least
acceptable of his guests. He smiled upon the table, his head
thrown back.

He could see Catherine, who was talking to Jabez, while
Joe, for the moment silent, seemed to ponder. Gwen was
looking with bright eyes from Joe to Rhoda; and Rhoda
was dreaming. Her face was open to Ferdinand; she glanced
at him now and then with a loving half smile.

"It's not as though people were *sensible*," Gwen was protesting with energy. "They're not. Quite the opposite." Frowning, she relaxed and leant back in her chair. "I mean——"

"Nobody said they were sensible," Rhoda answered slowly. "It's not a question of sense. It's a question of——" She paused, shrugged her shoulders, and with a grimace, and in a lower tone, completed her sentence with the word "taste."

"We shan't get far with taste," said Gwen. "If we're going to talk about a community and its conditions of life——"

These two children! thought Ferdinand. What did they know of conditions; and what did they know of taste? They had been arguing, and he had been amusedly listening to their argument; and the sum of the argument was that Gwen was a practical little person while Rhoda thought beauty more real than justice or wages or the vote. Ferdinand had been pleased, and touched, to hear her speak so much in accordance with his wishes. He had looked around the table for applause, and had observed that Jabez was not listening to Rhoda, but was staring straight before him, as a man might do who refuses obstinately to hear what is abhorrent to him. Well, that did not annoy Ferdinand. He might resent the obvious disdain; but he had never supposed that Rhoda would convert Jabez to her views and he did not even wish that she might do so.

"It seems to me," he said, so that all those who were at the table could hear him, "that most of you young people are too impatient. You want something violent to happen —something exciting—as if you were all tired of the old things. You're——" He paused, searching for the condemnatory word. It came from Catherine.

"Bored, Father," she prompted, in a tone that was full of mischievous laughter.

Ferdinand shuddered.

"Is that it?" he asked. "As I look round at you all I feel that there isn't one of you that has the old-fashioned virtue of contentment." He allowed his glance to embrace those eager faces. "And I'm sure you're missing a great deal of the relish of life. You're dissatisfied; you want change—incessant change. To what end? Now, for myself, I am a lover of things as they are——"

"No!" cried Joe and Catherine simultaneously. Ferdinand saw them laughing at the chorus; and then Joe supplemented that cry with the words: "Things as they *were.*"

It was something of a shock to Ferdinand to be told that he was out-of-date.

"How is that?" he inquired.

"*We* are things as they are. The dissatisfaction, the boredom you speak of. We embody it. You represent 'the old-fashioned virtue of contentment.' You love the past."

There was some truth in what Joe said.

"But, my dear Gascoyne," objected Ferdinand, "the mistake you make is in thinking that the present is confined to *young* people. You think *you* are the present day. We're *all* the present day—all of us who are alive." Even as he said those words Ferdinand felt his heart sinking, either because the silence about him had an echo of disagreement or because he did not feel himself convinced by his own speech. This led him to add, in a murmur: "It may be, indeed, that you're the future."

They all turned to Joe, to see how he would answer.

"Most of us don't live in the present at all," said Joe. "We may physically exist in the present, but actually we live in our thoughts, which are elsewhere. Now, *you,* Mr. Meadows, live in the past. Your memories, the older things about you, all sorts of associations—these make up your present. Not ours. We haven't got those memories and associations. It's hard for you to realize, but most of us haven't even an historical background. Our conceptions are purely arbitrary. That's why young people are so dogmatic. The world's a very simple place for them. They think of themselves as the only complex things in a simple world. That's why they're such egomaniacs. As far as I can see, I'm probably the only one of us who lives in the present."

"Rubbish!" cried Gwen. It was nearly a snort. Her face was expressive of sisterly impatience. But Joe was used to sisterly impatience, and was even expert in provoking it.

"I'm neither afraid of the future nor expectant of it. I'm an evolutionist. To me, the general pressure of events and the general conflict of impulses presents a spectacle and creates the future, as it has created the present. Not design, but unconscious pattern. We all contribute to the pattern, although we seem to be working for our own ends. We're like the people one sees ploughing and pushing barrows and stooping about in the fields as the train rushes by. *You* don't realize it, but I *do*. I don't reverence the past, and I don't worship the future. Both are superstitions. I accept the world as I find it."

"We all do that!" Rhoda turned upon him with a show of impatience as great as that exhibited a moment earlier by Gwen. "It's nothing peculiar. We have to!"

"No!" Joe shook his head. "You don't, for one. You find yourself surrounded every day by social conveniences that have been developed by many generations. You don't realise your advantages. You take them for granted, because you've never experienced any contrast; but all the same you're dissatisfied with what you've got. You try to get something else. You're demanding, all the time, something that isn't there." He met her glance fairly, and it was Rhoda who looked away. "You don't *love* the Present; you're impatient of it. You don't *love* the Past; you ignore it. You love the Improbable. You're seeking it all the time—the Improbable, the Unlikely, the Indescribable. It's a constant pursuit, because the present doesn't interest you and you haven't found your métier. Talbot, here, has found his. He doesn't love the Past or the Present, and he doesn't pretend to. He has his teeth firmly set in What *Should* Be. It's spoiling his life. Gwen, who's superstitious and reads her tea leaves every morning, loves Magic, Fate, What *Must* Be."

"What cheek!" exclaimed Gwen. "Superstitious!"

Catherine was smiling to herself as she listened to this harangue.

"You say that about Rhoda," she objected quietly. "But what you mean is that everybody young has a love of romance."

"We all love romance," Joe answered, with equal quietness. "Old and young. We aspire to it. Some of us live it."

"The imaginative live it," Catherine said.

"They're not dissatisfied," Joe retorted.

"No. Why should they be?" It was a murmur only, and nobody paid the smallest attention.

"You haven't included Catherine in your denunciation of us all," Rhoda swiftly interrupted. She was a little—Ferdinand thought, excusably—flushed as the result of what she had herself suffered. She was gazing at Joe with her head high, as if she had been hurt. "Is she to escape?"

Ferdinand noticed that Catherine looked quickly down at the tablecloth when this question was put, as if to ensure that whatever the response might be it should not take her unawares. He saw that Joe was at first not inclined to answer, and that he then, with a laughing side glance at Catherine, jerked up his head and his long nose in the most whimsical of gestures.

"Well, now, Catherine," answered Joe, with an air of mock frankness, "is a most peculiar case. She doesn't live in the Past. She gives her mind to the Present. Whether she has any interest in the Future—" he hesitated, smiling—"whether she has any interest in the Future, I can't say. She may like the Indescribable as much as you do. She may be as expectant of the Must-Be as Gwen. She may have a passion for What *Should* Be." His quick eyes were roving from face to face, resting lightly, hurriedly, upon each, and hardly ever reaching Catherine. "But anybody more completely baffling to the philosopher doesn't exist." He ended lamely, as if he either could think of nothing more to say or was afraid to express his thought.

"I'm rather interested in the Present, I think," ventured Catherine in that silence. "But I expect you're looking for extremes, and I don't think I'm absorbed in it."

"I doubt if you're absorbed in anything," said Joe.

Ferdinand saw Catherine's lids quiver; he saw her smile very tranquilly—as it seemed—and then, as Rhoda turned from her observation of Catherine and offered a shoulder to Joe, he noticed that Rhoda's eyes were bright with tears of vexation. Ferdinand drew a deep breath. His own interest, he found, had been, not in the specific labels which Joe Gascoyne had applied, but in the emotions which, as he guessed, they had aroused in those who had been labelled. And he was puzzled, also, to find a reason and a meaning in much of what Joe had said. Was there a reason and a meaning in all of it? Had these youngsters a key which was denied to Ferdinand? Was Joe as learned in character as he seemed; or had he, too, been guessing?

II

"Spoiling my life, eh?" said Jabez unexpectedly.

Everybody else at the table started. Jabez had listened quietly enough to all that Joe had advanced in the course of his high-spirited speech, and none of them had supposed that he would take amiss the few words regarding himself. Ferdinand was the first to grow apprehensive.

"That was a manner of speaking," he suggested.

"Aye," thoughtfully murmured Jabez. "Yes, I realized that. With Gascoyne everything is a manner of speaking." He shot a smouldering look across the table at Joe. "But whether he does right to sneer at something he doesn't under-stand——"

"I wasn't sneering," explained Joe.

"You were putting what could be called practical idealism on a level with astrology," persisted Jabez. "You think that because a man wants to help his fellow men he's no better than—he's no different from—a man who collects postage stamps. You say he's only following his inclinations."

"I think he's following his inclinations. I don't say that his inclinations aren't more valuable to the community than the inclinations of a stamp collector."

"But there's no virtue in doing what you think is right?" asked Jabez.

"We're all trying to do what we think is right," answered Joe. "Do *you* feel specially virtuous?"

"No," said Jabez. "But I think some people don't worry much about what they're doing. If they did, we should all be reformers."

"That rules out the artists altogether, doesn't it?" said Joe.

"We-ell?" Jabez, it was clear, was quite prepared to rule out the artists. "It might rule out the evolutionists. I don't know that that would be a bad thing."

"It would give bigots a tremendous lift," said Joe.

Ferdinand looked from one to the other in alarm. How serious was this sparring? Was there a rivalry between them other than that which their respective intellectual standpoints created?

"Oughtn't we to have some sort of tolerance for each other's views?" he hastily demanded. "I think that in social life we must make recognition of others and the points of view of others our first concern. Wouldn't you admit that?" He turned pleadingly to the combatants.

"What tolerance have you for *my* views?" asked Jabez.

"Every tolerance, I hope," whispered Ferdinand.

"Until I express them. If I were to begin putting each one of you in his place, as Gascoyne does, I shouldn't find much tolerance."

"Try!" cried Joe suddenly, with an encouraging smile. "There are no enemies here, Talbot."

"Are there none?" Jabez stared straight across at Joe. "No, there are none. You can none of you hate."

"*I* can!" exclaimed Rhoda.

"So can I!" supported Gwen.

"Women are the hope of the world!" declared Joe. "*They're* serious enough."

"Their hatred is no good to me," retorted Jabez. "When they say, 'I hate you,' or 'I hate injustice,' or 'I hate life,' what do they mean? They mean——"

"Well, within *reason!*" cried Joe.

"They mean that they're cross," continued Jabez. "That's all. Everywhere I go it's the same. The people who say 'I get so wild,' or 'It makes me see red,' or 'Usurers,' or 'Blood-suckers,' they're only pretending to be indignant. They don't know what indignation—moral indignation—is. I've been sitting here listening to Gascoyne and realizing the selfishness of mankind. Gascoyne doesn't care what happens to the world, as long as *he's* all right. He's one in a thousand millions. He comforts himself by thinking it doesn't matter what he says or does. The world will go on, a pattern, a mote dance, whether he lives or dies. He's not an evolutionist. He's a pessimist. He belittles us all so as to excuse his own laziness. Well, we're not all as selfish as he is. We can some of us give ourselves a little discomfort by helping forward the improvement of the world and the people who live in it."

"What's your aim? Isn't it happiness for all?" asked Joe.

"Health, food, and clothing; leisure——"

"We're showing you the way. And you don't like our leisure. You see that it doesn't produce happiness. Only dissatisfaction."

"Aye, and clever gabble."

"Daddy, don't let them quarrel," whispered Rhoda suddenly. Ferdinand, distracted from his attention to the two young men, saw that her face was perfectly white.

"They're not quarrelling," answered Ferdinand in the same low tone.

"Yes. Underneath," she whispered. "They hate each other."

III

Well, that frightened Ferdinand. He did not believe it but it frightened him all the same. Swiftly, he tried to improvise an interruption which should not be too abrupt. But he was less quick than Catherine, who must have seen the whitening of Jabez's face. Jabez was a man who whitened in anger; Joe, upon the other hand, if he had been angry, would have flushed. He had not flushed. He was not angry. It was to Jabez that Catherine addressed herself.

"You mustn't be impatient with Joe," she warned. "Jabez, you *must* try and believe in the good faith of those who don't agree with you."

The cool words made their instant impression. Their pacific sincerity was unmistakable. Ferdinand breathed more freely as he watched the rigour fade from Jabez's expression. As he looked down he saw that Rhoda's hand, lying upon the edge of the table, relaxed and began to tremble. So Rhoda had been more frightened than himself! Upon an impulse, he covered that slim hand with his own fingers, pressed it, and allowed his hand to remain extended even when Rhoda withdrew hers to safe concealment under the table.

"Yes," Jabez acknowledged, biting his lip. "It's a fault." He was entirely recovered. Catherine's words had been magical in their effect—less by reason of the words than by the tone and the spirit of the speaker. "It's hard for me to feel he's not putting it all on." He sat back in his chair. "And another thing, I don't get his point of view. If he's sincere, it seems as if nothing matters."

"Doesn't art matter?" asked Rhoda breathlessly, defiantly.

"What *is* art?" Jabez did not look at Rhoda. His jaw was thrown forward. "Jargon, isn't it?"

"If you showed Talbot the finest work of the human spirit, he'd ask what use it was to a starving child," Joe said, "and there wouldn't be any answer, because to Talbot all the advantages of life are material."

"They're what hedonists like yourself take care to seize pretty firmly," retorted Jabez.

"Oh, a hedonist!" cried Joe. He burst out laughing; but in so good-tempered a manner that while Jabez looked sour he did not lose his recovered calm.

"Well, we can't *all* stand aside and laugh," Jabez muttered. "Somebody's got to do something. You talk about art—but you're not an artist. You don't *do* anything. You accept what you find; but you don't appreciate what you owe to reformers even in your own surroundings. You say nothing matters; but if you were starving you'd care little enough for art or pattern. You'd join in the tussle."

"I'm in it. I'm working for my bread. But in my leisure time I like to do what interests me. Instead of going to watch football matches and greyhound racing or the flickers, I read, I talk, I look at pictures, I listen to music. I try to educate myself. Where we come to absolute conflict is in this. I believe that men—the poorest men, as much as the richest, and probably more than the richest—make what they want to make of their lives. In the main they're dominated by their affections; but if they have the will and the inclination, I think they grow rich, or learned, or wise (quite a different thing), or they create beauty for the rest of mankind. To me, it's all a question of will—and genius. If a man wants wealth or power, it's within his grasp. But he must want it *enough*. Without will and without genius you yourself——"

"Oh, genius!" exclaimed Jabez. "You needn't bowl out——"

"Why not? I believe it. Without will and genius, you'd still be a clerk. You're not. Your ambition wouldn't have been anything without will. You'd have given in, as thousands of others do, to the pressure of life. You didn't give in. You persisted. You don't know when you're beaten."

"Don't I?" Jabez had paled again. "I wish I didn't!" His head drooped. He was sad and dispirited.

"Then you rise again. Others don't. As I was saying, the real difference between us is that you want to remove starvation from the world. You think that if poor people were less poor the standard of *spiritual* life would rise. Now you know very well that's not true. You know very well that communal kitchens and maternity benefits and pensions and the destruction of the wealthier classes won't affect the real life of man at all. The real life of man——"

"Yes, what's *that?*" asked Jabez doggedly.

"Is falling in love, and having children, and creating works of beauty," answered Joe.

"Falling in love, eh?" repeated Jabez.

"You're not *quite* an idiot, then, Joe," declared Gwen approvingly to her brother.

"All the rest's nothing at all, I suppose," sarcastically remarked Jabez.

"There's liberty," admitted Joe.

"Oh, there's liberty! What about slavery?"

"No man's *mind* need be enslaved."

"Good God!" Scornfully Jabez sat upright in his chair. "What cant!"

"It's not cant!" shouted Rhoda suddenly. She was now trembling violently. "It's *not* cant!" She faced Jabez, her eyes glowing, her bosom heaving. "Why be so smug? You know perfectly well that Joe's not a hypocrite. I'm disgusted with you!"

Jabez did not look at her. Indeed, to Ferdinand, it appeared as if an expression of disgust crossed his face. Instead of replying, he sighed deeply.

"Poor Jabez! You've got no supporters at all, have you!" said Catherine. "But you mustn't think you have no friend.

We all illustrate what Joe says about mankind. We're dominated by our affections. We don't quite agree with you; but
we all—like you very much." She hesitated before making
the declaration, but as she made it she smiled very kindly.

Ferdinand heard Gwen utter, very softly, an exclamation
of some kind. It might have been the smallest of groans. But
he was too much concerned with fear for Rhoda's composure to take very much heed of what was going on at the
other end of the table. His one desire was to break up this
uncomfortably outspoken dinner party, and carry them all
upstairs, to a room over which Peace and Harmony, as represented by the creation of his own taste, presided.

"Shall we go?" he gently interposed. "Catherine?"

IV

Once they were upstairs, in that delightful room in which
Ferdinand took unfailing pleasure, the talk became easier and
more general. Jabez seemed to exert himself to dismiss all
memory of the heat of the earlier discussion. He approached
Ferdinand, indeed, and stood very sturdily near the fire, setting down his coffee cup as soon as he had swallowed its contents. For a moment neither he nor Ferdinand could think
of any common ground; but at last Jabez said in a rather
smothered voice:

"You have a very beautiful home, Mr. Meadows. I never
come here without feeling that. And a very happy home, too,
if you'll excuse me for saying something uncalled-for."

"I hope it *is* a happy home. I think it is," responded Ferdinand, in a tone of politeness.

"Since I came to London I've found two happy homes;
but none so beautiful."

"Only two!" was all that Ferdinand, archly, found to say.

"Only two," confirmed Jabez seriously.

"Your own home: is that a happy one?" asked Ferdinand. The reply was a shaken head.

"I haven't got a home now," Jabez returned, after a pause. "I've never known a home—in the sense in which you use the word. A crowded dog box, full of noise and uproar. No room, no quietness; only a sort of ugly burrow for sleeping in. That's where I'm going now."

"You're leaving us?" cried Ferdinand, in surprise.

"I go backwards and forwards. I travel about the country. One day I hope to have four walls that I can call my own." The deep lines in his cheeks were deeper; his mouth was tightly closed as soon as he had finished speaking. Ferdinan's glace travelled to the brow, which had its distinction, and to the oddly set head with its crisp hair. It was impossible for him to deny that this was a man who affected him strongly. Affected him, it might be, with aversion, but none the less affected him. His muscles were braced in Jabez's presence; he was on guard, as he might have been at the approach of a menacing dog, a mastiff, or a bull terrier, as to whose purpose he was in doubt.

"You must come again when you're back in London," Ferdinand said. "You won't, I hope, take too seriously what Gascoyne has been saying this evening. He's something of a debater, I think."

"I like him," was Jabez's short comment. "He's genuine."

What! Was this the hatred proclaimed by Rhoda? Ferdinand felt himself start in surprise. Was she merely melodramatic, after all?

"He's a very amusing fellow," said Ferdinand.

"He's more than that," Jabez growled. "He's a man I'd trust." For a moment it appeared that this was all he was going to say; but after a silence, he added: "A man could lose to him without defeat." It was a singular utterance, which Ferdinand did not pretend to understand.

"Lose?" he vaguely murmured. "But why 'lose'?"

Jabez turned sharply. His face had changed.

"Aye," he answered, with more animation. "Why lose?" Then his hands went deep into his trousers pockets and his head settled down between his shoulders. He did not speak again; but at Ferdinand's side stood staring at Joe, who was talking to Catherine.

He seemed to be absorbed in the sight of these two, and Ferdinand, following his gaze, noticed for the first time that Rhoda had not come into the room with the others. She now appeared, and Ferdinand for an instant was startled, because he thought at his first glance that she looked as if she had been crying. That thought was dismissed when she joined Joe and Catherine, for she was smiling with more cheerfulness than Ferdinand had observed her to show since the dismissal of Punch Teed. He half turned to Jabez to see whether Jabez continued to show interest in the group before him; but Jabez had apparently forgotten the others, for he had turned away and was regarding the little copy of Verrochio's study which reminded Ferdinand of his dead wife.

V

That evening Rhoda sang a little, playing her own accompaniments. She sang Cui's enchanting song about the fountain at Tsarskoye Selo and some old folk songs; and Ferdinand was quite lost in his delight at her charming voice and the taste with which she sang. He did not observe the others, but sat alone, by the fire, drinking in these delicate sounds and recalling the voice of his wife, to which in the past he had listened with tender rapture. And when Rhoda closed the pianoforte Ferdinand was dreaming, so that he did not hear what was said or see what was done. Nor did he press Catherine to sing, being quite content with what he had heard, and desiring nothing better than the still lingering echo of lovely notes in the passages of his memory.

It was therefore with some surprise that he looked up from his reverie to find the party all on foot, ready for departure. Gwen, in fact, standing beside him with outstretched hand, was the cause of his awakening.

"So soon?" stammered Ferdinand, rising to his feet.

"So late!" responded Gwen. "It's midnight, Mr. Meadows; and Joe and I are workers, you know. I believe you've been to sleep!"

"I've been dreaming," Ferdinand said faintly, with a smile.

"So have we all," was her reply, as she pressed his hand. "Good-night!"

Joe was behind her, with twinkling eyes and a look of incredible gravity. Last of all came Jabez, who gripped Ferdinand's hand with a strength that caused Ferdinand to wince.

"*A bientôt*," Ferdinand said, cordially enough.

"Thanks." But the brief word was accompanied by a look that was long and grateful.

Within two minutes Ferdinand was alone with his daughters.

"So we're safe!" he rather plaintively proclaimed, arching his brows and shaking his head. "I feared for a time——"

They did not pretend to misunderstand him.

"Joe was very foolish," Catherine said. "He can't restrain himself. He talks too much. Much too much. And so insensitively. He must have known that Jabez was insulted."

"Well, as for that"—Ferdinand expressively raised his shoulders—"I always deprecate *any* argument at dinner. Political argument—— But, after all, it wasn't so much argument as a sort of slanging match. I feel the real cause of the trouble was that Gascoyne was talking for entertainment—the entertainment of the table, while Talbot—I suppose as a result of his associations—doesn't understand the art——"

Catherine cut him short.

"Joe knows Jabez as well as anybody can do who only

half knows him; and he ought not to have introduced anything so provocative. There wasn't any need for it. Just
senseless baiting. Besides, poor Jabez was at a disadvantage.
He knew that he couldn't say what he thought; and he's not a
conversationalist, as Joe is. Joe could talk anybody into
hysterics; and he ought to have known better."

"I don't agree," ventured Ferdinand. "I thought Jab—I
thought Talbot was bad-tempered and gauche. He *is* gauche.
A man of more skill would have demolished Gascoyne on
Gascoyne's own ground. But Talbot's a very serious fellow.
I should say he's a prig."

"Father! How ill-natured of you!" Catherine stared.

"Don't you agree?" Ferdinand was amazed at her indignation.

"Certainly not. He's serious; but why idealism should be
priggish, I don't know."

"You astonish me!" was all Ferdinand could say. "Really,
my dear Catherine——"

She was not smiling. She looked even a little angry.

"I think you ought to have more charity," she said. "You
were the host, and to you Jabez's comfort should be as important a matter as Joe's. But you're prejudiced against
Jabez . . . because he's—I suppose, because you're antipathetic to each other."

"Antipathetic!" cried Rhoda, who all this time had said
nothing. She was at the door, about to go, listening to the last
words of the evening. "I should just think you *were!*" And
with that the door closed behind her, and Ferdinand had
only a memory of her white face above the poppy-coloured
dress, and of the burning eyes which shone from above those
marble cheeks.

"I've said the wrong thing," stammered Ferdinand. "Always—always! How unfortunate!"

"Poor Father!" Catherine lingered. "But you're quite
right. It *was* unfortunate. Father. . . . D'you know—" she
hesitated just long enough to give additional meaning, by her

delay, to the words that followed—"I think you'll have to try and like Jabez just a little more than you do at present."

She, too, was gone, a fair, gray, swirling shadow; and Ferdinand was left alone, to recall her parting words and to try to understand their meaning.

CHAPTER V

CROSS–PURPOSES

I

FOR the next week Ferdinand was confined to the house with a severe chill; and his solitude gave him many opportunities for the play of his anxious thoughts. In vain he tried to absorb himself in books. Books can solace a man in sorrow; but when he is in fear they do little else than exasperate him. The pages of Sir Thomas Browne, of William Penn, of Henry Vaughan, became vague blurs against which his doubts stood out very black and clear. So Catherine was in love! He was unprepared for the discovery. He had thought —what had he thought? Nothing! He had refused to think. Not for him had been those matrimonial plannings to which the mothers of daughters were supposed to give so much attention. For him, the girls were children still. Their heads were clear, as were the heads of children. Their hearts——

What sick fancies these were! For the hundredth time, sitting by the fireside in his book-lined study, convalescent but enfeebled, Ferdinand struggled against them. He would read. The book was held resolutely before his eyes. He forced himself, sitting in front of that warm fire, shielded from every draught, to follow the printed words.

But seeds themselves do lie in perpetual shades, either under the leaf, or shut up in coverings; and such as lie barest, have their husks, skins and pulps about them, wherein the nib and generative particle lieth moist and secured from the injury of air

187

and sun. . . . Legions of seminal ideas lie in their second chaos
and Orcus of Hippocrates; till putting on the habits of their
forms, they show themselves upon the stage of the world, and
open dominion of Jove. . . .

If Catherine left them——— Strange that he had never considered such a possibility! Inconceivable that she could leave
them for this fellow. And yet was not the history of human-
kind filled with tales of such fruitless and incomprehensible
sacrifice? She could have no notion of what life with him
would mean. Sordid, hideous surroundings, such as she, who
knew nothing ignoble, could not endure; exacting, jealous
neighbours, watchful of every action, every word, lest it contained or could be twisted into some reminder of their in-
feriority; constant association with a splenetic, glowering
nature, soured and malevolent. Jabez was neither of her class
nor her quality. His thoughts were base, not in their ends,
but in their preoccupations. He was bounded by his experience, and in his experience beauty had no place. No place!
Catherine! Good God! A flush of heat swept Ferdinand. He
was forced to throw down the book which he had been holding in his hand. Good God! That such a fate should attend
her!

It was at the moment when Ferdinand had resumed his
frenzied pacing of the room that he saw Catherine's face
in the doorway. She had turned the handle silently, so that
she should not disturb him; but upon finding that he was alert
she came right into the room, closing the door behind her.
Ferdinand could hardly bear to raise his eyes; and when
he did so instantly averted them again, as if he had been
dazzled. How lovely she looked! Her dress was of blue, a
light colour that glowed when the sunshine caught it; and her
fairness was beautiful. Her lips were now parted; upon her
face was an expression of eager sympathy in which laughter
in some extraordinary manner had its place. Ferdinand's
heart rose in greeting. Troubled though he was, he could

not resist her, but smiled in return, pathetically, appealingly, as if to say, "Don't leave me! Don't forsake me! I am growing old; I need you! I need you; I am growing desolate!"

"I thought you might be resting," said Catherine, "so I crept in. You're not resting——"

Resting! Good God!

"No," said Ferdinand; and his voice, by a miracle, was steady. "No; I'm not resting. I feel rather restless, in fact." There was a calmness in his manner, and a dignity; he could not yet throw dignity away in order to abase himself before her. And the calmness gave Catherine no hint of his tortured state. Perhaps she thought him, as he was, still weakened by the chill, his eyes still painful. A chill would account for many strangenesses of mood, of tone. How unfortunate, while pride had still its power!

"It's being indoors so long, I expect," she added cheerfully. "I asked Dr. Bright if you could go out. But he said there was rather a biting wind to-day. He thought perhaps to-morrow."

"Ah!" Ferdinand could not trust himself any farther than that. "To-morrow!" She seemed unconscious of his effort. Her own face, so fresh and so animated, gave no sign of awareness or of doubt or preoccupation. She was calm— calmer than he, even at the height of his pretence. Yet within, he thought, she must be excited, full of expectation, of doubt. No, she would be calm, would be smiling, unreadable, if she knew that she had but a year to live. The courage! The equanimity! The maddening coldness—— He set his teeth. Courage!

"Wouldn't it be lovely to hire a car and go for a drive in the country?" continued Catherine. "You could see how all the hedges and trees are budding——"

"Lovely indeed," Ferdinand said, straining for cordiality.

"Or a walk in the Park."

"You tantalize me!" he protested.

"Till to-morrow," was Catherine's answer. She approached

him. "Your fire needs making up; and your book has dropped; and your cushions are——"

To-morrow. That meant another white night, during which he would toss, at times languidly, with the fever not yet wholly dispersed, at times with excitement and dread, working himself into a condition of frenzy. It was impossible that he should endure another such night. At all costs he must know the truth.

"Catherine!"

She did not hear. She was upon her knees before the fire; and one of the fire irons, disturbed by her movements, crashed gently within the fender. When she glanced up again, smiling, ready to rise from her task, Ferdinand's desperate courage had gone. He could no longer hope to provoke a clearer understanding between them. Whiter than before, and with his knees trembling, he stood looking down at those slender shoulders, and at the quick hands, the slim neck, the soft hair. Every movement she made was full of life and purpose; in Catherine were none of those lassitudes which gave Rhoda, alternatively with her vehemence and her caressing charm, a languid grace which was as enticing of confidence as it was indicative of voluptuousness. Confidences with Catherine were impossible; she had too quick a sense of the ridiculous, or too much sagacity, for such prolonged and luxurious excursions into sentiment. Well, was she for this temperamental merriment or insensitiveness the less subject to disillusion? Ferdinand shivered at her danger. It was beyond his control. She was no longer a child, to be persuaded. What was the truth?

II

"Would you like to have your tea in here?" she asked. "Or will you go into the drawing room? I promised to go out to tea to-day, and so I hope you won't mind being alone. Does it matter very much?"

It mattered very much. The thought of being alone, at this especial moment of crisis, was painful to Ferdinand. Indescribable loneliness harassed his feelings. He could hardly bring himself to reply.

"Is Rhoda not in, then?" he asked, with sinking heart. He was to be alone with his bitter fears.

"Rhoda went out after lunch for a walk, and she has telephoned to say that she won't be here for tea."

"How seldom she's in, now," complained Ferdinand.

But Catherine, however indulgently, would not allow him to be unjust. She shook her head in reproach.

"This is the first afternoon she's been out since your cold began. It was really I who urged her to go, because I thought she was looking rather ill."

"Ill?" He was startled.

"As if she needed a change."

"Then where *is* she?" He was conscious of being querulous, and was ashamed. An excuse rose to his mind. "I'm growing into an old man," he thought, and was sorry for himself. Underneath his self-pity was another thought, self-contemptuous: "I'm sorry for myself. Whenever I ought to act decisively I pretend that I'm ill and unfit to tackle the problem. I'm not old; but weak, feeble, contemptible." He had not heard Catherine's reply. Aloud, he repeated: *"Where,* did you say?"

"Apparently she met Mona Talbot, who asked her to go home. Mr. Talbot isn't very well, either; and you know how fond he is of Rhoda. Mona thought it would cheer him up to see her."

So she could go to cheer Mr. Talbot! Talbot—that name caused Ferdinand to tremble anew.

"I'm not well," he said in a low voice. "I don't feel——"

"You'd like me to stay at home? Then I'll just——"

"No!" She had risen as she spoke; and Ferdinand's protest had been explosive, for the purpose of restraining her movement.

"I can easily telephone that I'm not coming. If you're not well——"

"I'm quite well. I don't know what's happening to me!" cried Ferdinand, in exasperation. "I'm beginning to whimper and grizzle. It's contemptible. Contemptible! I'm only sorry to give myself away like this, Catherine. I'm ashamed. I really don't——" He was speaking with fastidious distaste for his own mood. His hands flew together, and the fingers were tightly interlaced. "I beg that you won't stay in. I should like it, of course; but I should suffer a great deal of self-blame. Please——"

"It's quite easy for me to stay, Father. I'd rather."

"And I'd rather you'd go. Don't you see that if you let me keep you I should feel miserable? I've always dreaded the time when I might be one of those elderly people who spoil the happiness——"

"Aren't you silly!" was all she said.

"I may be; but that doesn't alter my feeling. One may know that one is silly and still be silly. One may fight against it, and still be silly. And I don't wish you to encourage me in silliness."

"By staying? It isn't a sacrifice, you know."

"It *ought* to be, at your age!" groaned Ferdinand.

"That's the silliest thing of all, Father. The idea that one's own father is a bore is awfully old-fashioned. It's the sort of thing Bernard Shaw was saying twenty years ago. In the new age we're going to rediscover our parents. It will be very salutary to us to realize that they're still rational human beings."

"Have you ever doubted it?" asked Ferdinand.

"I used—when I was at school—to take you for granted."

"Don't you now?" he begged anxiously.

She shook her head with enchanting firmness. There was no coquetry but the utmost candour.

"You know I don't," she said. "Why pretend?"

"But I never seem to get any nearer to you!" cried Ferdinand, in desperation. "With Rhoda I can feel—at least, I always have *felt*—that some common ground is possible. With you, never!"

It was Catherine's turn to flush.

"You hurt me when you say that, Father!" she protested. "It's *awfully* stupid!"

"Aren't you conscious of it yourself?" Ferdinand demanded. "Surely you must see that I never know what you are thinking and feeling? At most, you give me a hint, a glimpse, tantalizing——" He turned away from her in excitement, unclasping his hands and throwing them out before him. "I told you I wasn't well," he continued. "I'm talking foolishly. I'm still not myself. I need a change, distraction. Forgive me."

"But I haven't anything to tell you," began Catherine, in a wondering tone. "You can't want me to make something up, Father. Surely it isn't a kind of false gabble of sentiment you want? That would be ridiculous!"

"Nothing, eh?" he muttered. "I'm not so sure. But go, go, my dear. Keep your engagement. Give me that foretaste, at least, of the new age. Treat me as you'd treat——" He checked himself.

"As I'd treat——?" prompted Catherine

"Rhoda." But that had not been the name which had trembled upon his lips. He did not dare to say the fatal name. Why not? When dread was his bugbear, why did he not have done with it? He could not tell.

"Oh, Rhoda," Catherine responded, in an odd, low voice, and with something of her old mischievous smile. "I'll do my best. And you'll have your tea in here? Alone?"

"Alone." It was as a knell to his ears; but he smiled in return, dismissing her; and spent the moments until tea was brought in gazing at the fire, by no means recovered from his fit of unwonted melancholy.

III

After that solitary meal he felt his mood vaguely lightened; but for the time only. There was a shadow upon the room, for although the day had been bright, with a tearing wind, his window faced the east, and the sun's rays had already sunk below the level of that space which he commanded. A springtime chill was upon the outer air, and even within doors something of crepuscular gloom made the air less cordial. Night was approaching with stealth. Soon all would be gray; a breeze would stir the awakening branches, and its sound would carry the mournful contrast between ardour and passivity to many hearts besides Ferdinand's. He brooded, his head low, one hand extended towards the sinking fire, the other pressed lightly upon his knee. Strange, he reflected, how sentimental, how weak and trivial one became after illness. In such a state as his even death had less than its customary threat. Death at least would mean peace, and this peace, which all men desired, was to him at the instant so plainly the solution of every trouble as to have incomparable charm.

Suddenly he started upright in his chair, aghast at such folly.

"How shameful!" he exclaimed aloud. "One would suppose that I was confessedly at the end of all usefulness in life. As if I was old and dying. What a thought! I should have sunk low indeed if such a thing were true." What was that movement? Did he hear a sound? Was this a fresh current of air upon his cheek? The air was cool; the shadows were creeping closer. Had Catherine returned?

Not Catherine, but Rhoda. It was Rhoda who stood there in the twilight. She was watching him; she came closer, her skirt making as she moved the slightest rustling noise.

"My dear?" Ferdinand glanced over his shoulder and saw her standing behind him.

"How dark it is in here," she murmured almost fretfully. Then, with more rapidity: "Doesn't it make you sad?"

"Not the darkness, my darling," he responded gently. "Come closer. I can't see you. Catherine said you were out. She's gone out herself. I don't know where. She didn't say. Did you find Mr. Talbot better?"

"Mr. Talbot? Ah, yes, he's better. Did Catherine tell you? I met Mona. I went home with her. Just for a little while. Are you better? It's cold in here. Very cold and dark. I don't think you should sit in the cold."

"I didn't seem to need the light," Ferdinand said. "I've been sitting here thinking. Reading, too; but I'm tired of reading. Catherine says I may go out to-morrow."

"Catherine? Oh, yes; I suppose she asked Dr. Bright."

Rhoda was beside him, kneeling upon the hearthrug and ruefully staring at the sunken fire. Her attitude was so similar to Catherine's, and she was so unlike. The same slim shoulders, as touchingly young, but in movement, where Catherine had been still. Rhoda was never entirely still, as Catherine was. There was subtle movement, subtle change, all the time. In the past Ferdinand had found this quick restlessness, betokening the eagerness of her mind, a charm the more; now, because he was unstrung, he was irked by it. She had lost her charm for him. She was the cause of some at least of his troubled imaginings. It had been Rhoda who first stirred the pleasant waters of Ferdinand's life into turbulence. That her unconsciousness of change, or her effort to ignore the change, added to his sense of lost serenity was a further cause for his aversion. He blamed himself, but he could not control that tiny thread of horror which lay behind all his loving thoughts of her. Rhoda's voice, as she responded to him, was still low, as if she had been thinking with melancholy of other things, and as if the shadows were hushing her into silence.

"We'll all go," Ferdinand said. He imagined that he could see her acquiescent nod. "Are you cold?"

"A little." No more. He could faintly picture the outline of her face, thinner than it had been, and in some manner altered, although he could not be sure of the actual character of the alteration. Was it thought of Punch Teed that made her sad? A longing? A heavy cloud upon his spirits made Ferdinand sigh deeply; but he strove to check the sigh, lest, hearing it, Rhoda should penetrate his mood and his secret.

The room grew darker. Shadows crept more daringly from every corner and from behind every extrusion. The great square of the window faded from opal to gray, from gray to deeper gray. Still it glimmered, while the fire became more glowing by contrast with the surrounding darkness. Ferdinand sat with his hands together and his head low; and Rhoda, from kneeling upright, sank down until she half reclined before the fire.

"Isn't it strange," she said, in a hushed voice, "strange and terrible that nothing will ever stay quite still? The friends you make, and the things you do, are always changing and re-forming into new shapes until they're unrecognizable. This fire is like that: the colour comes and goes in it, as if it is breathing."

"Everything changes," Ferdinand agreed absently. Impatiently, he wondered why it should be necessary to proclaim as a discovery this unhappy knowledge, which yet was so definitely a comment upon his own uneasy reflections.

"We can't even prevent ourselves from changing," Rhoda said. "I've tried to keep as I was. I've tried hard. It's impossible." She was speaking, it seemed, less to Ferdinand than to herself. "Daddy, do *you* change as much as that? Are *you* as volatile? Or is it only when we're young that we change all the time?"

"All the time," echoed Ferdinand, absorbed in his thoughts. "All our lives."

"Is there no end? I think I've been wrong. I've tried to remain a child. You can't help growing up. I wonder if it's wrong to try and stay young. One isn't young any more. Isn't it better to reach out at life and be adventurous?"

"Experimental? No, no!" protested Ferdinand, his distress at that association of words and ideas rising fast.

"It's a colder world. Baser. You think that, don't you?"

"I think that to be deliberately adventurous is to be experimental."

"I suppose so. And yet how's one to judge? There's so much that one doesn't know—until one tries. That's horrible to you, isn't it? You don't like the idea of adventuring—experimenting. You've always waited. Things have come to you. They come to some people, but not to others. I wish I could look on. Things would come to me, then. But I can't. Some things come to me, but not the things I want. Not the things I want." Her voice had sunk, in this repeated phrase, to a whisper.

"What things are they, my darling?" Ferdinand asked. He hardly heard the answer to his questions.

"Precious things." It was a breath.

"Perhaps they're only hidden," he ventured. "Not denied."

She shook her head. Very sadly indeed, she refused to accept the comfort he offered.

"No. I shall never have them. I want them too much. I used to think—I think life can be very cruel unless one is cruel one's self, or very cold. If one is cruel one's self one can cause pain to others."

"One can do that without being cruel," Ferdinand said.

She uttered a sound that might have been a smothered, bitter laugh.

"Don't I know that!" she murmured.

"But you, my dear——" Ferdinand roused himself from the bitterness of his own mood—"at your age everything is possible. Everything. You take things too much to heart. A month, a year——"

"Oh, Father!" There was anger in her protest. "What's

the good of truisms? They're so false. You're thinking that everything seems tragic to a child. You think I'm just disappointed. A day or two, you think, and I shall be happy again. Well, I *am* disappointed, but it's with myself. I'm discouraged, Father."

"With everything before you!" He was incredulous.

There was a silence, during which it was evident that she was endeavouring to recover her self-control. She slowly rose from her position upon the hearthrug and stood thoughtfully, with her head bent. At length, in a tone which she did her best to make level, but in which the quiver was none the less audible, she answered:

"I can't tell you what's in my mind, Daddy. I wish I could."

"You could tell me anything," Ferdinand begged.

"I used to think so. But I can't. You wouldn't understand. Isn't that strange!"

"Not altogether strange," Ferdinand said. "For I haven't the key."

"The key to everything——" Rhoda began. "No, I won't say that. It wouldn't be kind. And you're not well, Father. I've been boring you. Silly of me. I didn't mean to do that. Only, you see, there's nobody——"

She stood looking down at the fire. Ferdinand heard the faintest of sighs. When he looked again, he could not see her; and only the almost soundless click of the door latch told him that she was going.

"Rhoda!" he called.

Too late. There was no answer. She had passed from the room, and he was once more alone.

CHAPTER VI

CATHERINE GOES TO A PARTY

I

HAVING left her father to drink his tea, Catherine ran out of the house and met the full strength of a sweeping and boisterous wind. It took her breath away, brought colour to her cheeks and a sparkle to her eyes; and then, as she walked southward, it seemed to be bent upon the task of hastening her progress. Sunshine glimmered from a cloudy sky, and the lower film of black scud was to be observed flying helter-skelter before that fervent blast. There was a curious pearly light everywhere about her, clear, pure, and sweet. Every building looked taller and more graceful in this light. It was a day to lift hearts and tingle the blood of the young; and Catherine's step was as buoyant as the day itself. It was as though she had escaped.

And yet, having begun her journey with such suggestive briskness, Catherine was no sooner out of sight of the house and out of the direct course of the breeze than she began to loiter a little. The colour in her cheeks was heightened by all sorts of exciting reflections. For a time she held her head low, in thought, and when she again raised it she glanced about her with quick delight in all the incidents of life which were in movement within range. Many of the squalid shops attracted her as she came abreast of them, and so did the aspidistras and brass bowls in some of the Bloomsbury windows. A dirty little dog pushing his nose into some greasy newspaper near the curb was one episode; another was a frowsty tabby cat which blinked repressively from a doorstep in answer to her gay greeting. The shops, the houses, the people, the posters upon the hoardings, were all scrutinized with the same swift yet sympathetic consideration by those quiet, calm, gray eyes. Just so would they have been seen by a child upon her way to or from school, who dawdles and runs and again dawdles, with the object of delaying the end of the journey. Was Catherine as cold, as assured, as unreadable as Ferdinand believed? He had never seen her thus.

At length an impulsive glance at her wrist watch caused Catherine to exclaim. She was already late for her engagement, and, reluctantly, she must delay no longer. Farewell to the joys of loitering, of objectless gazing! No gems were ever as precious to the seeing eye! Others, from the tramp to the holiday maker, might revel carelessly in such joys; not Catherine! One who lives under the punctual tyranny of hours and minutes may not long enjoy the truant's inestimable rewards! With a very sober face, Catherine walked with greater purpose. Some of the animation was gone, to be replaced in turn by perplexity, sorrow, returning gaiety, pain, and doubt, as each of these emotions became uppermost in her thoughts. Sometimes gravity aged her, and sometimes perplexity, giving way to laughter, made Catherine look younger even than her years. Many of the passers looked back at her, as if they had been startled into interest by that expressive mobility.

She had told her father that she was going out to tea. What she had not told him was that the tea was a tea party given by Joe and Gwen Gascoyne in their flat in Bedford Row. And it was to Bedford Row that Catherine now directed her steps. To reach that straight and impressive double row of flat-faced houses she walked through Lamb's Conduit Street into Theobald's Road; and once more her pace slackened. Almost, it appeared, with an effort did she enter at length the fine doorway and march past the offices of solicitors and others to an upper floor. Then, quickly, she pressed a small bell-push, and heard the thrilling whir within. She was breathing rather quickly from her climb when the door swung back.

It was Joe Gascoyne who appeared in the open space—Joe, with a melancholy and yet whimsical look upon his droll face, a sharp-winged collar, sponge-bag bow tie, and a cutaway coat which made him leaner than ever. He was immensely tall, towering above her, his eyelids blinking, his straight hair carefully parted and brushed.

"Hullo!" cried Joe. "At last! But where's Rhoda?" He looked sharply past Catherine to the darkness of the staircase. His heavy eyebrows moved, as they always did when his mind was not at rest.

"Did you expect her, then?" stammered Catherine, hesitating in the doorway—almost shrinking back. "I thought she——"

"Certainly we expected her!" Was he disappointed? Annoyed? It was impossible to be sure. Joe could pretend anything, from shock to equanimity. "What's happened?"

Still he held the door, as if—— Catherine, by no means at ease, explained.

"She said she had telephoned to Gwen. Can't I come in, please?"

Joe stepped back. Behind him rose a thin haze of gray smoke from a dozen cigarettes and pipes; and from this haze came the noise of quite a number of tongues in persistent action. Catherine heard the tinkle of spoons against china, and a cackle of choking laughter. Then Joe's tall figure surged up again as he closed the outer door. It blotted out the smoke, while his voice, close to her ear, threw all the other sounds far back into a dimness of debate. Joe's hand was at her elbow, so that they stood together for the merest instant in the narrow little passageway from which all the rooms in this flat opened. Catherine heard her own heels strike the linoleum with a kind of pattering sharpness.

"Yes, you can come in," Joe said. "Though why——
However, there's a fearful row; and there's some fearful
nonsense being blethered. Outrageous! Put your things in
Gwen's room, please. I'll wait here. The atmosphere's perfectly abominable. It's just as well Rhoda didn't come, perhaps."

Just as well? Joe was not ordinarily ungracious. Catherine, stepping within Gwen's bedroom, was a shade paler than
she had been a moment before. But she was still smiling.

As she slipped off her coat, the smile left Catherine's
face; but that might have been because Gwen's room was
plain, ugly, and square-toed. It was, indeed, cell-like in its
lack of ornament.

"What a good sleeper Gwen must be!" thought Catherine
half aloud. "Otherwise she'd dream of penal servitude."

Here were no armchairs (but that was because all chairs
had been concentrated for the party), and no charming pictures or frills or curtains. Everything was plain, with an
ugly plainness. But for the presence upon the dressing table
of an enormous powder puff and the absence of all sporting
implements the room might have been that of a boy. The
walls were bare except for three or four brightly coloured
reproductions of celebrated English paintings; the bed was
of iron, enamelled black. Upon the floor were three infamous
rugs in many hues. And yet it was in this room that Gwen
spent fully one third of her daily life. There was no sign
here of her boasted love of physical comfort. Perhaps that
flourished only by day!

Catherine stayed in Gwen's room as short a time as possible, and then returned to Joe with an impetuousness which,
it was evident, took him by surprise. Joe, in fact, was discovered by Catherine standing with his hands deep in his
trousers pockets, his feet together, his shoulders thrown forward, and his face distorted into an aspect of the greatest
malevolence. So might a black-browed devil gaze upon a saint
in torture.

"Joe!" cried Catherine, in surprised protest. "What a diabolical look!"

"You think so?" The expression vanished. "There is a reason, as Grape Nuts says. Come along!"

"The reason!" she demanded.

"You'll know soon enough." He passed her into the first veils of tobacco smoke and followed morosely behind. They were in the midst of the hurly burly. The room was occupied by a dozen or more young people, all sitting or standing in attitudes which might have been supposed to represent intellectual acuteness, all smoking, all blinking the smoke from their eyes, and all talking with assurance in a rather superior manner. Their voices were loud; their pronunciation was exaggerated; they looked as if their mouths were always open, even in sleep. "Observe the intellectual white mice," whispered Joe, "performing their fanciful tricks."

Laughing, Catherine directed her attention to the scene before her. She saw a tall, fair young man standing upon one leg, one arm raised and bent over his head so that his left hand could pluck at his right ear. Another, shorter and darker, was kneeling upon a chair before him. Both were talking simultaneously. She saw two young women sitting down with crossed legs, scattering cigarette ash around them, replacing the cigarettes in their mouths, and grimacing to keep the smoke from their eyes. Both were talking simultaneously. Everybody seemed to be talking simultaneously. The noise was deafening. "I *know!*" everybody was saying emphatically. "It's *so* bad." Only they did not say "know" and so," but "kneau" and "seau." Catherine could not hear them praising anything. Indeed, she felt that the expressions of aloofness, and even of conceit, which she saw all about her could never have been associated with praise; for dissatisfaction had already given the lips and nostrils and eyelids of all these youngsters a permanent curl of superciliousness.

"Well?" asked Joe.

Catherine shook her head. She caught sight of Jerry

Anderson in a corner—the Jerry she knew—and she smiled with relief. At least there was one person known to her in this crowd of unfamiliar faces. And she had no sooner recognized Jerry than she saw Gwen, who had left her great teapots in order to greet the newcomer. Gwen came plunging up like a young colt, her dress green and shapeless, a cigarette dangling from the corner of her mouth. She looked like a naughty caricature of the dry-lipped virgins who cultivate ideas to the sacrifice of charm.

"Who d'you know?" she bawled into Catherine's ear.

"You!" cried Catherine.

"I'm busy for a bit. Sorry! Who else?" It was impossible for normally low-voiced human beings to converse in such noise. All they could do was to shout the brief questions and answers into each other's ears. "I've got a job for Joe; so don't let him cling to you!"

"Then Jerry!" Catherine uttered the name in a tone of considerable urgency. She had just seen a most unhealthy-looking young man, of great length and sallowness, eyeing her with every sign of choice; and she could estimate danger well enough to read in this regard a menace to her immediate comfort. The young man, she could tell, unless he were defeated by some such strategy, would bear down upon her the moment she was alone and would begin to ask questions, oddly condescending and impertinent, and to Catherine in the highest degree boring, in a high-pitched voice of bewildering self-consciousness. Whereas Jerry, whom she knew, and whose novel she had lately and very critically read in manuscript, could be made either to listen or to entertain, as she wished.

"Jerry it is!" shouted Gwen. raising those amusing sisters to Joe's expressive brows.

Jerry rose cheerfully from his place in the corner. He looked fairer and more delicately handsome than ever. He had still that flattering, caressing, ingratiating air of modesty, and that lid-fluttering charm which was one of his chief

social assets; and there was a pressing gentleness in his
greeting such as Catherine had experienced with pleasure
many times before. She joined him and was swallowed up,
she felt, in the corner, with the one person present who
could be managed without inconvenience. Jerry was also, as
usual, primed with a conversational opening, and this, as he
clasped Catherine's hand in welcome, he proceeded to disclose.

"I'm going to write a play called *Dinner,*" he began without preamble. "It's in three acts. The first act is the drawing
room, with everybody arriving; and it ends with the butler
saying, 'Dinner's served.' They all file out. Act two shows
them all, a minute later, filing *into* the dining room and taking places at table. All through the second act nobody moves
at all. They're sitting round the table. They all discuss the
latest detective stories and recite their own verse. Then, you
see, one of the young women gets drunk and begins to confess her sins. Very rhythmically, you know. I think perhaps
blank verse. Be rather jolly! They're all subjugated by her
charm, and she'll do it very much *à la* Tchekhov, with a good
splash of Dostoevsky. There's a gradual crescendo. At first
the other guests are worried; then they're infected. Who
wouldn't be? Then the act ends with the butler flinging open
the doors back into the drawing room. Act three shows them,
a minute later, filing into the drawing room. The wife—one
of the women is the hostess, you see—the wife says to the
husband, 'You are the hero of that girl's adventures, Pedro.'
And she takes up a revolver that the audience has been staring at all the evening and shoots him. What?"

"I shan't come," Joe said. "I couldn't bear it, Jerry."

"I couldn't bear you to be there, dear Joe," answered
Jerry gracefully, his lids quivering. "Unless, of course, you
played the butler! That's an idea, you know. By Jove, I
think you'd do it excellently!"

"I've always wanted to go on the stage, Jerry," said Joe.
"But in serious parts."

"You'd be lost! You should be in comedy, at least."

But Joe had gone. He had heard the door bell, and it was his laborious duty to admit each comer to the party. Catherine watched his disappearance and sat beside Jerry, looking out at the smoke and the sprawling figures with a cheerful countenance. She heard Jerry's voice, and for a moment she did not take any notice of what he was saying, so interested was she in the girl who came into the room as she gazed. This girl was younger than Catherine herself, and painfully thin. She was rather dark, very pale, rather pretty; and as she stood beside Joe, waiting for Gwen to greet her, she looked up at him in a manner which attracted Catherine's attention. There was a mixture of timidity and confidence, an overrunning into smiles, and a darkling plunge into sobriety which gave to this little fragile creature a very pathetic interest for any onlooker. Could not the truth regarding her attitude to Joe be plainly read? She was so young that she had no suspicion of the clearness with which her feelings could be seen by others. Quickly Catherine, with her expression unchanged, glanced at Joe. It gave her a curious sensation to observe that he was in a low tone saying something jocular to this stranger, much as he had done, a few moments earlier, to herself. With the slightest of smiles Catherine turned again to Jerry. And from Jerry she received, perhaps, the most unexpected shock which had ever been administered in the course of her short life.

"*What* was that?" Catherine demanded, in a peculiar voice. Her lips were parted in amazement. "I didn't——"

Jerry's hands, which, as she looked downwards, giving him all her attention, she could clearly see, were trembling. His manner was entirely changed. No longer did he tell her the improvised story of a play. No longer was his tone strained to the degree appropriate to one who seeks to amuse. It was dry and broken, a little hoarse. The story he was telling was that of an unhappy young man.

II

"I want you to listen to me," Jerry was agitatedly saying, in a very low voice, speaking so close to her ear that even in that din the murmur was intelligible. "Catherine, can you hear?" She inclined her head, not speaking, and the voice continued: "I feel I can't go on any longer. I've simply got to find a way out or I shall go mad. I don't know if I can make you understand. I never can tell how much you know—about anything. You don't talk. You listen. Then listen! A little while ago—months, I suppose—I met this girl (nobody you know). She was clever, pretty—I don't deny all her virtues. Perhaps she's good, too, in her way. I was interested. She had done a lot of interesting things, little plays, little pastorals, things of that sort; she'd acted a little. I used to meet her. It seemed all right. I mean, nothing in it except the usual—— Then she seemed to change." He shrugged his shoulders. "I didn't know what the matter was. I thought—I don't know what I thought. It doesn't matter. One night I discovered. She'd been drinking—something like the girl I was speaking about in the play. Out came a lot of stuff about the kind of life she'd led—I can't tell you. That doesn't matter, either, except that it bored me to hear. Nothing very unusual, nothing very good or bad or interesting. Just enough to make me feel sorry for her, and a bit impatient. I said something—perhaps more than I ought." He stopped, moistened his lips, and reflected for a moment. "What I said I'm not sure; but, well, she started crying, and —you can guess the rest. I needn't tell you what's been going on. Anyway, since then—Catherine, I want you to marry me. It's the only way I can escape. She's bent on making herself secure. She's hounding me to death. You'd think I was the first—— My God! Catherine, I've thought it all over; and it's the only way I can find."

"But, Jerry! To do what?" begged Catherine.

"Don't you see, I can't *stand* her," Jerry cried hoarsely. "I can't stand her, now. She bores me to death. I can't tell her so."

Catherine whitened. She stared straight before her as one visualizing a scene.

"You could tell her—oh, Jerry, it's ridiculous. No girl could possibly——"

"You don't know! You don't know!" he whispered. "She's round my neck. She pretends I've ruined her. It's absurd, of course; but that's what she says. She can't work; she's got no money; and she——" He groaned.

"Surely you can say that you don't want to see her any more?"

"I can't." If Jerry had not been so much alarmed, his situation and his alarm would both have been ridiculous. Perhaps he saw that, for he suddenly implored: "Don't laugh at me, Catherine. Marry me!"

Catherine's head—she did not know it—was shaken very vigorously.

"But, Jerry! it's not fair to her. Naturally, I don't know what the exact circumstances are; but it seems to me that you *do* owe her something."

"What, my own ruin?" He was passionate.

"Some little loyalty. Certainly, frankness."

"I've tried frankness—cautious frankness. You don't know your own sex, Catherine."

"Or the other, it seems," responded Catherine gravely. "No, I know little enough."

"Oh, you blame me?" demanded Jerry. "You don't know her type."

"One doesn't generally think of individuals as belonging to a type until one is tired of them."

"Yes, I agree. I'm tired of her."

"And you expect her to acquiesce. Jerry, *she's* not tired."

"No, she's probably drunk," he brutally said. "Catherine, think it over. Catherine!"

What more Jerry would have said was not indicated. He was given no opportunity of saying it; for at this moment their conversation was interrupted. Joe stood before them with the little girl who had last entered the room. Catherine met the girl's rather large brown eyes, which were wide open with some emotion akin to astonishment.

"Jerry!" said Joe, in a stern voice. "Allow me to introduce you to Miss Priscilla Loop."

Catherine's last glimpse of Jerry showed him rising, biting his lips, and then, as he encountered those liquid, sympathetic eyes, fluttering his own lids, putting his head charmingly back, smiling with a good deal of his old easy flattery. Jerry did not look in Catherine's direction as she departed from his side.

III

"The fact is," Joe said, "that I've had enough of this. I think I'll see you home now."

"No, no!" cried Catherine. "You can't do that. You're the host."

"Well, I'm not, really. It's Gwen's party, and I was the doorkeeper. Everybody's here now, and I'm finished work. Are you ready to go? I can't stand these barren highbrows. They talk too much rubbish for me."

"But you don't listen to them," objected Catherine. "As far as I can see you do all the talking yourself."

"It may be so," he agreed. "In self-defence. They've got such horrible voices. Have you noticed? There isn't a decent voice in the whole of Bloomsbury. They all either squeak or bray. I don't know why the development of the brain should atrophy the vocal chords."

Catherine laughed.

"So you're dissatisfied even with Bloomsbury!" she answered mischievously. "Joe, dear, you're the perfect highbrow."

Joe looked uneasy.

"I don't like you to laugh at me," he grumbled. "It seems blasphemous. Now, suppose we just slip out and walk along to Woburn Square. You wouldn't be blamed. And to tell you the truth, I want to escape. You provide the alternative, d'you see?"

With a very strange glance, in which discomfort mingled with laughter, Catherine averted her eyes.

"I sometimes feel a hunger for flattery, Joe," she observed, "and you gratify it."

"It's not flattery," Joe said. "It's simple enthusiasm. You see, I particularly want to go now. I have a reason. I don't want to stay."

"That only means that you're shy."

"I'm not shy. I'm as little shy as you are."

"Ought I to be?" demanded Catherine. "Why?"

"You're too self-confident. People lean on you. I do, myself. But seriously, Catherine, do help me to escape. Gwen —Gwen has her eye on me. If I'm with you she'll feel safe."

"Safe!" Catherine stared a little.

"It would take too long to explain. If you could just get up and go over to Gwen—don't look at her, because she's looking at you just now—and say you have to go, and you'll be quite all right, and see yourself out, and won't she bring Joe to supper one night——"

"Poor Gwen!"

"She's romantic."

"She's very loyal. I don't think it would be kind to her. Besides, Joe, it wouldn't be good for you. On the other hand, I think I should like to go, because Father's still very poorly, and I felt rather a wretch for leaving him. But you must stay and play your part. Besides, it's ridiculous, Joe. There's nothing here that you could possibly want to escape from. You're not a dunce!"

"No, I'm not a dunce," agreed Joe. He seemed cast down. "I sometimes wish I were. But I see you haven't any real pity for me. It wouldn't matter to you if my days were numbered!"

"I should be sorry for it," admitted Catherine.

"Would you really?" His quick eye scanned her closely. Then: "Although I seem to be looking at you, I am in reality observing that Gwen has risen. She is coming to separate us. She is bringing over a most terrible young man to introduce to you, and she's going to launch me on to those two dames by the window. Farewell, old friend; in death remember that you might have saved us both."

Catherine glanced up. What Joe had said was unfortunately true. Gwen was bearing down upon them with the tall and distressing youth who had first stared possessively at Catherine upon her arrival. She jumped to her feet with something like consternation.

"Dear, dear!" said she. "I really must go!"

IV

She had left Bedford Row and was halfway down Great James Street, between those tall and mouldering houses which so irresistibly remind the beholder of Dickens and his London, when she heard quick steps behind her and found Joe Gascoyne once more at her side. It was a most singular meeting, for Joe had lost his air of nonchalance, and was as one who had fled from danger. Catherine, for her part, quite unmistakably flinched.

"Oh, Joe!" she protested. "You *shouldn't!*"

"I had to!" he panted. "My dear Catherine, you have no idea——"

"It's such cowardice!" she said. For a moment she was almost ready to send him back. Then the preposterousness of the situation was too much for her. "Come along quickly, then," she proceeded. "You know perfectly well what I think of you!"

"The worst, I know," Joe returned. He had recovered something of his composure and stalked by her side, very erect, with long strides. "I'm not going to apologize for myself. Well, I wanted to talk to you. There are things I want to say and to ask. For one thing, you're excited. Why?" Her denial did not affect him. "You *are* excited," he repeated. "What I believe some people call 'upset.' Any reason? You won't tell me. Very well; then tell me this. What's the matter with Rhoda? Why didn't she come to-day?"

"I don't know," said Catherine frankly. "Please believe me, Joe. I really don't know."

"And if you did you wouldn't tell me. Is that it?"

"It depends. She said she would rather stay at home."

"And did she stay at home?"

"No. I made her go out for a walk."

"Ah. You don't know where she is, then?"

"Really, Joe!" Catherine was smiling, but she gave him nothing at all. Joe continued walking by her side; his head was bent, and there was a considering stillness in his manner.

"Well, it doesn't matter," he said quite lightly. "You're a very difficult customer, Catherine. I've always said it. You allow me to be your friend, but you don't allow me to help you. Naturally, I resent that. Do you know it?"

"Is it that you want some help, yourself?" she asked, after a moment's pause. "Tell me, Joe."

"I can't. Confidences should never be one-sided. However, I'm mystified."

Catherine waited. Even he, who was less versed than she in the preliminaries to confession, would have realized that Joe was about to impart a confidence.

"Yes," was all Catherine said.

"Everybody mystifies me. What do you think of Talbot?"

"Talbot!" It was an echo. Joe looked away from her. "I don't know what you want me to say," Catherine proceeded. "As *what?*"

Joe nodded.

"Aren't you guarded!" he cried. "Do you *never* let yourself go? However, you're quite right. I meant, do you like him?"

Catherine mischievously said:

"Supposing I were to say 'no'?" She was laughing. "You'd be surprised, wouldn't you, Joe? I think you and he make a bad pair."

"He likes me," Joe answered. "I like him, too."

"I'm so glad." That was sincere enough. Catherine looked straight before her, down through the pearly light which was beginning to drape Guilford Street in delicate shadow, while the yellow lights of a taxi at the end of the street flashed and were gone.

Joe resumed:

"But I think his manner is unfortunate. He doesn't do himself justice. He sometimes appears sour, which he isn't. He's a nice chap." It sounded as though Joe felt this commendation, in face of her silence, to be rather up-hill work. "I'd like to help, if I could. You know, Catherine, I probably seemed fairly stupid and selfish the other night. We can't always help ourselves. We're driven into wrong actions and unjust speeches——"

"Also into flight," Catherine remarked.

"That's true enough!" He stopped suddenly, wondering why she had diverted him from his apology. "Ah!" he cried, in triumph. "You're interested! You think I'm wandering from the point! It's *I* you want to hear about. Well, I'll tell you. You must know that Gwen——"

"Oh, Gwen," Catherine said, under her breath. "Joe, how easily you blame others!"

"Gwen," persisted Joe, "for some reason, is anxious to break up our home."

"She must be in love, Joe!"

"How *artful* women are! Now, you can believe me when I tell you that I cannot spot the young man. There isn't anybody she knows that I'd give a rush for. You can't possibly tell me that Gwen, who's a vigorous and impudent young person, is thinking of marrying such lads as we saw to-day. Can you?"

Catherine shook her head.

"I'm as much in the dark as you are, Joe," she said.

"Of course, it's springtime. But even so—— Can you tell me this, Catherine? Does there come a time when the thought of marriage becomes epidemic? Do you young women think of nothing but marriage? Do they think of marriage more in the month of April than at any other time? I'm seriously troubled over this."

"I can see that you are, Joe," was all that Catherine said.

"Gwen wants to get rid of me. I'm sure of that. She's even provided the bride——"

"She seems a charming girl," Catherine responded.

Again Joe was startled. He smiled, checked himself.

"Well, you saw how I ran!"

"But you'll go back, Joe."

"Pooh!" cried Joe. "That wasn't what I wanted to ask you. You've put it completely out of my head with your nonsense. Catherine, are you happy?"

She seemed surprised, as well she might be, at this abrupt change of tone and topic; but she answered with entire—or perhaps almost entire—frankness.

"I'm discontented, Joe. I don't think I've ever been really discontented before, but I am now. I'm dissatisfied with myself and with everybody else. I want something to happen."

"You'll get that," he remarked. "It's always the presage of a storm."

"But I don't like change for its own sake. I expect that I'm as puzzled as you are, really."

He nodded. They both nodded—very wisely.

"I wish you were more emotional," Joe said, looking into the distance.

"Yes, I'm sorry I'm not." Catherine did not show by the

flicker of an eyelash that there had been anything peculiar in his remark.

They had walked quickly, and they were approaching that little chain of squares of which Woburn Square forms a part. The light was exquisite. All the cloud which had obscured the sky during the afternoon had passed into the distance. What could be seen above was a sky the pallor of which held all the gleaming beauties of the opal. Against the sky the recently lighted street lamps had their own odd attractiveness. And Catherine and Joe, still walking with rapidity, could see the dark line of the houses, and the little iron balcony outside the first-floor windows of Catherine's home.

"I shan't come in," Joe said. "I shall lose myself!"

"Poor Joe!" Catherine murmured. "It's very sad."

They parted. Joe walked away, and Catherine ran up the two steps and let herself into the silent house. Neither looked back.

CHAPTER VII

TEA WITH MRS. BALTHAZAR

I

FOR a week, now, Ferdinand had been released from confinement in the house; and his first act, following this liberation, had been to resume the habit of walking far and wide about the London streets. During one of these walks, he came, as if by accident, through Lincoln's Inn Fields and entered Holborn, as he had done once before, by way of Great Turnstile. And, being arrived at this familiar spot, what could have been been more natural than his next proceeding? Finding himself immediately outside the flower shop kept by Mrs. Balthazar, he presently, with an air of purpose, walked straight into the shop and stood dreaming. For in this bower of sweet-smelling flowers, amid the fern and the tender foliage of young plants, with forced early roses, the merest buds, glowing and scenting the air with divine fragrance, with spring flowers still exquisitely drenching the air and offering their loveliness to the intoxicated eye, Mrs. Balthazar stood, scissors in hand, trimming the stalks of those blooms of which she was making a bouquet. To any beholder the spectacle would have had its attractiveness; to Ferdinand at this moment, miserable and self-distrustful, it was nothing less than an enchantment.

"Well!" cried Mrs. Balthazar. "Well! I *must* say! What's for you, sir? Come to see me, have you?" She put down her scissors, wiped upon her little black apron the hand in which they had been held, and offered it frankly to Ferdinand.

"How d'you do?" asked Ferdinand.

"You don't look any too flourishing, yourself," was the reply. "Bin ill, have you? I *thought* so! You'll just come right in and have a cup of tea with me and tell me all about it. You've got to!"

She led him to the door of that cupboard-like inner room with the bare table and the strip of carpet.

"I really——" began Ferdinand.

"Sh!" Archly she forced him to enter; and Ferdinand for the first time beheld the wretched little cubicle, lighted by a single electric bulb, in which Mrs. Balthazar spent such time as the requirements of her shop did not fill.

"There! You take this chair, and I'll have the other. Kettle's just boiling. A tablecloth—so; and here's a cup—it's cracked, but you won't mind that! And a plate! Well, it's very nice to see you. But I could tell you'd been ill. I expect you haven't been out much lately, have you? No, I thought not. I noticed you hadn't been in."

The quick talk was accompanied by quick action. As she spoke Mrs. Balthazar had opened the door of a small cupboard and had taken from it cups and saucers, plates, a brown teapot, an insignificant jug, and a cake such as may be bought for sixpence at any small baker's in the neighbourhood. The cloth was laid, the kettle, which had been singing upon a lighted Valor-Perfection oil stove in one corner of the room, began to steam violently, and tea was concocted in a trice. Ferdinand, half delighted, watched the deft movements of his hostess until she sat down near him. It was then his turn to make an observation upon her looks.

At first glance he was shocked. At his entry, he had been too much preoccupied to look closely at Mrs. Balthazar; but now that he could see her clearly he realized that if he had been ill and unhappy she must have been even more wretched than himself. Apparently she wore the black dress in which he had always seen her; but whereas the face above that dress had once been doll-like, it was now ghastly in its pallor, and its lines were greatly sharpened. She was older. Perhaps she had always been older than Ferdinand had supposed; but, if that were so, a mistake could no longer be made. Her cheeks were drawn; her eyes, which had been demure, were never still. She had an air almost of desperation. And yet, to Ferdinand, Mrs. Balthazar's manner was as simple and as caressing as it had ever been.

"Have you been ill, too?" Ferdinand asked.

She gave him a queer glance.

"Nothing to speak of," she said. Just about this time of year I always begin to feel the winter a bit, you know. Have you noticed how you do? Afterwards, I mean. You go through the winter all right; and then—I don't know— something seems to *give*. And auntie's been ill. See, you don't know auntie, do you? An old lady?" She cocked her head.

"I think, perhaps——"

"Well, perhaps you've seen her." Mrs. Balthazar began to pour out the tea. Ferdinand watched that thin brown stream, almost golden in the light from above. "She's deaf, poor soul. And I don't know how it is, or why, but the radiators in this place never will work. So poor old auntie— she's rheumaticky—she's just felt a regular old dismal Jimmy. You know, she hasn't seemed to care for anything."

Ferdinand took from her hand his own cup and saucer. As he did so he shook his head.

"I'm so sorry," he said gently. "You must have been very unhappy."

"Yes, I have," admitted Mrs. Balthazar. She bent her head, but not quickly enough to prevent Ferdinand from seeing that her blue eyes had filled with tears. Alas, he could tell that tears had been often in those eyes of late. Poor woman! He looked away. There was a pause, at the end of which a sigh indicated that Mrs. Balthazar had recovered her composure.

"Wouldn't it be possible for you to take a holiday?" Ferdinand asked.

A shaken head was his first answer.

"There's only the two of us. Who's to carry on the shop? That's the worst of it! I'm stuck here. No getting away—ever. I wish I could." There was something fierce in that last admission. "That's the worst of having a place like this. It's our living. Well, I mustn't grumble, because it *is* a living."

"I'm glad to hear you say that," Ferdinand exclaimed. "Glad indeed! I—I feel that you're very plucky. Very plucky. The last time I came in here——"

There was an abrupt interpolation which checked his reminiscence.

"Oh, don't!" she cried, in a voice of despair. Her hands were raised and pressed against her mouth.

Surprised, Ferdinand stopped himself. He murmured apologetically.

"I beg your pardon."

Mrs. Balthazar's head was shaken. For a moment she could not speak but sat staring down at her cup, quite obviously trying by will to dismiss from her mind some unbearable memory.

" 'Twasn't you," she said, at last, clearing her throat. "You know it wasn't."

Ferdinand moved his plate nervously, averting his glance from her.

"I wish I knew what to say to comfort you," he stammered. "You see, I'm—it is so very difficult to offer anything that isn't clumsy consolation. If I could say or do——"

Across that white face before him flitted an expression which he did not understand.

"Here am I worrying you when you're just out of bed," she murmured. "I ought to know better! But you're so kind, you make me cry. You oughtn't to do it, you know." She thought for an instant. "Let's talk about something else, shall we? I didn't mean to interrupt you."

"Certainly we can talk about something else. But if you knew how tired I am of——" Again he abandoned the effort to force a confidence. It seemed to Ferdinand that there was something fatal in his desire to learn the truth.

"You're tired!" she exclaimed. "And I'm bothering you. It's too bad of me to do that!"

"You misunderstand me. I only wanted to be your friend!"

"Friend," Mrs. Balthazar breathed. She put forward her hand, and with the fingers touched Ferdinand's hand, which was resting upon the table, halfway between them. "That's a lovely, cosy word! I haven't really got a friend in the world. That's what makes everything so hard. I don't expect you know—you couldn't know—what it is to go on, day after day, with nobody to take an interest in what's happening to you."

"Do I not?" said Ferdinand, in a low voice. He still felt those fingers upon his own. They crept farther, until his whole hand was covered by hers. And Mrs. Balthazar's head drooped even more than it had done. He heard her breathing quickly. Lower and lower drooped the head; her shoulders moved. At last sobs shook her body; and Ferdinand pressed his free hand upon hers, very warmly, in cordial sympathy.

II

Several moments passed. The rumbling of heavy traffic in Holborn made a continuous roar, while within, in this poky little room, which smelled of the oil lamp, steam rose faintly from the teacups and from the uneasy kettle. Ferdinand, completely absorbed in the pitiable spectacle before him, felt descending a dull melancholy from which there could be no escape. When he withdrew his covering hand and sought to release the hand which still lay imprisoned, he was conscious that Mrs. Balthazar shivered. At his insistence, she suffered his hand to be free and pressed her own to her cheek, hiding from him as well as she could the tears which trickled from her eyes. Broken words forced themselves from those swollen lips.

"So *good* to me . . . I'm so lonely——"

Poor woman! Poor woman! thought Ferdinand. But what could he do? There was nothing.

"I ought to know better," he heard her wailing. "I'm ashamed of myself." With her handkerchief she attempted to dry her eyes. "It's your being so nice——"

"Is there nothing I can do?" thought Ferdinand aloud. "I feel I ought not to leave you like this."

"Don't leave me," she wailed. "It's been such a mercy——"

"But, you see——" The sense of the suffocating confinement of that room oppressed Ferdinand deeply. He shuddered at it. The thought of this unhappy woman being forced to endure her sorrow amid such squalor, such unmitigated straitness, was abhorrent to him. "It seems to me that if you could only tell me of some way in which I could help you——"

Drearily the head was shaken slowly from side to side—with finality, it seemed.

"You can't," came a muffled voice. "Nobody can do that."

"But I can try," he gently persisted. "Don't you think I could do that?"

Mrs. Balthazar struggled to speak. In vain. For a moment no words came. Then, startlingly:

"Can you mend broken hearts, then?" she almost shouted. "Of course you can't; nobody can. You can't help me!" Having spoken with such bitter hysteria, she recovered herself with a frantic effort. "Look how I'm talking to you," she moaned. "I don't know what I'm saying. I don't get any sleep. I lie awake all night, listening to the sounds, and wondering if there'll ever be any end to it all until I'm dead."

"You, too," said Ferdinand quietly. "I've been lying awake, myself, and listening to the sounds."

He heard her awed whisper.

"Have you?" The handkerchief was lowered. Mrs. Balthazar's tear-brimming eyes stared at him. "You've been doing it too? But why? Are you miserable too? I thought you'd been ill."

"Both ill and unhappy," said Ferdinand.

"O-oh!" Her exclamation, half-incredulous, half-pitying, was long drawn out. "And I've been—isn't it funny we should *both*—I suppose lots of people are like us. You don't think of that, you know. You only think of yourself when you're miserable. At least, I do. Perhaps you're different."

Ferdinand wondered. Had he been thinking only of himself? He had thought he was concerned only with Rhoda and Catherine.

"I may as well tell you," Mrs. Balthazar continued, "that what's made me so wretched is—— No, I won't. It's a shame. I won't. I've been grizzling quite enough. It's time I pulled myself together." She gave herself a jerk of reproof and proceeded: "Well, now, what's been worrying *you,* then?" She dried her eyes; and Ferdinand could see them plainly, swollen as they were, with tears still glistening in the lashes. "Is it your daughters? Don't tell me they've been worrying you! Why, you poor thing! If they've been worrying you, they're not the girls I thought for. That I *must* say."

"They're both good," protested Ferdinand, stricken with a dread of his own disloyalty. "Both of them. I mustn't give you a wrong impression."

"No, no!" cried Mrs. Balthazar quickly. "Of course they're—I only meant, were you troubled about them? I've thought such a lot about them."

"Only by incidentals," Ferdinand murmured. "Really, nothing—I couldn't——"

"You don't want to talk about them." She was as swift as a cat. "Not to me."

"Oh, please!" Ferdinand raised his hand.

"I quite see. I know what it is. I mean——" She seemed to think for a moment. Then, as if to divert his attention, she asked, hardly: "Nothing to do with Mr. Teed, is it?"

"Mr. Teed!" stammered Ferdinand. "Why, what do you mean?"

"I just wondered." Her blue eyes were strangely fixed. "I knew he knew you."

The two of them looked directly at each other; and Ferdinand was the first to look away.

"I don't know," he said almost inaudibly.

"I think it is," responded Mrs. Balthazar.

"No." Ferdinand shook his head. "No; you're quite wrong. That was ended—ended."

He could see Mrs. Balthazar looking at him steadily from between her lashes. Her head was thrown back, so that he saw the creamy fullness of her throat, the sharp line of her chin, and the bitterly pursed lips. There was no beauty in that face; but only cruelty and jealousy and suspicion of himself.

"I wonder," said Mrs. Balthazar. And again: "I wonder." She shivered slightly.

CHAPTER VIII

A CRISIS

I

His first thought as he left the heavily scented shop was that he had escaped. His second was that he had needlessly run away. His third was that in spite of every circumstance he must presently return.

A great deal could still be discovered, Ferdinand felt sure, from Mrs. Balthazar. She had suffered, and she consequently had a distorted view of life. But she also had the wisdom which comes to those who have suffered. She was still beautiful. She had sympathy and understanding. Poor woman! Pity was very active in Ferdinand's heart. As he walked homeward he brooded much upon Mrs. Balthazar: upon her loneliness, her grief, her courage. She attracted him very strongly. She almost fascinated him. Outside his own family he did not know of anybody who had awakened in himself so much interest and pity.

The problem served him for some moments of his walk homeward. Then his mind swerved and he began to think once more of Rhoda and of Catherine. In spite of his denial that Punch Teed had been a cause of his own misery, he was by no means certain of the fact. Had Rhoda really broken with Punch? Or was that hint of Mrs. Balthazar's justified? His fears rose again in tumult. Could it be that Rhoda was still seeing Punch clandestinely, surreptitiously? He had been lulled into tranquillity. Nay, his mind had been diverted from this by the appearance of another danger. Not Rhoda, but Catherine, had been the occasion of his later alarm. Were they both heading for disaster? For almost the first time in his mature life Ferdinand began to hurry home. He did not run, but he walked as young men in love may walk, very swiftly and apprehensively, with nerves active and with eyes straight ahead. As a consequence, he was to become the witness of a scene which disquieted him no less, but rather more, than anything which had already passed.

He was hastening onward when from a turning a little way in front, upon his right side, came two figures, walking at a medium pace in the same direction as himself. Ferdinand was so astonished at the sight and so filled by it with stormy dismay that he very nearly came to a stop. The two persons who thus forced themselves upon his notice went onward, absorbed in conversation. They did not look up or about them, but proceeded as if their path were set and familiar; as if what they said was of urgent interest. They were close to each other, strangely intimate in bearing, as if they had some common secret in which no other person might claim share. Following them, his pace reduced to a speed less than theirs, Ferdinand saw the two pause for a moment at the corner of Woburn Square, still deep in speech. He saw them exchange a last word, clasp hands gravely, and separate. Jabez Talbot went across the square and away, while Catherine went on, ran up the steps before the Meadows's house, and disappeared instantly within the door.

Ferdinand's heart was throbbing rapidly. He could feel it beating in his throat. A secret? A conspiracy? This was worse than anything he had anticipated. He was more than alarmed; he was angry. Slowly he proceeded to the house, and entered it as Catherine had done, and was lost in the soft luxury of its silence.

II

But once indoors, although the calm of the house had an influence upon him, Ferdinand hurried to his study. The serious faces of those two as they parted were still in his vision; the air of whispered confidence galled him. With the door closed, he began to walk up and down the room, a thousand speeches and ejaculations rising to his tongue. What! Was it to be said that his daughter must furtively meet her lover, permit him to walk with her through the streets, and then dismiss him at a distance from her home lest their transactions should be espied? It was intolerable! Such conduct was for other times, other persons. This young girl or that (he would not be too rigorously censorious) might have her afternoon walk with a lover, and might hide the fact from her parents; but not one of his daughters. For Catherine and for Rhoda their father's house was ever open. Neither had been forbidden to introduce to the house a single one of the acquaintances, the friends, with whom they associated. There had been no attempt at stern parental control, and there would never be. Had he not trusted both his girls? Had he not treated them throughout with love and sympathy? Surely he had not failed in that first duty? And yet, first Rhoda and then Catherine had shown a readiness to deceive him. He could not bear it. He *would* not bear it. He had been caught unawares with Rhoda. He was not to be deceived by Catherine. Bitterly he reproached them both, his heart full of pain and anger.

Again, what was the truth regarding Jabez? He was supposed to have returned to the North of England. Ferdinand had been allowed to think that he was still in the North. If he had not, with his own eyes, seen Jabez that afternoon, in the street, within fifty yards of his own home, Ferdinand would have believed that he was three hundred miles away. But he had seen Jabez. It was enough. The duplicity was not only Catherine's. Nay, it might be that she had acted under instruction! A politician, they called Jabez. A politician—a rebel! A leader, a manipulator, of men. Well, Rhoda had been right. From her first meeting with this man she had despised him; and her judgment, although it had rested upon intuition alone, had been sound. She had been right while Catherine, usually so sagacious, had been wrong. It was another proof that the instinctive judgment of an impulsive woman was to be preferred to the more intellectual understanding of one who was less impulsive.

What had Joe Gascoyne said? Something to the effect that Catherine ordinarily repressed her emotions but that in time of stress these emotions might well become ungovernable and carry her straight to disaster. Was that a true saying? Had Joe foreseen this happening? Had he meant that Catherine, for all her ostensible calm, was inflammable to the torch of such a nature as that of this agitator?

"Ah, I wish I knew!" cried Ferdinand, striking his hands together in despair. "I wish I knew!"

He stared out of the window at the little square of garden behind the house, his spirits black, his temper spoiled. It seemed to him that in the last few weeks his happy life had been torn wantonly asunder. His interest, his peace, had alike been bound up in the happiness of his two girls. Now he had lost both. For Rhoda his feeling was diminished; for Catherine——

"Yes, Father?" It was Catherine's voice, behind him.

Ferdinand wheeled around to see Catherine standing within the room.

"You're there?" stammered Ferdinand.

She nodded, smiling, archly expressing an exaggerated surprise at his surprise.

"I looked in on my way downstairs to see if you were home. I've just come in, myself."

"Yes," Ferdinand said. "I was behind you!"

Did her face change? Was there the slightest increase of colour? He could not tell.

"Oh," cried Catherine. "Did you see me?" No shame! Ferdinand could not speak. He inclined his head. His eyes were fixed upon her coldly, bitterly, accusingly. "You saw Jabez, then?" Was it bravado? That was an offence the more. Even the suspicion of it increased his coldness. "I wish I'd known." She seemed as frank as ever—as deceptively frank. "He was on his way to some committee meeting, so he wouldn't come in."

Was it true? Was it a lie? What more easy than such a lie?

"I thought he was out of London," said Ferdinand.

"Did you? He goes and comes, you know." She was— perhaps deliberately—paying no attention. Her eye had strayed to the picture cover of an art magazine which lay upon Ferdinand's desk.

"I was told he was out of London," persisted Ferdinand. An anger, the rising, uncontrollable anger of the gentle person who believes himself to have been deceived, seized him. In an entirely different tone from that in which he had hitherto spoken he continued: "I naturally believed it. So when I saw you with him I was—still quite naturally, I think —very much surprised."

"We must have forgotten to tell you, Father," answered Catherine very quietly. But she had looked up, so that she must have recognized the change in his voice. "He came back about a week ago. I hadn't seen him until I met him by accident in the street."

"By accident!" exclaimed Ferdinand harshly. He was frowning upon her in distaste.

"Why, Father——" began Catherine.

"I must speak to you, Catherine," cried Ferdinand. "I really cannot endure this silence, this confusion and uncertainty." He took a quick turn about the room before he proceeded, but in truth he was not, for that moment, quite master of himself. "As to this—this—as to Talbot. As you know, I've never set any limit to your acquaintance. I have seen strange faces in this house, and heard some strange speeches; but I have never offered objection to them. Because I relied upon your taste, your sense, your social tact——"

"I don't know what you're talking about, Father," said Catherine in a bewildered way.

"You *must* know. Talbot has been introduced into this house. Against my will, I've tolerated him——"

"He's our friend, Father!"

"*Your* friend."

"*My* friend, then," corrected Catherine, her eyes sparkling.

"You said something lately that made me believe you——" It was impossible to proceed. "Something suggestive of—of another relationship. Was I wrong? Did I misunderstand you? Am I wrong? Am I tormenting myself needlessly?"

Catherine was silent. There was a smile; but a smile of something akin to pity, of something that might have been contempt or intrepidity rather than amusement, upon her lips. At last, quietly, she said:

"*Are* you tormenting yourself, Father?"

"I'm in constant pain. Catherine, can you give me your promise that this man—that Talbot—— Think, my darling! I couldn't endure that he should break up our happiness. Catherine, I appeal to you——" Ferdinand did not know what he was saying. He was horrified at the sense that he had lost essential self-control. "I'm not a young man. I'm growing old. I can't *bear* these uncertainties."

She had turned away from him.

"I think you're awfully unjust to Jabez," she said warmly. "You seem to want to see him punished for something—for some jealous opinion you've formed of him."

That was what Ferdinand heard. The words made his emotion ungovernable.

"Some *jealous* opinion! Catherine!"

"Is it not that?"

"Never. Such a thought has never entered my head. I've appealed to your pity. I appeal to your judgment. Give him up, Catherine! Let him go back to his own people! He can never be anything to us but a cause of distress. I appeal to your judgment, Catherine. Have you no respect for mine?"

"Poor Father!" said Catherine gently. "Of course, I respect your judgment. But it isn't your judgment that's speaking."

"It *is* my judgment," persisted Ferdinand. "Do you suppose that I would ever jealously interfere with your happiness?"

"My happiness?" She seemed incredulous. "Oh, but it's not *my* happiness that's in question, surely? We were speaking of you and Jabez."

"I don't understand you," stammered Ferdinand.

"You want me to refuse to let Jabez come here?" she asked. "Is that what you mean?"

"To refuse to meet him—speak to him——"

She shook her head resolutely. Ferdinand had never seen her so immovable.

"No, no, Father. I couldn't do that. It would be horrible. You don't really mean such a thing. You couldn't! It would break poor Jabez's heart. You mustn't be cruel, you know."

"Is my heart to be broken, then?" demanded Ferdinand passionately.

"No!" cried Catherine. "Father, dear; you hurt me! I hope nobody's heart is to be broken. But, really, you're being intolerant. You're asking too much. And you're unjust to Jabez. He hasn't had a chance to win your liking. Give him time, Father!"

Ferdinand could endure no more. He waved his hand to bid her go.

"Please," he said. "Please!"

Not until she was gone did he turn round again; and when he once again felt himself alone he sat down before the fire, under the shadow of those tall bookshelves, filled with sombre and gleaming burden, and felt as if his heart had indeed already broken.

PART THREE

CHAPTER I

ILL NEWS

I

To LIVE with those from whom one has in some manner effected an estrangement would seem to be a very difficult task. Nay, it *is* difficult. But it is not as impossible as some would have us believe. Ferdinand found, as he had found before, that after an hour, or a day, or a week, the wounds are hidden. Silences, indicative of pain, or of a forbidden topic, may arise; but if we all parted as brusquely as fashionable husbands and wives have a habit of doing there would be nothing left for the world but a return to nomadism. The house in Woburn Square had never been one in which either lamentations or rejoicings were noisy; it was now more silent than ever. For Ferdinand had quarrelled with neither of his daughters, but was estranged from both. Yet even in this estrangement there was no interruption in their ordinary loving domestic intercourse. Meals were eaten, thoughts were uttered, a visit to the theatre was undertaken, there were as usual walks and talks. What proceeded unseen was known only, and in secret, to each of them.

Ferdinand's own position was at its hardest when he awoke in the morning and saw the sun's early brilliance gleaming across the carpet beside his bed. He then had such a feeling of expectancy, and immediately afterwards such a recognition of loneliness, that he was sometimes overset. But every day lent its aid to the situation. By the seventh morning Ferdinand, walking more briskly as the result of better health, better rest, and the sun's morning radiance, came into the breakfast room with something of his old

agreeable and reflective calm. Immediately after him followed the breakfast dishes. Three or four letters were upon
his plate; the *Times* and the *Morning Post* were ready for
perusal; the fire glowed; the sun shone through the mellow
curtains. It was enough. His heart mounted.

Catherine was already in the room, and she was studiously
reading a letter. Rhoda was no more than a moment behind.
She entered the room impetuously, as was her wont, and by
her coming seemed to quicken the impulse of the atmosphere,
so that both Ferdinand and Catherine looked up with smiles
and new interest.

"Morning, Daddy," Rhoda said, as she eyed her own
empty plate. "No letter for me! Who's yours from, Catherine?" She did not sit down at once, but moved to the fire,
bent towards it, a graceful figure, turned away, and idly
picked up one of Ferdinand's newspapers, opening it and
glancing at random down the long columns.

Catherine finished reading her letter; Ferdinand adjusted
his horn-rimmed spectacles and picked up the four envelopes
addressed to himself. All were bulky; and all contained re-
quests that he would contribute to some fund of an estimable
character.

"I wonder," he said, without reflection, "whether our
Socialist friends realize how little of the wealthy man's
wealth stays in his own pocket."

It was a matter of no importance; but as soon as he had
uttered the words Ferdinand regretted them. He should have
known better. It was no part of his wish to throw out any
such affront to Jabez—or even to say that which would serve
to recall a thought of Jabez. Therefore, with a start of an-
noyance, he felt that he had blundered. He looked surreptitiously at Catherine, who did not appear to have heard what
he said. She was standing up and was preparing to serve
Ferdinand with his breakfast. He hoped she had been deaf
indeed. Although his heart was beating a little more quickly
at the knowledge of danger, he could not entirely restrain a

faint smile of relief, and even (perversely) of mischief. For, as Ferdinand believed, it is quite true that many demands are made upon the wealthy man by those who are not official tax gatherers; and the four envelopes contained appeals which were not altogether lacking in a note of peremptoriness. *Noblesse oblige,* they all indelicately, in effect, reminded him.

Because of his preoccupation Ferdinand did not observe that Rhoda was reading her newspaper with more than common intentness. He had heard, it is true, a sharp exclamation from her, but he had paid no heed. Rhoda was capable of uttering just such a cry in face of any report of cruelty, injustice, or impudence. But as she quietly replaced the paper upon the table Ferdinand looked directly up into her white face, and he was startled to observe its pallor and the sharp hardness of the line of her cheek. True to his habit, he glanced quickly from Rhoda to Catherine, for the purpose of ascertaining the reason for this frozen whiteness; but Catherine, smiling unconsciously, was at this moment handing him across the table a plate containing nobly scrambled eggs on toast. He therefore received no help from Catherine; and when he glanced again, very cautiously, at Rhoda, who by now was seated in her place, the pallor had been suffused by a deep flush which remained perceptible for several minutes. Ferdinand had no clue to Rhoda's mood, and so he began, comfortably enough, to eat his breakfast. He noticed, however, that although Catherine gave her sister the letter which had arrived that morning for herself Rhoda did no more than glance perfunctorily through it, and in silence returned the letter to Catherine. She did not speak throughout the meal. Yet upon her arrival she had been full of zest. What was the explanation? Mechanically Ferdinand took up the paper which Rhoda had laid down, and began his highly methodical examination of its contents.

Quite early he found the cause of Rhoda's exclamation, her pallor, and her flush.

Those were the days preceding the enactment in England

of a law suppressing the lavish reporting of divorce cases. And Ferdinand's eye quickly caught an entire column devoted to the account of a case which had occupied a judge and special jury during the greater part of the previous day. The case had its disgraceful details, but these interested Ferdinand not at all. The one fact which impressed him, and caused him quickly to turn the page without allowing his shock of surprise to be seen by either of his daughters, was the citation of George Teed as corespondent. Was it the George Teed they knew? There might be others. There *must* be others. He read again. Impossible to doubt that it was Punch. Well, was it surprising?

"Good God!" thought Ferdinand. "What an escape!" And then the dagger of doubt was plunged into his heart. Had she escaped, after all?

He did not dare to look at Rhoda lest he should read in her face a confirmation of his fear.

II

Ferdinand's food remained before him, untasted. Although his eyes roved over the printed words, they carried no message to his brain. He was in consternation. This was something which he could never have foreseen; it came from without. It was disagreeable. It was worse than disagreeable. In an instant Rhoda, and Rhoda's happiness, were once again paramount in Ferdinand's thoughts. And he could not make the slightest movement, since he knew that Rhoda must be watching him. To refer to the matter was impossible; to ignore it would be disastrous. What was he to do?

"Father," called Catherine quietly. "Your breakfast is getting cold."

With an exclamation, Ferdinand crushed the paper and allowed it to drop to the ground.

"I——" he began. He could not eat. And yet if he did not eat his agitation would become apparent. Automatically he took up his knife and fork, paused, shuddered, and set down the knife and fork. "I wonder whether you would give me some fresh coffee, Catherine," he said at length. And then, chockingly, he lied. "I was engrossed in a most—most interesting——"

It must be obvious—he thought—to both of them that he was lying. Could he look, to see? Swiftly, confusedly he glanced from one to the other, and once more averted his gaze before either could suppose herself examined. Rhoda, with scarlet face, stared across at the fire, lost in reverie; Catherine, veiling incredulity with skill, received his cup of cold coffee and refilled it. There was silence. It lasted unbearably while Ferdinand drank his fresh coffee; and when the task was done he rose to his feet.

"If nobody else wants the papers I shall take them to the study," he said.

"How mysterious you are, Father." Catherine was gaily rallying. Then she must have seen something which made her pause, for she instantly added: "However, do take them."

At this Rhoda languidly set her knife and fork across the plate, stood upright, and moved slowly towards the door. Her face was hidden from the others. But the deliberateness of her movements was remarkable. She seemed to be holding herself with perfect rigidity, her shoulders stiff and her head as erect as that of an automaton.

"It's such a beautiful morning," said she, with drawling casualness, "that I think I shall go out." But she did not, in saying this, turn and address the others. Her hand was upon the door. She was almost gone.

"Will you wait for me?" cried Ferdinand appealingly.

She did not hear him, or she pretended not to hear him. She was out of earshot, leaving Ferdinand, still grasping both newspapers, and Catherine, still sitting at the table, confronting each other, each with an air of accusation. The door was closed; her farther progress, unseen and unheard, was hidden from them.

"What *is* in the papers?" demanded Catherine, with gentle imperiousness.

"Distressingly enough," Ferdinand answered her, "there is bad news of Punch. He has been involved in a divorce suit." "The conditions very disagreeable," he would have added, but Catherine interrupted him.

"Never! Let me see!" She took from his hand the first of the sheets, found the place, and breathlessly read the report. During the perusual Catherine's cheeks also flushed slightly, less at the case than at the unconscious perceptions of all that the news involved of shame to Rhoda; and when she had finished reading she returned the paper to her father. "Rhoda had seen this, had she?"

"Evidently. Didn't you notice her face?"

"I didn't see. I was stupidly thinking of something else. What was she doing? Was she crying? Only red?"

"Ought I to say something to her?" asked Ferdinand. "I feel really—— Poor child! She may be in despair." The thought alarmed him. "Catherine, do you think——" He was so much frightened that he could not proceed. "I'm afraid," he declared.

"Of what?" demanded Catherine.

"She seemed too calm."

Catherine shook her head decidedly. And having done that she was inclined to hesitate.

"It may be so," she agreed.

"I wish we knew!" cried Ferdinand. "I wish I knew what to do. And what this means to her."

"It may mean no more than embarrassment," said Catherine thoughtfully. "She would feel very much embarrassed —very much humiliated. You must remember that this must have been going on——" Her voice failed as she became lost in reflection.

"Going on?" questioned Ferdinand, in agitation. "Catherine, please!"

"Going on at the same time," Catherine answered in a strange voice and with a strange look.

Ferdinand shivered. He had not conceived that possibility. "Intolerable!" he exclaimed.

Catherine said no more; and Ferdinand, with fresh food for distressed consideration, moved quickly about the room. His task was not simplified. It was made more difficult than ever.

"What am I to do?" he suddenly demanded. "What am I to do? Can you tell me, Catherine? I really don't know what to do. It seems to me that the easiest thing, as usual, would be to do nothing whatever; but if I do nothing the consequences may be tragic."

"The consequences, with Rhoda, may always be tragic," Catherine said. "Whatever is done."

If only, Ferdinand thought, one could achieve clearness. If a question could be asked and answered truthfully. But where pride was involved any lie seemed preferable to the truth. In his perplexity he became momentarily impatient.

"Then what is to be done?" he cried loudly. "An understanding seems impossible. Impossible!"

"I shall see her at once," said Catherine, in a decided tone. "You'd better take the papers to the study. I'll ring for the table to be cleared and then I'll go to Rhoda." In a lower voice she added: "It will be useless."

"Why should it be useless?" asked Ferdinand. "You're her sister. Why should it be useless?"

He had posed, it seemed, an unanswerable question; for Catherine, with a shaken head, passed him and disappeared, leaving Ferdinand more than ever at the mercy of his fears and entirely without clue to the labyrinth of sisterly relations.

III

There seemed to be nothing for him to do, and he therefore slowly made his way upstairs and into his study. Once there, he cast aside the papers with a gesture of disgust and stood with bowed head listening and thinking of all that had happened and all that might happen. It occurred to him that if in such distress he could have appealed to some higher power his mind would be tranquillized; but for many years his faith in the direct interposition of God in human affairs had been inactive. The force of habit was so strong that he could not now cry aloud his agony. Whatever might come, he must endure it by the strength of his own nature; and that feeling which was strongest within him was not so much dread of what might occur as a sense of his own powerlessness to avert danger from his most loved child.

It was strange how this news had swung him back towards Rhoda. And yet not strange, since she had all along been his greatest cause of anxiety. For Catherine his love had been as great, but it had not been intensified by this anxiety. Catherine had seemed aloof, self-confident, beyond his influence. His love for her had been chilled. Lately he had rediscovered her, but she was disappointing him. Well, after all, Rhoda was his favourite child. She was now, as she had always been, the one in most danger. And he had lost her. He could not help her. The spell which had bound them together was broken through her attachment—was it in fact an attachment?—to another, younger, man. He, the father, however, loving, was discarded. It was his business to stand aside, and he could not stand aside. He loved her too well. It was his duty to protect her, and he could not protect her because agitation made her wilful. Bitterly did Ferdinand realize this. He had no power, since the claims of love, however unconsciously and however involuntarily, were repudiated. He could do nothing save listen.

At last his listening was rewarded. The door of the room was opened and Rhoda came in. She was dressed for walking, in a very plain brown costume with a brown hat which bore a bow of orange ribbon.

"Catherine says that you asked me to wait for you," she

said abruptly. "I'm sorry I didn't hear you, Daddy. You must have spoken very quietly."

The painful scarlet had faded from her cheeks leaving them without colour; and as she spoke she was quite obviously determined that he should not compel her to meet his glance. There was neither life nor expression in her face. Her carriage was repressive. She appeared to Ferdinand, not as a child in sorrow, but as a woman in agony.

"Rhoda, my darling——" he eagerly began.

"I'd rather not come with you to-day, Daddy. You'll forgive me, won't you?"

She spoke coldly, but with a kindness which deeply wounded him.

"I thought perhaps—companionship——" stammered Ferdinand.

"Not to-day. Another time. Do be kind, Daddy, and not look so hurt."

"I? Hurt? My darling!" He would have taken her hand, but she drew back, so clearly unwilling for any contact that Ferdinand drew back in turn. "Whatever you wish," he said, but not as coldly as she. "I hope you know that I should never want to press my company upon you or do anything——"

He heard her sigh, saw the faint shrugging of her shoulders.

"I know you're all kindness, Father," she answered steadily, but with a considerateness which amounted to impertinence. "I want to go for a walk alone. It may seem strange to you——"

Ferdinand was startled at that tone.

"Everything is strange to me," he exclaimed. "But go, child; my own thought was for you."

"Thank you." She was evidently grateful. Tears darkened her eyes. "I know, Daddy." She turned away and was going.

"You've seen Catherine?" Ferdinand asked quickly.

Rhoda did not stay. Over her shoulder she answered his question.

"It was she who said you wanted to go with me. Don't you remember?"

"Of course." Ferdinand opened his hand, which had been clenched. "Did she say anything else?"

"Nothing else," was the response. The door closed. He was once more alone.

CHAPTER II

AN APPEAL FOR HELP

I

THAT afternoon Ferdinand avoided any nearness to Mrs. Balthazar's shop. As he approached it he deliberately made a détour, which took him farther east and along Gray's Inn Road. Here, where the old houses of Holborn Bars look down upon later squalor, and where the buildings of the Inn peep over a wall at the filth and dust of incessant traffic, he found fit accompaniment to his mood. A stale smell hung in the air, rolling onward from a brewery in the Clerkenwell Road; ugly blocks of workmen's dwellings stood grimly drab above the tram lines by the corner of Rosebery Avenue; and even the old houses in Theobald's Road, in one of which Benjamin Disraeli was born, were black and gruesome to Ferdinand's eye. This was an ugly streak of London, spoiled by the rumbling dray and the heavy passenger vehicles, the vile smoke from soft coal and the constant issue of vapour from motor exhausts. The town was visibly decaying. Ferdinand felt that it was already dead, that it was putrefying under his nostrils.

And as he had this thought he looked up and saw that he was almost abreast of the end of Bedford Row. The glimpse he had of that wide and pleasant street was in some measure consoling; for here, in the heart of squalor, were peace, dignity, and beauty. More than that; he knew that in Bedford Row, in one of these tall and shapely houses. lived Joe Gascoyne. And to Ferdinand Joe represented disinterestedness. No danger threatened from that cool dry mind, incapable of the fevers of love and the fervours of enthusiasm. True, Joe was young; but his youth was that of an older genera- tion, when young men were wise and responsible beyond their years and not, as now, raw under the veneer of sophis- tication.

So it was clear that Joe would give Ferdinand the con- solation he needed. Alas! Ferdinand did not know in which of these straight, flat houses Joe was to be found. If he had known! Deliberately he turned into Bedford Row and walked past several of the doorways, here and there examining the names which were painted upon the doorposts and those which had been engraved upon small brass plates. In vain did Ferdinand scan such names as he saw; that passion for privacy which distinguishes the true-born Englishman had caused Joe to suppress any mention of himself at the door of the house in which he lived. Ferdinand, becoming short- sighted as dusk interposed a film between himself and the world, was baffled. He abandoned his search. His hands, to which the crook of an umbrella gave a point of junction, were behind him. His felt hat was pressed down upon his head, sharpening by its hard line the gravity of the clean fea- tures below. Unconscious of the forlorn aspect presented by his sober thinness and the ever so slightly discouraged sink- ing of his ordinarily erect shoulders, he was about to turn and go home when, from the mouth of that curious little passage- way, Hand Court, appeared the very man of whom he was in search.

No contrast could have been more subtly complete than that which Joe and Ferdinand presented. Whereas Ferdinand had a judge's pallor and gravity and the slow walk of a man of middle age, Joe, with his heavy eyebrows, his gleaming, piercing glance all around, his long nose and expressively mischievous mouth, was full of a kind of liveliness. One could tell that his mind was quick and active, that his humour was vivacious and irreverent, and that his leanness was the result of good health rather than asceticism.

"Ah, Gascoyne," Ferdinand said. "Just the man I was looking for!" He grasped Joe's hand, standing and smiling with a warmth that was greater than usual. He saw the black eyebrows so nearly opposite his own give a twitch of surprise and was then enveloped in Joe's beaming glance of welcome.

"You've been to the flat, have you?"

"I didn't know where it was. I was still looking for it when you burst from that—" Ferdinand raised his head in order to examine more particularly what to him had been an unexpected thoroughfare—"that very mysterious little court."

"It connects Bedford Row with Holborn. But I'm sorry you shouldn't know where we live. A few doors only—on *this* side—" Joe indicated with his open hand. If he was surprised—if he was astounded—at the apparition of Ferdinand and at the desire of Ferdinand to visit himself, he gave no sign of it, but bent towards his guest in the most gracious and charming manner. "I rather think Gwen won't be there; but if the place is more than normally untidy you'll forgive it, I'm sure."

"We shall be alone?" questioned Ferdinand, rather anxiously, rather pathetically.

"Yes." Joe was already leading the way towards one of the houses, and a moment later stood aside in order that Ferdinand might mount the stairs before him.

"Good!" breathed Ferdinand. "I'm glad of that. I rather wanted——"

He could not see Joe's face as they proceeded up the stairs, for Joe was behind him. But he heard Joe's voice saying:

"Go slowly. We're up at the top of the house. You'll be breathless."

II

They had arrived, and Ferdinand, ushered into the living room, became aware of a guarded fire, and a tea table laid for one person. Armchairs, bareness, the table, and the fire represented all his first impressions of Joe's home. But the elevation of it was exhilarating. He knew that they must be high above the ground. The light was peculiarly cold and penetrating, for the room faced the west, and it was receiving the last pallors of the day.

"My dear fellow," Ferdinand began. "I shall be interrupting you most abominably!"

He indicated the laid table and did not immediately take the obviously inviting chair to which Joe had drawn attention.

"Of course, you *can* do so," responded Joe. "But on the other hand you could join me. How does that strike you? It only means a plate and a cup and saucer; some sugar——" He was hurrying from the room as he spoke, and he returned a moment afterwards with all the additions he had named. "The kettle will boil in no time on our patent gas, and we can have tea. If we're doing that, we're bound to agree. I always feel that one can never quarrel over tea."

Ferdinand followed Joe with his eye, enjoying the sense of harlequinade as that tall figure made its quick movements about the room. How lithe the man was! And how resourcefully unembarrassed! Ferdinand himself was embarrassed. But that was because, obeying his impulse, he had come upon an errand; and because, being here, the enormity of his proposed act of confidence was becoming gradually apparent to him. Nothing, however, in Joe's manner suggested that Joe was expecting a confidence. He behaved as he might have behaved to an old friend, perhaps to a former school master. Approval of Joe began to steal into Ferdinand's mind. For Joe——

A very strange thought assailed Ferdinand. It was so strange that it took his breath away. He remembered that Rhoda had once spoken warmly in defence of Joe. She had been very clearly his champion. She had been his supporter in the argument with Jabez. If only—— That was the first time such a notion had arisen in his mind. Even so, it had come there merely as an alternative; but as an alternative so infinitely to be preferred to what might be that it shone brightly by contrast. If only Joe, by interposing, could——

"Well, as to quarrelling," smiled Ferdinand, "I don't think we're likely to do that. Because I've come with all friendly intent, with the object of asking your advice."

Joe betrayed himself. He betrayed the fact that he had been speculating upon the occasion of Ferdinand's visit.

"Advice!" he cried. "How exciting!" His long hands came together in gleeful contact. "One second; I hear the kettle." He swooped from the room; there was a faint clatter, a pause, and then he was back again, carrying a teapot and tea cosy, which he proceeded to set upon the waiting tray. "Now," said Joe. "I'm all attention!"

And with that he turned in his chair and faced Ferdinand. Ferdinand, meeting those bright and searching eyes, and confronted by that alert attentiveness, was momentarily discomposed. Faltering, he looked down, uncertain where the story he had to tell should be begun. Aware, too, that it must be told in such a way as to disguise everything which was of moment to himself. Not an easy task! On the contrary, a task of such extreme difficulty that he might have been excused for flinching as he confronted it.

III

"Now that I come to speak to you," he said frankly, "I'm rather at a loss. I see that I am perhaps going beyond the strict limits of propriety." He hesitated still.

"Do you mean," asked Joe, "by 'the strict limits of propriety' the extreme limits of your confidence in myself?"

This inquiry checked Ferdinand; but it did not make his task more difficult, and in this respect it helped him.

"Perhaps I mean 'the strict limits of propriety,'" he suggested. "I have great confidence in you. But I also have a feeling that you won't be willing to limit your attention to what I tell you."

"You think I shall guess a great deal—wrongly," said Joe. "It's not my discretion you mistrust."

"No. It is your perception that I fear."

"Then tell me nothing," urged Joe. "Because once you've talked to me as you were going to, you'll feel I'm like Poe's Raven. It isn't worth it."

"And yet," Ferdinand persisted, "I shouldn't have come to you now if I hadn't been in great need."

"Then tell me all you can," replied Joe promptly. "And I won't tell you what I guess. But in that case you'll be sure to overrate my perception and imagine that I know more than I do. I can't imagine anything more uncomfortable."

Ferdinand, in spite of his unhappy state, could not restrain a smile at this shrewd prophecy.

"Very true," he admitted. "However, I must risk it. If you knew what advantage I expect to gain you would be amused. But in fact, Gascoyne, I want to ask you about two men whom you know."

"Two," murmured Joe. "I wonder which two."

Did he know? Ferdinand glanced in vain at that mobile face, the expressions upon which were so rapid that they could never be seized and interpreted. A mysterious face, wholly unreadable by himself. Were others more skilled? He wondered.

"First," said Ferdinand, forcing himself to the plunge, "I want to ask you about Punch Teed."

Joe jumped. He gave a lurch forward in his chair and answered without reflection.

"Oh, a bad young man. A bad young man."

Ferdinand shivered. This was no more favourable a beginning than he had expected.

"But how dangerous?" he asked quickly.

"To whom?" countered Joe. There was a long silence.

Ferdinand perceived clearly that he could not maintain discretion in talking to Joe. He had been foolish. He had already said too much.

"To my own peace of mind," he hesitatingly responded. It was an ambiguity. It would not serve.

"As affecting the girls?" said Joe. Then, with entire frankness: "I must tell you at once that I don't know," he continued. "I know nothing."

"But the man?" pressed Ferdinand.

"As far as you and I can speak of him, he's no good. You don't want me to give you reasons."

"No. And yet I should like to know what step I could take. Gascoyne, I must trust you, I see. I want to keep him away from my house. More, I want to take some decisive step——"

"But nowadays," Joe answered quickly, "one can't take steps. That's the trouble! The authority of the male is gone. He may possess all the wisdom in the world; but he hasn't any longer the power to enforce his wisdom. The Law, sentimentalized by so-called Progressive Members of Parliament, denies it to him. That is what makes men nowadays appear merely inept in relation to recalcitrant wives and daughters. The days of the cudgel—— However, you don't want me to talk of that. It's the commonplace of adolescent conversation. You can try and keep him out of the house: no more."

"You've seen this latest?" questioned Ferdinand. "The divorce, I mean."

"Divorce means nothing, at the moment. It's smart. It might heighten his attractiveness."

Again Ferdinand shivered.

"I can't contradict you," he said. "I should like to be able to do so."

"But why?" asked Joe. "It might happen to any one of us to be involved in divorce."

"Oh!" cried Ferdinand. "Surely you don't mean that?"

Joe smiled. "I think I do," he answered. "But of course I may be wrong."

There was a further pause, at the end of which, after much thought, Ferdinand proceeded:

"Well, that's not my only problem. There is another—to me, quite as serious. I mean, Talbot."

"Talbot," repeated Joe. Now at last Ferdinand caught a glimpse of emotion. Joe's face changed for an instant. The mention of Jabez Talbot's name had aroused him. "Oh, Talbot's quite different."

"Different, but perhaps equally a problem," persisted Ferdinand. He could see by the quick movements which Joe gave that his meaning was being sought for. Well, surely it was pain enough? But perhaps in this case Joe was not quite so completely detached? "I don't ask, you understand, for the same reasons or similar reasons. But you remember that we once spoke a little of his opinions; and you, I remember——"

Joe shook his head.

"You don't understand him. You don't get on with him. He's like the rest of us. He's very honest, very ill-educated, much troubled. He wants to do right by the whole world. Especially by his own people."

"Then *let* him," cried Ferdinand impatiently. "I wish he would do so."

Joe looked up and directly at Ferdinand. And his glance was sombre.

"If you can show me how such a man as Jabez can carry out his humanitarian ideas without interfering with *us,* I shall be surprised," he said. "He wants to change the world. You and I want to keep it as it is. We're his enemies. We resist him, and he attacks us. But that is because we enjoy the power, and he wants to enjoy it. We're in his way. Therefore we must go. And he knows he's helpless until he can convert us to the doctrine of hara-kiri."

"I'm not in the least interested in his ideas," returned Ferdinand. "I merely don't require his company."

"Oh!" Joe gave a cry. "You want also to keep *him* out of the house."

"Worse," said Ferdinand bitterly. "I want to keep him out of the family."

Joe had grown quite pale.

"I see," he murmured. "Yes, I see." He moved sharply, so that his face was in shadow; and for several minutes afterwards the two of them sat opposite to one another, as if silently overwhelmed by the picture which Ferdinand had called up.

IV

Ferdinand was the first to speak.

"And I came to see you this afternoon, because I happened to be passing this way, and I thought you—being a young man—might be able to tell me how it can be done." Joe shook his head vigorously; but Ferdinand, while not ignoring the gesture, insisted upon completing his statement. "Both my girls are of age; they can do as they choose. I can beg them to do as I wish; I can forbid them to do anything else; and they can ignore me. In effect, they do so. Because the young people of the present day are not to be persuaded. They feel that they know best. And, as you say, one no longer has any power. As for myself, I'm not a man of strong will. Possibly, even, I have supported the very things that have limited my own power. I can plead, but I can't insist. To insist would seem to me—as well as to them—antediluvian."

"Of course you can't insist," declared Joe, pouring out the overbrewed tea and handing a cupful of dark brown liquid to Ferdinand. "We're agreed on that. You speak as if there had never been any young people until now; but there have always been young people, and self-conscious young people at that. Ours are only more self-glorifying than most, because they've jumped the claims of the middle-aged youngsters who lost a lustrum in the war; but in fact they're no more silly and talkative than the pre-Adamite young. And you can't do anything, because you're dealing with something as uncontrollable as the seasons and the spheres. But at the same time I'm bound to say I think you've brought the whole trouble on yourself."

"Oh, dear!" Ferdinand murmured. "This is very unwelcome."

"I knew it would be. But you had a couple of charming kids, and you couldn't leave them alone. You cosseted them; you taught them to love you and look to you for everything; and then you tired of them."

"No!" cried Ferdinand, in what, for him, was a loud voice.

"At any rate, you turned them loose on the world."

"As they grew up I certainly wanted them to have some social life."

"Well, they're torn between old loyalty to you—or love—or whatever it may be called—and the natural instincts of their young bodies. It's bound to be so where motherless girls are concerned. The father swallows them. Then he disgorges them. He's really responsible for their emotional vagaries. I'm sure of this."

"Then what else could I have done?" asked Ferdinand, astonished and horrified. "You make me appear a perfect monster."

Joe shrugged. Perhaps he had expected a defence—or at any rate something other than a question.

"I don't know," he admitted. "Certainly you're not a monster. You've half killed them with kindness; and this is a revolt against that, too. It doesn't *do* to treat women with kindness. They're incapable of understanding it. But you could have given them another mother. Treated 'em rough. Anything *except* make them revolve round *you.*"

"Oh, come!" cried Ferdinand impatiently. "You speak as though everything were so simple. It's nothing of the kind. Besides, you think of both girls as having had similar experience. It's not so. Rhoda——" His speech was checked. It was suddenly clear to him that Joe had all the time been speaking only of Rhoda. "In both cases," he went on, "I've allowed a great deal of freedom. But indeed that isn't in question. My one idea has been to make both of the girls happy. But, of course, I've exercised a certain amount of control. After all——" He became incoherent. Indignation was rising. His heart was swollen in his breast. He felt that he was being cruelly accused.

"If that's your idea of control, then you must take the consequences," Joe said. "All I know is that apparently it has produced some recent inconvenience to yourself."

"Inconvenience!" cried Ferdinand. "Good God!"

"Anything else? The girls are still at home. They're safe. They're not ruined. Jabez won't ruin either of them, at any rate."

"You use the word 'ruin' very loosely."

"Choose another word. Spoiled, deceived, enslaved——"

"That may be so. But, assuming this appearance of danger is, as you say, false, or even only temporary, I'm still alarmed, Joe. I can't help being alarmed."

"Needlessly, in Jabez's case. He's as honest as bread and meat. In Punch Teed's, I can't say."

"Simply—yes, I understand. But in the case of Talbot. Have you thought of the poverty, the squalor—the effects of such a life on a sensitive girl? I can see the future too clearly."

"I can't see the future at all," admitted Joe bluntly. "Perhaps it's as well. But it seems to me that your picture doesn't arise from what we've been saying."

"Doesn't it? I wonder. Would *you*," began Ferdinand, "would *you* look on Talbot as the ideal—or even as a suitable—husband for Catherine?"

"For Catherine——"

That was all. Joe did not answer for a moment. He sat in his chair, with his hands clasped, his head lowered, and

his eyes very nearly closed. Then he looked directly at Ferdinand and said:

"What's the matter with him?" His voice, it seemed, was
harsh with a kind of vicarious resentment. He was very cold,
very composed; and his gaze was steady and accusing.

"To me, everything," answered Ferdinand.

"Nonsense!"

"I must insist—everything."

"Then I don't understand what qualities you need in a
husband. He's got the only qualities I value. Almost all of
them, at least."

Ferdinand frowned deeply and touched his lips with the
fingers of his left hand.

"Would you feel as calm if he were going to marry
Gwen?" he asked.

"Oh, Gwen," laughed Joe. "Gwen will follow her own
course, anyway."

"You have no authority over her?" pressed Ferdinand.

"None. Don't want any."

"Yet you're *in loco parentis*. And yet Gwen, your sister,
can hardly be less dear to you than my girls—or less dear
to you than they are to me." Even as he spoke, his heart sank
deeper and deeper, for he knew that Joe would not be found
wanting an answer to his questions. He was right. There was
an answer.

"The cases are different." Joe said briefly enough. "Gwen
knows the world. She's lived a different life. She's been
mixing with these people all her life. She's alive to all their
ways. If she slips, it will be from infatuation. That's a thing
one can't guard against, in old or young. But it won't be
from ignorance, from innocence. I've taught her a great deal.
I've laughed at her, and let her laugh at me. There's no train-
ing like it. You've never laughed at Rhoda or taught her to
laugh at you. Or Catherine either, for that matter."

Ferdinand, who had leant forward in asking all his questions, fell back once more in his chair.

"All this is true; and yet how little you know," he muttered. "How little you know! So much and so little!"

Joe smiled, as it seemed to Ferdinand, with cool indifference. His air was almost one of indulgent kindness.

"Almost nothing at all," he acknowledged.

"No; even that isn't true. I think you know a great deal. I think you know much more than you're ready to tell me."

"I think a great deal more than I *can* tell you. If I were to begin to tell you everything I think, you'd have the right to call me a prig. Also, I should annoy you very much. Also, I couldn't help you any more than I've done."

"Oh, yes," Ferdinand said courteously.

"I don't feel that my opinion is generally very welcome. I give it, sometimes, out of sheer determination to be unpleasant; but on the whole I think it's better to be usefully silent. The rest is only ornament, you know."

Ferdinand thought: "He despises me!" A shudder ran through him at that thought. More than a shudder. He looked furtively at Joe, to find him sunken in his chair, without any of his habitual animation. Joe seemed to be looking at some vision of his own, a miserable one, which crushed him. But even as Ferdinand watched him Joe jerked his shoulders and sat upright, a faint smile upon his lips. And as he saw this Ferdinand felt his own heart sinking, sinking. He felt sore and ashamed, as Joe had foretold, with the notion that he had exposed himself to an unfriendly eye. The knowledge came to him that whereas we can never understand the causes of our own misfortunes we can always very clearly see the cause of the misfortunes of others. From shame arose self-condemnation; from self-condemnation a resentment of criticism; and from resentment a coldness. A coldness that made Ferdinand shudder again. His glance at Joe was chilled, malicious; but something within him was broken. Presently he could not keep his eyes level, but dropped them. He was bitterly mortified.

"I misjudged you," continued Ferdinand, at length. "And

yet I'm not sure that I did. No; I merely thought it possible
—it was an impulse—that you might be willing to help me."

Did his voice tremble? He hoped it was steady. He hoped
it gave no sign of his humiliation.

"I *have* helped you," retorted Joe, with quiet cruelty. He
was in earnest. Ferdinand thought him still more pale than
usual, though he appeared unmoved. "But as yet you can
hardly tell how much. I've helped you by doing something
to clear your mind."

Ferdinand rose from his chair. Instinctively he put his
hands behind him, in concealment.

"You think it was clotted?" he said coolly. "Quite true,
you *have* helped me. Perhaps by oblique means. Perhaps I
can't see at the moment how much. Yes, I may see more in
this when I think it over."

"I'm sure you will," agreed Joe, with a quick air of cordiality which was not quite a success. "I shall come to call on
you very soon, to find out how much use I've been."

And at that the consultation came to an end; and Ferdinand groped his way down the stairs, more depressed by
several degrees than he had been when he ascended them.
He had made his appeal for help; and it had been rejected.
With his heart burning, a little patch of pink in either
cheek, and a dryness of the lips which he could not over-
come, he stood hesitatingly upon the pavement below. One
impulse drove him this way and another drove him that.
Finally he turned to the left, towards that little court from
which, an hour before, Joe had emerged. It led towards Holborn. It led—did Ferdinand realize it?—towards Mrs. Balthazar.

CHAPTER III

DANGER

I

IT LED towards Mrs. Balthazar. Everything led towards Mrs. Balthazar. Stealthily there had come into Ferdinand's mind the insatiable craving of the affrighted soul for pity. He would have been ready to stoop for that. He would have stooped even to Joe Gascoyne. Only from Catherine and from Rhoda would he now deliberately hide his heart. Towards them, Ferdinand was all pride.

And so he turned to the left and stepped into the dark little court, where a newspaper shop snuggled upon one side, while the shop of a dealer in antiques radiated its own gloomy charm upon the other. At the end of the court, under a house beneath which the passageway ran, he could see red omnibuses glittering in the reflected lights of shop windows, and people walking, their faces suddenly ghastly in the white light. Then they were past, both people and omnibuses, and Ferdinand himself was within the range of that bitter brilliance, corpse-like under its eye.

Even now he hesitated. He was a shy man, drawn vaguely and aspiringly towards something which he believed to be necessary to his peace of mind. His dry lips parted; he swallowed quickly. Should he venture thus to seek sympathy from a stranger? A stranger, too, who was not his social equal? The doubts arose only to be dispelled with indignation. What! A stranger? No stranger, but a friend. Not only a friend but one who knew unhappiness. She was a friend, and a sympathetic friend. As for social equality, Ferdinand raised his shoulders. Surely the Devil himself had whispered that thought into his ear. Was he not living in the Twentieth Century, when democracy reigned without fear? There were nowadays no social orders—only the wise and the jealous! And besides, the impulse was too strong to be resisted. Friendship, consolation, understanding, Ferdinand must have. Without them he would perish. He crossed the busy street.

Another pause followed as he saw the dim shadow of Mrs. Balthazar's shop. It was all but in darkness. A single bulb burned somewhere in the background; but the window was unillumined, the fronds of fern were ghostly in the dusk, the place had the air of being deserted. For perhaps a minute Ferdinand stood near the doorway, drawn hither and thither by his wish and his fear. His fear made him draw back, shrug his shoulders in pretended indifference, and pooh-pooh his own eagerness; his wish plucked him back whenever he would have gone upon his way. At length, in an access of courage, he entered, waiting timidly, turning his eyes uneasily towards the window, and then down towards some very pale pink roses which rested there as if they were growing. The roses reminded him, in their silent beauty, of Catherine. He thought instantly of all his suffering because of her danger; and his face became haggard. An impatience seized him. He could not keep still but was forced to walk about in the cramped space among the flowers and the fern.

And then Mrs. Balthazar came from the little cupboard-like room behind the shop, peering slightly, as if at first she did not identify her visitor. When she did so, she gave a small cry.

"Oh!" said she. "I *thought* I heard somebody come in. Somebody very quiet. It was *you!*"

It was strange for Ferdinand to think how greatly her manner towards him had changed. At the first, he remembered, it had been very quiet and dignified, and as if she had some fastidious, defensive suspicion of him. Now it was all gentleness. Ferdinand had the feeling that she had resisted a quick readiness to come forward and lay her hand upon his arm.

"Perhaps you're busy," Ferdinand suggested, his heart lightened. "I wonder if you are."

"Busy? Where's all the people, then?" She looked with delightful pertness about the shop. "No; I'm not busy. And besides——" Ferdinand could hardly see her expressive pout. "You come into my little cubbyhole. It's cramped but it's warm. No, I've been reading a book. That shows how busy I am. I'm glad to see you."

She led the way into that stuffy cupboard, and there, as she had said, a book lay upon the table. She could not have read very much of it, because the book lay open at its first page. It was clear that she had been determined to read, perhaps to clear her mind of unhappy thoughts; but the thoughts had been more powerful than the printed words. No wonder she was glad to see Ferdinand!

Now that he could observe her more distinctly he felt sure that she had been suffering. There was as great a change in her appearance since that first occasion as he had distinguished in her manner. There was greater gentleness, greater appealingness. She looked as though, if one were to be very kind to her, she would begin slowly and helplessly to cry. And, as ever, he shrank from provoking any demonstration of such feeling. Nevertheless, he was greatly touched by the pathos of Mrs. Balthazar's bearing; and his pity must have been evident to her, for as she spoke again he saw tears glistening in her eyes.

"There, that's better!" she exclaimed, as Ferdinand seated himself. "You wouldn't believe how glad I am to see you. I've still got Auntie ill, you know. Poor old thing, she's been quite bad. And trade's bad. Everything's bad. And I haven't seen anybody I like for ever such a long time. I begin to feel quite neglected. But now *you've* come, it's different. I shan't grumble and grizzle any more. How are you? You look a bit better than you did; but not well, you know. There's *something*. I shan't forget how kind you were the other day. I wasn't well. I was silly. It's not like me. But you get mopey, being in a place like this, especially if you're alone. You hardly know what you're saying. At least, I don't. I expect you always do. That's the benefit of a college education: you always know what you're doing and saying."

She smiled as she spoke, and bent forward. Ferdinand thought that he had never seen anything more prettily appealing than her manner. It united a kind of deference to an ingratiating familiarity.

"Oh, yes, I'm better," he said. "But, like yourself, dispirited. There seem to be times when all that one does—even when it is done with the best intentions—recoils in failure upon one's own head, as if intention counted for nothing whatever. Have you noticed that?"

"Yes," she sighed languidly, as if she had not fully understood.

"I sometimes feel that I'm growing old," proceeded Ferdinand, subtly cheered by her incredulous laughter at such an idea. "As though I were a little unfitted to cope with the—I think it must be called *mock* turbulence—of the day. So much is going on that I can't enter into."

"What nonsense!" cried Mrs. Balthazar. The tears had gone from her eyes, which had grown bright and interested. "Why, you're not *old*."

Ferdinand raised his shoulders in humorous deprecation.

"Some people would think I was," he murmured.

"Well, *I* don't!" she asserted warmly. "I think you're in the prime of life. That's what I mean! People seem to think that as soon as you turn forty—I don't mean that *I've* turned forty——"

"Oh!" Ferdinand lifted both his hands in protest at so unneeded a disclaimer.

"Well, they do, *really*. You know, they think youth is everything. So silly of them!"

Ferdinand was aware of her close regard and of a curious sharpening of those delicate features. But he was gratified by her obvious readiness to defend him against any irresponsible charge of age.

"I think they *are* silly," he admitted. "But more than that I feel that the way young people have nowadays of regarding all—what I may call moral problems—is a little disconcerting. Do you feel that, too?"

"Oh, I *do*," Mrs. Balthazar agreed. "Very. It's so—well, I don't know what to call it."

"Not quite cynical," continued Ferdinand.

"No," she hesitatingly agreed. "No, perhaps not. And yet, you know, it *is*, in a way."

"A sort of hardness—eh, cruelty——" He paused, endeavouring to find the correct word.

"Both hard *and* cruel," cried Mrs. Balthazar. *"Very* cruel. But then, I think they *are* cruel. Of course, you know, I've seen a lot of that—I mean, if I were to tell you all the cruelty I've known in my life—" the tears once more started to her eyes, but she proceeded, ignoring them—"I believe you'd be sorry for me—just a *little* sorry for me."

"I'm sure I should," said Ferdinand. "I am already."

"Are you?" It was so quickly, faintly said, with such a gentle glance, which resembled that of a child, that Ferdinand unconsciously shook his head in warm-hearted pity. "I believe you are. Just fancy you being sorry for *me*."

"I think we ought to be a little sorry for each other," murmured Ferdinand whimsically.

"Do you?" It was almost a sigh. Mrs. Balthazar's eyes closed for a moment. Her left hand, which had rested upon the edge of the table, slid imperceptibly forward, in the direction of Ferdinand. He saw it there, lying so very much nearer to him, the arm white, shapely, and plump, the hand slightly reddened and darkened by work and constant contact with the flowers and baskets; and his own hand, which had hung unseen by his side, took to itself an independent life, so that it rose to the level of the table, and came to a stop there. Both he and Mrs. Balthazar were smiling—she a little breathlessly—when there came an interruption to their talk. The sound of the front door of the shop being pushed open and the sound of a walking stick tapping upon the floor without caused Mrs. Balthazar to jump to her feet.

"Sh!" She put her finger to her lips, slipped through the doorway, and was gone.

Ferdinand, sitting there for a moment longer, was urged by unexamined emotion to stand upright, leaning with one hand upon the back of the chair. He allowed his eyes to roam about the little room, from the open book to the bare walls of matchboarding, from the chair and the radiator to the rug or strip of carpet beneath his feet. What a narrow life this was for any woman, he thought! How could she live and breathe here? Wonderful as she was (to be the product of such surroundings), what might she not have become if circumstances had been kinder? What infinite treasures might not a life of ease open to such a one? He could imagine her sparkling before every new wonder with which she might be brought into contact. Not the excited rapture of a child, sweet and thrilling, but the thankful marvel of a starved mind and heart, before such beauty as had never been conceived. Wonderful experience. Wonderful, enviable. . . . There was no end to the fascination of that imagined picture. Ferdinand was lost in contemplation of it. And then he was astonished to feel that his heart had begun to beat rather more rapidly than was its wont.

He had hardly realized this before the shop door was shut and Mrs. Balthazar reappeared. At sight of Ferdinand standing her expression changed from one of gaiety to one of arch disappointment. But she did not urge him to sit down again. Instead, she remained standing where she was, her lips parted, looking up at him through her eyelashes with an air of quaint wisdom and expectancy.

II

"That was a man wanted some roses," she explained. "I let him have them cheap to get rid of them. Shan't get my money back, I don't expect. Not on them. That's *you!*" She smiled again, very archly. "Aren't you an encouragement to business!"

"I'd better go before I quite ruin your exchequer!" exclaimed Ferdinand. But he did not move.

"My what? Oh, you needn't go yet. I was only joking about that. Besides, we haven't nearly said all we were going to say, have we? You remember—" she faltered—"you remember, you were just going to be a little sorry for me." Her head was cocked.

"So I was," admitted Ferdinand. "So I *am.*"

"But you don't know why!" She came a step closer, looking up into his face.

"On general grounds," Ferdinand said.

"Oh!" She was rueful. "Is that all? I thought perhaps it was something else."

"Something else?" reflected Ferdinand. He was not looking at her for a moment; and when, baffled, he glanced again, he was surprised to find that she had come close beside him. "But you were to be sorry for me, too," he said aloud. He was smiling; the tips of his fingers were tingling. "Wasn't that the arrangement?"

"Yes." She was holding her head so that he could not see her face.

"Well?" asked Ferdinand.

Mrs. Balthazar caught his arm, and pressed it to her side.

"You're lovely!" she exclaimed. "Just lovely! And as *good!*" Her clasp of his arm was light. It relaxed. And when Ferdinand did not move but looked down in silence upon that fair head and the white neck, it tightened once more. He could feel her shoulder below his own, soft and firm. What confidence she had in him! What gratitude she gave for his trifling help! Gratitude, confidence. . . . Perception of something more than the moment came to him. Something that aroused dormant feelings within his heart. It was as though he began to awaken from a dream. He listened almost anxiously, almost desirously for the opening of the shop door. There was no sound without but that of the rumbling of traffic in Holborn. Within there was his own breathing, steady, regular, but more rapid than usual. Involuntarily Ferdinand drew away—not with abruptness, but with a gentle stealth that was far more expressive of the perception which had arisen in his mind. Mrs. Balthazar looked up.

Her eyes were tearless. They were limpid. Her lips, to any but Ferdinand, would have been irresistible. But she made no movement except that she quickly released his arm, still smiling. If she sighed Ferdinand did not hear her. He only saw the smile deepen; and smiled gravely in his turn, tempted, resolute, again tempted. Could Mrs. Balthazar know that? Had she the unerring knowledge of the woman of—should he say—experience? The diabolical knowledge of male vacillation? He could detect no knowledge—other than all knowledge—in her contemplative glance. There was no scorn; no impatience; no disappointment in that glance. If she felt one or other or all of these emotions she had the unfathomable gift of concealing them. Her smile was without malice.

"I feel much better!" she declared. "Do I look it?"

Ferdinand was compelled closely to scrutinize her face, now once more, under the stress of her increased happiness, almost as lovely as it had ever been.

"I think you do," he at last proclaimed.

"Only *think*? Is *that* all?" The eyes danced. "Not sure, then?" Ferdinand could not speak. He could only bow. Mrs. Balthazar turned away. "There's something about you—" she said—"I don't know what it is, but somehow you *make* me feel happy. I simply can't help it. I suppose it's because you're so kind. So *good*."

Was there a dryness at last? His ear was alert for that. He would have caught more than the reality. At least Ferdinand did not run away.

"I have always tried to be both kind and good," he said. "But I think perhaps that is what has caused all my troubles. It sometimes happens that kindness and goodness aren't appreciated at their true value by others."

"How shocking!" cried Mrs. Balthazar. "Aren't people awful! But—" she hesitated—"have you *always* been kind and good? All your life, I mean?"

"Oh, I couldn't remember," laughed Ferdinand. "You mustn't ask me to go back so far."

"I hope you haven't," she commented unexpectedly. "You know what I mean—I mean, one likes somebody to be a little *human,* now and then."

"I hope I'm that," said Ferdinand quickly. "I've always tried to be."

She gave him a swift look, smiled, and went to the door.

"Wait a minute," she called. "I'm going to bring you something."

For a second time Ferdinand was left alone in the cubicle. But he did not now glance about him but sat with narrowed eyes staring directly at the wall. He saw nothing. Before him, in imagination, were two blue eyes, a pair of soft lips, a white neck. He heard a soft voice in his ear, felt a soft arm holding and pressing his own arm. So vivid was the memory that when Mrs. Balthazar returned from her excursion to the shop, Ferdinand was quite startled by her reappearance. She seemed like a dream that had turned by some very earthly miracle to reality.

III

"I've brought you a rose," she said. "I think you ought to have one. There! Isn't that a lovely one? It's the nicest I've got. Now, hold still; I'm going to pin it in for you. Wait while I get a pin and then you'll see what you'll see!"

Ferdinand, staring at the rose, was transfixed. It was one of those pale pink roses that he had seen in the shop upon his arrival. And it reminded him still of Catherine. He could not draw his eyes away from the rose because of that association. Catherine, the rose, Catherine——

"Here we are!" cried Mrs. Balthazar. "Now!"

She took the rose in her hand, reached up to the lapel of Ferdinand's coat, passed the stalk through the buttonhole, tiptoeing in order to perform her task quite perfectly. Catherine—the rose—Catherine—— Catherine—the rose—— Although he held his head stiffly back, Ferdinand could not prevent his eyes from glancing down at that little round face, the lips pursed seriously, and at the raised arms and busy, nimble hands. Catherine—the rose—— She was so quick; and the task was so long. It seemed endless. Memory of Catherine faded. The rose would not stay as Mrs. Balthazar set it. She pressed closer and closer to Ferdinand in her intentness, her hands upon his breast, her lips drawn adorably together, her eyelids low, so that he could just catch a brightness through the lashes. No more of Catherine. Even the rose was forgotten. Involuntarily, Ferdinand put out his own hands, so that they lightly touched her body. He smiled; he saw Mrs. Balthazar smile. She smiled with a curious demureness which made him half ready to speculate—a demureness that recalled his first impression of something almost sleek in her movements. And as he noticed the smile, and the pressure of her body, Mrs. Balthazar finished arranging the rose in his buttonhole and freed her hands, lightly patting his breast as a sort of caress. She did not withdraw her hands, but looked quickly up, lifting her face higher than before.

Ferdinand's sight was blurred by a moisture which rose inexplicably to his eyes. He looked down at that tempting smile, at the pursed lips, the little pointed nose. He hesitated. Mrs. Balthazar's hand crept to his shoulders, rested a moment, and so, upward, to his cheeks. He stooped. Their lips did not meet; but while Ferdinand's brushed that soft cheek clumsily Mrs. Balthazar gave him a light kiss not far from the right-hand corner of his mouth.

"There!" she said hastily, breathlessly. "There's a flower and a kiss for you. Just to show how much I like you! Aren't I a bold, bad woman? That's what you think of me, isn't it?"

She did not move, but kept her hands to Ferdinand's cheeks, her breast against his own.

She was smiling; but her eyes shone and her mouth was hard with defiant defensiveness.

"No," said Ferdinand, taking her hands and stepping backwards. "That's not what I think."

"No? What, then?" It was a sigh.

"I think you are kind to an old man—an unhappy old man."

"Old!" She laughed. "Who told you you were old? Those girls of yours? You know why they do that, don't you?"

Those girls—Catherine—Rhoda! Memory rose urgently within him. Catherine—Rhoda—and he, here! Shock after shock of perception ran through Ferdinand. He had caught the roughness of Mrs. Balthazar's tone, the roughness which indicated that she was interposing herself between Ferdinand and Catherine, Ferdinand and Rhoda! Ah! Not thus was he to be wooed! To acquiescence in this too easy, too pleasant forgetfulness of sorrow succeeded vehemently a sense of shame, a sense of suspicion. He held himself so still, and his face so rigid, that Mrs. Balthazar could not read what was passing in his mind. She could be quick to seize any movement of aversion (and physical aversion there was none); but she could not guess at the loyalties which lay deep in Ferdinand's heart. Confidently, she continued:

"Don't tell me! They make out you're old because they like the young men best! They don't know! Do they? You're turning away; don't you like me, then? You're not looking at me!"

There came an unexpected tapping—three slow taps and a

rattle, like a signal—at the door of the shop. It was Mrs. Balthazar who freed her hands. She pulled herself sharply away from Ferdinand. Her face had grown perfectly white. He heard her give a painful cry, saw her shrink back farther and farther. For an instant—and all this passed in but a single instant—she seemed to be bereft of all presence of mind. Then, in a whisper, she said:

"You must stay here. You must be very quiet. There's somebody there. Keep quiet! Stay here——"

"No!" cried Ferdinand. "I won't. I must go."

"Sh!"

Unheeding, she pushed him sharply with her hand, as if to force him to stay concealed; and then, as the door of the shop was opened, she almost ran from him. There was no time for more, no time for delay. He must go instantly, without explanation or understanding. Quickly as Mrs. Balthazar moved, Ferdinand was as quick. He followed her from the little room into the green dimness.

Standing just within the door he could see the tall figure of a man, but the man's face was hidden, and Ferdinand was too confused and too eager to be gone to do more than receive a vague impression of height and bulk. He hastened, keeping his head low; and he did not even look up as he came abreast of the stranger.

"Good-night, good-night," muttered Ferdinand. "Thank you so very much, Mrs. Balthazar."

It was over. She did not reply or move, but seemed as if she were paralyzed by the interruption. The man by the door stood aside to let him pass. Ferdinand, walking quickly, gained the street, where the flood of human beings, homeward bound from work, seemed to gather and carry him onward, unresisting, as so much flotsam upon its surface. He was trembling violently. The excitement of the scene in which he had been engaged, the disturbing conflict which had arisen within himself at memory of Catherine and Rhoda, the sudden change of Mrs. Balthazar's manner at that strange tapping, and the appearance of the tall stranger—all crowded his mind with feverish bewilderment. As he walked he tottered; his hands shook; there was nothing in his heart but pain and horror. Too plainly, even in his confusion, he realized from her collapse into furtiveness that there was mystery in Mrs. Balthazar's actions. Did it relate to himself or to this other? To himself—ah, Ferdinand's cheeks burned. That he should thus have sunk—that he should thus know the ignominy of flight. . . .

With ejaculations of dismay and despair of which in his tempest of feeling he was unconscious Ferdinand made his way through the crowds. He was even thankful that they were there to envelop him, as a mantle, and hide by their numbers his almost hysterical access of self-loathing. Thoughts mounted in his mind with such rapidity that he was convulsed by their tumult. Choking, suffocated, he hurried through the ghastly whiteness of the night-illumined streets, intent only upon escape and forgetfulness.

CHAPTER IV

BREAKING POINT

I

IT WAS quite dark by the time Ferdinand reached home. Heavy clouds were assembling, and a wind which was as cold as that of any winter day had sprung up. Ferdinand, arriving at the house shaken and buffeted, went directly to his study, more thankful to be there than he had ever been. With the door closed and the blinds drawn, he could feel— at least momentarily—safe. But what was he to do? In which- ever direction he looked the same threatening darkness con- fronted him. He was without friends. He was deserted. That which had hitherto represented his whole interest in life was about to be shattered. Not Ferdinand, but Catherine, but Rhoda, had been his first thought. And the result was seen. Bitterly he turned again and again in his mind the question of their ingratitude.

"Always! Always!" he ejaculated aloud. "Have they no *sense?* Is nothing due to me for all the loving care I have given them? None. Never!" He had known it for years. A hundred instances of this obtuseness of theirs rushed into his mind. At such a time examples are never wanting, treasured as they have unconsciously been, far below common under- standings, waiting malevolently for their hour of opportunity. And yet he loved these children as much as he had always done. "It would seem that my love is an offence!" groaned Ferdinand in anguish. "Unforgivable! To be repaid by every cruelty!"

His thoughts took another turn. His mind, inflammable as cotton waste, in which the flames dart and gather before they blaze into savage triumph, took fire. He lived over again the moments of his visit to Joe. Humiliation possessed him. Here again nothing but criticism, a refusal to admit right and sympathy. Gascoyne—he had himself used the word "prig"—was none other. He had guarded himself; but such feeling as he showed had been with the girls. To *them* he would grant liberty, but not to Ferdinand. Good God, was there nothing at all in the life of the day but indulgence of the young?

Another turn. Swiftly came that vivid picture of Mrs. Balthazar. Ferdinand could see her in her slimness, the milky throat rising from her black dress, the veiled eyes. He could feel her gentle hands and the softness of her lips upon his cheek. Irrepressible impatience seized him. He started to his feet, pacing up and down the room, his two hands upon the lapels of his coat. Wild distrusts ran through his mind— vehemently, like the shocks of a March wind. Was she pure? Was she true? And if not? If not? What was it to him? Pooh, a mere acquaintance; a flower seller; a little woman of whom he knew nothing, as to whom he cared nothing. Did he not? Nothing! Nothing! Nothing!

So explosively he cried aloud, with memory of Mrs. Balthazar's fairness rising before his eyes, memories of his yielding to her charm causing him yet to tremble. The stranger whose coming had led her to abandon all, who was he? A lover? Ferdinand was racked. Well, and if a lover? A younger man than himself. But she had said, of younger men—she had said of himself—— Ah, he was old. That crude, that cruel suggestion of hers, that Catherine and Rhoda, like the commonest of their sex, had use for nothing but youth, rankled afresh. It was supported by his recent agonies. But she—Mrs. Balthazar—despairingly did Ferdinand strike one hand against the other. He was old; he was old. His head was gray, his spirit was shaken. The perception was very bitter. It was like acid upon his ardour.

Supposing—that was the intuition which he was refusing

to allow himself to receive—supposing Mrs. Balthazar had been made unhappy; supposing in her distress she had sought to turn himself to account. . . . The thought was maddening. But if it was maddening, there was a reason which could be found. It would not be maddening if he, this old man, believed himself to be old, believed himself to be too old to succumb to the temptations of—of what? Of love? Absurd! It was absurd.

"It is absurd!" cried Ferdinand aloud, trembling, and his cheeks hot with embarrassment.

"Is it absurd?" whispered a voice within him. "Then who has been made absurd?"

In such a mood the strangest, the wildest, the most terrible thoughts come to young and old. The shames to which human beings are subject as a result of their own imaginings, their own self-accusation, are inconceivable by other human beings, who see only the outer shell and never think to look beyond it.

II

At length, wearied and aghast, he felt that he could no longer bear his solitude. At all costs he must leave this room, which had grown stale with his unhappy struggle. Elsewhere, he might find Catherine; and Catherine, although she might mock at his wishes, would at all times tranquillize him. She would speak of indifferent subjects, and he would forget all these ugly imaginings until he was once again alone, doomed to sleeplessness and self-torture. He started towards the door.

Everything in the house was still. Listening, he could hear nothing but the ticking of the grandfather clock which stood near him in a corner by the stairs. Silently he closed his own door and moved across the landing to the door of the drawing room. Here, too, all was silence. The room was but dimly lighted, and Ferdinand's heart sank at the thought that his desire for company was to be baulked. But as he was about to withdraw he caught the faintest sound, just such a sound as might have been made by a light sigh. It checked him. Was somebody there? He looked towards the sunken fire; and as his eyes grew more used to the darkness he saw that Rhoda was half sitting, half reclining upon the hearthrug, her head resting against the seat of an armchair, her shoulders huddled, and her arms extended so that her hands lay listlessly together.

Should he go? Apparently Rhoda, so absorbed in her own reverie, had not heard any sound of Ferdinand's entrance. She was so still that she might have been sleeping. But that she was awake Ferdinand was convinced. He knew that she must have sighed. Only the craving for company which had driven him from his own room now urged him to stay; and he deliberately, in closing the door, allowed the lock to click in order that the noise might announce his approach.

"Are you there?" Ferdinand then said, advancing into the room. His simulation of nonchalance was pathetic enough; but it would serve. No very strict examination would be held by Rhoda. And as for Ferdinand himself, pride forbade that he should allow any trace of his emotion to be seen by either of his daughters.

"Daddy?" Rhoda gave a jump and sat upright, so that she was supported by one hand. Her head was thrown back and she looked at him from an upturned face. "You startled me."

"How dark it is in here," Ferdinand said fretfully. "Have you got a headache?" He stooped to tend the fire and took his seat upon the other fireside armchair. "I thought I should find Catherine here—not you. Have you been out?"

All these brief speeches were addressed to her nervously in the effort to build up a conversation. And so he did not wait for answers to his questions, but sat back in the chair, his eyes half closed. He had been so much agitated that his mind would not function properly. He thought of words, of topics, and forgot them before they could be introduced. His fingers pressed and wound about each other so feverishly that they hurt, and he continuously bit his under lip. But this, of course, Rhoda could not see. Nor did she show any interest in his inquiries. Ferdinand saw, as the flames began to rise about the recently added coal, that she was sitting upright, with her back against the chair and the weight of her body supported still by one hand. She was looking neither at Ferdinand nor at the fire, but at the little patch of darkness created by the fender's interposition. Her face was very serious, as if she were deep in thought.

At last Rhoda moved. Her hand had grown painful. In a strange voice she answered Ferdinand.

"No, I haven't been out. I haven't seen Catherine."

"She's probably with Mona."

For the first time, Rhoda looked at Ferdinand. The mention of Mona had aroused her.

"Yes?" she said listlessly. "It doesn't matter."

Ferdinand, listening, was stirred to vague irritation by her indifference. He, too, moved, drawing his hands apart with difficulty and forcing himself to sit still in his chair. A few months ago, how impossible this strained silence between them would have been! Rhoda's vivacity, in those days, was incessant; how different, now, was her hostile shrinking from any intimacy of conversation!

"Excepting as it shows her inclination," he struggled to say, "I've made it clear to Catherine that I don't approve of what she's doing. More, I can hardly do."

"What inclination is that, Father?" asked Rhoda, suddenly alert. "I don't see what you mean."

"You surely can't be blind to Catherine's actions," Ferdinand coldly answered.

"I am, indeed," she returned, closely watching him.

"To her meetings with that fellow," continued Ferdinand. "Although no doubt she doesn't parade them. Rhoda, I'm extremely uncomfortable about Catherine. She's admitted to me——"

"What has she admitted?" demanded Rhoda harshly. She

had roused herself and was sitting there quite tense. Ferdinand could see her marble face in the firelight.

"You know perfectly well my antagonism to Talbot. I haven't to express it. His personality, his opinions, his behaviour—— And yet for some reason Catherine has developed this partiality——"

"Ridiculous!" exclaimed Rhoda vehemently. "My dear Father!"

"I've *told* her that it's ridiculous," began Ferdinand. "She seems not to be able to see it."

"But the *idea* is ridiculous!" cried Rhoda. "It's not possible. I don't mean what you've told Catherine. I mean that what you *believe* is ridiculous. I'm telling you that you're mistaken.

"I wish I were," said Ferdinand sharply. "Unfortunately I'm not."

Rhoda shrugged with impatience.

"It's impossible to argue," she cried. "It's absurd to do so. But really, Father, you're quite mistaken. I can assure you."

"I'm *not* mistaken," replied Ferdinand obstinately. "I've *seen* them together. Besides, as I say, Catherine has quite clearly made the admission to me. I'm not in the habit, I hope, of imagining absurdities or manufacturing opinions. In this case I wish I were."

Rhoda's head was bowed. She did not answer him. She had clearly made up her mind not to answer him further. Ferdinand, because this resistance had aroused his temper, went on talking.

"It was a very unfortunate day for us when Talbot was brought here. It wasn't done at my instance. It was an accident. *You* had met him, and had seen that he was a dislikable person. He had been rude to you, and you had resented it. Then, it appears, Mona, thinking to heal the breach, begged to be allowed to bring him here. I remember the evening. It was the evening Edmund Piercy said that——"

Horrified at the proximity of a fatal reference to Punch

Teed, Ferdinand checked himself abruptly. He felt hot at the danger which had been so narrowly averted. His embarrassment caused him to stammer for an instant before he proceeded.

"From the *first* Catherine seemed to be impressed by him. She talked to him all the evening. I thought nothing of it. I supposed it to be common courtesy to a stranger. But since then, at first from her hint, and then——" He dropped into vague thoughts. "But *you* were right, my darling; you were right all the time. You saw that he had a bitter, invincible ignorance, an ugliness of temper. There's a great deal to be said for that faculty which is so much laughed at nowadays —the faculty of feminine intuition."

Rhoda did not at first answer him. At last, sarcastically, she said:

"I suppose Catherine—although she's a woman—has none of that."

"Less, I think, than you, my dear. Catherine thinks more than you do, but she feels less."

"But you say she has feeling for Jabez."

Ferdinand started—less at the point than at the tone in which it was made.

"I should have said that she feels less acutely."

"I wonder if that's true," pondered Rhoda. "Poor Catherine! I wonder if she really feels anything at all. She seems so contented. It would kill me to be so contented. Perhaps she's dead already."

"My dear!"

"Yes, I know you're shocked, Father. You never can realize that there is so much going on that you're unaware of. The thought of saying of a live person that she's dead seems to you horrid. It's like saying of a dead person that she's alive—rather morbid. Isn't that what you feel?"

"Catherine is not dead," replied Ferdinand.

"Not even in my sense? Sometimes I wonder if any of us are alive—any human beings at all. If we were alive, should we all be so hopeless and so dissatisfied? I used to think that it was only in dreams that one knew complete helplessness; but that isn't true. We're all so wretched——"

"Wretched, my darling! Are you still unhappy?" begged Ferdinand. "I do so wish it were possible for you to be happy again, as you were——"

"As I was?" prompted Rhoda mournfully. "When was I ever happy?"

"Surely until a very little while ago."

"No!"

"Rhoda!"

"You see, it's quite impossible to convince you of something you don't want to believe. And you can't realize that I——" She was choking. Quite suddenly Ferdinand knew that Rhoda must all the time have been in as great distress as himself. She was now so excited that her excitement could not have been aroused by anything he had said. More quietly she resumed, after a moment: "I was trying to say to you that you don't understand me. You still think of me as a child. You think that if I'm unhappy for an hour a little treat, or some sweets, or some flowers, will dismiss all that and make me happy again. It isn't so. I'm not happy because I'm dissatisfied. And you think that's *nothing*. You think it will pass. You don't know."

"Tell me!" urged Ferdinand.

"How can I? If I tell you that I *must* have love, you won't understand me."

"But you have it, my dearest."

"Preserved love. Condensed. Good enough for Catherine and for women such as Catherine. But for me, useless. I'm all feeling. There's nothing else there. It's my life. And I'm stifled, helpless! Wherever I turn I meet suffocation. If I try to escape—as I *have* tried—I meet—I meet shame—shame!" Her voice broke.

"Shame? Never!" cried Ferdinand. "You've always misunderstood that!"

"And now you come and speak to me of Catherine and Jabez, telling me of this and that, speaking of Catherine as if she were alive, when you must know that she hasn't any feeling but only a cold, prim little heart. She'd be sorry that I should suffer, but she'd suggest some medicine or another blanket. She would think I could be cured by a brisk walk or a dance—when all the time it's my spirit that's in torture. Oh, I despise her, I despise her. She's cold, she's sly. She hates me—no, not hates, not hates. She couldn't hate, because she has a cold heart. Poor Catherine! I *think* she's dead, Father. I think she *must* be dead. Don't you? Or do you think—yes, I'm sure you do! I can see your face. You're uncomfortable. You think I'm just a little distraught. Just a little mad. Isn't that so, Father? I'm sure you don't understand what I'm talking about. No, I can see you don't!"

"No, I don't understand," Ferdinand agreed.

She sprang up from the hearthrug.

"You never *will* understand!" she cried accusingly. "You refuse to understand!" Her hands were raised to her face. He could imagine them pressed in the darkness against her lips.

"Neither you nor Catherine do I understand," he said.

"Catherine!" exclaimed Rhoda. "Catherine! Always Catherine!" Her breath was sobbingly drawn.

"My dearest!" Ferdinand also rose, his hands outstretched towards her.

"D'you think I don't *see?* D'you think I don't *feel?* It's Catherine, now. You think of her. You don't love me any more. You despise me!"

"Rhoda! How can you speak so ridiculously!"

"It's true!" In anguish she faced him. "I know. I knew at once. I've seen. You used to love me——"

"I love you both!" cried Ferdinand, in extremity. "Good God! If I didn't, should I be so unhappy? I love you both equally."

"You used to love me best. I was your little girl! You

were always thinking of me, making games for me, loving me. Now, everything is changed. It's nothing to you if I'm unhappy—miserable——"

"And yet I've no other concern!" exclaimed Ferdinand. "Rhoda, you're hurting me unbearably!"

"You're hurting *me!* Everything's changed. Your love, your sympathy—everything is gone. I used to be able to tell you my thoughts, knowing that you would understand them. Now that's impossible. Not your fault only, Father; some of it is mine. I've been growing up. But the position now is quite hopeless. You haven't even seen, as I've done, how it has come about. I've seen it too clearly. You began to lose interest in me nearly a year ago. I was too demonstrative, perhaps. Well, I held off. I loved you too much to want to risk boring you. So I was more careful. I watched your mood more. But still I felt you loved me—loved me better than Catherine, better than all the world. And then, as you know, I met Punch. I told you about that. You didn't understand. You were shocked. It was something quite unthinkable to you. And it nearly broke my heart."

"It nearly broke mine," whispered Ferdinand.

"You see? It isn't thought of *me* that worries you. It's not thought of my growth or my need. Only the *convenances*. But for those I might suffer without your caring. But as soon as you thought I'd in some way disgraced you, you turned away from me. I think you hated me, then."

"Rhoda!" But he was horrified at the perception which underlay her words—the half truth of her passionate reading of his aversion.

"You turned to Catherine. *She,* you thought, would never disgrace you. She was quiet and prim. She was *good*. She could give you the feeling of stability you cared about. Not I. You left me alone. When I tried to appeal to your love you checked me. I was something—not unclean, but disagreeable. You could have nothing to do with me until I had been punished—purified. I was an outcast. I knew that. I was made to realize it. You had nothing to give me unless I admitted my sin. My sin! Where was my sin? It was in your mind—not in mine."

"It was never in *my* mind," protested Ferdinand.

"Disgust of me—aversion—you couldn't disguise it. You used to look at me out of the corner of your eye. In distrust. What should I be doing next? Something improper, something disgraceful! You were ready to wash your hands of me if I offended again. It was Catherine you approved. Catherine, who would never step outside her little boxed life. And so every day you and Catherine sat together, talking of my misdeeds—although my misdeeds were only in your own thoughts and were never real."

"Rhoda, all that you are saying is absolutely false. You've been suffering and you've attributed thoughts and speeches to Catherine and to me which neither of us has ever been aware of. We have *never* discussed you. I have *never* varied in my love for you. I admit that I was displeased—shocked, if you like—about what you had told me. It was a revelation of something I had never suspected. But I forgave you——"

"Forgave!" She was scornful.

"Yes, forgave!" cried Ferdinand defiantly. "For I can't admit the modern doctrine that children owe no duty to their parents. I think you had a duty of frankness to me. You were not frank. You deceived me——"

"I know. I admitted it. I was ashamed. I still *am* ashamed."

"It's your shame that has suggested all these suspicions of me. These suspicions are unjust. Rhoda, my dearest, you're excited now. You're ill. So am I. We're in no mood to talk quietly of these things. You're saying what you'll regret having said. So, perhaps, am I. Let's say no more, now, but talk quietly later, when we're both calmer."

"When I'm asphyxiated, Father. No, no. It's only when I'm worked up that I can bring myself to speak at all. It used not to be so——"

"And Catherine," pursued Ferdinand. "You're equally unjust to her!"

"Catherine, whom you now suspect as you suspect me! You think that Catherine is carrying on some clandestine intrigue with Jabez. You've been watching Catherine, it seems, as you watched me. You've found out that Catherine is as sly as I am. You're alarmed on *her* account now. It doesn't occur to you that the whole atmosphere of this house is stifling—even to Catherine! So you're suspicious of her! Well, you probably have reason to be. Even though Catherine is dead, she has her own thoughts. She's kinder than you, Father. She sees more clearly. She would never abandon me as you've done."

"I've *never* abandoned you!" cried Ferdinand. "Never. Never."

"She might pry, but she'd never judge, as you do. Because she knows all the temptations there are. She doesn't *feel* them. She's too cold for that. But she isn't as harsh. Father, if you *knew* what I go through! If you had the power to understand what suffering can be! But instead of sympathy, I am given suspicion—judgment. Oh, I can't bear it; I can't bear it!"

She was sobbing terribly. The violent flood of words, of accusations, had come to an end. Her face was buried in her hands, and her body was shaken with heavy sobbing which rendered her inarticulate. Ferdinand could not touch her. He had neither the power nor the impulse. This storming creature, so unjust, so vehement, was not the Rhoda he had known and loved. It was a woman from whom he was powerfully estranged—a woman, when he had known her only as a child. He stood quite still, frozen, his teeth chattering, before this avalanche of accusation. His mind was closed to it, so that he caught only here and there an intelligible charge, and for the rest he was bewildered beyond all bearing. To see Rhoda, shaken as she was by those sobs of agony, to hear in confusion the echoing words of pride and dislike which had tumbled headlong from her lips, made him feel faint with anguish. He had no ability to distinguish between what was true and what was false in her suspicion of his conduct. He could only struggle desperately to maintain such composure as remained to him after the scenes of the day.

Presently Rhoda moved. She withdrew her hands from her face, which was swollen with crying, and wiped her eyes. Then she looked at Ferdinand. It was a single glance, intended to satisfy a single doubt. He was hardly aware of it, because, in the effort for self-control, he was himself looking steadily down, his hands clenched, his teeth clenched. He did not raise his eyes as she moved, but kept them low. And Rhoda, as quickly looking away again, did not speak. Instead of speaking, she walked stumblingly across the darkened room to the door. Even here, she paused, as if to speak again, her hand outstretched, fumbling for the door knob, but after an instant's hesitation she disappeared. The door was silently closed. Ferdinand did not know of this second pause. If he had known, he might have made one further appeal for her pity. Instead, he remained behind, trying to prevent his lips from trembling, conscious that disaster had come unexpectedly and irretrievably upon him.

CHAPTER V

WHAT HAS HAPPENED?

I

THE minutes passed, but Ferdinand did not heed them. He was sunk in apathy. In what manner he had again reached his study he did not know, but he found himself sitting there while the clock ticked and night slowly crept deeper and deeper into his consciousness. This old house seemed to settle as the evening chill penetrated to its heart. At last mechanically Ferdinand looked at his watch, and with the utmost weariness dragged himself into the bedroom to change his clothes for dinner. He had no spirit left in him, but was a prey to lethargy. He shrank from meeting Rhoda afresh. If Catherine had been absent he felt that he could not have endured the meal. Feebleness such as that of laden old age hung upon his limbs, weighing them down. His hands were cold. In vain, every now and then, did there dart through his brain a hope of some miraculous awakening which should turn his misery into the relic of an unhappy dream. He was old, feeble, a coward; and if his vanity demurred at such charges, there were always other charges, as cruel, to take their place.

Hesitatingly he returned to the drawing room. To his relief it was empty. The room was now brilliantly lighted, and the fire had been made up. The two evening papers lay, as usual, upon a side table. The curtains were drawn; there was a purring air of comfort in the room, as if, lazily stretching in the warmth, it was conscious of its own beauty. Without

283

realizing what he did, Ferdinand picked up the newspapers, adjusted his glasses, and began idly to glance through the columns of print. But this occupation did not distract him, and very soon, in disgust, he cast the papers aside, staring sightlessly at the picture which hung at the other end of the room.

While he gazed, Mona Talbot came into the room, with Catherine.

Ferdinand started. For an instant his interest was directed, not to the two girls, but to the space behind them. Only when the door was closed and when he recognized that they were alone did he move forward to greet Mona. But his heart was beating more rapidly as a result of the fear which had seized him that Jabez was one of the party. If Jabez had been there, what could he have done? Again nothing? The reflection flashed into his mind that he had only one resort, which had been suggested to him by a remark of Joe's, made, as it were, aside. Well, that resort had yet to be tried. Would it succeed? Then, was Catherine observing his embarrassment? She should have no triumph! He would behave as though Jabez did not exist.

"Delightful surprise!" he said, taking Mona's hand. It was a large hand. The knuckles were wider than his own. Mona had been built upon a large scale, although her gauntness was constant. Her coarse, untidy hair was upon a level with Ferdinand's eyes. He never missed it. But he liked her. For him beauty in the friends of his daughters was not a necessity. Indeed, the absence of it had always enhanced the charm of his two girls. Were they aware of this?

The resort, of course, was that of a direct appeal to Jabez. The more Ferdinand thought of that, the more excitedly did he wish to put it to the test. He would write to Jabez, asking him to call. No, he would offer him lunch at the Club. As man to man . . . Ferdinand could not meet Catherine's glance lest she should read lurking jubilation, make a swift counter move—ah, if there were but time! He did not hear Mona's good-natured response to his greeting. What had she said? It was difficult to remain calm under such an inspiration. He could not keep still, but moved his hands, smiled, played with his watch chain.

"We've not seen you for so long!" Ferdinand's tone was caressing. He felt warmly cordial towards Mona, who had never caused him the smallest trepidation. Now, there were few of his acquaintance of whom so much could be said. She, with innocence shining from her plain face, beamed in acknowledgment.

"Well, you've been ill, Mr. Meadows," she said. "You mustn't forget that."

Ill? Had he been ill? Of course. He remembered now. But really, with all that he had so lately suffered—— How strange that the face of Mrs. Balthazar should come flying before him at that moment! The vision caused him to flinch. Mrs. Balthazar . . . His flight at the coming of the stranger was an ignominy the more. For a moment memory crushed him. He was ashamed. It was as if everything had recently conspired to make him feel unhappy. Was it just that he had been ill? He caught at the explanation. Yes, he had been ill: illness had caused him to distort all that had happened. He had seen it awry, swollen, like some frightening shadow, which lurched and threatened, but from which returning health would bring escape.

"But I'm better now," he answered Mona. Then, to Catherine: "Is Mona our only guest?"

So he had been unable to conceal his dread! He knew it at once. What a mistake! Before Catherine, too! He wished the question unasked. He looked away from her, endeavouring to pay no attention to her reply.

"Edmund Piercy is coming, Father. But he said he might be late."

Edmund Piercy—well, Edmund was not frightening. Stay, what had he in his mind concerning Edmund? The Law? No; in that respect Edmund could not be other than reassuring. For Ferdinand had not broken the Law. No, it was something which Edmund had said. Something—it was something about Punch Teed. He had said that Punch Teed would shoot himself. But that must be forgotten, obliterated. It was surmise, one of the wilder guesses of youth.

"Capital!" laughed Ferdinand, to cover his own delay. "This will be a delightful evening, I know!"

"Have you seen anything of Rhoda?" came unexpectedly from Catherine. The question made Ferdinand jump.

"No, no," he stammered. "At least, an hour ago—a long time ago."

"Strange," was all Catherine said. And then she spoke of something else to Mona Talbot.

Why strange? What did Catherine mean? He could not ask her; but continued standing and smiling constrainedly at the two of them, not understanding a word of their talk. Why strange? And where was Rhoda? Instinctively he looked towards the door. It began to open. He looked very quickly away. To confront Rhoda at this moment would be painful. He would feel shy, stern, anxious.

It was not Rhoda. Ferdinand's heart fell. This was not Rhoda but Edmund. It was Edmund who came booming into the room, heavily arch, almost amorously arch in his manner to Catherine. How was it possible, with such polish, and so much manner, to remain so uncouth? Did the Bar teach nothing of the niceties of bearing? It would seem as though it did not. But where was Rhoda? Why did she not come? Was her fear of a meeting still greater than his own? Ferdinand was filled with contrition. Poor Rhoda. Should he go and speak to her?

Another flutter at the door. Dinner was served. No Rhoda: how late she was! And how foolish thus to delay her coming! So far from distracting attention, such a late arrival would draw every eye. Her discomposure, he knew, could not escape notice. Poor Rhoda! Ferdinand sighed with some impatience in which pity was a principal ingredient.

II

They sat at table with Rhoda's familiar place upon Ferdinand's left hand unoccupied. Beside Mona, too, there was a noticeable emptiness, although no knives and forks were laid there. Ferdinand could not refrain from glancing every now and again at this vacant patch of tablecloth. And each time he did this he gave a quick blink in Catherine's direction, never quite seeing her, but always wondering what she was thinking. She wore a sapphire-blue dress, cut very plainly, and her hair had been freshly waved. She looked—he thought —almost more lovely than she generally did. But the tilt of her chin carried a hundred suggestions to Ferdinand's brain. It meant an obstinacy which he could never conquer; it meant calm effrontery; it meant—had she no heart? Rhoda had said that Catherine was dead. Dead—heartless—was that true?

And where was Rhoda? Why did she not come to dinner? He moved restlessly, impatiently.

"My dear, oughtn't we to send up to Rhoda's room?" he asked, at length.

"It was in darkness when I came down, Father. She wasn't there then, for I looked in."

"How extraordinary!" began Ferdinand. "Had you any idea——?"

"Miss Rhoda has gone out, sir," said the parlourmaid at Ferdinand's elbow.

"Out? Did she say where she was going?" Ferdinand looked up into the parlourmaid's expressionless face. Apparently Rhoda had said nothing. A vague alarm seized Ferdinand.

"I expect she's gone up to see *me!*" exclaimed Mona. "Well, *there's* a thing to do!" She began to laugh. "It's like Box and Cox. Because you see, I didn't tell Pa and Ma where I was going. I forgot all about it. Well, I think they've got the best of the exchange, if you ask me."

"Oh, we can't allow you to say that!" interposed Ferdinand gallantly. "Thank you, Annie. I expect Miss Rhoda is dining with Mr. and Mrs. Talbot."

"Is your cousin at home?" asked Edmund Piercy, directing his fish-like glance at Mona.

"Up in the North, Mr. Piercy," returned she.

"Ah!" Ferdinand did not know that he had breathed deeply. Was Catherine as clearly aware of the empty space as he had been? Of course, she must be! A wave of exasperation swept him. He pressed his lips together firmly for an instant. Aloud, he said: "He goes and comes, I suppose." But he did not dare to look at Catherine. This was exciting news. It brought relief—yes, but it also delayed the execution of his new plan. As fast as his spirit had risen it was depressed.

"I've been helping him—at least, I hope I've been helping him—over the Trades Unions Acts," boomed Edmund, elongating his chin as if he were going to make a joke. "You know that the men who draft Acts of Parliament always do it with an eye to the continued prosperity of the legal profession."

Ferdinand thought: I wonder if he ever forgets that he's a lawyer. *I* never do. Pompous young man! Then, addressing Edmund, he added: "It must be a satisfaction to you to clear up an ambiguity."

"Oh, no," said Edmund in triumph. "The satisfaction lies in the ambiguity." He laughed, in two or three deep grunts, and looked around the table, beaming pontifically.

"Now, Edmund!" remonstrated Catherine. "Are you *really* helping Jabez? Or are you just confusing him? You know you mustn't lead him into a quag!"

"He couldn't," objected Mona briefly and proudly. "Jabez is too clever to be cheated."

"Yes, yes," said Ferdinand a little testily. "I'm sure everything has been made perfectly clear to him."

"As clear as I could make it," confessed Edmund. "And

yet, you know, there are so many issues that it would be hard to make any law watertight, foolproof——"

Something more he said, like a voice in a cavern, but Ferdinand could not listen to these platitudes. We all make our own platitudes, and those of other men are intolerable to us. Ferdinand's mind was flying to Rhoda, to Mrs. Balthazar, to Joe Gascoyne, to Jabez; and wherever they momentarily rested they found only cause for embarrassment. He felt that he must be upon the verge of a nervous breakdown. What if he should be ill again? What if he should lose grip of himself? A sickening fear of insanity crossed his mind. He pushed away his wineglass, and the wine spilled like blood upon the white tablecloth.

"I saw our poor friend Punch, to-day," Edmund was saying. "This affair is particularly unfortunate for him. It seems that his father has taken it very badly."

Ferdinand shivered.

"Most distressing, most distressing," he murmured in distaste.

"The father—a very good sort of fellow, I believe—Gascoyne knows him—has always been out of sympathy with Punch. There's insanity there, I think—on the mother's side. Some form, at any rate. He's refused to help Punch any more. And Punch lately lost his job—nothing to do with this, of course—so he's in a bad way. He talks of cutting loose and leaving the country."

"Leaving the country," echoed Ferdinand.

"So he said. I think he'll go, to. He has a little money of his own. You see, this case—Punch gets the blame, because she's a young woman, only married a year or two, and belonging to a family. The whole thing is very disgraceful to both of them; and Punch's father is rather of the old school."

"The old school—what is that?" asked Ferdinand with a bitter note in his voice. The old school! Good God! Was respectability, dignity, honour, so completely outmoded?

Edmund grew still more ponderous.

"The old school?" he asked, entirely missing the irony of Ferdinand's question. "I should describe it as a school in which one practices with considerable freedom one's self and is very censorious of the freedoms of others." He drew down his chin, beaming.

"What!" Ferdinand spoke the word under his breath. It seemed to him that Edmund was looking along the table with cynical knowingness. "Surely that is a new definition of the old school?"

"It seems to be a fairly common understanding," returned Edmund drily.

Ferdinand started. His eyes fell upon the red stain which had been made upon the cloth by his spilled wine. Without replying to Edmund, he leant back in his chair, surveying that red spot. His mind gave a twist. He could see himself hurrying from Mrs. Balthazar's shop, could hear again her sharp instruction to remain where he was, could recall the pressure of her hands, the strange tapping at the door. At last:

"The young are not very charitable towards their elders," he said mildly. Looking directly before him, down to the bottom of the table, he saw Catherine smiling unconcernedly, and his heart leapt.

III

Their visitors were gone, and Ferdinand was alone with Catherine. As soon as they were alone he returned to the one topic to which they had been unable to refer while others were present.

"Rhoda?" Ferdinand said agitatedly. "I don't like this."

Catherine shook her head.

"She isn't at the Talbots'. I telephoned after dinner."

Ferdinand felt his blood run cold.

"She's not there!" he exclaimed, in a rising voice of fear. "Then where *is* she?"

"I don't know, Father. She said nothing to anybody. Nothing to me. You must have been the last to see her."

"Where can she be? Where can she be?"

"It's certainly very odd. I telephoned to the Gascoynes; she's not there. I haven't asked anybody else. There hasn't been time. Besides, I didn't feel anxious about her."

"Do you now? She was very strange when she was——"

"Strange? What d'you mean?" There was a new sharpness. Catherine seemed suddenly to have become rigid. "Father, tell me what she said—what she did!"

Under that clear gaze Ferdinand moved uneasily. He felt his lips to be dry and moistened them with his tongue. Yet he would not admit Catherine to knowledge of his own deadly alarm.

"Oh, come, come; she's sure to be all right," he exclaimed. "I ought not to have said——"

"You said she was strange. Was she unhappy?"

With a struggle Ferdinand forced himself to admit that she was.

"Yes," he said unwillingly. "She was very unhappy. I'm afraid that I, too, was strange. I didn't feel well—I'd had rather a shock—no matter. That is, I didn't succeed, as I ought to have done, in calming her. She was very agitated, very angry with *me*——"

"With *you*." Was there relief in Catherine's tone? Ferdinand looked up at her, to see a white face. Catherine resumed: "Just let me run up to her room again, to see. If she comes in while I'm there, we'll explain. But I'm rather worried about her."

Ferdinand was alone. The moment he was free to do so he gave way to the fear which he had been trying to conceal from Catherine. Where could Rhoda have gone? Supposing she were not in her room; and supposing she did not come home—what then? What was to be done? Had she gone heedlessly out of doors and, in her state of trouble and agitation, met with some street accident? Was she merely paying a visit to some one of her friends? Was she deliberately frightening him, with the object of reviving his living interest in her? The last alternative he would not, could not, allow himself to include in his suppositions. Indeed, it was unthinkable.

At last he could bear solitude no longer and went up the stairs to Rhoda's room. There, amid the snowy freshness, he saw Catherine standing at the open wardrobe. She was very still and stared at Ferdinand as if she were dreaming when he entered.

"Nothing?" he asked sharply.

"I was looking in here," murmured Catherine in an even tone.

"For dresses? Oh, but surely——"

"I've just rung for Annie. Oh, there you are, Annie!"

Ferdinand stepped aside and saw the white cap and cuffs, the expressionless face of the servant.

"Ought we——" he began warningly.

"Annie, did you notice if Miss Rhoda seemed to be carrying anything?" proceeded Catherine, taking no notice of his cry. "A bag, I mean?"

"Yes, Miss Catherine—a bag," answered Annie. She might have been an automaton, so still did she stand, so quietly did she answer. Her face was the colour of cream and was as free from lines as the face of a nun. She did not smile or frown, but looked steadily at Catherine, ignoring Ferdinand. There was no sign of life in her, or of the insatiable passion for gossip with which the kitchen must ring daily and hourly.

"She didn't say anything, Annie?"

"No, Miss Catherine. She didn't see me."

Didn't see her! Sinister words, full of significance! Ferdinand turned away, in horror.

"Thank you, Annie."

Noiselessly Annie disappeared. Ferdinand and Catherine stood facing each other, both pale, both filled with the same thought. Rhoda had left the house with no intention of returning that night. So much was clear.

"I saw that she had been in rather a hurry," explained Catherine. "Everything was tossed aside. Father, I think you'll have to tell me exactly what it was that Rhoda said to you."

Ferdinand stared at her. The lethargy which he had felt earlier in the evening, after the talk with Rhoda, was stealing back upon him.

"I—I don't know," he stammered. "It would be impossible, Catherine——"

She came close to him, took his arm, looked up into his face.

"Poor Father!" said Catherine very gently. "Poor Father! Let us go downstairs. Because, you see, I've got to know something of what Rhoda said so as to know what to do."

"Do?" dully asked Ferdinand. "Do? Oh, my God!"

He had remembered Edmund's story of Punch. He had remembered those exact words about Punch's intention to leave the country. What if Rhoda were gone with Punch? The thought startled him into passionate excitement. He put his arm about Catherine as together, very slowly, they crept down the stairs again to the tranquil drawing room. What if Rhoda had gone with Punch? He had a sudden picture of the black sea, of two figures, shrouded, while a ship made white foam in the blackness; the groan of cordage oppressed him; then Punch and Rhoda together, agitated, furtive, close in the shadow. The horror of that imagining was so great as to be unendurable in silence. With a fevered exclamation, he broke away from Catherine, striding across the room, striking his hands together in frenzy.

CHAPTER VI

SEARCH

I

As HOUR after hour passed without news the strain upon their nerves grew even greater. It was impossible for either to communicate to the other the most secret of their common fears; and for his own part, having once thought of Punch Teed, Ferdinand could not clear his mind of that almost certainty. Late as it was when he arrived at the conviction, and much as he wavered as to the wisdom of his action, he set out upon a journey of despair. It was easy enough to ascertain the address of Punch; a taxi was at the door in a few moments. Alone, therefore, and racked by extremity of misery and apprehensiveness, Ferdinand was driven through the dark streets of London. He was taking the one chance apparent to him of saving Rhoda from a lifetime of embittered regret.

His cab sped through deserted streets; and Ferdinand, bending forward, seemed as if he must urge the vehicle to further speed by actual movement of his own body. All the while, exclaiming, crying out in a loud voice of agony, he was insensible of every indication of the cab's progress. When it drew up in the darkness, before an unlighted block of flats in Chelsea, he at first could not bring himself to descend, so forlorn appeared the prospect of awakening life in a building so sunk in night silence. But the peering face of his driver, faintly illumined by the light beside the meter, brought the need of action once again to Ferdinand's mind. He sprang out, leaving the taxi door swinging, sought the bell push of Punch's flat, and waited.

Silence. He could imagine the shrill twitter of the bell far within. Trembling, dry-lipped, he waited. With his hand again raised, he paused; to ring too urgently would be to betray the nature of his errand, to alarm Punch and cause him to remain hidden. But—if Rhoda were there indeed— what guilty stirrings the noise would create! What fears, remonstrances, agitations! Silence. Again he rang. Then frantic energy overmastered him, and he pressed the bell again and again. The little push emitted little sounds under the pressure of his finger. No result. No result, and Ferdinand was distracted. With his eyes close to the brazen tablet of bells, he saw that one would summon a housekeeper; and when all his ringing of Punch's flat produced no response, he pressed the housekeeper's bell.

Ah! There was a faint streak of light from below. Then a brilliance within the closed door, which he could see through the glass sections. A loud noise of locks; the opening of the door; the sight of an angry, sleepy face and a tousled head. A man, huddled into a coat and trousers, presented himself —a man with gaping mouth and inflamed eyes, half smothered in drowsiness, but vindictively resentful of disturbance.

"Mr. Teed. Mr. Teed," cried Ferdinand. "I can't make him hear."

The sleepy face reddened; the swollen eyes blinked again. But the man saw from Ferdinand's dress and Ferdinand's agitated manner that this was no casual, mischievous interruption of his rest.

"Gone, sir," came in a cracked voice. "Gone away."

"Gone!" exclaimed Ferdinand. "He can't be! You're sure? My God! When did he go?"

"This evening. I dunno where he's gone. He come down, gimme a letter for the agents——"

"Was he alone?"

The man shrugged. His face was distorted by a grin.

"That I can't say, sir," he said slyly.

"Come, now!" cried Ferdinand. He took a Treasury note

from his pocket and gave it to the man. It was an aid to memory. "Was he alone?"

"Well, sir, I ain't sure, sir," said the man. "I rather *think* that there was a young woman with him. Well, as a matter of fact, I got them a taxi, so I *know* there was. Thank you, sir."

Ferdinand tottered. In a faint voice he put a further question.

"Did you see her face?"

"No, sir. I see her with a cloak all drawn up round her." He gathered his own coat the closer, in order to show how the cloak had concealed the wearer's face. "Of course, I don't say nothing about Mr. Teed, sir. He was always open-handed, sir."

"Do you know where he's gone?"

"No, sir. I didn't hear what he said to the taxi man."

"You can't help me to find him? Think! It's a matter of life and death."

"No, sir. I'm sorry I can't, sir. He never said nothing. But he'd got luggage with him, sir."

Beaten, sightless, Ferdinand made his way uncertainly back to his cab. He had no longer any hope. What could he do? As they returned home he no longer bent forward, eager for the greater and even greater speed, but sank back into a corner of the taxi, his head sunken upon his breast, his arms rigidly down before him. He was hardly conscious.

II

There was no news at home, where Catherine waited.

"Come, child, you'd better go to bed," Ferdinand told her. "There can be no sense in waiting up, losing your sleep."

"I've been wondering if we should telephone to the police, Father."

"The police? Oh, no, no!" The thought of such a thing was insufferable.

"If anything has happened to her——"

"There may be a letter. Tell me, Catherine; had Rhoda a cloak?"

"Do you mean, was she wearing one? I don't know, Father. And I've sent Annie to bed. Rhoda certainly *has* a cloak. Why do you ask?"

"No reason, no reason." Ferdinand brushed aside her question. In vain.

"But you *must* have had a reason," protested Catherine gently. "Where have you been, now? Father, I think you really must tell me what you've been doing. Short of telephoning to the police, I can think of nothing that I can do. I've searched again for any letter. There isn't anything."

"How cruel! How cruel!" exclaimed Ferdinand. "Without a word! It's bitterly cruel!"

Catherine said nothing for a moment or two. Then, thoughtfully, she put her further question.

"I suppose you've been to Punch Teed's," she said, "and somebody has seen a woman in a cloak?"

Ferdinand bowed his head.

"Both gone," he groaned. "Both gone to-night. I could discover nothing."

"Was it Rhoda?" she persisted. "Are you *sure?*" When he did not answer she continued: "If you're not *sure,* I don't believe it. After all, it might have been somebody else. No, I *can't* think she'd do that, Father; really, I can't. Besides, I believe it was over. I think we shall hear she's safe somewhere. I feel sure of it."

Ferdinand shook his head miserably.

"I wish I could think you were right," he said. "But even if you *are* right, that doesn't solve our dilemma. And it doesn't—Catherine, it doesn't make *me* guiltless!"

Catherine said a very curious thing. She said:

"That's absurd, Father. You're not guilty of anything— except of being our father. And if Rhoda has run away it's because of something in her own mind, not because of anything you've done or failed to do. She may have said something unkind to you—she may even have blamed you—but nobody else will blame you for something Rhoda has done. It would be too ridiculous."

This she said with so much sweetness that Ferdinand started from his misery. The hardness of her words was lost in the kindness of her manner. Catherine's hand was outstretched; he took it. Then, drawing her nearer, he kissed her cheek, now so haggard under the piercing brilliance of the room's light. Ferdinand could not speak; but he pressed her hand, which he still held, and sending her from him he began to wonder whether what she had said might possibly contain truth.

Once more alone, and fast sinking back into the state of despair from which he had been aroused by Catherine's reassuring speech, he was conscious that some dim memory was struggling into his attention. He became a prey to the unrest which such an effort arouses, listening, his thoughts moving quickly from one point to another. The bright lights of the room tried his eyes, and he moved across to the door with the object of extinguishing them. And as he stood there with his hand upon the switch, watching the darkness that winked as each bulb was extinguished, the memory was born.

Mrs. Balthazar had more than once mentioned Punch Teed. What if—his excitement came and went with the quickening beat of his heart—what if that tall figure, half seen in the gloom of the flower shop and ignored by Ferdinand as he hastened to liberty, had been the figure of Punch!

If so, to what did the supposition lead?

Ferdinand left the switch and moved quickly and lightly about the room. He had discovered, he believed, another possible means of tracing Rhoda. He did not ask himself whether Rhoda, thus found through the interposition of Mrs. Balthazar, would respond to his eager search. His one desire was to find her. And this gave him the hope of which his aching heart had urgent need. His impulse to call Catherine was checked. But soon—very soon—as soon as it was light—he knew that he had another journey to make in pursuit of news.

III

It was still early when Ferdinand left the house for the second time. He had been unable to sleep and had made no attempt to go to bed; and now that he was out of doors, in the chill of the morning, with the streets only half-awakened to the full life of day, he knew that he might find Mrs. Balthazar's shop still closed. But as he walked onward he began to meet those ardent workers who precede the general flock of clerks and assistants in progress to their daily tasks; and presently the pedestrians became more numerous, and more and more omnibuses filled the air with noise. Ferdinand walked more rapidly and was lost in the jostle. At length he was in Holborn, and he could see that some of the shop blinds were being pulled up. The sun shone down cheerfully through a haze of smoke; there were many sounds of activity; already there were loiterers and those who stood together, earnestly talking after a greeting or before a farewell.

He was near to Mrs. Balthazar's shop, where the blind was raised, and the windows—as the result of so chill a night—were faintly steamy. Within—and Ferdinand did not now hesitate to enter, since the time for hesitation was past —there was, as ever, a mass of green, while the atmosphere was moist and suffocating. His first thought in the silence was that nobody was in the shop or in the little room at the back; and the warm air was so full of exciting and disagreeable associations that he found it hard to conquer his emotion. At last, however, as he rapped with his walking stick, the door of the little room slowly opened. Ferdinand's heart was like water.

But it was not Mrs. Balthazar who shambled with difficulty from the room behind the shop. Not Mrs. Balthazar, but the old and ugly woman whom he had seen here once before. She was dressed as she had then been dressed, in a dirty black frock over which a dirty blue pinafore had been thrown. A knitted shawl of crimson wool was about her shoulders; and as she shuffled one foot slowly and painfully before the other, Ferdinand was shocked at the thought that anybody so old and so ill should be at work. The grotesque resemblance of this old woman to Mrs. Balthazar could not be missed; but her eyelids, behind black-rimmed spectacles which framed them, appeared to have sagged, so that their inner redness was revealed, while her mouth gaped open, showing in the midst of that ash-coloured face broken and discoloured teeth within the bruised lips.

"Ur," grunted the old woman. Then, with her hand raised to her ear and breathing loudly she panted out: "Speak up, sir; I'm deaf. But there ain't anybody here but me, and I——"

With that her breath seemed to catch, and she staggered. Without Ferdinand's aid in reaching the round-seated chair which stood near by, she must have fallen. But he had gone at once to her side, had caught her, and had gently led her to the chair, where she sat, breathing in a hissing, disgusted way, as if she was filled with hatred of life. Only then did Ferdinand notice that as the old woman rested in the chair, her stick firmly clutched and yet totteringly incapable of giving any support, tears had begun to stream from those terrible eyes and run heavily down the ashen cheeks.

They ran unchecked, splashing down upon her dress, while the ugly old woman rocked to and fro, her mouth open, her hands trembling, apparently incapable of doing anything to help herself.

"Is Mrs. Balthazar not here?" exclaimed Ferdinand. And then, more loudly, he repeated his question. He stood bending by the old woman, his hand gently upon her shoulder. "You ought to have somebody to look after you, you know."

"I know that," groaned the old woman. "I know that. I

ought to have somebody to look after me." She nodded her
heavy head as if she had hardly strength to check its feeble
motion. "I know. I'm ill—I ain't fit to be about. I ain't. But
if I don't come who's to look after the shop? Who's to do
anything? Eh?"

"Haven't you got somebody? Where's Mrs. Balthazar? Is
she not here?"

Wearily the old woman shook her head. The tears slowly
trickled from her eyes. She was hideous; the drops that fell
upon her grimy hands were smeared together. But she was
unhappy, and Ferdinand could not resist the appeal of unhappiness.

"I can't leave you like this!" he called. "Can't I get somebody to come and give you a hand?"

"Who *is* there?" she grumbled. "Who'd come and help
me? She's gone. She's left me."

"Gone?" cried Ferdinand. "Mrs. Balthazar?"

"What? Yes; she's gone. I don't know where she's gone.
Oh, they're selfish; they're selfish, these bits of girls. They
think only of themselves. The old ones—" she panted—"the
old ones—they can starve; they can starve." Her voice died
away into a barely audible mumble. Her head lurched forward. Again she might have fallen if Ferdinand had not
supported her. "But the young ones, they think only of themselves."

"Look here," Ferdinand said in her ear, shrinking from
her repulsiveness but resolute in his knowledge that something must be done for her protection. "I'm going to get
somebody to help you. To *help* you, d'you see? Do you think
you could——"

In the same low mumble the old woman was all the time
continuing to mutter to herself, shaking her head in despair,
the trembling hands holding fast to her stick, which was
pressed close to her breast.

"It's no good. It's no good," she groaned. "I may as well
give up! The old ones are useless. They can starve; they

can go. What does *she* care! She don't care—not *her!* All she cares about . . ." The muttering became indistinct. It ceased.

"I'm going to leave you for a moment," said Ferdinand again. His glance, wandering about the shop, had encountered a wall telephone, which he had never previously seen; and with the sight of that telephone he had received an inspiration. "There; see if you can hold yourself upright. Can you? Splendid!" Carefully, he released his hold of her, resting the limp body against the frail back of the chair. Then, still looking behind him, lest she should slide helplessly from her place, he stepped towards the telephone and asked for a number.

For Ferdinand the meaning of those mumbled words had been piercingly clear. Mrs. Balthazar—— "The old ones are useless. They can starve; they can go. . . . Oh, they're selfish, these bits of girls. They think only of themselves." Was this ugly old woman with the bruised lips and the gaping red-rimmed eyes, the dirty, stubby-fingered hands and the tear-soiled cheeks, any different from himself? He stood regarding her with pity.

A voice spoke in his ear. He started into alertness.

"Is that—is that you, Catherine?" he said. And then: "Catherine."

CHAPTER VII

NEWS

I

WHERE was Rhoda? Where was Mrs. Balthazar? Every inquiry produced the same result. Both had disappeared. No word came from either; and there was no clue to the whereabouts of Punch Teed. He, too, had vanished. That day passed without news; and a second day. The household in Woburn Square gradually returned—or so it appeared—to its usual tranquil course. Meals were brought to table, were eaten, or were half-eaten, and were sent away again. Ferdinand, having done all he could think of as likely to assist in the finding of Rhoda, and having shrunk from calling in the police to give publicity to his search, was feeling the reaction after so much nervous strain. Lethargic and exhausted, he crept from room to room of the house, sometimes standing deep in thought, and sometimes walking rapidly about in moods of panic. There was no peace for him at this time, but only an overpowering sense of impotence.

Ferdinand and Catherine said little enough to each other when they met, and although Catherine was always hopeful, reassuring, and considerate, she was uncommunicative. If she was taking any steps upon her own account to discover where Rhoda was hidden, she did not give Ferdinand news of her successes or her failures. She had taken in hand the succour of Mrs. Balthazar's aunt, who was now in hospital, while a capable young woman took temporary charge of the shop; and having in response to Ferdinand's appeal performed this task of rescue quietly and without fuss, and having restored the household to its normal routine, Catherine became once again, for Ferdinand, a source of baffling exasperation.

Was she human? Was what Rhoda said of her true? Had she no heart? Somehow it was a relief to him to fire into resentment over the problem of Catherine. It took his mind from terror for Rhoda's future. He began to remember Catherine as a child. Even then she had been cold, indifferent, good-natured—and therefore inhuman. How be good-natured unless one despised? Rhoda did not despise! She was as Ferdinand was, sensitive, emotional—weak, if you will, thought Ferdinand, if to be sensitive and unresourceful is to be weak—but full of pride. Was she full of pride when her vanity had fallen a victim to Punch? The doubt drove him frantic.

One time, as Catherine was leaving him alone, Ferdinand called out to her.

"Catherine!" he cried. "Is there anything else you think I should do? Is there anything you can suggest? I seem to have racked my brains to no purpose, until they yield me nothing. And yet we *can't* sit doing nothing. It's really impossible to accept a situation of this kind."

Catherine closed the door again and came back into the room.

"I don't think there's anything you can do, Father, except wait," she answered. "I know that's very difficult; but at least Rhoda knows where *we* are, and I think she may come back at any moment."

"Come back!" cried Ferdinand. "With Punch? My God!"

"Perhaps alone, Father, quite happy and well."

"You don't believe it! Nor do I!" He began to walk about the room. "But where *is* she? And why doesn't she write? This cold-blooded cruelty——" He broke off, inarticulate. "I can't make it out. That poor woman sitting in the shop said something—she said, 'The young ones think only of themselves.' It's true. It's true. You can't deny it, Catherine!" He stood, challenging her.

Catherine, standing as erect as he, was a little flushed, but not, it was clear, with anger. With steady eyes fixed upon him, she answered:

"Both you and she have just suffered, Father."

"But from that very thing," asserted Ferdinand. "That very selfishness I speak of. Where is the thought, the love, the kindness?"

"It may be that they're in conflict with something still stronger," Catherine said.

"You defend them," cried Ferdinand, recovering himself, and with difficulty speaking calmly. "In face of all you know, you defend them."

"I'm not very old myself, Father," answered Catherine.

The answer came as a shock to Ferdinand. It was delivered with a composure which he vainly sought. Whatever he might say to Catherine, he knew that it would always be met by this coldness. In despair he turned away, conscious of defeat.

"Besides," continued Catherine, "I don't think either you or Mrs. Mears mean what you say. *You* love Rhoda and Mrs. Mears loves Mrs. Balthazar. You've both been deeply hurt. But as soon as Rhoda comes back——"

Ferdinand turned round at that, explosive with pain.

"She *won't* come back!" he exclaimed. "I know it!"

"I think she will, Father," said Catherine very steadily. "You wait. And see whether I'm right."

Something in her voice caused Ferdinand to stare at her; but she delayed no longer, and he was again left to debate with himself the matter of their disagreement.

II

That night Ferdinand did not sleep at all. A storm of wind was raging, and throughout the house could be heard mysterious sounds, creakings and stirrings which, as he was inclined to doze, made his nerves quiver with messages of dread. Supposing Rhoda were far beyond his reach, as he feared; supposing a message of sorrow came from her at last, recording fugitive happiness, certain prelude to disillusion and despair? He felt that if he could hear of her safety the rest could be borne. If he could hear of her desire to return home he was willing to devote the rest of his life to the cherishing of her broken happiness. No thought of any wrong she had done interrupted his pure concern for her good. He might cry out in his agony that she was selfish, and that she had sacrificed his peace of mind for a foolish infatuation; but in truth such cries found no echo in his heart. His heart was faithfully hers; he desired nothing in life but Rhoda's tranquillity.

Impenetrable darkness began very strangely to give way to a shadowed calm. The outlines of chairs, and even the smaller ornaments upon his mantelpiece, were imperceptibly made more and more clear. Black faded to gray, and from gray to the pallor of the dawn. Soon light filled the room, lifting all from a common murk to sharp detail of form and shadow. Suddenly, like a flying spear, came a swift shaft of brilliance—the first silver of the day; and with that glimpse of sunshine Ferdinand rose immediately from his bed, walking to the window, and looking out upon the trees and bushes and the greenness of that fragment of lawn in the garden below. A few sparrows were chirping among the tender leaves; smoke was rising and was being beaten downwards by the remaining winds of last night's storm. Above, the sky was a mass of light cloud, moving endlessly, fascinating to Ferdinand's raised eyes in its motion and impenetrability.

It was still so early that he knew he would find every other room in the house darkened by drawn blinds, but he was thankful for the coming of day. The secret fears bred by darkness had filled him with fever, but now, at least, whatever news or absence of news the light might bring, he could escape from the frightful imaginings of those last silent hours. He need no longer be wholly alone, terrifying himself with every supposition that a sick fancy could impose upon his apprehensiveness; for Catherine would be at his side—Catherine, to whom, as every hour passed, he the more surely looked for support and understanding.

Another hour—another two hours—and his vigil would be ended. More quickly Ferdinand wrapped his dressing gown about him and sat down to wait for the moment of relief. His eyes closed. It seemed to him that his ears remained alert to catch every sound of movement within the house; but when he again looked up the time had passed and it was eight o'clock. Not sleep, but some merciful suspension of his faculties had caused the moments to fly. Heavily, he rose to his feet and moved across the room.

In half-an-hour he was upon the stairs, making his way down to the lower floor, where he knew the table would be laid for breakfast. He was still too early, and the room, as yet, was empty. But as he went to the front window he heard from somewhere in the neighbourhood that sharp rat-tat which in London is the postman's unmistakable signal. Craning, Ferdinand pulled aside the curtain and looked out of doors. There was no sign of the familiar uniform. But when the sound came again it was nearer than before. In front of him the big trees were in rich leaf, still unspoilt in their brilliant green. The flagged pavement was dry; the leaves moved hushingly in the breeze. There was subtle promise in that sweeping together of the leaves. It caused Ferdinand's heart to lighten until the eagerness, the hope, the almost certainty, was an added pain.

At last he caught sight of the postman, marching along with his hand full of letters and a bag over his shoulders. A moment and the man was lost to view—a tall thin man with his face half hidden by the great peak of his cap. Crack-crack, said a knocker. Again the postman came into view. He was abreast of the house, looking up at it. Ferdinand could see the little brown moustache and the lips beneath it. He

could hear the quick step and see how the man swung pro-
fessionally past the railings and up the step at the front door.
Trembling, he hurried from the window, across the room,
and out into the lobby. There, descending the stairs at a
run, was Catherine. There was a rustle, a clatter, crack-
crack! Ferdinand's left hand went to his heart, which was
suffocating him.

Then Catherine turned from the box, holding one letter,
apart from the others, directly towards Ferdinand.

"Is it?" he panted. "My dear, for God's sake——"

With trembling hands he snatched the letter from Catherine, saw once more the loved handwriting, an English
stamp, a Northern postmark, and tore open the envelope.
So blinded was he by excitement that he could see only a blur
upon the sheet of paper which crackled between his fingers.
Despair seized him afresh; this was the cruellest blow of all.

"I can't read it," he groaned. "Catherine, I can't *read* it!"

"Come, Father." Gently, she led him back into the room
from which he had espied the postman.

Here, where the light was very clear, Ferdinand could
see the agitated words which had been traced by Rhoda. And
as he did so his heart stood still. He looked, half stunned,
at Catherine; and his first impulse was to crush the letter in
his hand, to conceal it from her. While Catherine, waiting
expectantly at his elbow, tried to gain a glimpse of that
precious missive, Ferdinand was crumpling it close to his
breast, and staring at her with an expression that was more
akin to pity than to any other emotion.

"Father!" she prompted. "Nothing can be bad news! She's
alive; she's well——"

Struggling hard, Ferdinand withdrew the letter, and with
pain straightened it out. He could hardly bring himself to
confide it to her, and when at length Catherine had possession of the letter he turned from her so that he might not
see her face as she read the overwhelming words.

DEAREST FATHER [the letter ran] :

I'm a beast, and I know it. I've behaved rottenly. I couldn't do otherwise for fear you'd come and break down my resolution. But by the time you get this Jabez and I will be married. You'll hate it, and I hate to give you pain. But you see we love each other. Forgive me, Father. Not Jabez, because it isn't his fault. He wanted to tell you and is angry with me—it's awful; but I said nothing but this would do, and now you *must* forgive me for being such a beast. It's been an awful struggle.

Love,
RHODA.

There followed a hurried postscript:

Father, do send me a telegram quickly. I shall be wretched until you do.

Ferdinand, turning back to Catherine against his will, was amazed to see her face bright with joy.

"It's splendid!" she cried. "It's splendid! What a relief!"

"Catherine!" exclaimed Ferdinand, dumbfounded.

She restored the letter to him.

"It's what I hoped, Father!" she said more sedately but with shining eyes. "I can't tell you how glad I am!"

Ferdinand continued for some moments to regard her in stupefaction.

CHAPTER VIII

JOE COMES TO BREAKFAST

I

BREAKFAST was served as Ferdinand stood looking at Catherine; and the slight clatter of the dishes aroused him from the state of bewilderment into which he had fallen. As long as Annie was in the room, he did not speak, but as soon as the door had closed behind her he gave voice to the extraordinary doubts by which he had been assailed.

"Catherine," said he with great earnestness. "You won't, I'm sure, deceive me. But are you *really* glad of this? Whatever you say, I shall believe."

Catherine answered as frankly.

"I'm more glad than I can possibly say," she told him. "Jabez is a splendid man, loyal and true. He isn't very elastic or very humorous, but he *is* sincere. And he's got a power that will make Rhoda happy. All her extravagance of feeling won't shake him. On the other hand, she'll fill his life with excitement. They'll probably quarrel a good deal—perhaps they won't—but they'll make each other happy."

"But *you*, Catherine," began Ferdinand. He struggled for breath. "Surely this is an amazing piece of unselfishness on your part? I mean—from what you said——" He could proceed no farther. Only when he saw that she was smiling did Ferdinand resume. "Perhaps I've made some ridiculous mistake. I thought—I thought——" He flung out a hand, raising his shoulders. "You said one day——" It was impossible!

"I can't imagine what I said, Father!" cried Catherine. "I didn't know I talked so much."

She was positively impudent!

"Then I misunderstood you. I had formed the impression that *you*——"

"Oh, that I was in love with Jabez? Father!" She rallied him. "No, no; you were wrong."

"You spoke so highly of him!" stammered Ferdinand. He continued to watch Catherine, who was so happy.

"I still do, Father. I should have thought that in itself——" Catherine also, it seemed, could leave her sentences unfinished. "When did a young woman ever praise a man she loved? Certainly not in the last twenty years. No, you were wrong, Father. But you see Rhoda fell in love with him at sight; and Jabez fell in love with her. He talked to me for the same reason that made Rhoda abuse *him!* It was because he couldn't find anything to say to her except the forbidden words."

"The forbidden words?" vaguely repeated Ferdinand.

"Now you're being dull, aren't you?" retorted Catherine.

"These subtleties . . ." stammered Ferdinand. "I really —of course I realize what you mean."

"Only they're not subtleties at all."

"Do you mean that you were never frightened of Punch?" asked Ferdinand.

"Oh, yes, I was!" she corrected. "Because Rhoda didn't know everything about herself. I was more frightened than you were. I was frightened because you were always so much against Jabez. And he was so shy. And Rhoda is such an idiot. A lovely idiot, of course; but quite capable of going off at a tangent. When you're in love with one man and he is shy you sometimes fly off to another who is *not* so shy."

She stopped, laughing.

"You are so learned," murmured Ferdinand, with a dark glance. "Surely, Catherine——"

"I'm not speaking for myself," she admitted. "Is that what frightens you?"

"I'm very frightened, I must admit. Even you are prepared for quarrels. But what of Rhoda?—leading such a life as that." He could not express his fears.

"She's not a mollycoddle, Father. She'll love it. So will he. She'll make him a beautiful home; and he's always wanted that, poor man. You think of him as a terrible 'red,' but really he's an artist. The more you know him the more you'll love him."

"I? Love!" Ferdinand was aghast. He shook his head from side to side. "Bad as it is, I'm tremendously relieved. It might have been so much worse. But the thought of Jabez——" He shuddered, looking round the room. "You're more optimistic than I could ever be, Catherine! But that, I suppose, is your nature. It seems to me that you and Jabez might have intellectual interests—sympathies. But it appears I was wrong. I have been much wrong. I suppose I am often wrong—perhaps always wrong. Dear me, it's a very disquieting thought."

"Yes, you were very wrong," Catherine murmured. "And our breakfast is getting cold."

Ferdinand made a movement of impatience.

"Breakfast!" he said fretfully; and then he sighed. "Sometimes I wish you didn't confuse things so much, Catherine. We were speaking of something so much—so much more interesting. I suppose you don't feel the contradiction." Nevertheless, he seated himself at the table and unfolded his napkin.

"Perhaps I don't," answered Catherine gently.

"You're not romantic."

"I don't think I am."

"It's very strange. Because you are really more beautiful than Rhoda. And yet, with this——" He seemed to have lost himself in speculation; but at length, meditatively, he concluded: "I wonder if you will *ever* marry, Catherine."

Catherine, busy at her own end of the table, smiled calmly.

"There seems no reason why I ever should, Father," she answered.

II

They had not spoken again when a faint knock at the front door struck their ears, and a moment later Annie ushered into the room an unexpected visitor. It was Joe Gascoyne, who still carried his hat and his walking stick. He was debonair as ever, and although he was rather pale he was entirely collected. Ferdinand heard, somewhere far behind attention, the ugly skirr of a taxicab's gears, and knew, of course, that Joe had hastened to them upon some urgent errand.

"You've had news?" Joe began unceremoniously. He looked, not at Ferdinand, but at Catherine.

"A letter, just now," she answered quickly.

"All right?" Joe jerked his head faintly at Ferdinand, but still did not address him personally.

"Quite."

"Good!" Joe put his hand to his brow and sat down plump in a chair. "Good-morning, Mr. Meadows," said he.

Ferdinand saw those black eyebrows working. He looked below, at the mischievously pointed lips.

"Good-morning, Gascoyne," he answered with dignity.

"So you're pleased!" declared Joe. "Well, that's something." He affected to sigh.

"I hope we have never been other than pleased to see you, Gascoyne," Ferdinand ventured.

"I was speaking of something quite different, sir," said Joe. "I was speaking of the marriage which has just taken place between your daughter and Master Talbot."

"Just taken——" Ferdinand looked at his watch. "Oh, excuse me." He rose quickly from the table. "Catherine, excuse me. I think perhaps I'd better——" He glanced anxiously from one to the other of them. "If I send a telegram now——"

"You'll be just in time!" cried Joe. "But you must be quick!"

He, too, had risen; but he did not follow Ferdinand from the room. Instead, as soon as Ferdinand had passed the door, he drew his chair forward to the table, setting down, en route, his hat and stick.

"Catherine," he said imploringly, "I'm famishing. For God's sake, give me some breakfast!"

Obediently Catherine peeped within the covered dish.

"How did *you* know, Joe?" she demanded sternly.

"Had a letter from Jabez. These people seem to me to take us jolly well for granted, I must say! He bowls it out to me as a matter of course and tells me to come round and see *you*. Well, of course, I—well, I mean, I think it's a bit thick. He ought to do his *own*——"

Joe broke off and received a plate from Catherine upon which lay two small fillets of sole.

"It was very nice of you to come so early," Catherine said.

"The letter arrived as I was sitting down to breakfast. I came away at once, in a taxi, which I loathe. That shows what I'm prepared to do for you, Catherine."

"We're very grateful," was all she said demurely. "Poor Father has been almost out of his mind."

Joe ate his fillets of sole and drank the cup of coffee which was handed to him. Presently he said:

"On the whole, I think he's been lucky. It might have been so much worse. However, you won't thank me for telling you that."

He returned to his breakfast. At intervals, he looked at Catherine, but they did not continue to discuss the situation. Catherine asked after Gwen; Joe commended the coffee, which in this household could be recognized as coffee, whereas in Gwen's charge it might have been almost any half-cold liquid. At last he glanced at his watch, drew his black eyebrows together, and mysteriously grew taller and taller until he stood upright. He then possessed himself of his hat and stick, upon the latter of which he leaned. Almost, it seemed, as an afterthought, he said in a casual tone:

"Of course, I needn't tell you that I'm in love with you?"

Catherine gave a little jump and sat quite still.

"Oh," she said, with almost perfect coolness. "I was afraid it was Rhoda."

"You *weren't!*" cried Joe. "Now what *is* the sense of saying a think like that?" He gazed intently at her, with indignation. Catherine's cheeks grew pinker. "However, you said 'afraid,'" added Joe. He set aside his hat and stick. "And I may tell you that—well, I wondered if you'd set your heart on Jabez."

"Oh, no," said Catherine quickly. Her fingers rested upon the tray before her. "How silly!"

"On me, then?" persisted Joe.

It was strange that both should appear so calm when the hearts of both were beating so rapidly.

"Yes, on you," agreed Catherine. "It's been rather a strain."

As she spoke she rose to her feet, and Joe, with one long step, was at her side.

"Marvellous creature!" he ejaculated in a tumult, holding her hands and kissing her. "I adore you."

In a moment:

"Poor Father!"

"He'll be alone."

"I hope not. I hope Mona——"

"Good God! Do women think of only one thing?" exclaimed Joe. "Is your Father——?"

"But for that thing," Catherine said, "they'd be only inferior men."

"I love you," answered Joe. "The rest doesn't matter. I ought to be gone, and I stay here. See what power you have over me! And I expected you to send me away! Well, I've been wrong."

"You talk so much, Joe!"

Joe could not forbear laughter at her reproof.

"Devil!" he cried. "But what a relief! Golly, what a re-lief!"

Laughing, trembling, they kissed again. They were happy.

CHAPTER IX

LAST WORDS

I

FERDINAND was waiting in the drawing room, his back to the fire. Sunshine was blazing through the windows and giving fresh vividness to every colour in the room. Upon his right hand stood the grand piano, bearing a vase of flowers; to his left was the smaller of the two reputed Vermeers, partly in shadow, revealing its vista of cobbles behind the averted face of the young woman who listened; directly before him, radiant, was that ageless painting of the old woman spinning. For such beauty as the room held he was reverently thankful. Nothing could have given him greater and purer delight. To Ferdinand's eyes, in this mood of recovered tranquillity, the two pictures assumed ethereal beauty.

Ferdinand, too, was listening. He awaited the return of Rhoda. She was to come, now that all the trouble had passed, confident in the loving regret of those whom she had deserted. There were to be no recriminations. Happiness, love, and contentment were henceforth to be supreme, with neither tears nor anger to impair the quietude of reunion. Ferdinand, dressed carefully, his thin face held high, his hands, nervous and tender, hanging beside him, pictured the meeting. He was unquiet, but he forced himself to be still. When the sound should come from the square below which assured him of their arrival he would descend the stairs silently and would be the first to welcome Rhoda. Just so would the momentary shyness of both be conquered, or at least smothered, and thereafter a new life would begin for them all.

He knew that for a time he would miss her; but Catherine

would be there, always at hand, always calm, considerate, and without agitation. Catherine might be too still, too passionless, but she would tend him. The very quality which made her unattractive to young lovers was the quality most to be valued in a companion for one, such as himself, whose days of stress were over. In her care Ferdinand saw himself gradually growing old, in this beautiful house which was filled with memories and now was to be filled with peace. His mind ran much upon Catherine as he waited. He praised her calmness, her coldness, her simple beauty, her resourceful freedom from every tempestuous emotion. She had presence of mind; she had the far-seeing comprehension of one who who had been born wise; in her company he was to age gently, mellowing as the seasons mellow, not weary, but ripe with happiness.

As he so reflected Ferdinand drew a deep breath. He listended again. It seemed to him that the spring afternoon was particularly buoyant, and the sunshine warm and eager, as befitted the occasion. There came in at the open window many of the echoes of London in springtime. There were the sharp, plaintive chirpings of sparrows, the faint rustle of the sturdy green leaves; motor vehicles sent aloft their muffled buzzing; a slamming door and the clatter of something dropped upon the pavement blended with the deeper humming of distant traffic. Everything now had power to increase Ferdinand's anticipation of delight.

Still there was no sound from which to draw knowledge of Rhoda's coming. His legs were growing stiff. For a moment he made as if to walk about the room; then, with a smile, he abandoned that plan. He would sit down. One could listen as well sitting as standing. So, in his old chair by the fire he rested, waiting for that welcome noise. The birds chirruped and the leaves swayed; Ferdinand could hear them growing louder and fainter, in strange long waves, as if the air had its rhythms as potent as those of the sea to lull the ear and the mind. Smiling, he leant back in the chair, soothed

by the warmth and the sunshine and the sounds; and in a
moment was fast asleep.

II

When Ferdinand awoke he thought that he was still dreaming, for the sunshine had moved and he was quite in the
shadow. The fire was burning very brightly and cheerfully,
and the little noisy flurrs of gaseous flame were making much
ado behind the bars. It was a merry sound, and the brightness stimulated him. He turned in his chair, still smiling,
and met the watchful eyes of Rhoda. At first he could not
believe that she was there, kneeling in her old attitude upon
the hearthrug, close to his side, but after that breathless instant of surprise he was elated by the certainty of her presence.

"Why, my child!" Ferdinand exclaimed. "Bless me, I was
asleep! What a welcome!"

She was in his arms, her warm lips pressed upon his cheeks,
her hands tenderly pressing his head closer and closer to her
bosom. Never had Rhoda been so eager, so loving, so tumul-
tuous in her embrace.

"You forgive me, Father?" she whispered, her eyes wet.

"Yes, child, yes! But forgive—what a horrid word!"

"Once you thought it the right word," she told him, with
reproach.

"I forget," Ferdinand answered. "I quite forget. You must
forgive me for that."

"But I was cruel! I was really horrible. It makes me hot to
think of it. Forgive me, Daddy."

"It is our own cruelty that we can't forgive," murmured
Ferdinand. "And you're happy now. Catherine says you are
going to be very happy. That's true, isn't it? My darling!"

She still held him tightly, until Ferdinand, becoming incapable of drawing his breath, drew gently back, still holding the loving arms, and at length the quick, warm hands.

Seen thus, Rhoda was greatly changed. All the sullenness which of late had troubled her face was vanished, and in its place was a radiance in which Ferdinand could cordially rejoice.

"Will you miss me a little?" breathed Rhoda.

"All the time."

"You'll be lonely."

"Catherine will take care of me."

"Catherine—oh! But Catherine won't. She won't be able to."

"Won't be——?" He was bewildered by such a strange assertion. "I don't understand you, my dear."

"She's going to be married, too. To Joe!"

"To Joe!" Ferdinand felt himself whirling. "But this is——"

"It's true, Father. Poor Father! It's too cruel. But listen, I've got something else to say. Why shouldn't *you* be happy, as well? Why shouldn't you marry Mona? It's the dearest wish of my heart!"

Ferdinand, in consternation, put her away from him with a convulsive gesture. He could not suppose her serious. Then, as the suggestion was borne to his mind, he felt a return of that terrible agitation from which he had so lately escaped.

"I? Oh, my dear child!" he stammered. "No, no! It's impossible!"

"Hush!" She pressed her fingers to his mouth. "Here's Jabez! Here's my husband!"

It was true. The door had opened, and Jabez stood within the room. Ferdinand had a distinct memory of his first sight of Jabez, exactly in that position by the door. But there had been others present; a crowd had intervened; they had not measured each other. Now, as he slowly struggled to his feet, Ferdinand had good reason to be thankful for his own commanding height. Jabez, shorter, stoutly built, with his broad brow and his lined cheeks, would else have dominated him. For Jabez had all the aggressive reserve of a physically

strong man. He was watchful. He made no movement until
he knew that it was to be peace and not war between them.
Ferdinand, steadily regarding his supplanter, while Rhoda
hung upon his arm, extended the hand which was free from
Rhoda's control.

"Welcome," he said a little hoarsely.

"He's not angry with us, Jabez!" cried Rhoda, looking
proudly and gladly from one to the other. "He couldn't be,
with you!"

"I'm glad of that," Jabez answered, looking distrustfully
at Ferdinand.

"Come," said Ferdinand. "We are to be friends, you
know."

He felt his outstretched hand seized with a grip of iron.

"It's very good of you, Mr. Meadows," retorted Jabez.
"You'll find I'm grateful."

Ferdinand knew that they could never be friends, but he
pretended to believe that this knowledge was a fantasy. He
looked fastidiously at Rhoda, who was so delicate, so full of
quicksilver, and wondered how she could endure this dour,
hard-grained Northerner with the bitter mouth and the waiting manner of a stump orator who gives his audience time to
see every point. An almost imperceptible shrug lifted his
shoulders. Then:

"I came to say that it's time we went, my dear," Jabez
continued.

"What!" protested Ferdinand. "Oh, I can't allow that!"

"I'm sorry, Mr. Meadows."

"I shall appeal to Rhoda!"

"Oh, Jabez, is it *really* time?" came from Rhoda.

"You've only just come!" cried Ferdinand. "Both of you,
surely——" The thought that his wish was to be immediately disregarded was deplorable.

"Very sorry, Mr. Meadows; but we've promised to go to
my uncle's; and we've a train to catch at half-past six. I'm
speaking to-night at Reading."

"So soon!" Ferdinand looked in dismay at Rhoda. "Rhoda, my darling, this is terribly sad. Why, I've hardly seen you." Wistfully he implored her sympathy. But Rhoda gave no sign of protest. Nay, she was contemplating Jabez as though she marvelled at his clemency. Ferdinand was amazed. Her submissiveness struck deep into his heart. He had lost her forever.

"I shan't be a minute!" She flitted to the door, leaving the two men standing together by the fire.

They were silent as she left them. They remained silent until her return. Only at parting did Jabez once again seize Ferdinnad's hand and compress it.

"Thanks!" he said. That was all.

Ferdinand followed them down the stairs, where Catherine was waiting. Within three minutes they were out of the house, the door closed, everything still and peaceful, as though they had never arrived. Was Ferdinand dreaming. Had be been dreaming all the time?

III

So, after a little while, it seemed to Ferdinand that he might as well go out of doors himself and take, as usual, an afternoon walk. He had no longer any place at home; and in the streets, in the turmoil of the London traffic, he would be able to indulge his thoughts unchecked. He had much to think about.

From Woburn Square, as if by instinct, he made his way eastwards and eventually came into Southampton Row, passing through his favourite Queen's Square to Devonshire Street, and so through to Holborn. It was a Saturday afternoon, and the streets were almost deserted. All those who ordinarily made them a moving blackness had gone by train and omnibus to their homes, or were watching the last agonies of the season's football, or were in the theatres, laughing, weeping, concerned deeply with all those trivial or imaginary happenings of the moment, which seem to be the most important of all. Only here and there did Ferdinand encounter a solitary wanderer like himself, and always the loneliness of such strangers struck him with a curious pang. He was alone, as they were; he was wandering, as they were.

At last he came to the shop above which the name of "Balthazar" was still newly painted. It was empty. The blinds were drawn; steam was upon the windows. He could imagine the clammy atmosphere within. Poor Mrs. Balthazar, where was she? What would be her fate? One day soon, perhaps, she would creep back, having found, as all do, that the tide of passion ebbs in due course. Almost with a shudder, Ferdinand turned away, proceeding until he reached the narrow alley known as Great Turnstile. It broadened; he was in Lincoln's Inn Fields. The high wall which hides the Inn was upon his left hand; upon his right were the gardens. And as he walked Ferdinand communed with himself.

He recalled what Rhoda had said of Catherine and his consequent amazement. He recalled the tone in which Jabez had announced that he and Rhoda must leave the house. There was a moment during which he glimpsed his own future loneliness. He grew sad. Never again could he hope to enjoy the old tranquillity which had been his, the loving care of his two girls, the tender anxiety which had saved the days from ever being dull. It was a great loss. The sense of it made him grave. And then, quite suddenly, as if the birds had begun to sing more loudly, Ferdinand was conscious of one overmastering emotion. It filled his head so that his heart seemed to be bursting. He was sorely tempted to run, dancing, amid Lincoln's Inn Fields, his hands meeting high in the air, as do the hands of Harlequin, in "Carnival." For the emotion which had seized Ferdinand so unexpectedly was the emotion of relief. He was free. He had no burdens. The incessant anxiety which had weighed him down was removed. Rhoda was no longer in his charge. The responsibility was shed. In future Jabez would have the care of her. As for Catherine . . .

He was free. They had no conception of what freedom would mean to him. Nobody could have any conception. He planned in elation. He would travel; would savour the beauties of the world; there should be nothing he had not seen and known. This was triumph! This was liberty! He could hardly believe it, could only exult, scheme, imagine. . . . All who saw this grave, silent man passing quietly along the flagged pavement of Lincoln's Inn Fields would have supposed him preoccupied with serious problems of the law. None could have divined that he walked sedately with difficulty; none could have guessed that as he walked Ferdinand was entering upon a new phase of life, the inevitable sorrow of which was hidden momentarily from him by a sudden illumination so blinding as to exclude every shadow.

THE END

Date Due